A TIME TO KILL,
A TIME TO HEAL

WAR, TREASURE, DECEPTION, MURDERS, AND TWO ENDINGS

BY D. J. WEST

DORRANCE
PUBLISHING CO
EST. 1920
PITTSBURGH, PENNSYLVANIA 15238

Dorrance Publishing Co
585 Alpha Drive
Suite 103
Pittsburgh, PA 15238
Visit our website at *www.dorrancebookstore.com*

ISBN: 979-8-89211-293-2
eISBN: 979-8-89211-791-3

A TIME TO KILL,
A TIME TO HEAL

WAR, TREASURE, DECEPTION, MURDERS, AND TWO ENDINGS

DEDICATION

FOR MY WIFE, BETTY

ACKNOWLEDGEMENTS

Special thanks to Sara Camilli for editorial and other much appreciated assistance and encouragement during the development of this work. Thanks also to the following family members and friends who read various pieces and drafts of the manuscript, providing needed information, encouragement, and constructive criticism along the way: Mark West and Lisa Woodson, Dr. Anne West, Lisa West, Dr. M. Geoffrey Smith, Carl and Mary Ellen Anderson, Ray Camilli, Dr. Gary and Kathie Calandra, and Clara and John Carlson.

To every *thing there is* a season, and a time to every purpose under the heaven: A time to be born, and a time to die; a time to plant, and a time to pluck up *that which is* planted; A time to kill, and a time to heal; a time to break down, and a time to build up.

Ecclesiastes 3:1–3 (KJV)

*A*s a distant church bell began to peal, the dying man's eyelids flickered, and he once again became conscious. Whispering to the woman at the bedside he said, "Lena?"

"No, Dad, it's Woody," she said, using the nickname he'd bestowed many years ago when she'd been obsessed with a school project about the lives of woodpeckers, the pileated one being her absolute favorite.

"Oh…yes, of course. Please, ask Lena to come in."

"She…she's not here, Dad."

"Oh?" A look of disappointment, followed by a pause, then, "Well…when will she be back?"

A look of pain on her face as she stammered, "I…I'm…uh…really can't say."

Another pause, then in a whispery voice, "Okay…then please get your Mom. There's…something…I really need to…" Suddenly racked by a fit of coughing, he became critically short of breath, unable to speak. Quickly, she reinserted his nasal cannula that had fallen out and increased the flow of oxygen.

Allowing him time to calm down a bit, she said in a voice reflecting her own grief, "Mom's with Lena, Dad. Don't you remember?"

The old man's body went slack. He closed his eyes as tears trickled down his cheeks, and after a time finally said, "I guess I'll sleep a little more now."

Kissing him, she whispered, "You do that. I'm going to leave for just a few minutes. I'm just going to the bathroom, then brew some coffee, and make a couple phone calls. I won't be long."

While she waited for the coffee, she called Allie at El Hogar to check how things were there and to say she wouldn't be in today. "He's really gone downhill the past two days. I...I don't think he can last much longer."

A few minutes later, as she was about to pour a second cup, she heard a hoarse scream followed by pitiful crying from the bedroom. Rushing in, she found him on the floor, his arms and legs pulled tight, crying and moaning, his cannula once again hanging free.

"Dad, Dad, what's wrong? Calm down, please calm down. You've had a bad dream. Yes? Here, I need to put your cannula back in again. Now, long, slow breaths. That's good. Just keep breathing long, slow breaths. I'll call the doctor and ask him to order something to help you feel better."

Still gasping between words, he began to yell again. "NO...NO DOCTOR! CALL...FATHER...OTERO. I MUST...MUST...TALK TO HIM...NOW!" Completely out of breath yet again, he ceased trying to talk, but continued to moan softly, tears running down his face.

Crying now herself, she ran to the phone to do what he'd asked, telling the person who answered that her elderly father was terribly distraught, near death, and had begged to have Father Otero come as soon as possible.

A short time later, Father Julio Otero knocked on the front door, and when she opened it, he said, "I came as fast as I could."

She showed him to her father's bedroom. He lay there, eyes closed, but apparently awake because he whispered, "Thank you for coming, Father."

To which the priest answered, "It's my calling to serve where needed. God be with you sir." Then, "Just a brief conversation with your daughter first, then I shall return to you."

Stepping into the corridor and softly closing the bedroom door behind him, he said in a very soft voice, "I recognize your father. I've seen him several times when visiting the boys at El Hogar, but we've never been introduced, and I don't recall ever seeing him in church. Is he, in fact, a member of the Catholic Church?"

"I've never known him to attend church since we've lived here, but I do know he was raised in the Catholic Church. As for you having seen him at El Hogar, after retiring some years ago he's done a great deal of volunteer maintenance work for us there, as well as helping the boys with their homework, especially in math."

Waiting in the kitchen as Father Otero returned to speak with her father behind the closed bedroom door, she nervously paced back and forth, had some more coffee she didn't need or want, then she paced some more. It seemed like two hours, but when Father Otero finally opened the door and beckoned to her, she realized it had actually been at most twenty-five minutes. Entering, she saw her dad lying still and looking very calm. Father Otero said, "I hope you understand the rules of confession do not allow me to share what he said to me?"

She answered, "Of course. I'd never consider asking."

Lightly touching her arm, he said, "I can tell you he's been deeply troubled concerning a number of things in the past, and he seemed very relieved to be able to discuss them with me." She just nodded, knowing she already knew at least most of what had been eating away at his conscience for so long. As though he could read her mind, Father Otero then added, "Do not grieve for what you suspect or may already know, my daughter. Your father is now finally at peace. His soul is with God."

Five days later, attired in black, she stood with her husband, friends, and several work colleagues, as her stepfather was laid to rest next to the grave of her mother.

PART I

1939 – 1954

CHAPTER 1

01 SEPTEMBER 1939, DRESDEN, GERMANY[1]

Klaus looked up from the report he'd been writing as the classical music on his radio was suddenly interrupted by a news bulletin. "*Achtung! Achtung! Der Führer…*" By the time the reporter had finished saying that Germany that morning had launched a full scale land, sea, and air invasion of Poland, Klaus felt physically ill. Dead forever now, a hope he'd tried to keep alive in the face of increasingly worrisome signs. Forcing himself to breathe deep and slowly to counter a rising feeling of panic, he thought, *God in heaven, couldn't he have settled for just pushing through one more hard line agreement to recover East Prussia and Danzig like he did with the Sudetenland, and then quit? Scheissen! We're in it now, another massive war with France and Great Britain, and almost certainly with Russia too, in spite of that nonaggression pact with Stalin. And if we don't win this time, we'll be crushed forever.*

In the kitchen, Klaus poured a double measure of schnapps, downed it in a single swallow, and then followed it with a second. The liquor burned his throat and stomach and made his eyes water but settled his nerves a bit. Look-

---

[1] READER NOTE—Dates are expressed as day/month/year and time of day in terms of the 24 hour clock (e.g. 1800 hours) in chapters where the story takes place in Europe prior to, during, and several years following WWII. When the story moves to the U.S., dates are given as month/day/year and time in terms of a 12 hour cycle (e.g. 9:15 p.m.).

ing out the kitchen window he could see a group of his neighbors already milling about in the street below. A couple were cheering and waving flags, while several others wore expressions ranging from hopeful, to confused, to frightened, as he now was. One elderly couple, whose son he knew had been killed in France just days before the end of the Great War, stood stoically in their doorway, watching and looking very sad. *They already know the hell many of us will soon know as well.*

Turning away, Klaus's eyes fell upon a photo of his wife Magda and their son Horst. It summoned thoughts of happier days; his graduation with honors in 1934 from the Dresden Technologic Institute (DTI), marriage to Magda that afternoon, an offer at their reception that evening of a well-paid position from a friend of his father. From there, his mind summoned an image of himself proudly holding his newborn son, Horst.

All good things, yet…When he'd first started his studies at DTI he'd still hoped aging President Hindenberg would somehow find a way to make the Weimar Republic a stable democracy. But while things had gone well for him in school, the same could hardly be said for the country. The economy was in tatters and political chaos had reached a point that finally allowed Nazi leader Adolf Hitler to become head of the government. And a year later, with Hindenberg's death, he'd made himself into an absolute ruler, *der Führer*.

Klaus had never identified with the Nazi party's racist policies or agreed with the thuggish behavior of its Brownshirt adherents. Looking for anything positive now, he had to admit he hadn't been sorry to see *der Führer* forcefully suppress the Communists, given that he'd always thought of Russia as an existential threat to Germany. He'd also felt some redemption in Hitler's refusal to comply with many of the restrictions that had been imposed on the country under the unjust Treaty of Versailles, and he had been impressed by how dramatically the man had been able to reduce the sky-high rate of domestic unemployment in 1934. For all that, there had been unhappy changes, including the passage of laws that severely restricted the civil rights of virtually anyone to voice criticism of the government. It was hard to tell now what people really thought about the government. They might be divided on an issue but had reason to be frightened and hesitant to speak in any critical way. As time went on, he'd become more and more disturbed by the highly discriminatory and increasingly violent way *der Führer* and his adherents pursued each new objective.

He'd been shocked by the utter savagery of Kristallnacht. And from there he should have stopped the mental movie, because in the next image from a month later he saw himself at his wife's bedside, crying, as she lost her fight with an overwhelming case of pneumonia just days before Christmas, 1938.

Forcing himself back to the present, Klaus's mind was now a whirlwind of questions and conflicting thoughts. Pacing back and forth, he thought, *What now? This is utter insanity. What should I, what can I do? All able-bodied German men are now bound to be called to military service. But I'm the single parent of a small child. Gerda's been a godsend with Horst, but she already has a part time job and should be allowed to finish her education to become a teacher. I'm the only real parent Horst has, and my parents are both gone. But I'm a qualified engineer employed in an industry of great importance to the war effort. Perhaps…I could be exempted, stay here, have things continue as before? But NO, KLAUS! What a selfish, unpatriotic attitude. Father would be ashamed of me. He left his business and proudly served the Kaiser in the Great War, charging me to care for my mother when I was only a little older than Horst. And even when he returned home, disappointed by the outcome, he often reminded me of my duty as a good German citizen to always support and defend the homeland. What to do now?*

Suddenly he remembered something else. *Damn! Gerda took Horst this morning for a picnic in the park, some time at the playground, and then to her place for an overnight stay to give me time to finish my report. Has she heard what's happened? What is she thinking? I must call her.*

Klaus ran to the phone, but on lifting the receiver heard only a strange buzzing sound. The connection at the base of the phone seemed intact. Either there must be a fault outside or in the body of the phone itself. Grabbing his jacket, he was about to run the three kilometers to his sister's apartment, when there came a loud knocking at the front door on the first floor. Klaus headed downstairs, but before he got there the knocking was repeated, louder this time, followed by a voice shouting, "Klaus, you *depp*, you in there or not? I tried to call. The phone rang, but no answer. Just about everyone is downtown right now talking about what's going on, and I have some really interesting news." It was Dieter Kleinschmidt, his best friend, calling him by a rude name, a practice they'd continued since they'd been kids.

Klaus shouted back, "Hang on, *Schwachkopf*, I'm coming. The phone isn't working at my end." Pulling open the door, he embraced Dieter with a bear hug.

Pulling away, Dieter took a hard look at his friend, saw his tousled hair, his haggard and flushed face, smelled his alcoholic peppermint breath, and said, "You look like hell, Klaus. Did someone just die?"

"No, but a lot of people soon will. What he did today could turn into a disaster."

Dieter looked somber for bit, nodding agreement, but then said, "Yes, but the point is he's *done* it, so we've got to figure out how to survive the ordeal and come out ahead, and von Schallenberg has a suggestion as to how we might do that."

"Herr Dr. Professor Heinrich von Schallenberg, our eminent mentor at DTI?"

"One and the same, Klaus. He doesn't seem at all stressed by what just happened, happy, in fact. Apparently, he's worked his way up to a position of some influence in the party, and now wants to help us, his favorite students. That's what he called us. Did you know they appointed him overall Director of the DTI earlier this year?"

"No. I also didn't know he had strong Nazi sympathies when we were students."

"I know. If he did, he didn't show it a lot. When did you last see him?"

"It was…it was at Horst's baptism, more than four years ago. He couldn't attend Magda's funeral because he was out of the country, but he sent flowers and a letter of condolence."

"Well, he's definitely thinking about your and my welfare now in light of what's just happened. He said to me he knew how much you must have been struggling since Magda's passing, and that you're most likely trying to decide how to continue to be a good parent to Horst, and still fulfill your patriotic duty to Germany. He even said that if you *really* want to go that way he could probably get you an exemption from military service, but since you've always expressed such a strong feeling of patriotism for the homeland you might be hesitant to do so."

"My God, Dieter. The man knows my mind better than I do."

"I told him I'd call and ask you to join us. But when I couldn't get you on the phone, he urged me to try to find you and let you know he'd like us to join him for dinner at his home this evening at 19:30."

"At his home? That exceeds any social invite we got during our student years. I'd better clean up and dress up."

"*Jawohl*. You definitely need to do that, given the way you look right now. I'll call from my place to let him know we're coming, then I'll pick you up at, let's say…19:00? I figure it's about a twenty-minute drive."

At 19:23 Dieter turned his brand new Volkswagen onto the circle drive that fronted Professor von Schallenberg's mansion-like home, parking it at the far end of the portico extending from the front entrance. Adjusting their ties and smoothing their hair, the friends knocked on the large ornate wooden door. It was immediately opened by a tall, rather cadaverous-looking man in a black suit, clearly the butler, who said, "Welcome, gentlemen. Herr Dr. Professor von Schallenberg awaits you in the dining room. Please follow me."

As they entered, the professor jumped up, glass in hand. "Please join me in a toast to the glory of the new Reich." While he didn't add an extended-arm *Heil Hitler*, they immediately noticed the red, white, and black swastika banner hanging on the back wall. The butler appeared again with drinks, and raising their glasses they shouted, "*Prost*." Then the professor said, "Business first, gentlemen."

Sitting together at one end of the large table, he said, "I started to tell Dieter this afternoon about something I think could be of advantage to you both." Then he told them he'd learned of a decision to organize a new battalion in the armed military component of *der Führer's* paramilitary organization, *der Schutzstaffel* [SS], called *der SS-Verfügungstruppe* [SS-VT], a name later changed to *der Waffen-SS*. It was to be an artillery battalion, recruited and trained in Dresden. Because of its focus, the battalion would need and value officers with a solid engineering background. Even after it was ready, he thought the battalion might be kept local for a time as part of the home guard before being deployed. And on that point, because of the kind of overwhelming *Blitzkrieg* Germany had put together and just loosed upon Poland, he was convinced that would so cow other potential opponents, the war would be over in a year or even less. "With my recommendation, gentlemen, your service in the SS-VT could also bring very favorable attention from people able to advance your careers after the war."

Having made his pitch, the professor continued, saying, "You're among the very best students I ever taught. If you are interested, I can ensure you appointments as officers in that battalion." Dieter's eagerness was immediately apparent, while Klaus, always the more serious of the duo, sat silent for a time, looking rather like Rodin's *Thinker*. Looking at Klaus, the professor finally said, "Relax, Klaus. As I said, this is the military arm of the SS, not *der SS-Totenkepfverbände* (SS-TV, Death's Heads Formations that ran the German concentration camps prior to and during WWII). And this arrangement could not only work to your benefit professionally after the war; it would give you more time with your son while fulfilling your military obligation." Then looking at Dieter with a bit of a grin, he added, "And for you, it would give you more time to spend time with your girlfriends."

As Klaus continued to ponder, the professor said, "Although you two don't look or act at all alike, I know you both have real talent. Klaus, as physical looks go, you're the model of the true Aryan, tall, with blond hair, pale blue eyes, and that chiseled jaw line. And Dieter," he said, chuckling, "you're fine too. Even though you're fifteen centimeters shorter than Klaus, with that height, your brown hair, and blue eyes you resemble *der Führer*. Just add a mustache and I swear that from a distance you could pass for him. Neither of you will have any trouble being accepted into *der SS-Verfügungstruppe*."

More drinks and conversation followed. Dieter was ready to say yes from the beginning. Klaus took longer, but with some unspoken reservations, finally nodded, and agreed to accept the Professor's offer.

Had they made a good decision? It must have seemed so with Germany so clearly on the rise. Of course, they were both intelligent enough to know nothing is ever certain. Even if the conflict proved to be as brief as the professor so confidently predicted, there was always a possibility one or both of them could be seriously injured or killed. But having made the commitment, surely the thing to do now was to push away all such thoughts and get on with the task. For Dieter, that seemed easy. It was more of a challenge for serious, reflective Klaus. Still, in his worst imaginings, he couldn't have anticipated how the journey he was about to start would not only change his life forever, but years later bring mortal danger to his son and a granddaughter he would never know.

CHAPTER 2

03 FEBRUARY 1944, LEAVING LENINGRAD, RUSSIA

Klaus lit two cigarettes, passed one to Dieter, and said, "Just one more day and we can leave this godforsaken place. I can't wait to reach Riga, have decent quarters, and not be shot at every day."

"Amen," replied Dieter, as he avoided a huge pothole and turned the Kommandeurwagen into a broad circle drive fronting the Catherine Palace. "And if we're lucky, maybe we can leave with some pretty *souvenirs* in our pockets, eh Klaus?"

Professor von Schallenberg's rosy prediction more than four years ago that the war would be over in a year at most now sat bitter in their mouths. The only part of his prediction to hold true was that Klaus had been able to spend six more months in almost daily contact with Horst, and Dieter had enjoyed a similar period to entertain his myriad girlfriends before the battalion completed training and was finally deployed to eastern Poland. And that hadn't seem so bad at first, as at appeared it was there only to passively stand guard against any thought Russia might have to test the Molotov-Ribbentrop Pact.

What eventually happened, of course, was while Hitler had quickly conquered much of continental Europe, two things the Nazi party had hoped for, and many had truly expected, did not happen. Great Britain hung tough, refusing to make any concessions to Germany. And Wilkie lost to Roosevelt in the 1940 election for U.S. President. In spite of these disappointments, Hitler, who'd always intended to be the first to violate the Molotov-Ribbentrop Pact, decided to go forward with an invasion of Russia. He'd gradually built up a huge body of troops and machinery along the entire western border of Russia, and on 22 June 1941 launched a massive invasion (Operation Barbarossa). It went well at first, but like Napoleon's venture two centuries earlier, the invasion ultimately bogged down. And when Japan bombed the U.S. fleet in Hawaii on 07 December 1941, Hitler's problems multiplied. When the United States immediately declared war on Japan, it also abandoned any semblance of neutrality regarding the conflict in Europe by declaring war on Germany and Italy.

For Klaus and Dieter, Operation Barbarossa quickly became a hellish experience. As soon as it began, they were made battery group commanders in battalions assigned to different sectors where both came under frequent fire over most of the next two and a half years. During that time both received field promotions so when they finally met again in December 1943, they both held the rank of major. (Note: here and elsewhere Klaus and Dieter are referred to using the equivalent English term for their rank; in fact, as members of *der Waffen-SS* Klaus's and Dieter's final rank in German would have been *SS-Sturmbahnführer.*)

Now beyond war weary and just recently released from brief hospitalizations for minor wounds, they'd recently met again for the first time in more than a year. Shortly thereafter they felt as though they had won the lottery, as both received orders to report to Riga, Latvia, there to be engaged with recruitment and training of troops to rebuild two badly depleted *Waffen-SS* divisions. A year earlier, Soviet troops had finally managed to break a small pathway into Leningrad through a longstanding German blockade. And though Germany attempted to sustain its siege of the city for a time, on 27 January 1944, Hitler decided to order a strategic westward withdrawal to allow some of the most depleted elements of Army Group North time to rest, restore troop strength, and prepare for an overwhelming counteroffensive he hoped would surely defeat Russia for good. Along the way, he ordered the retreating troops to ransack Russian museums, churches, palaces, and homes of the wealthy, and to look for art, jewelry, or other items of value to be shipped back to Königsberg to enrich the Reich.

On their way to Riga, Klaus and Dieter had been ordered to pause briefly at the Catherine Palace, there to search for any smaller articles of value that might have been overlooked by a previous search detail. Several days earlier, an SS officer, assisted by a team of regular *Wehrmacht* soldiers from Army Group North, had labored around the clock to dissemble and ship to Königsberg an entire chamber called the Amber Room, a priceless piece of art, featuring gilding, carvings, 450 kilograms of amber panels, gold leaf, gemstones, and mirrors, and also included statues of angels and children. Some considered the Amber Room to be the eighth Wonder of the World.

Once inside the palace, their initial find occurred after Dieter yelled, "Catch!" suddenly throwing to Klaus a baseball he always carried. The throw was high, and in trying to catch it Klaus jumped up and back, hitting a large gilded mirror. It fell to the ground and shattered, revealing a sizeable oil painting on the wall. "Seven years bad luck for you, Klaus."

Getting up and taking a close look at the painting, Klaus said, "I don't think so. Magda taught me a lot about classical European art, and I think this could be a genuine Rembrandt. I have to think someone was in a burning hurry and hoped the mirror could serve as a temporary shield until he or she could come back to properly package and transfer it to a safer place. In fact, if they did this once, maybe there are others covered the same way." The friends spent the next half hour tossing more mirrors to the ground and ultimately found three more paintings: another Rembrandt and two that Klaus suspected had been painted by Vermeer.

An hour later in a basement storeroom of the palace, the friends made another discovery. In it were twenty-five eighty kilo barrels of flour. Following Hitler's order to destroy as well as to plunder, they set about opening and pouring out the contents to make the flour unusable. Part of the way through, Klaus watched with amusement as Dieter struggled in vain to turn a barrel over.

"Where has your strength gone, Dieter? Too much time spent milking the cow?"

Replying with an obscene gesture Dieter said, "Give me a hand, Klaus. There really is something odd about this one. It's much heavier than the others."

Together, the men managed to turn the barrel on its side and open the top. Out flowed flour, but packed in the bottom they found something quite different, thirty small sacks, each closed with a seal bearing the likeness of Tsar Nicholas II.

Klaus picked one up, surprisingly heavy for its small size. Breaking open the seal, he poured out the contents and exclaimed, "Gold coins, Dieter! There must be thousands of them in those sacks. We're wealthy, or we will be if we can find a way to hide most of these from that prick Hofstetter when he comes later this afternoon."

Klaus counted the contents of the sack. It held two hundred fifty fifteen-ruble coins. All bore a likeness of Tsar Nicholas II, were dated 1897, and appeared never to have been circulated. Klaus grabbed a handful and put them in his pocket. Dieter did the same and then returned the rest to the bag. Klaus picked up another bag and hefted it.

"I'd guess close to three kilos. Assuming they're 90 percent gold, the melt value of all these coins ought to be…" He closed his eyes and did some mental arithmetic. "Something…something like…400,000 Reichsmarks! A fortune, Dieter. How are we going to spirit these away?"

Dieter thought for a moment. "We could use the spare wheels and tires. The Kommandeurwagen has two, one on top and the other under the hood. We can deflate the tubes, take the tires off the wheels, stuff the coins inside, then remount the tires on the wheels and reattach them to their mounting brackets."

"And if we have a puncture on the way back to camp?"

"Let's hope we don't. I'll drive very carefully."

Making multiple trips, Klaus and Dieter carried the bags upstairs, laid them on the floor by the paintings in the foyer, then took a break and went outside for lunch and a cigarette.

Next, the friends headed upstairs, having been told the previous search detail hadn't had time to work through six bedrooms in the east wing of the palace. Carefully working through them one by one they discovered nothing of interest in the first five. The last chamber was substantially larger and also much darker because, unlike the others, all the windows were cloaked with heavy drapery. Entering, Klaus tripped on the doorsill, but broke his fall by clutching at an ornate armoire, slightly displacing it from the wall. Regaining his balance, he used his flashlight to inspect the interior and the two drawers at the base but found nothing of interest. He was about to cross the room and open the drapery to allow a proper inspection of the whole room when his light caught the image of a small sculpted figure of the double-headed Russian imperial eagle on the wall behind the armoire. Close inspection revealed a hinged seam between the dual heads and the rest of the eagle's body. *Interesting.* He grasped the heads, pulled lightly, heard a grating sound, and saw a small panel under the armoire slide open. *A royal hiding place for something valuable?*

"Dieter, come look at this."

Beneath the open panel Klaus's flashlight revealed a small oak chest, its cover also adorned with an image of the Russian eagle. He pushed the armoire further into the room to gain access, then knelt and lifted the chest from its hiding place. It was locked, so he forced the blade of his knife between the cover and base, twisted it, and broke the lock open. He'd anticipated the chest might well contain precious jewelry, and he was right. There was jewelry, quite a lot of it, but he whistled as he saw something far more interesting. Lined with purple velvet, the chest was divided into three parts. While the center section held a collection of gold rings, earrings, several necklaces inlaid with diamonds and sapphires, and an array of loose gemstones, in the two sections on either side lay six ornate, bejeweled, egg-shaped *objets d'art*.

"Dieter, I do believe we've just stumbled on the missing Imperial Fabergé eggs, or some of them at least."

"Missing eggs?"

"Magda told me about these. She learned about them in one of her classes at the Art Institute. She told me that over a number of years Tsars Alexander III and Nicholas II commissioned the House of Fabergé in St. Petersburg to create a series of unique bejeweled eggs as gifts for their wives and mothers. After the Bolsheviks killed the Tsar, his wife, and children, the eggs and all other items of value belonging to the Romanov family were taken and stored in the Kremlin Armoury. The Soviet government later sold some, but an audit later showed eight of the eggs had gone missing. Finding these now in this place makes me strongly suspect we've just found six of those missing eggs."

"They look pretty Klaus, but are they really very valuable? I'm thinking the jewelry is what we want."

"It's a fact the Soviets didn't get much for the eggs they sold during the depression. But each one of these eggs is absolutely unique, so after the war is finally over, I predict collectors will be willing to pay a fortune for them. They could end up being worth more than all this jewelry and the gold we found this morning put together."

The men stood silent for a moment to let that thought sink in. Klaus struggled, but only briefly, with the ethical dilemma of keeping their find secret as opposed to sending it on to the treasury of the Third Reich. The seemingly endless war, as well as the attitudes of many higher echelon officers had made him cynical. He thought, *If we give these up, they won't make it to the Third Reich anyway. They'll only end up in Hofstetter's pocket. Better us than him.*

"Dieter, let's keep the eggs and half the jewelry for ourselves. We'll let Hofstetter have the paintings, half of the jewelry, and as many sacks of the gold as we can't manage to cram into the spare tires. He's sure to take his cut before sending whatever is left to Königsberg or Berlin."

Klaus walked to a window and used his knife to cut strips of cloth from one of the drapes. Meanwhile, Dieter ran outside to remove the spare wheels from their mountings on the Kommandeurwagen. Klaus met him there a few minutes later, carrying the six Fabergé eggs and two collections of jewelry and gemstones, each enclosed in a protective wrapping of drapery. Then he made several trips to and from the palace foyer, each time carrying several sacks of the gold coins. Together, they managed to stuff the eggs, the jewelry, and twenty-four of the thirty sacks into the tires. The remaining sacks of gold, the chest holding half the jewelry, and the four paintings found during the morning were left in the foyer for Colonel Hofstetter. With some difficulty, Dieter managed to remount the heavy packed wheels to their brackets on top and under the hood.

At 16:00, a large Mercedes staff car followed by a 2.5 ton, 6x6 truck came to a stop where Klaus and Dieter sat on the palace steps. Four regular *Wehrmacht* soldiers got out of the truck, while the driver of the Mercedes, an SS Lieutenant, walked to the passenger side door, opened it for his commanding officer, and saluted.

SS Lieutenant Colonel Wilhelm Hofstetter emerged, a short, balding man who peered unsmilingly through a pair of old-fashioned wire rim spectacles and carried himself with an officious bearing. Conceding their difference in rank, Klaus and Dieter stood at attention, extended their right arms in a salute, and said, "Heil, Hitler." Klaus thought, *What an odious little martinet. That showy pre-war black uniform he still insists on wearing instead of the standard grey-green makes him an easy target. But then, no big loss if that should happen.*

Hofstetter briefly acknowledged the salute, then addressed Klaus and Dieter, "What have you found for the Third Reich today, Majors?"

"It's been a productive day, Colonel. I think you will be impressed."

Hofstetter remained stern faced as he, his adjutant, and the four soldiers followed Klaus and Dieter into the main foyer of the palace. The Colonel's eyes lit up, and Klaus saw the corner of his mouth twitch as he examined the paintings by Rembrandt and Vermeer. *I'll bet at least one of those finds its way into his personal collection.* After a cursory examination of the jewelry and the six sacks of coins, Hofstetter turned to Klaus and Dieter and said, "This is *all* of it?"

Knowing the colonel would expect him and Dieter to withhold at least something, Klaus smiled, jingled the pockets of his tunic, and replied, "Well, *almost* all of it, Colonel, except for a handful of coins and a small present for my girlfriend." Withdrawing his hands from his pockets, he displayed a dozen gold coins and a pair of diamond studded earrings. Dieter followed suit, showing that he too had some of the coins and a couple pieces of jewelry. The colonel made no comment, but whispered something to his adjutant, who turned and left the palace. Through the open doorway Klaus and Dieter watched as the lieutenant examined their vehicle, looking under the seats and under the hood. They held their collective breaths and were relieved to see the treasure-laden spare wheels pass inspection.

Returning to the palace, the lieutenant whispered a message to the colonel. Apparently satisfied, the colonel ordered the crew of soldiers to inventory everything in the foyer and to construct protective framing around the paintings to ensure their safety while being transported back to Berlin. Turning to Klaus and Dieter, Hofstetter simply said, "You are dismissed." The friends responded with another salute and quickly left the building.

As Dieter put the Kommandeurwagen in gear and pulled away, he glanced over his shoulder and muttered, "*Scheissen! Was ein Arschloch.*" (Transl. Shit! What an asshole.) Klaus just smiled and began to hum the "Deutschlandlied," the Song of Germany, the national anthem since 1922.

That evening, as several other SS officers celebrated their pending relocation to what they hoped would be a more congenial post by drinking themselves to stupefaction with stolen Russian vodka, Klaus and Dieter remained sober and considered how best to safely and secretly transport their treasure.

"We can't risk driving all the way to Riga without a functional spare tire," said Klaus.

"Those sacks of gold coins weigh a lot, but they aren't very large," said Dieter. "I think six would just about fill a medium size metal ammunition box and then weigh about the same as a full box. There's a dump in the field out back with a bunch of discarded empty boxes. Let's pack the eggs, gold, and jewelry in them. No one should question our carrying ammunition boxes in the Kommandeurwagen."

Dieter parked directly in front of their tent, then walked over to the waste dump and scavenged five empty ammunition boxes. In the meantime, Klaus loosened the nuts holding the spare wheels to their brackets on the roof and under the hood of the Kommandeurwagen. Looking to make sure no one was watching, the men wrestled the wheels to the ground and rolled them into the tent. Half an hour later when the treasure had been transferred, Dieter put empty spare wheels back on the roof and under the hood.

CHAPTER 3

Shortly before dawn, Klaus and Dieter joined a column of armored vehicles and troop trucks heading west to the Russian city of Pskov. Most of the soldiers in the vehicles, members of Army Group North units hit with heavy losses, sat quiet, gray with fatigue, as the mud-spattered column proceeded under heavy snow flurries. Other elements of Army Group North remained in position to the east and continued to sustain a strong defensive position in most places. But with Germany having been soundly defeated in Africa, losing important support with Italy's surrender the previous year, now heavily engaged with Allied forces in central Italy, and snippets of news from the Western Front suggesting the Allies might soon launch a major cross-channel offensive from Great Britain, Klaus and Dieter couldn't help but wonder. Was it *really* possible for Germany to fight on so many fronts and still win? *Der Führer* had promised his troops this temporary withdrawal from Russia to allow time for rest and regrouping would later allow them to launch a massive counteroffensive sure to destroy Stalin. Germany could still win the war and have a bright future, couldn't it? The friends kept working hard to convince themselves of this because they needed to believe it. The alternative was too frightening to confront at this point.

Seventy kilometers south of Leningrad, the concern Klaus voiced yesterday happened. Obscured by snow and mud, the right front wheel of the Kommandeurwagen hit a large hole, blew out the tire, and bent the wheel. As soon as Dieter could ease the car to the berm, Klaus jumped out and removed the spare wheel from the bracket on the roof. Dieter set the brake, got out, and jacked up the front end. A few minutes later, they were able to rejoin the column.

The rest of the journey was unremarkable, with the column reaching Pskov shortly after 19:00. Klaus and Dieter carried the five ammunition boxes to their tent, ate their rations there, then slept fitfully, fully clothed, with their pistols close at hand.

The next day they reached Riga, and reported to the new training base commander, SS Colonel Karl Meier, who confirmed their duty over the next months would be to help oversee the conscription and training of new recruits for the 1st and 2nd Latvian Legions, also known as the 15th and 19th *Waffen SS* Divisions, which had suffered very heavy casualties. For this they learned they would be based at a new training base close to the Salaspils work camp, where Klaus had temporarily been billeted in 1941 while awaiting assignment to a different artillery battalion before going on to the Russian front. Then, the best news. They were granted three days of leave in Riga and, as a temporary billet, given private use of a large home recently seized from a Russian sympathizer.

Klaus and Dieter couldn't help smiling. Three days! The top three things on their minds: where to safely cache the treasure, beer, and sex, although not necessarily in that order. At the house, they immediately looked for a safe place to store the eggs and other booty. In the study, Dieter discovered a large wall safe behind a painting. The lock had been broken and the safe stood empty. Although it was large enough, it was too obvious.

A moment later Dieter found Klaus looking at a large fireplace in the drawing room. The opening was shallow but quite wide and stood nearly a meter and a half high. Stooping a bit and craning his neck to look upward, Klaus noted the rounded breast leading to a narrower neck directly above the back wall. Extending his hand through the neck he found what he was hoping for, a broad horizontal shelf in the much wider smoke chamber feeding the chimney.

"Look at this, Dieter, I think this can serve us until we can settle on a more permanent hideaway."

"How…?"

"This is a Rumford fireplace. The large shallow firebox reflects a lot of heat into the room, but of course there's a lot of smoke too. Rumsford's solution to that is this curved breast starting at the front above the firebox that channels the smoke through a narrower passage before opening into a large smoke chamber that then connects to the chimney. This creates a Venturi effect that accelerates the flow of smoke into the chimney…"

"I know about the Venturi effect Klaus, but…"

"The point I was about to make is that the base of the smoke chamber is flat and runs the full width of the fireplace. That narrow neck still looks wide enough that I think we can slip those ammunition boxes through it one at a time, letting them stand side by side on the shelf in back."

Having checked one item off the list, their next priorities were beer and female company. The friends knew they could just stop at one of the military brothels and spend fifteen minutes with a tired whore for as little as five to ten RM. (In 1943, the Reichsmark (RM) was pegged at 4.2 RM per U.S. dollar when a Troy ounce of gold was worth about $34.) But that held little appeal, and price was scarcely an issue when you had a handful of fifteen-ruble gold coins in your pocket. Another officer at SS headquarters had told Dieter about a place called Bierstube Böttcher that had a large stock of good German beer, music, and attractive feminine companionship willing to spend the whole night with a client for the right price.

That evening, at a corner table in Bierstube Böttcher, Klaus and Dieter sat, smoking, listening to music, and working on a second liter of the dark lager that hadn't been available in Russia at any price. Several more junior officers sat at two nearby tables, talking, drinking, and playing cards. As they enjoyed the ambience of the place, two attractive women entered and surveyed the men there. The men at all three tables looked up and smiled. The women smiled in return, but quickly reading the ranks, strolled over to Klaus and Dieter.

Placing her hand lightly on Klaus's shoulder one said, "You are new here are you not, Major? I'm Karina." Then turning to her companion and Dieter, she added, "And Major, this is my friend, Alise."

Alise smiled and said, "Would you gentlemen care for some company this evening?"

Klaus rose, pulled over two chairs from a nearby table, and said, "By all means, ladies. Please join us. I'm Klaus and this is Dieter. We've just returned from the Russian front and are celebrating our escape from hell."

Dieter signaled the waiter and ordered a bottle of French champagne for the table. The first went quickly, so Dieter ordered another. By the time it was mostly consumed, the girls were giggling, and conversation had largely given way to more physical sorts of communication.

Karina snuggled close to Klaus, put her lips to his ear, and whispered an invitation to take the party upstairs to the apartment she shared with Alise.

Dieter ordered a third bottle of champagne in a bucket of ice to take with them. Then the foursome made their way, somewhat unsteadily, to a staircase at the back of the building. Upstairs, Alise took the champagne from Dieter and whispered, "For later, *liebchen*. We don't want to drink too much right now, do we? Let's dance a little."

The girls had a windup gramophone, and Karina put on a record of slow dance music. Approaching Klaus, she reached up, clasped her hands behind his neck, pulled him to her, kissed him fully on the lips, and pressed her body close against his as they swayed gently to the music. Alise followed suit with Dieter.

As the record ended, Karina said, "It's very warm in here, Klaus. Take off your tunic. Then come help me select something more comfortable," as she led the way to her bedroom. Dieter glanced at Klaus with a look that said, *This is what we came for, buddy. Good luck.*

The bed in Karina's room had a coverlet decorated with the outline of a large red heart. Klaus sat on the edge and removed his boots as Karina entered her closet and emerged a minute later wearing a short, sheer red negligee that left little to the imagination. Then she bent, clearly displaying her flower, as she rummaged in the drawer of the nightstand looking for something. Klaus felt a growing tightness and quickly moved to shed his shirt and trousers.

Turning, Karina looked at him and said, "Goodness, Major, how you've grown in the last few minutes. Here, let me help with the *lettre francaise*." Kneeling, she unwrapped the condom and pulled down his undershorts to reveal his bulging member. Klaus nearly lost it at that point, but closed his eyes, thinking intently about the time outside Leningrad when he'd nearly been killed by an exploding mortar.

Properly attired, Klaus extracted Karina from her flimsy negligee and cast her onto the bed. He took her quickly and intensely, after which they separated briefly, giggling and gasping for breath.

"Round one, Kari," said Klaus. "Prepare for round two."

This time, he slowly caressed her, running his hands lightly over her entire body, stopping to gently stimulate her erogenous areas, lightly kissing her breasts, neck, ears, and lips. As a prostitute Karina was used to being taken hard and fast as Klaus had done at first, but this time she found his approach unexpectedly pleasant. Slowly, she felt herself becoming more and more aroused. Reaching down, she guided him inside, then holding him close, she kissed him, and lifted her hips rhythmically with increasing frequency until, with a moan, they both climaxed. After a short rest, one more round. Then the lovers finally separated and fell asleep.

For Klaus, sleep wasn't restful. Around 05:00, he awoke shaking, sweating, and in a dark mood because of the dream he'd just had. In it, Magda had appeared. At first, she looked vibrant, healthy, and happy. But then he saw her change, become ill and take to her bed, coughing and desperately trying to breathe. Finally, with her last breath, she whispered to Klaus that she loved him and told him that he would now have to be both mother and father to their son Horst.

Looking over at the sleeping Karina, Klaus suddenly felt dirty and disgusted with himself. He just had to leave. Rising quietly, he put on his underwear, shirt, and pants, left three of the fifteen-ruble gold coins, worth about 160 RM, on the table by Karina's bed, and tiptoed to the parlor to recover his hat, jacket, and boots. Now fully dressed, he cracked open the door to the other bedroom, peered inside, and saw that both Dieter and Alise were still asleep. Returning to the parlor, he took a scrap of paper and pen from his jacket pocket, scrawled the words *Café Antons*, and left it for Dieter to find when he finally woke up. Then he descended the stairs at the back of the building. For now, he only wanted to walk, walk and think. Dieter could pick him up later at the cafe.

Walking briskly, partly at random, but with his ultimate destination in mind, Klaus finally reached the cafe as dawn was breaking and the place was just opening for business. Nodding to the proprietor, he took a table near the door, ordered an espresso, and lit a cigarette. The waiter quickly brought the coffee and with it a week-old copy of the *Berliner Lokal-Anzeiger*. Klaus thanked him and pretended to scan the paper, but his thoughts were elsewhere.

Magda! More than five years now since his wife had passed and he couldn't seem to move on. The dream he'd had last night had occurred before, but waking from it in the bed of a prostitute made him ashamed. Not only did his dalliance with Karina seem wrong, he also felt guilty about Horst. *It's been so long since my last leave to see him for just a few days. He's growing fast and I'm not there to help him. I must get leave and see him again soon.*

An hour and a half later, Dieter pulled the Kommandeurwagen in front of Café Antons to find Klaus working on his third espresso and pretending to eat a croissant.

"What the hell happened with you and Karina? Was she not good? But, no, she must have been since you left her way more money than she expected. So why did you leave? She doesn't understand and neither do I."

Klaus looked at this friend and just said, "Magda." Then he told Dieter of his dream.

Dieter leaned over, placed a hand on his friend's shoulder, and said, "Yes, you and Magda were the perfect couple. You loved her like no one else and were utterly faithful to her in life. Her death was a tragedy, but she's gone, Klaus. You've got to get on with your own life. Do you really believe her spirit floats about in the ether watching and passing judgment on everything you do here? If so, then I think you must resign your commission immediately and enter the nearest monastery."

Klaus shook his head, smiling just a bit at Dieter's sarcasm. "No, of course not. But…"

"But what, Klaus?" Dieter clapped him on the shoulder. "Come back with me. Alise and Karina will cook breakfast for us, and we can stay with them again tonight. Tell Karina she didn't do anything to upset you. Tell her…tell her you're sorry you had to leave so mysteriously, but you had an important early morning assignation with a secret agent, and thought you could return before she woke up. Everything will be fine, except that you've set the pay scale pretty high for an evening with a couple of whores, even if they are very pretty and compliant."

Klaus shook his head again. "You go back, Dieter. I…I just can't. It isn't Karina's fault, but I wouldn't feel right being with her again. Give her my regrets. Enlarge a bit on that fiction you just invented. Tell her the contact I met at the cafe provided top secret information critical to the security of the Fatherland. I can't even share it with you but have been ordered to leave immediately on a special mission."

Dieter rolled his eyes and shook his head, but realizing he wasn't going to change his friend's mind, rose to leave. "Klaus, we've got just three days before we have to go to the training camp. After that, there will be little or no opportunity to visit Alise, Karina, or any other pleasant companion of the female persuasion. I'm going to spend the next couple days with Alise. What do you intend to do?"

"Go ahead, Dieter. Enjoy yourself. While you're happily screwing your brains out, I'll apply myself to protecting our future. Once we're at the training camp, it won't just be female companionship that's lacking. We'll have little or no personal privacy of any kind, so we have to find a secure place to hide the treasure. This morning while I was walking, I got an idea, but we're going to need some tools and special supplies." Klaus rose, drew Dieter close, and whispered the details of his plan.

Turning to the waiter, Klaus pointed to money he'd placed on the table. Then the two men left the cafe. This time, Klaus drove, dropping Dieter around the corner from the apartment that Karina and Alise shared. As he walked away, Klaus called, "Right here, at 15:00 tomorrow." Dieter nodded and threw a casual salute.

Klaus's first stop was at a shop he'd passed that morning. Inside, he had a brief but animated conversation with the proprietor, a Mr. Svens Balodis, who assured him he'd be happy to fill the major's order. However, he couldn't possibly have it ready by tomorrow. But when Klaus offered to pay twice the usual price, the impossible suddenly became doable.

The following day, Klaus parked the Kommandeurwagen around the corner from Bierstube Böttcher and waited for Dieter. At 15:05 he appeared, still buttoning his jacket and looking as though he'd had little sleep the previous night. As soon as he got in, Dieter surveyed the collection of items in the back and said, "A gasoline auger? Are we going ice fishing, Klaus?" Klaus just smiled, put the car in gear, and headed southeast out of Riga in the direction of Salaspils. A little over an hour later, he pulled off the dirt service road and parked out of sight behind a line of trees. Then he directed Dieter's gaze to a location some fifty meters distant.

"Even if there's fighting around here in the future, I think our stash should be safe buried over there. Let's get this done quickly. When the war is over, we can recover it at leisure. But just in case things don't go quite as we hope, let's each take one of the eggs now and keep it close as a talisman. Afterall, *Der Spatz in der Hand ist immer besser als die Taube auf dem Dach* (Transl. The sparrow in the hand is always better than the dove on the roof). Since all the eggs are hinged and hollow, I've loaded each one with several pieces of jewelry and loose gemstones. Take your pick, Dieter."

CHAPTER 4

The next several months seemed to Klaus and Dieter like a vacation on the Mediterranean compared to their former service in Russia. No one was shooting at them, and while accommodations at the training camp were decidedly basic, they weren't uncomfortable.

In February, as they were just getting settled at the training base, the main body of Army Group North was defending a position at the northern end of the Panther line in Russia, extending from Lake Pepius on the border of Estonia past the city of Pskov to where remaining elements of the much weakened 15th and 19th *Waffen-SS* were stationed by the Sorota and Velikaya rivers. That line managed to hold firm against several Soviet attacks, strengthening hope that the units withdrawn at the end of January could soon be reinforced to a point, making an effective anti-Soviet counteroffensive possible.

In April, Klaus applied for leave to visit his son and sister in Dresden and was told he could take a week it at the end of June. However, that was cancelled the day after the Allies landed in Normandy the first week of June. And two weeks later, the base outside Riga was put on ready alert over news of a marked increase in partisan activity behind German lines to the east. His request for leave received a final death notice on 23 June, when to everyone's shock Stalin launched Operation Bagration, a sudden, massive attack that quickly broke through German lines to the south in Byelorussia, and continued on and on, eventually liberating all of western Russian and pushing German forces out of eastern Poland.

Two hours later all personnel at the base were ordered to be ready to deploy eastward later that day. Klaus and Dieter were immediately directed to assume positions as battalion commanders and to accompany the new, recently trained troops to rejoin elements of the 19th and 15th *Waffen-SS* already at the front. Given no time to even consider recovering the treasure, and unable to meet and speak privately as the two battalions were deployed some distance apart, the friends tried to stay in touch by sending coded messages, each urging the other to obtain *souvenirs* if and when the opportunity arose. In August, Dieter and the 15th *Waffen-SS*, having again taken very heavy casualties, was transferred west to Prussia, to take on more new recruits being trained near Danzig (now Gdansk, Poland).

The 19th *Waffen-SS* continued to engage the Soviet army throughout the summer, but the division was progressively forced to retreat toward Riga. As it fell back, Klaus tried, without success, to disengage long enough to recover the treasure he and Dieter had so confidently hidden several months earlier. Further advances finally brought the Soviet army within artillery range of Riga. And on 9 October, some 200,000 German and Latvian troops, including the 19th *Waffen-SS* Division, were forced to abandon the city and withdraw northwest to the Courland Peninsula. The Soviets followed, fully occupying Riga on 13 October. Over the next six months the Soviets launched six major assaults against the German forces, resulting in heavy losses on both sides.

After long refusing to consider a complete withdrawal, Hitler finally decided to evacuate seven German divisions from the Courland Peninsula. Klaus, having lost all contact with Dieter and no longer able to convince himself there was any way whatsoever Germany could win the war, desperately sought a way to somehow reach his son and sister in Dresden. He requested, and was granted, permission to transfer out of the 19th Waffen-SS and join one of the seven divisions being relocated to fight in Poland and later on in Germany.

On 17 January 1945, Warsaw fell to the Soviets, and from there, with a marked advantage over the German Army in terms both of manpower and artillery, they continued to push west and south, advancing thirty to forty kilometers a day. By the end of March, the Soviet army was positioned just sixty kilometers east of Berlin along the River Oder. Further south, Budapest fell to other units of the Soviet Army on 13 February, and on 13 April it captured Vienna.

CHAPTER 5

It was nearly over. Hitler's thousand-year Reich had lasted just twelve years. On 16 April, 1945, the Soviet Army launched another major offensive, pushing west across the Oder and Neisse Rivers, aiming at Berlin. By 24 April the city was encircled on three sides, and the Battle of Berlin was about to enter its final chapter. Germany had only limited forces within the city, approximately 45,000 soldiers belonging to several weakened *Wehrmacht* and *Waffen-SS* divisions, plus the police, the Hitler Youth, and several thousand older men in the *Volksturm*, many of whom had served in the army when they were younger.

Dieter and remnants of the 15th *Waffen-SS* reached Berlin on 20 April, at the end of a long fighting withdrawal from Danzig, and were assigned to help man the second of three rings of defense around the city.

Klaus, and the few surviving members of the unit to which he'd been attached, reached Berlin on 23 April. Following the Battle of Seelow Heights above the western edge of the Oder River, Klaus had hoped it might be possible for him to head south to Dresden. Since hearing about the firebombing in February, he'd been frantic to know if his son and sister had survived. For a brief time, he'd even considered desertion, but then his sense of discipline kicked in. Surviving German troops from all points of the compass were being pulled inward to set up multiple rings of defense around Berlin. Klaus's group was directed to the city center.

When Klaus learned the 15th *Waffen-SS* was in the city and that Dieter was still alive, he tried to reach him. However, the army's communication network was now so degraded he was unable to make contact. In fact, over the next several days, defenders in various parts of the city often had to rely on the civilian telephone system, asking anyone who answered a call to provide an eyewitness account of what the enemy seemed to be doing at that location.

The morning of 30 April found Klaus pacing nervously back and forth in a room that had been converted into a bunker in the heavily damaged Reichstag. Alternately peering out a slit at the plaza in front of the building and back at a street map of the city, he kept trying to work out a route of escape from Berlin. At this point, the hope of all but the most diehard German soldiers was to hang on just long enough to allow Allied forces to reach the city from the West, and then surrender to them instead of the Russians. But in fact, no immediate help was coming from that quarter. The Allies were no longer pushing to the East but were drawn up along the Elbe River some 100 kilometers west of Berlin. German soldiers now in the city would have to find a way to escape and head west to reach them.

By late evening of 30 April, elements of the Soviet army had advanced to within a few blocks of the Reichstag and were preparing to attack the symbolically important building. Klaus grew ever more anxious. Keeping his pistol close at hand, he turned and nearly shot another SS officer who unexpectedly entered the room behind him as he was surveying the plaza.

"Klaus! Christ! Don't shoot! It's me, Dieter."

Dropping his pistol on the table, Klaus embraced his friend. "Dieter! My God! It's so good to see you again. I tried to reach you, but…"

"I know. I know. It's nearly impossible to get through to anyone now. My men and I were on the second ring of defense, but we were pushed back yesterday. Now we're trying to hold a line just a kilometer north of here. I ran into Captain Mueller there. He told me where to find you. Listen, Klaus, I have news…"

"Yes?"

"*Der Führer*. He's dead. Earlier today, he and Eva killed themselves."

Klaus stood silent, the news failing to elicit strong feelings of either sorrow or relief. It just was. The only thing left to think of now was his personal survival and that of his family.

"What can we do, Dieter? We mustn't be captured by the Russians."

"There are no good options. We can stay here, try to look like civilian refugees, and hope the Russians don't shoot us or starve us to death. Or we can try to escape the city, work our way west, and surrender to the Allies. I think I may try to pass as a civilian, just to see if that might make it possible to somehow slip out of Berlin and head west. Yesterday, when we retreated to our current position, I found some soiled work clothes and boots in an abandoned apartment. I could go get them and bring them here. We can shed our uniforms, put on those old clothes, and join one of the lines of refugees you've seen streaming past here all day. What do you think?"

Klaus hesitated. "What about our identification papers? We're dead men if the Russians even suspect we're SS."

"I've already lifted documents from a dozen dead civilians. None of them look a great deal like us, not like that *doppelgänger* aide of yours in the next room, but if we make ourselves sufficiently dirty and disheveled, then maybe the Russians won't look too hard at our ID cards."

Klaus and Dieter sat together for several hours. They shared Klaus's last four cigarettes and a half bottle of schnapps. Then Dieter left, promising to return before dawn with the work clothes and false identification documents. Behind the Reichstag, he began to trace in reverse the route he'd taken to reach the Reichstag and made it back without a problem. There he caught a brief nap, loaded a sack with dirty work clothes and the ID cards taken from the bodies of several dead civilians he hoped would allow him and Klaus to conceal their true identities. Just before dawn, he set out again, not knowing that in the past two hours a unit of Soviet infantry had occupied one of the blocks he had to cross. Hearing noise ahead, Dieter ducked into an alley, set down the bag of clothes, and cautiously looked around the corner just in time to be lit up by a powerful flashlight and hear a voice with a Russian accent shout in German, "*Halten sie!*" The light blinded him so he couldn't see the soldiers in this Soviet patrol already had their rifles raised to shoot when their sergeant shouted in Russian an order meaning, "Stop! Don't shoot! This officer has a dispatch case. We'll take him prisoner and deliver him to the colonel for interrogation."

Obeying with some reluctance, two of the soldiers grabbed Dieter and took away his pistol, while a third struck him across the face with the butt of his rifle. With blood dripping from his nose, Dieter was frog marched two blocks to a nearby building.

"Sir!" Sergeant Popov stood at attention and saluted.

Colonel Gennady Yakushin looked up from a map of central Berlin as Popov pushed Dieter through the doorway.

"Sir. We captured this German officer and saw that he carries a dispatch case. I thought he might have documents of importance so ordered my men to bring him to you for interrogation."

"Thank you, Sergeant. Bring him into my office." Colonel Yakushin inclined his head toward a wooden desk chair, and the soldiers forcibly threw the conscious but still dizzy and bleeding Dieter into it. Then they stood at attention, saluted, and left.

Gennady Yakushin looked at his captive and addressed him in German. "I see you are a member of the *Schutzstaffel*, the evil arm of your army specializing in murdering innocent civilians. What is your name, Major?"

Dieter made no response to the Colonel's assertion about the SS, and simply replied, "Dieter Kleinschmidt."

"Well, Major Kleinschmidt, let's see what's in your dispatch case." He peered inside and was surprised to see it held no maps, orders, or other documents, only Dieter's wallet and two small objects wrapped in cloth. Inside the wallet, he found Dieter's identity papers, several hundred Reichsmarks, and two photographs, one of Dieter posed with a pretty, blonde woman, the other a picture of a smiling SS major with a handwritten inscription that read 'For Dieter, Klaus Gustmann.'

"Who is this?" demanded the Colonel.

"A friend."

"A colleague? He is with you here in Berlin?"

Dieter remained silent. His gut twisted with fear and the blow to his head made him sick to his stomach. He was pretty sure no matter what he said they were going to kill him, and felt as though he was going to vomit.

Colonel Yakushin fingered the pistol at his hip and said, "Major, I asked you a direct question!"

Dieter swallowed, and finally croaked, "Yes."

The colonel had nearly decided there was nothing of significance to learn from this prisoner and was about to tell Sergeant Popov to take him outside and shoot him. But then he glanced at the back of the photograph of Major Klaus Gustmann. On it was written the following words in German:

Nach dem Krieg, ein Fest der gelben Kuchen, Eier, und Beeren

And underneath that, a line of letters and numbers that read: 5G65Va-65G127Oz-310G80SG

Yakushin translated out loud saying, "After the war, a feast of yellow cakes, eggs, and berries? I'm curious, Major. What does this mean? And this line of letters and numbers looks like a code of some kind. Tell me what that is."

Dieter hesitated.

As he waited for an answer, Yakushin unwrapped one of the two cloth-wrapped objects he'd found in the dispatch case. Out spilled a pile of fifteen-ruble gold coins. Unwrapping the other, he looked with amazement at an exquisite gold egg-shaped object inlaid with diamonds and rubies.

"My God!" Yakushin had heard of the Imperial Fabergé eggs missing from the Kremlin Armoury since the 1920s. Now he felt sure he must be looking at one of them, a rare item that should be worth a great deal of money.

"Where did you get this?"

Dieter didn't answer.

"Major, not only are you and your friend Gustmann murderers of many Russian civilians, but you've also committed a grave crime of theft against my country." He spread out the gold coins, held up the Fabergé egg, and said, "That reference to 'yellow cake' and 'eggs' now takes on new meaning. I suspect you and your friend may have others. And what does the word 'berries' stand for?" Thrusting the photograph at Dieter, the colonel demanded in a hard voice, "Tell me the meaning of this code. Does it point to where you've hidden the rest of the eggs?"

Dieter was now terrified and sweating profusely. He stammered, and said, "I…I…No, I know nothing about any other eggs…I…" then stopped.

Withdrawing his pistol, the colonel placed the muzzle firmly against Dieter's left temple and said, "You have a choice, Major. Tell me what I wish to know, and I will send you to a prisoner of war camp where you may *possibly* survive, or I will shoot you now."

Finally Dieter choked out, "Yes…there are…four more eggs, jewels, and gold coins. We…we found them in the Catherine Palace…took them to Latvia. They're hidden there."

"And that line of code tells where to find them?"

Dieter hesitated, and the colonel once again pressed his pistol against Dieter's head.

"I...I...yes, I will tell you."

There was a sharp knock at the door. Turning, the colonel shouted, "Go away. I'm busy." But a voice on the other side answered, "Colonel, sir. I have an urgent communiqué from General Zhukov, for your eyes only."

Muttering a curse, Yakushin walked to the door, opened it a crack, and said, "Just another minute, Lieutenant Sokolov. I'm nearly finished here."

At that moment, Dieter saw his chance. The window next to him was open. The colonel stood two paces away by the door and was partially turned away. Dieter jumped up and body slammed the colonel. Then he spun around, literally throwing himself out the window, did a somersault as he hit the ground, and took off running.

The colonel swore, ran to the window, and fired twice at Dieter's legs, missing both times.

Racing down the alleyway, Dieter almost made it to the corner before being seen by a Soviet sentry who cried for him to stop. Dieter put on a last second burst of speed but was cut down and instantly killed by a hail of bullets from the sentry's machine gun. Seeing this as he leaned out the window, the colonel screamed at the sentry.

"YOU GODDAMNED FOOL! YOU IDIOT! That prisoner had important intelligence information I was just about to get from him."

The sentry instantly came to attention and tried to apologize, terrified that he was about to be punished, perhaps even shot. But there was nothing to be done. The colonel waved him away and collected himself. *At least I have this egg. And this Major Gustmann may be nearby. Perhaps we can capture him and force him to translate the code telling where the other eggs and gold are hidden.*

Turning from the window, the colonel found Lieutenant Sokolov standing there, looking shaken, with General Zhukov's communiqué in hand. "Are you all right, sir?" The colonel grabbed the communiqué, read it quickly, and concluded no special action or reply was needed.

"Yes, Lieutenant. Everything is under control. I was just questioning a prisoner and he tried to escape, but the bastard is now dead. Thank you for the message. You may go now but send in Sergeant Popov. I have an assignment for him."

As soon as Popov arrived, the colonel ordered him to take a special patrol to hunt for an SS major named Klaus Gustmann. "If you find Gustmann, capture him and bring him to me. DON'T SHOOT HIM! He has very important intelligence information I must have."

Inside the Reichstag, Klaus fought a mounting sense of panic as he waited for Dieter to return. He hadn't been this frightened during the most intense moments of combat in Russia. This was different. The war was irrevocably lost, Germany defeated, and he felt trapped. There was nothing of importance left except survival, his own and that of his family. As the hours passed, Klaus was sure something must have gone wrong with Dieter's plan.

With cause, Klaus feared nothing more than being captured by the Russians and identified as a member of the SS. Fear grew to abject terror as he and his look-alike aide, *Obershütze* Otto Krummel, a regular *Wehrmacht* soldier, watched through the bunker just after dawn as a Russian patrol marched a bloodied quartet of captured SS officers into the plaza, forced the prisoners to kneel at the base of the obelisk topped by the Nazi eagle, executed them one at a time with a burst of machine gun fire to the head, and then spit on the corpses before turning toward the Reichstag.

Utterly numb now with terror, and driven by some primitive survival instinct, Klaus seemed to become two people, one who stood and mutely watched in horror as his other self drew his Luger and shot Otto in the back of the head. The observer Klaus struggled to comprehend the crime he'd just committed, while the other Klaus proceeded to exchange his SS uniform and identity card with those of *Obershütze* Otto Krummel. Next, he removed Krummel's aluminum canteen from its covering, cut through the side with his knife, and depressed it enough to slip inside the cloth-covered Fabergé egg that he, like Dieter, had been carrying in his dispatch case. Finally, he pulled the cut edges of the canteen back together and slipped it back in its cover. It wouldn't hold water anymore, but he was banking on it looking ordinary and not be taken from him if and when he got a chance to surrender to the Allies.

Hearing shouts and gunfire from the far end of the building, Klaus headed to the basement, seeking a place to hide. After surprising and killing two more SS soldiers, the patrol that had just executed the SS officers in the plaza met Sergeant Popov's patrol, and under his direction slowly worked through the building. After encountering and killing two more defenders while losing one of their own, they discovered the body of Otto Krummel, now dressed and documented as Major Klaus Gustmann. Popov sent a man back to report their find and a half hour later he returned with Colonel Yakushin.

The colonel looked closely at the body. The picture of Major Gustmann he'd found in Major Kleinschmidt's wallet matched the picture on the dead man's identity papers, and both looked pretty similar to the dead man's face. Turning the body over, the colonel noted the entry wound in the back of the dead man's head and the Luger pistol lying next to it on the floor. A suicide? Looking again at the entry wound, he decided it would have been nearly impossible for this man to have shot himself in the back of the head. Then he noticed something else, part of a small tattoo on the dead man's neck showing just above his collar. Pulling the collar down, the Colonel saw the tattoo was a string of small capital letters that read OKRUMMEL. Finally, he recalled hearing that many SS officers had a tattoo showing their blood type on their left forearm, a practice meant to give them a survival advantage if they were ever wounded and in need of blood. The Colonel pulled up the left sleeve of the dead man's uniform and looked. No tattoo.

"Sergeant, I don't think this is Gustmann, but someone else named Krummel who looks like Gustmann. I believe the real Gustmann killed this man to steal his identity. Keep looking for him. And if you find him, bring him to me immediately for questioning."

In the coalbin where he'd taken shelter behind a large pile of anthracite, Klaus remained numb with fear at the sound of the Soviet patrol inspecting the basement. As they left and their footsteps faded, his panic began to subside, only to be replaced by a feeling of such extreme guilt at what he'd done that he grew violently nauseous. Kneeling, he vomited repeatedly, finally falling semiconscious. How long he lay there he wasn't sure, but upon waking, he cautiously left the coalbin, hearing nothing now except distant artillery and rifle fire. It was dark outside, so as a dirty and disheveled *Oberschütze* Otto Krummel, Klaus cautiously left the Reichstag. Keeping to the shadows, he walked to the north end of the plaza toward what sounded like the engine of a German tank. It proved to be a Tiger panzer, accompanied by several *Wehrmacht* soldiers. Klaus joined them, learning they had recently encountered and killed several members of a Russian patrol, and were now hoping to break out of Berlin and head west.

The sound of rifle fire, mortars, and artillery seemed less intense in that direction. As the Tiger left the plaza and entered the Tiergarten District, they passed the lifeless body of an SS officer in an alleyway. Looking at the blood-spattered corpse, Klaus recognized with shock that it was Dieter. The dispatch case in which he'd carried his egg was not by the body. Someone, presumably a Russian, must now have it. Did he also have the coded information telling how to find the others? Klaus couldn't know the events leading to Dieter's death. Had he been killed outright or perhaps captured and interrogated before being killed? If so, had he broken and revealed the code to his captors? Klaus steeled himself against a surge of emotion and thought, *It doesn't matter anymore. Survive, Klaus. Just survive. Find Horst and Gerda and try to start a new life where no one knows us.*

After a long night, still posing as *Oberschütze* Otto Krummel, Klaus made contact with elements of Wenck's XII Army, then he continued on westward and several days later surrendered to American forces at the Elbe River.

CHAPTER 6

On 27 January 1948, following two and a half years of internment in a POW camp in the north of England, Klaus was released, given a Form D-2 prisoner-discharge certificate, a new German passport identifying him as Otto Krummel, a cheap suit, and a small sum of money. Two weeks later, as he stepped from the train at the Stadtbahnhof in the American sector of Berlin he felt a wave of dizziness, gripped by the memory of his last night in the city. Taking a deep breath, he forced the memory away. He had things to do.

All during his captivity, he'd been anxious to know if Gerda and Horst had survived the bombing of Dresden. He'd repeatedly requested his English captors to contact the International Red Cross to ask if it had any information concerning his first cousin, Gerda Gustmann, and her son, Horst. They had done so multiple times, but so far, nothing. His highest priority was to find them. If they were still alive and living in Dresden, he decided he'd get them to the American sector of Berlin. Then if the Russians hadn't already found it, he'd try to recover the treasure from Latvia and use whatever it took to get the three of them resettled somewhere in South America. Just maybe it would then be possible to rebuild their lives, live quietly, struggling to come to terms with his wartime experience, and avoid possible prosecution as a former officer in the SS.

Shouldering a rucksack containing his worldly possessions, including a battered canteen that didn't hold water, Klaus walked to an office run by the military governor of the American sector meant to help repatriated soldiers of the *Wehrmacht* find work and a place to live. At the entrance, he hesitated, then entered and came to attention in front of an American sergeant sitting behind the reception desk.

"Sir, I am *Oberschütze* Otto Krummel, recently released from internment at Camp Engelhardt in England."

Klaus presented his Form D-2 prisoner-discharge certificate, new German passport, and Otto Krummel's military ID certificate, whose picture he'd carefully scuffed to make it a little less distinct. The sergeant gave the documents a perfunctory look and told him to have a seat. Then he took a blank form from his desk and inserted it in his typewriter.

"Herr Krummel, I have a few questions for you. Your English seems good. Are you comfortable with that language, or do we need a German translator?"

"*Ja*. Yes, I am fine with the English."

Some of the sergeant's questions concerned Krummel's unit, his MOS, and his theater of service during the war. Klaus didn't really know the correct answers. He decided to give Otto a fictional service history based on his acquaintance with a member of the 19th *Waffen-SS* he and Dieter had helped to train. But wishing to avoid all reference to the SS, Klaus described himself (i.e., Krummel) as having served on the Eastern Front as a member of the 27th Grenadier Regiment of the 12th Division of II Corps in the XIV Army of Army Group North.

When the sergeant asked him about family and where he came from in Germany, Klaus truthfully answered that his parents and wife were deceased, then went on to say the only family members he had or at least hoped were alive and wanted to locate were his first cousin, Gerda Gustmann, and her son, Horst Gustmann, who had previously resided in Dresden. The sergeant recorded this information, including the address of the apartment where Gerda had lived, but looked grim and shook his head.

"You must know that much of Dresden was destroyed in a massive bombing raid. I hope your relatives survived." Then he said, "Herr Krummel, what skills do you have?"

"I hold a certificate as a qualified engineer from the Dresden Technological Institute."

A great deal of reconstruction work was being done in Berlin, so the sergeant brightened at Klaus's response. Of course, there was no possibility of providing hard copy documentation of this claim since the DTI and all its records had been reduced to a pile of rubble. However, that didn't discourage the sergeant. He also seemed to think it of little consequence that Otto's principal qualification was in mining as opposed to civil engineering.

"Herr Krummel, there's a construction site nearby in need of an assistant civil engineer able to speak both English and German, someone who can effectively communicate directives from the American supervisors to the German-speaking work crews. I expect you could fill that role." The sergeant wrote out a note, passed it to Klaus, and told him to report to the chief engineer at the site, Captain Howard Standish. Finally, having ascertained that Otto did possess a small sum of money, he provided the address of a rundown but serviceable pension near the construction site where he thought a couple rooms might still be available for rent. Klaus quickly reported to Captain Standish and got the job.

A year later, Klaus was still working at the reconstruction site. In some ways his time in Berlin had been a success. His English had improved from good to excellent, and the other German workers liked him. Captain Standish praised his work and had succeeded in winning a significant pay increase for his assistant engineer. But in private, he felt frustrated and despondent. He checked frequently with the local Red Cross office, but to date, they hadn't been able to provide any information about the fate or whereabouts of Gerda and Horst Gustmann. The only thing he'd learned with certainty was that the apartment block where his sister and son had been living in Dresden had been completely destroyed. Had Gerda and Horst been there at the time? Did they survive? The kind but tired clerk at the Red Cross office smiled at Otto and urged patience. Surely he realized there were thousands, no, tens of thousands, like himself trying to trace relatives displaced by the war. He had to have hope and patience.

Klaus often spent evenings at a local bierstube. Sitting in a dark corner with a stein of *dunkelweizen*, he watched and listened to people around him, paying special attention to patrons whose conversations suggested they might be refugees from Dresden. One evening in February, he overheard two elderly men in an adjacent booth talking about their luck in having been away from their apartment and in a shelter when the Allies firebombed the city. Curiosity overcame caution as he heard one man mention the address of the apartment.

The same building where Gerda and Horst were living. Unable to contain himself he got up and asked if the men had been acquainted with his cousin and her son, Gerda and Horst Gustmann? One of the men said yes, he'd met Gerda. In fact, they'd been in the shelter together during the bombing, and afterwards they'd both been relocated to apartments in another building that had sustained only minor damage. However, he didn't know anything about a son named Horst. He supposed Gerda might still be living there. However, when it became obvious the German Army was collapsing on all fronts, he and his friend had headed west, wanting to end up in a place controlled by the Allies rather than the Soviets. Klaus felt elated and frightened at the same time. *Gerda survived, but what about Horst?*

His mind was in a whirl. Klaus thanked the man, picked up his coat, and hurriedly left the bierstube. As soon as he could, he'd go to Dresden, find Gerda and Horst, and bring them to West Berlin. There was talk the Soviets might soon make it more difficult for civilians to travel back and forth between the Allied and Soviet zones of Berlin. Right now, it was possible, although guards in the Soviet sector made those crossings as uncomfortable as possible, questioning, searching, and often soliciting bribes before allowing people to proceed.

In his haste, Klaus collided with a man just about to enter the place, nearly knocking him over and causing his hat to fall to the pavement. He quickly apologized, bent to pick up the hat, and as he handed it back heard, "My God! Klaus Gustmann. You're supposed to be dead."

Klaus froze. This had been an ongoing fear, that he'd finally encounter someone who knew he'd been an SS officer and might, in return for a reward, turn him in to be prosecuted for war crimes. But when he looked closely at the man, he recognized Gustav Meyer, scion of the powerful Meyer family who owned the Meyer Steelworks. Gustav had been excused from military service because of weak eyesight and a limp caused by an early accident, but he was as dedicated a Nazi as anyone Klaus had ever known. He wasn't likely to betray Klaus to authorities seeking to arrest and prosecute former members of the SS.

Gustav invited Klaus to his apartment for schnapps. He wanted to know how Major Klaus Gustmann could be standing here now even though he was listed by the Soviet Army as having been killed during the last days of the war in Berlin. Klaus accepted the invitation, and once at the apartment told how he'd taken the identity of an ordinary soldier named Otto Krummel who resembled him and had been killed, although he didn't say how. As Otto Krummel, he'd been captured by the Allies and interned as a POW in England. Now that he was back in Germany, he hoped to reunite with his sister Gerda and son Horst. After that, he wanted to quietly resettle the three of them in South America. At that, Gustav became animated.

"Klaus, my friend, I think I can help you. Have you heard of ODESSA (*Organisation der Ehemaligen SS-Angehörigen*) and *Der Neuanfang* (Transl. New Beginning)?"

"I've heard ODESSA can help high-ranking members of the SS leave Europe and resettle under false names. That's exactly what I'd like to do as soon as I can find Gerda and Horst. I fear that as a former officer in the SS, especially because of the brief time my record would show I was stationed at the Salaspils work camp before going on to Russia, I might be subject to prosecution. But I was only a field officer with the rank of major, not a colonel or a general. And *Der Neuanfang*?"

"I can put you in touch with ODESSA. We need former SS officers at all levels who can work from a safe haven in South America to eventually implement *Der Neuanfang*, our plan for a glorious Aryan Fourth Reich in Europe." At that, Gustav, flushed with excitement, jumped up, turned to the wall on which hung a large red and white flag with a black swastika in the center, and extended his right arm stiffly in a salute. Klaus, who at this point felt no enthusiasm at all for such a project, quickly made a pragmatic decision to take help where he could get it, and joined Gustav in saluting the flag.

Two days later Klaus stood outside the bierstube as Gustav pulled up in a black Mercedes-Benz 770. They drove some twenty kilometers, finally stopping at a large home in the western sector of Zehlendorf. There, Gustav introduced Klaus to Diedrich Schmidt.

Over dark chocolate and peppermint schnapps, Klaus told Diedrich of his wartime experiences, including the discovery of treasure in Russia (the gold and jewelry, but *not* the eggs) that he and Dieter had hidden in Latvia, and how he now hoped to recover the treasure and relocate to South America with his sister and son.

Diedrich assured Klaus that ODESSA could help him. After further discussion, he suggested a plan whereby Klaus would travel to Latvia disguised as a Swiss consulting engineer, recover the treasure, and then leave Europe through Austria and Italy before being sent on to Argentina. On the way to Latvia, he should stop in Dresden and send his sister and son to West Berlin. Once Klaus was well settled, ODESSA would arrange for them to join him in Argentina. In return, Klaus agreed to give half the recovered treasure to his ODESSA contact in Latvia. Diedrich said he needed some time to work out details but told Klaus he should be ready to travel by the third week of March. The meeting ended at 01:30. The three men rose, shook hands, then turned to the wall and gave an extended right arm salute to the Nazi flag hanging there.

On the weekend before he was to leave, Gustav met Klaus at the bierstube to confirm all was ready for his journey. On Monday at 06:00 he would find a gray Volkswagen parked in front of his apartment that he could drive to and leave in Dresden. Then he handed Klaus a large duffle bag containing a business suit, a pair of wire rim eyeglasses, a false mustache, a black wig, makeup to give his skin an olive cast, and a Swiss passport identifying him as an engineer named Ruedi Bachmann. Finally, Gustav provided Klaus the address in Dresden where he was to contact his next ODESSA handler by asking for Herr Mannheim.

In case this venture didn't play out as he hoped it would and also thinking he might well be searched as he crossed the border into the Soviet zone, Klaus decided not to take his egg with him. If the mission was successful, he'd soon have several more along with a stash of gold and jewels. If not, at least he could leave the one egg he had as a legacy for Horst. Removing the egg from its hiding place in his tiny apartment, Klaus opened it up and took out a scrap of paper bearing a line of letters and numbers. These he copied on a second piece of paper and placed it in his wallet. After thinking a moment, he added the symbol and several additional numbers and letters to the line of code on the first piece of paper, then underneath wrote the following words, *Suche hier meinen Sohn wenn ich nicht zurückomme.* Placing that paper inside the egg, he then returned it to its hiding place.

CHAPTER 7

At 05:59 on Monday, Klaus watched as a gray Volkswagen pulled up to the curb. As soon as the driver got out and disappeared into the predawn darkness, Klaus grabbed his duffle bag and locked the apartment, whose rent was paid two months in advance. Then he descended to the street. Inside the car, he found the key the driver left on the floor and drove to the checkpoint separating the American from the Soviet sectors of Berlin. From there he'd be driving south through what would soon be called *Der Deutsche Demokratische Republik* (DDR). Stern-faced guards at the crossing made him step out of the car, closely examined his identity papers, and asked the purpose of his journey. He answered semi-truthfully, saying he'd recently learned his widowed cousin, Gerda Gustmann, was living in Dresden, and he wished to visit her. The guards briefly looked inside, under the hood, and under the seats of the car. They also probed Klaus's duffle bag, but finding no chocolates or cigarettes to take, curtly waved him through the checkpoint.

Unfortunately for Klaus, the surname of the man whose identity he'd stolen, Krummel, was quite rare in Germany. A day after he'd entered the Soviet zone, a record of his crossing caught the notice of Colonel Gennady Yakushin, now an MGB officer helping organize the Ministry for State Security (*Ministerium für Staatsicherheit*). Yakushin had long suspected the body of the SS officer he'd examined in Berlin in 1945 wasn't that of Major Klaus Gustmann. Now he wondered if this Otto Krummel who had just crossed into the Soviet sector of Berlin could possibly be that man. Summoning a Stasi officer, he ordered the man to track Krummel down in Dresden, put him under surveillance, and advise him as to where Krummel went and what he did.

Upon arriving in Dresden, Klaus parked the car several blocks away from Pension Lisl where he'd prepaid the proprietress for a week's lodging, telling her he was in the city to be interviewed for a post as supervisor at a Soviet construction project. Once in his room he studied a street map of Dresden, working to plot a course consisting of two walking segments with a tram ride in the middle where he hoped to find Gerda and Horst living. Closing his eyes, he imagined seeing them again. Of course, they'd be shocked as he'd been listed as killed during the Soviet invasion of Berlin, but he hadn't dared contact Gerda ahead of time. No one outside ODESSA was to have any advance knowledge of his travel plans for fear the mission could be compromised. Once Gerda and Horst got over the shock of seeing him, he planned to quietly explain as much of his plan as they needed to know, put them on a train to safety in the American sector of Berlin, then travel on to Latvia.

For the rest of this day, Klaus had a different mission. Leaving Pension Lisl, he walked four kilometers to the cemetery in Loschwitz where the Gustmann family had a small mausoleum. It held the remains of his paternal grandparents, his parents, his younger brother, who'd been killed in an accident as a child, and his wife Magda. Klaus had supposed someday it would hold his remains as well. Not anymore, of course. That summoned another thought that briefly made his blood run cold. *Could the Soviets possibly have sent 'my' body to Gerda, who would have interred it here? No! Surely, they buried Krummel's body in some mass grave outside Berlin or, more likely, they just burned it.*

Standing before the mausoleum, Klaus pondered the irony that this city of the dead had sustained almost no damage while the firebombing in 1945 had killed more than 25,000 people in one night and reduced much of the rest of Dresden to a pile of rubble. He took from around his neck a string necklace holding a key to the mausoleum door, a key he'd carried throughout the war and the years afterward as a POW in England. Clearly, no one had entered the place for a very long time, and the lock on the low barred door was rusty. Inserting the key, he had to work it back and forth several times before the lock finally yielded.

Crouching, Klaus passed through the low doorway and surveyed the interior of the small building by the flame of his cigarette lighter. He paused for a moment at each chamber to remember the relative entombed there. Then, passing by the empty space reserved for him, he fell to his knees and extended his hands to touch the door of the chamber holding the body of his wife Magda. Remaining there for some minutes, his eyes closed, his mind summoned images of better times: their wedding, the honeymoon, climbing and skiing in the alps, furnishing their apartment, their excitement and joy at Magda's pregnancy, the birth of Horst…. Finally, he pulled away, forcing his thoughts back to the present.

Next morning in the breakfast room, Klaus advised Frau Lisl Müller he had a series of meetings that afternoon and evening with managers of the new construction project in the city center. He likely wouldn't return until quite late, so might he have a key to the pension so he wouldn't have to wake her? The proprietress was adamant. It was out of the question for a guest to have his own key. She added that he should make every effort to be back before 22:00 when she always locked the front door. Klaus said he would try.

That evening at dusk, Klaus stood at the entrance to Gerda's apartment and knocked. He heard her approach the door, slide back the bolt lock, and then open the door a few inches with the chain lock still attached.

"Yes. Who is it?"

"Your brother, Gerda. Back from the dead."

"What sick joke is this?" Then peering more closely at him through the partially open door, she screamed and called out, "Klaus? KLAUS! Oh my God, it *is* you."

Gerda closed the door in order to pull out the chain lock, then opened it again, grabbed Klaus in a bear hug, and pulled him inside. She kept repeating, "Oh my God. Oh my God. They said you were dead. Oh my God."

Klaus returned the bear hug and smiled at his sister. "It is so good to see you again, Gerda." Then he looked about and said, "And where is our young Horst?"

Gerda's face fell. She pulled away, looked at her brother with a tortured expression, and said, "He isn't here, Klaus. During the last year of the war, I had to work a double shift at the munitions plant. I couldn't care for him properly, so I sent him to Prague to live with my cousin, Erica Kovach. Later, when we were bombed, I felt sure I'd done the right thing. So many people died, and our apartment building was demolished. At the end of the war I thought Erica would bring him here, but I heard nothing. Finally, I went to Prague and learned that Horst and Erica had been forced from their home and expelled from the city with a large number of Germans when the Russians came. No one seemed to know or care what had become of them. I heard some of the men were deported to labor camps in Russia, and maybe some whole families as well. I keep asking the Red Cross to look for them, but they haven't been able to find any trace of either Horst or Erica. Oh, Klaus, I…I…" Gerda burst into tears.

Klaus felt as though a steel band was tightening around his chest. He could barely breathe. Horst was missing. Had he been taken to a Russian labor camp? Was he even alive? First he'd lost Magda, then the war, now Horst, too? Without his family, without Gerda and Horst, what was left? The treasure suddenly didn't seem important. He sat heavily on the sofa and held his head in his hands, feeling hopeless. Gerda sat next to her brother and put her arms around him. They remained there silent for a long time.

Finally, Klaus's military training took hold and broke through their paralyzing ennui. Turning to Gerda, he said, "We simply *must* believe Horst is alive, and we *will* find him. We're all going to be together again, well off, and in a better place than this godforsaken country." With that, he told her about the cache of gold, jewels, and Fabergé eggs he and Dieter had discovered in Russia and later hid in Latvia but hadn't been able to recover when the Soviet army swept into Latvia. Gerda listened and cried again as Klaus told her Dieter had been killed in Berlin. Then he got to the part still giving him nightmares that was very hard to discuss.

"Gerda, I'm not Klaus Gustmann anymore, and you must never again call me by that name. I'm now an ex-*Wehrmacht* soldier named Otto Krummel. I was captured by the Allies and spent two and a half years as a POW at an internment camp in England. As Otto Krummel, I was given a new German passport. I came back to Germany and have been working as a supervisor on several U.S. Army construction projects in Berlin." Gerda said nothing, but her eyes widened with questions.

Klaus continued, "In Berlin, at the end when everything was collapsing, the Russians were everywhere, and from our bunker I watched as they lined up any captive officer wearing a SS uniform and executed them. I panicked, Gerda. Otto Krummel was my aide, a regular soldier, not SS. He was a good, obedient soldier, who resembled me physically in many ways…" Klaus's face took on an agonized look. He took two deep breaths and said, "I went crazy. I shot him Gerda. I took his life so I could take his uniform and his identity and try to avoid being captured and executed as an SS officer."

Gerda remained silent, her face showing a series of conflicting emotions. Her brother's crime was appalling Yet the war had inflicted so many terrible things on so many people she found she could neither forgive nor condemn him. He'd survived. He was here now. That had to be enough.

"I've made an agreement in Berlin with an organization called ODESSA. It helps former SS officers leave Europe and resettle with new identities in South America. They've agreed to help me travel to Latvia to recover the treasure Dieter and I hid there. In return for a share, I'll be extracted from Europe and resettled in Argentina where we can all start a new life. Our plan was for you and Horst to go to the American sector of Berlin and wait until I contact you from Argentina. Now that he isn't here, you must still go to Berlin since there are rumors the Soviets may soon close the border. After Latvia…" Klaus stopped and took a deep breath. "After Latvia, I'll return and find Horst. I'll tell my ODESSA contact I *must* first go to Prague before leaving Europe." Klaus looked at his sister with grim determination. "I must…I *will* find him, Gerda."

Two hours later, when it was fully dark, Klaus left the building by a rear entrance. Stepping through a missing segment of the back fence, he walked perhaps fifty meters along an alleyway to a point where it joined a through street. Several blocks later where that street intersected a major boulevard, he boarded a tram that took him within two kilometers of Pension Lisl. Walking the rest of the way, Klaus pulled his cap low over his face and affected the bent and slightly lame gait of a much older man. On that street as he passed the empty lot where he'd parked the car, he spotted the same black Volkswagen and man wearing a black homburg and overcoat he'd noticed earlier on his way to Gerda's apartment.

He realized the Stasi must have traced his car and now had it under surveillance to see if he would show up. No chance he'd ever go back to it now. What he hoped most was that the police hadn't yet linked him to his sister and placed her apartment under surveillance or managed to figure out where he was staying. Clearly, it was time for them both to leave Dresden. He decided to backtrack to Gerda's apartment, let her know the Stasi was closing in, and put her on the train to Berlin that night. Once there, she could stay in his tiny apartment using money hidden in the wall along with the box holding the Fabergé egg. He'd tell her where to look.

By the time Gerda's train left at 22:25, trams were no longer running, so Klaus had to walk more, nearly six kilometers, back to Pension Lisl. This time, as he walked past the place where he'd left the car, he saw the black Volkswagen had been replaced by a Russian ZIS occupied by a different man. Continuing his slow, slightly gimpy gait along the opposite side of the street for another two blocks, he turned right, then quickened his pace until reaching Pension Lisl. No other cars or people were visible along this block and all the windows in the building were dark. He would have to wake the landlady to gain entrance. Frau Lisl Müller would be incensed, but he was prepared to assuage her ire with a small box of Belgian chocolates and two packages of American cigarettes he'd hidden in the lining of his overcoat before crossing into the Soviet sector of Berlin.

In his room, Klaus set about turning himself into Swiss consulting engineer Ruedi Bachmann. He reflected on the irony that his early participation in theater as a teenager at the Gymnasium might now help save his life as he adjusted the dark wig to completely hide his blond hair, applied makeup to his face and arms, put on a pair of wire rimmed spectacles fitted with plain glass lenses, and attached a false pencil style mustache to his upper lip. Examining the result in the in the mirror, he decided his appearance really did approximate the picture (God knows of whom?) Diedrich had applied to Ruedi Bachmann's fake Swiss passport. As a Swiss citizen from Zürich, it made sense that German would be his primary language, although he wasn't confident he could speak it with a true *Schweizerdeutsch* accent.

Since the Soviets were beginning to industrialize the satellite states of Lithuania, Estonia, and Latvia, it seemed reasonable a consulting engineer from a nonaligned nation like Switzerland might be traveling there. Klaus felt his cover was sound. He was, after all, a qualified engineer. As a result of his prior military service in Russia and Latvia, he could also speak at least a few words of those languages. And because of his long internment in England and subsequent employment under an American supervisor in Berlin, he'd become quite fluent in English.

Shortly before dawn, Klaus packed his duffle bag, donned his overcoat, and quietly left the pension before anyone else was up. He walked rapidly for several blocks to a major boulevard and there boarded an early morning tram. At this hour it carried only a handful of passengers, none of whom showed any interest in him. Still, he decided to get off after a few minutes. He walked several more blocks to another major intersection, stopping twice in store entrances to look back and see if anyone was following him. Then he boarded a second tram and rode for several minutes to a location near the address where he'd been instructed to meet his ODESSA contact.

His knock on the door at 12 Bergdahlstrasse was answered by an attractive, blonde, blue-eyed, young woman.

"Yes?"

"My name is Ruedi Bachmann. I was told to contact Mr. Mannheim and advise him I may be able to help with *Der Neuanfang*." The woman beckoned him to come in and closed the door. Klaus stood silent, admiring the figure of this nubile female, but stiffened when she suddenly produced a snub-nosed pistol and made a request that clearly was an order.

"Please show me your identity documents, Herr Bachmann."

"Of course," he murmured, handing her his Swiss passport.

"And your other identity?"

Flustered, Klaus stammered, "What do you mean?"

"I think you have not always been Ruedi Bachmann, maybe for only a short time now. Herr Krummel?"

At that, Klaus opened his overcoat saying, "Yes, I understand now, but I'll have to open the lining of my coat to show you the other documents you wish to see."

"In here." She pointed with the pistol to a room on the right. "Remove your coat and place it on the table. There is a small scissors in the drawer you may use to open the lining, but let me see both of your hands as you do this."

Klaus complied, slowly removing from a cut in the lining of his coat the German passport identifying him as Otto Krummel. The woman reviewed it carefully. "Now, please tell me where you are headed and what you will be doing there."

Klaus replied with the oblique reference he'd agreed upon with Diedrich Schmidt about the gold and jewels he was to recover and share with ODESSA. "I am going to Riga to mine valuable minerals."

The woman finally seemed satisfied. She lowered the pistol and said, "I regret the inconvenience, Major Gustmann, but I'm sure you understand we have to be very careful."

"So may I now speak to Herr Mannheim?"

The woman smiled and replied, "There is no Herr Mannheim." Then, extending her hand to Klaus, she said, "I'm Erika, your ODESSA contact here in Dresden."

Erika handed an envelope to him and continued, "As Ruedi Bachmann, you will travel by train, first to Warsaw, then on to Riga. This envelope contains your tickets as well as letters referring to a meeting you've been invited to attend with the Soviet managers of a new cement plant in Riga." Having noticed Klaus's look of concern when she called him Major Gustmann, she added, "Don't be concerned, Major. From now on, your other contacts will only know and address you as Ruedi Bachmann. In Riga, your contact will be Andris Ozols. When you arrive at the train station, he will meet you and ask, 'Should the proportion of calcium carbonate in our cement be 40 or 50 percent?' You are to answer, 'Neither, it should be at least 60 percent.' Then he will help you recover the gold and jewels and take possession of the share you've agreed to give ODESSA. From Riga, you'll return to Warsaw by train, fly to Zurich on LOT, and travel by car to Italy where we've arranged passage for you by ship to Buenos Aires. Once you are settled there, we'll arrange for your sister and son to join you."

Klaus nodded to show he understood, but said, "I have a problem."

Erika frowned. "Yes?"

"My son Horst is missing."

"Missing? He's not here in Dresden with your sister?"

"No. Only yesterday I learned he was sent to live temporarily with my sister's cousin in Prague in 1944. He never returned." Klaus's voice became strained. "It's been five years. Gerda has tried repeatedly but hasn't been able to find any trace of Horst or her cousin. I *must* find my son!"

Erika's frown deepened. "Major, I'm very sorry hear of your worry, but... it's essential we carry out Diedrich's plan with no delay." Privately she thought, *He's probably dead, killed in the bombing of Prague or the Czech purge of ethnic Germans after the war, or maybe sent to a Soviet work camp.*

Forcing herself to smile, Erika touched Klaus on the arm and said, "I promise you we'll spare no effort to find your son. Don't lose hope, but for now you must continue on to Latvia."

CHAPTER 8

Klaus scanned the platform as he stepped from the train in Riga, wondering what his contact would look like. There were few other passengers. Most seemed to be lone travelers, only two being met by persons he supposed to be either family members or business associates. A uniformed guard stood at the end of the platform, watching as each passenger passed into the station. No one approached him on the platform, so after a moment, Klaus followed the others. The guard gave him only a cursory glance. Once inside, he stood a few minutes to see if someone would approach. When no one did, he decided to step into the small station restaurant to order coffee and a pastry.

The restaurant was empty except for a waitress who looked to be getting ready to close. She spoke to him first in Latvian, and Klaus, knowing a few words, managed to place his order in that language before telling her in German he was a Swiss engineer visiting Riga to help develop a new cement plant. She responded in German, welcomed him to Riga, and told him her name was Anna. She brought his coffee and a scone, then placed a sign on the door stating the restaurant was closed and proceeded to draw the curtains on the windows. Klaus wondered at that, but Anna said not to worry. There was no hurry. He could take his time with the coffee. She said her manager was expecting him and should arrive in a few minutes. She told him she had to catch a bus home so excused herself and left through a door at the back of the restaurant.

Ten minutes later, a tall, bearded man entered through the same door and introduced himself in German as the restaurant manager, Andris Ozols. He said he was glad the Soviets were bringing new industry to Latvia and to Riga, in particular. This would create much needed jobs to help the people recover from the war, and there would be a critical need for a lot of cement to aid this industrial expansion. Klaus agreed.

"Herr Bachmann, do you think it best to use 40 percent or 50 percent calcium chloride when compounding cement?"

Klaus started to answer, but then stopped. Calcium chloride? Ozols should have said calcium carbonate. Was this just a slip of the tongue, an innocent mistake? *Can I trust this man or is there a problem?*

Ozols looked at him closely.

Klaus hesitated, acting as though this was a question deserving careful thought, then chose words that let him cite the agreed upon figure without having to restate the name of the compound in question.

"Neither one, Herr Ozols, it must be at least 60 percent for the cement to have proper strength."

Ozols appeared to accept his answer. He replied, "We've arranged a room for you at a small hotel just across the street from the station. I'll take you there now to make certain you are properly received and settled. Tomorrow morning I'll come for you with a small van so we may recover the bullion you hid before Riga fell to the Soviets. Then I'll see you back on the train to Warsaw and give you instructions for meeting your next contact there."

Klaus nodded but was again disturbed by what Ozols had just said. He'd told Gerhard the treasure consisted of a couple dozen pieces of very valuable jewelry and perhaps seventy kilos of gold coins. But Ozols spoke of gold bullion, and enough of it to require a small van for transport? Was this another case of simple miscommunication between members of the ODESSA network, or something else?

Ozols accompanied Klaus to the hotel. The only person in the lobby besides the clerk at the reception desk was a heavyset man with Slavic features who sat in a corner. He seemed to be engrossed in his newspaper, but Klaus thought he saw him cast a quick glance of recognition at Ozols.

Klaus introduced himself and the clerk replied, "Welcome, Herr Bachmann. I hope your stay will be a pleasant one. Please sign the register and give your passport to me. I'll keep it here at the desk until you are ready to check out. Here is the key to your room, number twenty-one on the second floor. Is there anything more I can do for you?"

"It's late and I've had only coffee and a pastry. Would it be possible to have some bread, cheese, and a bottle of wine delivered to my room?"

"Indeed, Herr Bachmann. Although our kitchen is now closed, I'll send my assistant to obtain these items for you. They should be delivered within the hour."

Ozols accompanied Klaus to his room. After wishing him goodnight, he said, "Meet me in the lobby at 09:00. We can perform our task and have you on your way to freedom by evening." Raising his arm, he whispered, "Heil, Hitler," then turned and descended the stairs.

Klaus locked the door behind him, then sat on the bed and thought about the troubling conversation he'd just had. The man had made two misstatements. Were those mistakes significant? Was he trustworthy? If not, then he had to suppose the ODESSA network had somehow been compromised. Anna, and later Ozols, obviously knew enough to meet and recognize him. Klaus also wondered about the other man sitting in the lobby. He rose, walked to the window, and surveyed the area outside. Directly under his window a small roof projected from the side of the building at the first-floor level. He supposed it likely sheltered a side entrance to the hotel kitchen.

About an hour later, at 23:15, Klaus heard a knock and a voice called, "Herr Bachmann, I have the food and wine you requested." A young man stood in the doorway bearing a tray holding rolls, a large wedge of cheese, and a half liter bottle of red wine.

"I'm sorry for the delay, sir. We did have bread and cheese in the kitchen, but I had to go out to obtain the wine. I hope this will be satisfactory." Klaus took the tray, thanked the boy, and gave him a Swiss two-franc coin for his service. He started to turn away, but the boy had more to tell him. "Herr Bachmann, just as I was returning with your wine I met Anna, the waitress at the train station restaurant. She said to tell you Herr Ozols must change the time of your meeting tomorrow and asked me to give this note to you."

Klaus opened the folded sheet of paper to find a two-line message handwritten in German.

Herr Ozols kann nicht zum Hotel um 0900 am Morgen kommen. Stattdessen wird er Sie am Viertel vor Mittag begegnet——Anna

Klaus read the note, thanked the boy again, and gave him another Swiss franc. Ozols was asking to delay their meeting the next day from 09:00 to 11:45. Was that significant? Then he noticed that certain letters in the message had been lightly underlined in pencil.

$\underline{Oz} \underline{M} g \underline{b}$

My God! MGB! Anna's message was a warning that Ozols was an agent of the *Ministerstvo gosudarstvennoy bezopasnosti SSSR*, the secret police agency of the Soviet Union, otherwise known as the MGB. Feared throughout Latvia, Lithuania, and Estonia, the MGB continued to carry out mass arrests, deportations, and executions of people who had supported Germany during the war or continued to oppose Russia as members of resistance movements.

Klaus paced about the room. Had Anna already known Ozols was on the other side, or maybe a double agent playing both sides, when he first arrived at the station, or had she learned of his treachery only in the past couple hours? Perhaps the man he met wasn't even the real Andris Ozols, but an imposter. Anna left before he arrived and probably didn't see him enter the restaurant. Maybe he had intercepted the real ODESSA contact (the real Ozols?) and forced him to reveal the details of Klaus's mission, including the prearranged question he was to be asked and the proper response to it. If so, then Klaus was lucky his unfortunate contact had passed some misinformation to the imposter.

Klaus imagined the real Ozols lying dead or perhaps beaten and imprisoned by MGB agents. What to do? Clearly, he didn't want to see the man again. He must leave the hotel, but his Swiss passport was in a pigeonhole behind the reception desk. It would seem more than strange to seek out and rouse the night clerk, now surely asleep, and ask to have his passport back at this hour. Besides, he didn't know if the man could be trusted. He now felt pretty sure the other man he'd seen in the lobby had been there specifically to keep him under surveillance.

It seemed to Klaus that Ruedi Bachmann was trapped, but perhaps Otto Krummel could still slip away undetected. He decided to put away Herr Bachmann's spectacles, remove his dark-haired wig and faux pencil moustache, wash the makeup from his face and arms, and once again become Otto Krummel. But first, Klaus put on pajamas and walked to the bathroom at the end of the corridor. He wanted to show anyone who might be watching that he was just preparing for bed. Halfway along the corridor he noticed the door to room twenty-six was open just a crack, and as he passed, caught a quick glimpse of the Slavic man from the lobby before it was quickly closed.

The guests on each floor shared a common bathroom with a tub and toilet, but Klaus's room did have its own sink. After returning from the bathroom, he locked the door, pulled down the window shade, and washed off Ruedi's makeup. After becoming Otto again, Klaus ate the bread and cheese and drank the wine the boy had brought. Then he extinguished the lamp by the bed to give the impression Herr Bachmann had retired for the night. After that, he sat in the dark for several hours, occasionally peering around the edge of the window shade to see if anyone was in the alleyway. Around 02:00 he saw two men, who'd clearly had too much to drink, walk by singing and smoking. After that, the alleyway was silent and empty again.

When Ozols showed up in the morning and found him missing, the MGB would be looking for a dark-haired, mustachioed man known as Ruedi Bachmann, not Otto Krummel. But that didn't mean he was safe. He could still be challenged by the police, and a nonresident German (or any German, for that matter) with no legitimate reason for being in this Soviet puppet state was at risk of arrest and possible deportation to a Russian gulag or worse. He tried to think of someone who might help him and suddenly remembered Aleksis Skuja, a native Latvian. Alexis had been a captain in the 19th *Waffen-SS*. Klaus and Dieter had worked with him training the new recruits, and liked him. He was still alive and fighting when Klaus managed to be withdrawn from the Courland Peninsula. Many soldiers in the 19th had been killed during the battles there, and many who survived had ultimately surrendered to the Russians at the end of the war. But Klaus had heard quite a few had managed to escape into the forest where they became part of a resistance group in the Baltic States that called itself the Forest Brothers. With support from British, American, and Swedish sources, the Forest Brothers were now conducting guerrilla warfare against the Soviet occupiers. If Aleksis had survived, Klaus felt sure he'd be with the Forest Brothers fighting for an independent Latvia.

Klaus knew the Skuja family had owned a furniture store in Riga and lived in an apartment at the back. He wondered if the place had survived the war and was still in business. It was a shot in the dark, but the only thing he could think of to try at this point. If the store was still there and run by the family, he would introduce himself and ask about Aleksis.

At 05:00, Klaus decided to leave. After packing Ruedi Bachmann's clothes in the duffle bag, he dressed in a plain shirt, trousers, jacket, and cap, hoping to make himself look as much as possible like an ordinary workman. Using two bed sheets tied together, the duffle bag hanging from his shoulder, Klaus backed out the window and descended to the roof below. Cautiously easing to the edge, he dropped to the ground.

Klaus looked around but saw no one. He wondered if it might be possible to re-enter the hotel through the kitchen and recover Ruedi Bachmann's Swiss passport from behind the reception desk. It would be good to have should it ever became useful to become Ruedi once again instead of Otto Krummel. The door to the kitchen was locked, but he was able to spring the lock with the blade of his pocketknife.

Inside, Klaus cautiously worked his way through the dark room trying not to make noise. The kitchen abutted a small breakfast room hotel guests accessed through a door at the south end of the lobby. That door was closed, but it wasn't locked. Easing it open, he could see the lobby was empty, dimly lit by a small green shaded lamp on the reception desk. Dropping to his hands and knees, he pushed the door open and crawled behind several lounge chairs toward the reception desk. From a crouched position in back of the desk, he scanned the numbered cubbyholes on the back wall, found number twenty-one, reached in, and withdrew Ruedi Bachmann's passport. Then he quietly retraced his path, left the lobby, and closed the door behind him. In the kitchen, he recovered his duffle bag and walked out the door into the alleyway.

Klaus estimated the distance to Skuja's store to be about three kilometers. It was still dark. If anyone saw him walking with his duffle bag, he hoped they would suppose he was just a laborer on the way to work. Starting on Satekles Street, he turned left and walked down Merkela Street to where it became Kalpaka Boulevard, and then followed it until it intersected Strēinieku Street. Finally, a block down that street he could just make out the outline of the building he remembered as having housed the Skuja furniture store. It still bore a large sign saying SKUJA, but as he drew closer he realized it must no longer be in business since the front door and the windows on either side were boarded up. As he watched and wondered what to do next, the front door opened, and an old man emerged. Could it possibly be Aleksis's father? Bundled against the cold, the man pulled a rocking chair into the entryway, sat down, lit a cigarette, and proceeded to rock back and forth, staring into the semi-darkness as he smoked and drank his coffee.

Klaus crossed the street, approached the man, and using the few words of Latvian he knew said, "Excuse me. Are you Mr. Skuja?"

The old man raised his head, looked at Klaus without recognition, and after a moment replied, "Yes?"

"Mr. Skuja, my name is Klaus Gustmann. Your son Aleksis and I served together in the 19th *Waffen-SS* Division."

Skuja looked hard at Klaus but made no immediate reply.

"Is Aleksis alive? Is he here? I will be direct. I am in grave danger from the MGB and hope Aleksis can help me."

Skuja's expression showed concern mixed with suspicion. He didn't respond directly to Klaus's question, but finally said, "Follow me," leading him to a door at the rear of the building and showing him into a windowless room furnished with two rickety spindle backed chairs, a cot, and a small table on which stood an alcohol burner warming a small coffee pot. He motioned for Klaus to enter, sit on one of the chairs, poured a cup of coffee for him, and said, "Wait here." Then he left. Klaus heard the sound of a key and realized he was locked in.

Nearly an hour later, Klaus heard the sound of boots outside and a key being inserted in the lock. The door was thrown open admitting two swarthy young men dressed in fatigues and armed with rifles.

The taller one looked at Klaus and said, "Gustmann?"

"Yes."

"Come with us." He pointed his rifle at Klaus, and then swung it in the direction of the door.

Klaus rose and turned to pick up his duffle bag, but the other gunman picked it up first and indicated with his rifle that he was to walk ahead of him. The men marched him to a rusty KdF-Wagen and ordered him to sit in the back. His two escorts rode in front. The taller man drove.

Turning to Klaus, the man in the passenger seat said, "You claim to be a friend of Aleksis?"

"Yes."

"We'll see. If not…" He cast a mirthless grin at Klaus and drew his finger across his throat.

Klaus closed his eyes, hoping not only that Aleksis would recognize him but would feel charitable toward his wartime colleague. He knew Aleksis had always wanted an independent Latvia, but during the war also thought his country could forge an effective partnership with the Third Reich. Would Aleksis still be a friend, or would the defeat of Germany have made him a person no longer to be helped or perhaps even tolerated? He needed Aleksis's help, but he did have something to offer. Gold. There was too damn much gold in the cache for one man to carry away anyway. If Aleksis would help, he'd give him some bags of the gold rubles he'd previously promised to ODESSA. No need to mention the Fabergé eggs or the sacks of jewelry in the cache. Once he got them, he could easily secrete them with his clothes in the duffle bag. For the gold, he'd need a couple strong suitcases.

The sun had risen above the horizon as the car left the paved road and turned onto a dirt track leading into dense woods. A few minutes later, it left the road altogether and headed straight for some brush that was lifted away at the last minute by two armed members of the Forest Brothers. Klaus was directed to get out of the car and walk to the camouflaged entrance of what proved to be a three-room command center cut into the side of a hill.

Klaus stood in the first room, his armed escorts at either side. A man emerged from the back, stopped, and looked at him. Klaus looked back at the man. It was indeed Captain Aleksis Skuja, older, sporting a bushy beard, and limping from a wound sustained during the last days of the war.

"Klaus Gustmann."

"Aleksis."

"My God, Klaus. What are you doing here?"

"I would love to explain. At the moment I'm trying to escape the MGB and very much need your help. Can you loan me a vehicle, and then help me get out of Latvia? I can make it worth your while."

Aleksis looked past Klaus and said, "It's okay, Bruno and Kirils. Klaus is a friend." The two men gave Klaus a nod, turned, and left the room.

"I'm sorry, Klaus, for the way you were treated, but we have to be careful. The MGB is always trying to infiltrate. Last week we learned one of our members, who'd been with us for more than a year, leaked information to the MGB about one of our planned raids." Aleksis cleared his throat. "Lüks is no longer with us." Then he said, "Sit down, have coffee, and tell me your story. How is your sister Gerda and your son Horst? And how is Dieter?"

CHAPTER 9

Two days later, Aleksis was thinking about how best to get Klaus out of Latvia when two members of the Forest Brothers interrupted with an urgent message. An informer within the MGB had just let them know about an operation called Priboi that the Soviets were planning to launch in two days. There was to be a mass roundup and forced deportation to Siberia of Latvians, Estonians, and Lithuanians the Soviets considered enemies of the people. The news galvanized Aleksis. His parents and the families of many other Forest Brothers were sure to be targeted. A council was called to decide what could be done to protect them. Aleksis dispatched several men, directing them to gather and bring to the camp as many of the susceptible family members as possible. Three others left to ask local commercial fishermen for the use of their boats to evacuate at risk family members to Stockholm. Overnight, nearly a hundred people were brought to the camp. Alexis told Klaus he was to go to Stockholm on the same boat carrying his parents Arturs and Jana. The next day, under cover of darkness, Klaus and the others were transported to several pickup points along the western shore of the Gulf of Riga.

In Stockholm, the newly arrived boat people were quickly absorbed by the ethnic Latvian community founded by an earlier wave of refugees fleeing the war. Aleksis's parents invited Klaus to share their cramped quarters and treated him with kindness, their son having made clear he was a friend and colleague who had donated multiple kilograms of gold coins to help purchase more arms for the Forest Brothers. Klaus was confident the two heavy suitcases and duffle bag he'd taken on the trip to Stockholm would be safe with the Skujas. However, he didn't intend to stay long. Now that his connection with ODESSA had been broken, how was he going to locate Horst and get the three of them to South America?

Klaus wrote to Gerda and sent the letter to his apartment in the American sector of Berlin. He signed it as her loving cousin Otto. Daily, he walked to the city center, sat for a time in a coffee shop, read the newspapers, and listened to fragments of conversations in those languages he could best understand, German and English. He also understood and was able to read some Swedish, something he'd learned years earlier as a student intern at the immense iron mining operation in the far northern Swedish city of Kiruna. Three weeks after arriving in Stockholm an advertisement by Luossavaara-Kiirunavaara AB, the largest iron mining company in Europe, caught his eye. The company was seeking an assistant engineer for a position in Kiruna.

As he had every day the past week, Klaus stopped at the post office before returning to the Skuja's apartment and was elated when the clerk handed him a letter from Gerda addressed to Otto Krummel. It proved his sister had safely made it to West Berlin. However, as he read it, he grew worried. Gerda wrote that she'd been visited by a man named Gustav who claimed to be her brother's friend and suggested that something about his trip apparently had not gone according to plan. He wasn't specific, but pressed her hard to say if she had heard from Klaus or knew where he was. He told her not to worry, but since he acted so nervous, Gerda said he made her nervous as well. She wrote that she hadn't told Gustav about Klaus's letter and had denied knowing where her brother might be. Had she done right?

Klaus wondered. How deeply had the MGB penetrated ODESSA? Clearly, it had managed to get inside the cell in Latvia, but how far did the breach go? Could Erika in Dresden and even Gustav and Gerhard in Berlin have been compromised as well? He hoped not, but he was getting paranoid. He felt as though he couldn't trust anyone and would have to find some way to complete the journey on his own.

Klaus got a second jolt when he returned to the apartment and found Jana in tears while Arturs stood grim faced and did his best to comfort her. A newly arrived refugee from Latvia brought terrible news. Two nights ago, Aleksis and three colleagues had taken the gold Klaus gave them to a meeting with a supposedly trustworthy British agent from MI-6, only to find they had been betrayed. Agents of the Russian MGB were waiting. They took the gold and arrested everyone in the group.

Klaus realized he had to act quickly to make sure Klaus Gustmann, the name by which Aleksis, his parents, and the other refugees knew him, disappeared. He had no illusions about the ability of the Russians to make Aleksis tell where and from whom he'd gotten gold rubles. Once they knew that and where he was, they would come after him. Murmuring condolences to Jana and Arturs, Klaus headed straight to the downtown office of Luossavaara-Kiirunavaara AB. Introducing himself as Otto Krummel, he asked if he could be interviewed for the position of assistant engineer at the company's operation in Kiruna. He was lucky. The senior engineer from Kiruna was visiting Stockholm. He had just interviewed two other applicants, but found neither suitable, and so was willing to talk to an unexpected walk-in. As with Captain Standish in Berlin, Klaus was not able to provide written documentation of his graduation from the engineering program at the Dresden Technological Institute. However, he was able to answer all the senior engineer's questions and so convince the man of his competence. At the end of the interview, he was offered the job. Klaus said he was available immediately and was prepared to leave the following morning to travel to Kiruna.

Returning to the Skuja's apartment, Klaus said nothing about his interview or the job. He felt terrible for the Skujas, knowing that, at best, Aleksis faced interrogation, torture, and deportation to Siberia if not execution. That night, as the Skujas slept in their bedroom, Klaus rose from the couch where he slept in the living room, quietly collected his bags, and with some difficulty, ported them to the city center. At 05:30 he boarded a northbound bus heading for Kiruna.

CHAPTER 10

On a Saturday morning Klaus was reclining on his narrow bed in one of the tiny efficiency apartments the company made available to unmarried male employees. Tuning his radio to a classical music program, he stubbed out his first cigarette, lit a second, and for the hundredth time pondered his situation. It was a year and a half since he'd slipped out of Stockholm and taken the bus to Kiruna to work for the Luossavaara-Kiirunavaara AB iron mining operation. His experience there had been good in that he felt fairly safe and insulated from discovery by the MGB in this remote place 200 kilometers north of the Arctic Circle. At the same time it had been horrible in that he felt trapped, isolated, and constantly having to fight off anxiety attacks about his sister and son. He simply had to do something. *My God, man. You've got to get away from here, but where, and how to do that safely?* The plan to reconnect with his sister, locate Horst, and get resettled in a place like Rio de Janeiro was still out there. *But…you idiot, how in hell are you ever going to arrange and pay for that now the deal with ODESSA has gone bad?* As he continued to mull his dilemma, Peter Larson appeared in the open doorway. A shift boss, and Klaus's best friend among the mine workers, Peter had relatives in the U.S., and for some time had talked about wanting to emigrate and work there. Now he held a piece of paper and waved it at him.

"Look at this, Otto. The Cleveland-Cliffs Iron Company in the U.S. is advertising several administrative positions at their headquarters in Cleveland, Ohio. I'm going to apply. And it says here that one of the positions is for a mine safety engineer. You should apply for that. The salary is attractive, the climate will be better, and we'd be in a big city with all the amenities we don't have in this godforsaken place."

Klaus took the notice from Peter and read it through. *The United States? Really, Klaus? That's the last place you ever expected to go, but maybe…maybe you could make such a move work out after all.* He'd succeeded in changing his identity from that of an SS officer to an ordinary German soldier who had simply fought for his country. Perhaps the U.S. government and the CCI could view that as a forgivable service, one that wouldn't automatically prevent him from immigrating. For the third time, he had no paperwork to verify his graduation from the Dresden Technologic Institute. And if he had had it, it wouldn't have been of any use as the name on it would be Klaus Gustmann, not Otto Krummel. Still, that hadn't been a fatal impediment with either Captain Standish in Berlin or the Luossavaara-Kiirunavaara AB senior engineer in Stockholm. They had accepted his explanation that all records were lost when the DTI was destroyed during the bombing of Dresden and had been willing to hire him anyway based on the answers he'd been able to give to a battery of technical questions. Perhaps he could do this one more time in an interview with a recruiter from the CCI. He felt sure that Magnus Alvarsson, his immediate boss in Kiruna, would be willing to provide a positive recommendation.

Klaus looked up and said, "Okay, Peter. Let's do this."

Six weeks later, Klaus received a letter advising Otto Krummel his application for a position as a mine safety engineer with CCI had been viewed favorably. It went on to say an offer would be conditional upon a satisfactory face-to-face interview with a company representative and an agent of the U.S. Immigration and Naturalization Service (INS). A meeting with them was scheduled two weeks hence at the U.S. Embassy in Stockholm.

Klaus had been nervous as he waited in the reception area of the embassy. However, his interview with Mr. Ivor Halvorson, the CCI representative, went smoothly. Quizzed on structural issues and worker safety in deep shaft mining operations, he'd acquitted himself well. Halvorson shook his hand and said, "I'm satisfied you have a firm command of your subject, Mr. Krummel. I think it quite possible the company may offer this position to you."

Klaus was pleased but had an unpleasant presentiment as soon as Halvorson handed him off to the agent from INS. He looked at Mr. Harris, a short, balding man with wire rim glasses and an officious bearing, and thought, *Christ! He looks like a twin to that martinet Obersturmbannführer Wilhelm Hofstetter.* Harris led Klaus to a small windowless room lit by a single overhead fixture and furnished with a plain wooden table and three straight backed wooden chairs. One was already occupied by a swarthy, heavyset man holding a manila file folder.

Harris gestured to the single chair on the side of the table closest to the wall. "Sit there please, Mr. Krummel." It was a command, not a request. Turning to his companion, he said, "This is Mr. Woodlawn who has some questions regarding your past." Klaus felt his bowels turning to water. He knew almost nothing about the real Otto Krummel's past. *This is like a police interrogation room. They've even got me sitting with my back to the wall in a chair set lower than they are, so I have to look up at them.* He had counted on the war having made it all but impossible to obtain reliable records about the lives of ordinary German citizens. Consequently, he'd synthesized from nothing what he hoped would sound like a believable account of where Otto had grown up and gone to school, details about the members of his family, and what he had done before entering the German army. Would that be good enough? What if these INS agents somehow had detailed knowledge of the real Otto Krummel?

The first question had nothing to do with Otto Krummel. Woodlawn opened his file, scanned the contents for a minute, then looked up and said, "Major Gustmann…"

Klaus froze.

"…how are you acquainted with Aleksis Skuja?"

An hour and a half later, Klaus left the interview room, a free man who had just been offered a Hobson's choice.

Several weeks later, a manila envelope addressed to Otto Krummel arrived in Kiruna. A letter within advised him of his appointment as a CCI mine safety engineer. Also included was a visa authorizing him to enter the U.S., and tickets for traveling to New York by ship from Stockholm, then by train to Cleveland, where he was to report to a Mr. Axelrod at the headquarters of CCI.

CHAPTER 11

Klaus took a taxi from the train station in Cleveland to CCI headquarters. Smiling at the receptionist, he introduced himself and told her that Mr. Axelrod in Personnel was expecting him. Summoned a few minutes later, he politely declined the receptionist's offer to watch his luggage. Instead, he slung his duffel bag over his shoulder and lugged his two obviously heavy suitcases into Axelrod's office.

Klaus's enthusiasm for the new job cooled rapidly when Axelrod told him he wasn't to be based at the CCI headquarters in Cleveland after all. Instead, he had been assigned to serve as the safety engineer for a group of iron mines operated by the company in and around a city named Ishpeming in the state of Michigan.

"Ishpeming, Michigan? Where is this place?"

Pointing to a map on the wall, Axelrod showed him where the small city was located, some 600 miles northwest of Cleveland in the middle of the Upper Peninsula of Michigan. To Klaus, it looked nearly as remote as Kiruna. Was this going to be Lapland all over again? He started to protest, but Axelrod quickly raised a hand and said, "Mr. Krummel, I believe Mr. Woodlawn made it clear you would be working for us where you were most *needed*. As the engineer responsible for developing and implementing policies to improve mine safety, we want you situated where you will have direct contact with and can be viewed by the miners as a friend, not as a boss or some high-level company 'suit' they don't trust. We want you to get to know the miners personally, socialize with them, and share with us what you learn about the needs and thinking of our union employees, *if you get my drift*." Klaus got Axelrod's drift all right. Safety might well be the major part of his job, but the other part was to act as an informer for upper management, to look for and report back any plans by the miners to oppose corporate policies, possibly call a strike, or worst of all, promote the spread of communist ideology that Senator McCarthy and his associates were working so hard to expose and suppress. Klaus wasn't at all happy, but it seemed there was nothing he could do. They clearly had him by the short hairs.

The next day, Klaus boarded a New York Central train to Detroit, and then transferred to a second train bound for Chicago. From Chicago, he headed north on the "Peninsula 400," a Chicago and Northwestern train running along the eastern edge of Wisconsin to the Upper Peninsula of Michigan. Departing Chicago at 4:05 P.M., it reached Ishpeming, the end of its route, at 2:12 A.M. the next day. Descending to the platform, the extreme cold hit him full force, the thermometer on the station wall registering -14°F. *Damn! Just like northern Sweden.* Buttoning his coat tight and pulling his hat low over his ears, he slowly trudged with his weighty luggage to the Mather Inn where CCI had reserved a room for him.

The next morning, local CCI manager, Sam Thayer, met Otto for breakfast, welcomed him to Ishpeming, and walked him through the duties he was expected to perform. Then Sam drove him to a building close to the main shaft of the Mather D mine where he was to have his office. There he introduced Otto to Ruth Olson, a secretary, whose services he'd be sharing with two other administrative personnel.

The company had granted Otto a modest salary advance and two days of free time to settle in before reporting to work. Klaus wasn't quite sure where to begin, but he couldn't afford to take too much time as he'd learned he was already scheduled to carry out safety inspections and prepare written reports for two of the company mines the following week. In Kiruna, he'd lived in a dormitory-like facility and eaten at the company cafeteria. Here, he'd be on his own. Fortunately, Ruth, like a good first sergeant, was ready to take charge and help her new "shavetail lieutenant" until he could get more familiar with his surroundings.

"Look at this, Mr. Krummel." Ruth handed Klaus a page of want ads from *The Mining Journal*, pointing to one circled in red. "You're going to need a place to stay. You could just rent a room, I guess, but here's an ad for a small two-bedroom house on Iron Street that's available. My cousin knows the couple who just moved out. He says it's in decent shape, and the rent seems reasonable. Would you like me to call and find out if we can see it today?"

Klaus was surprised but pleased by Ruth's efficiency. "Please, yes. By all means, Mrs. Olson. I appreciate your help."

Ruth called the number listed in the ad, spoke briefly to the person who answered, then said, "Great," and ended the call. Turning to Otto she said, "We can see the place at two-thirty this afternoon. I'll drive you there. Next, you'll need a car and, of course, a driver's license." She looked at Otto uncertainly and said, "You do drive, do you not, Mr. Krummel? Perhaps you already have some kind of license?"

"Yes, of course." Klaus withdrew his wallet and showed Ruth the driving license issued to Otto Krummel when he was living and working in Kiruna, Sweden.

"Oh, very good. We'll go to the police station now so you can get your Michigan license. Then we can look for a car for you to buy. Have you thought about what make you would like and how much you want to pay?"

Klaus shrugged. He hadn't thought about it but considered the size of his salary advance and suggested, "Perhaps four to five hundred dollars? Not more, I think."

"Fine. When I knew you were coming and would need a car, I asked my cousin to look around. He called yesterday and said there is a nice looking 1947 Plymouth coupe with only 20,000 miles down to the Peltonen Plymouth-Dodge dealership. They want $575, but I betcha' you can get them to come down. We'll go there after the police station and before you look at the house."

Klaus shook his head and smiled. "You are indeed remarkable, Mrs. Olson. Thank you very much."

Ruth Olson's advance planning made it possible for Klaus to quickly immerse himself in the job. He soon gained the respect of his coworkers and his manager, Sam Thayer. Within a month, he'd inspected and certified the support structures installed in several new drifts, held informational meetings on safety equipment and procedures with three groups of underground miners, and begun to develop casual friendships with several individuals. Over the next several months he grew especially close to Eino Hakala and Richard Maki. The three often spent Friday evenings at the Roosevelt, enjoying beer, popcorn, and "bullshit" talk as Eino was wont to call it.

Just about everyone now knew Otto Krummel had served in the German army and, especially when Eino and Richard took pains to emphasize that Otto had only fought on the Eastern Front, most seemed content to let the past be the past and accept him. But there were exceptions. One Friday evening, a very drunk Ole Halvorson staggered over to the table where Otto, Eino, and Richard were sitting. Placing his clenched fists on the table, Ole leaned forward, stared directly at Otto. and shouted, "You fucking goddamn, Kraut, Heinie! You killed my brother Lars. I'm gonna take you out, you bastard."

Klaus tensed, his first reaction being to rise and defend himself, but then he stopped. *Calm yourself, Klaus. Do nothing to make people take a closer look at you than they already have.* He remained sitting, just returned Ole's gaze, and said nothing.

Eino and Richard came to his rescue. They jumped up, grabbed Ole, and pulled him away to the other side of the bar. Eino said, "Shut up, you dumb Swede. You're crazy drunk. Otto didn't have nothing to do with killing Lars. Lars died in Normandy. Hitler sent poor Otto to get his ass shot off in Russia. Now get out of here. Get some cold air. Get some coffee. Go home." He pushed Ole out the front door.

Ole staggered off down the street sobbing and still muttering, "Goddamn Kraut. Goddamn Heinie."

The house Klaus rented came partially furnished. Most of the items, though worn, were serviceable. However, he quickly concluded the bed was beyond recall. He spent his first night sleeping on the sofa, and early the next day resolved to use some of his advance to buy a decent mattress. At the store he also purchased a brass floor lamp and a comfortable overstuffed recliner chair and was pleased to learn his purchases could be delivered later that same day.

That evening, Klaus prepared a simple supper of sausage and hot potato salad accompanied by a bottle of Pabst Blue Ribbon beer. He planned to spend the rest of the evening in his chair beginning to read the six-volume set of Gibbon's *The History of the Decline and Fall of the Roman Empire* he'd purchased that afternoon at a used book store on Cleveland Avenue.

He was halfway through the second chapter of Volume 1 when there was a knock at the front door. Opening it, he looked down and saw a small blonde girl wearing a Brownie Scout pixie hat and a Brownie Scout vest over her winter coat. She held a bag containing several boxes of cookies.

"Hello, Mister. My name is Anna Albrecht. I'm eight years old, and I'm selling Girl Scout cookies. Would you like to buy some? Please?"

Klaus smiled. "Well, Anna. My name is Otto Krummel, and yes, I think I might be interested in buying some cookies." Then he noticed the woman standing a few yards away on the sidewalk. "Is that your mother, Anna?"

"Yes."

At that, the woman came forward and said, "Mr. Krummel? My friend Ruth Olson told me she's working for you and that you've just moved here and started to work for CCI. I'm Kristin Albrecht and this is my daughter Anna." She turned and pointed. "We live just a block and a half down Iron Street that way." She smiled. "Anna and I want to welcome you to the neighborhood, and hopefully sell you some cookies as well."

Klaus returned the smile. He looked at her sparkling blue eyes and blond hair fetchingly framed by the fur trim on the hood of her red parka and, without thinking, muttered, "*Rotkäppchen.*"

"Excuse me? What did you say?"

Klaus blushed. "Forgive me, Mrs. Albrecht. I apologize. Just an expression in my native German. I must remember to use my English."

"That's okay, but I'm curious to know what you said."

"I'm embarrassed, Mrs. Albrecht, but looking at you there in your red parka with the hood up made me think of the children's story about Little Red Riding Hood. I didn't mean to say it out loud. *Rotkäppchen* is the German name for Little Red Riding Hood."

Kristin laughed. "Oh my. What do you think of that, Anna? Do you think I look like Little Red Riding Hood?" She held up her basket holding another dozen boxes of the cookies Anna hoped to sell in the neighborhood. "And here we are at Grandma's house. Do you suppose Mr. Krummel is the wolf, Anna?" She turned back to Klaus, her eyes dancing. "What have you done with our grandma, Mr. Krummel?"

Anna looked a bit uncertainly at her mother. Clearly she was teasing Mr. Krummel. She hoped this wouldn't cost her a sale. Klaus, also blushing, didn't know what to say. Kristin reached out and touched him on the arm. "I couldn't resist teasing you just a bit, Otto. So now it's my turn to apologize. And please call me Kristin."

Klaus recovered his composure, managed a smile, and replied, "Kristin and Anna, I promise you Grandma is quite safe. And yes, this wolf definitely does need some cookies. What kind do you have Anna?" Anna showed him, and Klaus bought one box of each kind being offered that year: peanut butter sandwich, shortbread, and chocolate mints.

As Anna and her mother turned to go to the house across the street, Kristin called back, "Anna and I would like to invite you to dinner. Would next Sunday be all right?"

"Yes. I would be honored."

"Great. Let's say five o'clock. We live in the green house at 289 Iron Street. See you then."

CHAPTER 12

Klaus sat at the kitchen table, opened a bottle of Pabst, and reflected. Another month and it would be two years since he'd first set foot in Ishpeming and, like that day, it was damnably cold again. But weather wasn't really the issue. He was thinking again about the near miss in Latvia that could've cost him his life, and his frustration at still being unable to rejoin Gerda and find Horst. It had been three years since his single exchange of letters with Gerda. A second letter he'd sent to her from Kiruna had been returned marked as undeliverable. After that, repeated requests to the International Red Cross failed to yield any information about where either she or his son Horst might be. At times he'd been so frustrated and anxious he'd nearly said to hell with it, thought about just quitting his job with CCI, and trying to go back to Europe to look for them. So far, reason had intervened to stop him from doing something completely stupid. He didn't have enough money to do anything dramatic at this point even though he knew he was sitting on a fortune in gold and valuable jewelry. A small town like Ishpeming offered no access to a high-end market where such things could be sold for what they were worth. On top of that, he was in thrall to a faceless government contact he only knew as J. If he had decided to cut and run, he supposed J could easily stop him from leaving the country. What might his fate be then?

And worse, though the IRC had had no success in finding any information about his sister or son, a year ago it had forwarded to him a copy a letter it had received from a Frieda Krummel in Cologne who was trying to trace her husband, one Otto Krummel, who'd been a soldier in the German army. Might he possibly be that person or know anything about that person? Klaus immediately replied, no, stating he was originally from Dresden and was in no way related to a Frieda Krummel or knew anything about another person with the same name as his. But at the time, the letter precipitated another full-scale anxiety attack and feeling of guilt.

The night after receiving it, he'd tossed for hours before finally falling into a disturbed sleep accompanied by a terrifying dream he'd already had a couple times in the past. In it, after shooting Otto, the man didn't immediately collapse as actually happened. Instead, he'd turned, looked directly at him, and said in a pleading voice, "*Herr Major, warum hat Sie mich erschiessen? Meine frau...meine Kinder*" (Transl. Major, why did you shoot me? My wife...my children), before slowly sinking to the floor. Klaus awoke shaking, drenched with sweat, and barely able to breathe. Downing a large volume of schnapps helped some, but it took days for the intense feeling of guilt to subside. After one of those dreams, people tended to notice he seemed preoccupied and uncommunicative, but to the few who inquired, he only muttered, "The war..." Most accepted that, likely thinking *Battle Fatigue*, or maybe the more recently coined term, *Combat Stress Syndrome*. Some expressed sympathy.

But now, maybe, just maybe there was some light on the horizon. Two weeks ago, while searching the card catalog at the library for any holdings on the history of the Russian Czars and the Bolshevik Revolution, he'd engaged in conversation with the reference librarian. She admitted to also having a personal interest in the topic and told him she had a couple books on the subject at home she would be willing to bring in for him to read.

"That would be wonderful. What sparked your interest in this, if I may ask?"

"My dad, who lived in Chicago and recently passed away, willed to me a really ornate broach supposedly once owned by Alexandra, wife of Czar Nicholas II, that my grandfather purchased in the late 1920s from the Soviet government. I wanted to have it properly appraised, and when I did and received an offer if I wanted to sell, I was...well, let's just say, really pleased."

"Where did you go for that? Sounds pretty high end for Ishpeming."

"I learned of a reputable gallery in Chicago specializing in Russian art and jewelry called Siegelman and Friedland. I took it down there. They did the appraisal, then made an offer, enough to pretty much remodel our entire house."

"Impressive. Could you tell me how to contact those people?" Then in a sort of embarrassed voice, "I...I'm in possession of a necklace that came down through the family and was rumored to have been owned by some member of the Romanov family. I don't know the truth of that. It does look really nice. It's composed of an impressive array of what I think are diamonds and emeralds, although I can't personally tell for sure if they're real."

"No problem." Walking over to her desk, the librarian rummaged through one of the drawers in her desk, withdrew a card, and handed it to him. "Here. This has the Siegelman-Friedland Gallery address and phone number. Have at it, and good luck."

Klaus thanked her, and quickly headed home to pen a letter to the Siegelman and Friedland gallery. In it, he wrote that he possessed a diamond and emerald necklace once owned by his grandfather, who'd acquired it while holding a diplomatic post in Saint Petersburg in 1905. He went on to say he wished to have the necklace formally appraised and would consider selling if the price was attractive. He included a detailed written description of the piece. He concluded by asking if it would be convenient for him to visit the gallery during the second week of February when he was already scheduled to be in Chicago for a meeting of mine safety engineers.

A return letter from Siegelman expressed interest, so Klaus met with the two gallery owners. They vetted the necklace as quite likely having been a Romanov family possession and though Klaus thought Siegelman's face expressed some doubt about his story as to how he'd come to have it, he didn't press the point. The partners offered $10,000, and Klaus accepted on the spot.

Having concluded one transaction, Klaus casually mentioned he also possessed a beautiful gold egg-shaped object inset with diamonds and sapphires his grandfather had acquired in 1920 from a general in the White Army during the Russian Civil War. He wondered, could it just possibly be one of those fabled eggs the House of Fabergé had created for Tsars Alexander and Nicholas that had since been reported as missing from the Soviet Armoury? That got rapt attention and raised eyebrows from both men. Klaus now planned another trip to Chicago to have them look at it.

So now, maybe life in Ishpeming really wasn't so bad after all. It did seem the longer he pretended to be Otto Krummel, the more it felt like he was actually becoming him, a man who'd made friends and was well thought of at work. Except for the nerve-racking letter from Frieda Krummel a year ago, in some ways Major Klaus Gustmann was beginning to fade away, taking with him bad memories of the war and any passion he might ever have had for national socialism. Of course, another very important reason that life here had improved was the pretty blonde, blue-eyed widow named Kristin Albrecht, who lived just over a block away.

She'd been kind to him since the first day he hit town, bringing over baked goods, inviting him to dinner, and helping him find his way around the community. A month after he arrived, she convinced him one evening to go bowling with her and given his total lack of experience with the game, assured him his score of 126, compared to her 198, really wasn't that bad. The following week she'd stopped by his house to ask if he might like to attend services with her at the Lutheran church. He put her off on that one, saying he'd think about it, but two weeks later, when she invited him to a church supper, he accepted. He'd been devastated by Magda's death, but the war had required his full attention as long as it lasted. Since then, he'd been terribly lonely, wishing, but pretty well convinced he might never once again have a real family life. Clearly, Kristin seemed interested in him, and he found her attractive and fun to be with.

Klaus had grown close not only to Kristin but also to her daughter Anna, and she'd begun to treat him like a second father, having lost her first when she only three years old. The three of them were soon doing many things together, going to a movie, out to dinner, having picnics, swimming and fishing in the summer, skiing in the winter, and sometimes just sitting around the fireplace enjoying each other's company. Klaus had even begun to imagine possibly asking Kristin to become his wife. But could that *really* ever happen? The problem was his double life. Kristin and Anna didn't know who he really was. Could he find a way to let them know in a way that wouldn't destroy their relationship? They were definitely helping to keep him here. Without them, he might well have given in to one of his inclinations to jump ship and try to escape the hold J held over him.

Enough reflection. Opening another bottle of Pabst, Klaus turned to a task he knew he should have taken care of long ago, preparing a will, leaving his estate to Gerda and Horst. After Magda's death, he'd had a formal will registered with a lawyer in Dresden naming Gerda and Horst as co-beneficiaries, with Horst also designated as Gerda's ward until he reached adulthood. Now that Major Klaus Gustmann was officially dead, although Gerda knew otherwise, they were technically eligible to receive the proceeds of his life insurance policy, cash from his savings account, and several items of Magda's jewelry cached in a safe in the apartment they had occupied in Dresden. Of course, none of that was relevant now. The insurance company no longer existed, and both the bank and his house had been totally destroyed when the Allies bombed Dresden.

Given his present circumstance, the will that Klaus now prepared was brief, handwritten, and frankly strange. On the first sheet of paper he wrote: I, Otto Krummel, a resident of 176 Iron Street in Ishpeming, Michigan, USA, being of sound mind on this date, February 5, 1953, declare the following to be my last will and testament.

He then named Gerda and Horst as equal co-beneficiaries of his estate, giving their birthdates, full names, last known addresses, and identifying them as his cousin and her son, respectively. Klaus hoped the fiction could withstand scrutiny should it ever actually become necessary to probate the will. Even in death he felt compelled to hide his identity as SS Major Klaus Gustmann, fearing such a revelation might prompt the government to impound his wealth and so deprive his sister and son of the inheritance he wanted them to have. Of course, J (was he FBI or CIA?) knew who he was, but in the event of his death Klaus thought it unlikely J would be inclined to expose their prior relationship. Klaus added a specific bequest for Kristin Albrecht, willing to her a diamond-studded ring he planned to place in his safety deposit box at the Hematite Bank along with the will as soon as he managed to get it signed and witnessed. There it would reside with a life insurance policy for $5,000, listing Kristin as beneficiary.

Apart from the bequest for Kristin, the will said nothing about the rest of his estate. Instead, the text on the second page began with a stanza taken from a common German children's rhyme he felt sure both Horst and Gerda must know by heart.

Hoppe, hoppe, Reiter,
Wenn er fällt, dann schreit er.
Fällt er in die Graben,

Fressen ihn die Schlangen.
Fällt er in den Sumpf,
Macht der Reiter plumps!

After that, he picked out a dozen seemingly unrelated verses from the King James Bible, consulting a dog-eared copy left in the house by a previous renter. Raised a Catholic, Klaus didn't think of himself as religious, but in secondary school he'd taken a class on the Bible as literature. Gifted with a near eidetic memory he found he was yet able to recall and write out several useful verses from memory before skimming through the Bible to select others that would serve his purpose. Then he listed and underscored the selected verses, followed by the full text of each (not shown here).

Proverbs 1:8
Proverbs 13:22
Ezekial 28:4
Proverbs 10:2
Ecclesiastes 8:10
1 Kings 20:38
Deuteronomy 27:23
Matthew 15:39
Psalm 5:9
Ezra 10:31
1 Chronicles 2:47
Daniel 2:43

Finally, at the bottom of the third page, he added lines on which to print and then write his name, the date, and the names and signatures of two witnesses. Tomorrow he would take the will to work and ask Eino Hakala and Richard Maki to sign as witnesses.

Klaus was pleased with his creation. Although he hoped the will would never have to be probated, that he'd yet be able to find his sister and son and share with them the treasure while he still lived. But if the worst happened, then he wanted the court and its appointed executor to find the language confusing. He only wanted Gerda and Horst to be able to figure out where he'd hidden their inheritance.

CHAPTER 13

Klaus placed the newly drafted will on his desk, then opened a third bottle of Pabst and tuned the radio to WDMJ to catch a rebroadcast of a Duke Ellington concert in New York City. Lighting a cigarette, he leaned back and spent the next hour listening to his favorite jazz pianist and orchestra.

Finally calling it a night as the station began to play the "Star Spangled Banner" before signing off, Klaus got up and went to the basement. He checked the pressure gauge on the furnace and added two shovelfuls of coal. Then he went back upstairs and was nearly to his bedroom when he heard a knock at the side door. *Who could it be this late? Surely not Kristin.* Pulling the curtain on the kitchen window to one side, he saw a smallish man in a dark mackinaw standing in the driveway. The nearby streetlamp dimly illuminated his face. It wasn't anyone he recognized. He opened the door just a crack.

"Yes. Can I help you?"

"*Guten abend*, Herr Gustmann."

Klaus jumped backward with shock, stammering, "*Nein*, I mean no. My name is Otto Krummel. I know of no one named Gustmann."

"Oh, I think you do," replied the man in English.

Then he reverted to German saying, "Don't be fearful, Herr Gustmann. Your secret is safe with me. My name is Jürgen Holzer and I am from ODESSA. We're very sorry for the problem you encountered in Latvia, but that situation has been corrected. Anna asked me to tell you the traitor Andris

Ozols has been eliminated. I'm glad you were able to escape his trap, but we didn't know what happened to you after that. Only later we learned from Aleksis that you went to Stockholm and took temporary refuge with the Latvian community there. We sent a man to find you, but you had already gone, and no one seemed to know where. Now, thankfully, we're ready to help you resettle in South America. There is a job for you in Rio de Janeiro with a consulting engineering firm founded by several senior *Schutzstaffel* officers. They'll be pleased to have you join them. It's time to complete your journey, Herr Gustmann, give to ODESSA what you promised, and begin working with our brothers to bring *Der Neuanfang* to fruition."

Klaus's brain was a whirl of confusion, taking several seconds to frame a response. He'd just been thinking what he wanted most now was a chance to build a new life with Kristin and her daughter Anna. Any interest he might ever have had in helping create a Fourth Reich was totally gone. And something about Jürgen's words didn't ring true, the part about having learned from Aleksis about Klaus's escape to Sweden. The news reaching the Latvian community in Stockholm was that Aleksis had been betrayed by a double agent from MI-6 and arrested by the MGB. If Aleksis had told anyone about his escape to Sweden, he was sure it must have been the MGB, not ODESSA.

Finally, with a strained smile, Klaus said, "Indeed, you startled me, Jürgen. I was afraid you were from the FBI, and I was about to be arrested. It's been very stressful living here. It will be good to settle where I don't have to keep looking over my shoulder. I've been isolated in this godforsaken town with no idea how to find a friendly contact. Come in. Tell me about the plan for Argentina. When can this be done? What route am I to take and who will be my contacts? Am I to travel as Otto Krummel, or will I need another identity?"

Klaus and Jürgen sat at the kitchen table eating braunschweiger on crackers and drinking Pabst beer. Jürgen praised the liverwurst but wrinkled his nose at the beer.

"Nothing like a really good German beer."

Klaus had to agree, but over time he had adjusted somewhat to the featureless character of mainstream bottled American beers.

Jürgen didn't seem prepared to provide much specific information, saying his mission had only been to make a first contact with Klaus. He said Klaus would meet another member of ODESSA next week in Chicago who would provide him with all the details, tickets, and other documents needed for his passage to and settlement in Rio de Janeiro.

"I'll travel with you to Chicago and introduce you to your next contact. Since you won't be coming back to Ishpeming, gather everything you wish to take including, of course, the gold rubles, eggs, and other jewels you recovered in Latvia." Jürgen looked around the house. "I presume they are well hidden here or perhaps in a large safety deposit box in the bank?"

Jürgen's reference to the treasure as including eggs, jewelry, and gold rubles, and not gold bullion as the man calling himself Andris Ozols had seemed to believe, instantly made Klaus wonder how he could know this. Information about the eggs couldn't have come from either Diedrich or Aleksis as he'd never told either man about them. Aleksis could be the source of Jürgen's knowledge about the gold rubles because he'd had them in his possession when arrested by the MGB, but what about the eggs? *My God! This must go all the back to Dieter. The Russians who captured him must have found his egg and forced him to tell about the rest of the stash before they killed him. Still, Dieter hadn't told them exactly where to find it.*

Klaus suddenly became aware that Jürgen was staring at him, waiting for an answer to his question about where the treasure was kept.

"Neither place, Jürgen. It would be foolish to keep such valuable items in this house, and I don't trust banks. But don't worry. They're in a very safe place. I'll have everything with me when we meet to take the train to Chicago. But first, I need to lay some groundwork. If I suddenly disappear, that will draw attention and there will be an effort to trace me. Instead, I'll set the stage by resigning my job at the mine and tell people I've accepted a new position somewhere else. What to do think?"

Jürgen seemed a little startled, as though he'd given no thought to the need for Klaus to cover his trail, but quickly recovered. "Yes, I agree. That seems a reasonable plan."

"In the meantime, Jürgen, where are you staying? How can I reach you if we need to talk?"

"I'm at the Northland Hotel in Marquette under the name John Abercrombie. Leave a message for me there, and I'll contact you by telephone at your home."

With that, the two men separated. Klaus watched Jürgen drive away in a dark blue 1948 Chevrolet coupe, resembling one that had seemed to be following him yesterday. It had taken the same route and made the same turns he did, but then continued on and turned right toward the highway when Klaus turned into his driveway.

Alone now, Klaus thought, *As soon as Jürgen sees I have the treasure in hand or can figure out where it's hidden he'll try to kill me and take it. I've got to lay a trap for him first.* He unlocked the lower right-hand drawer of his desk and took out the .32 caliber Beretta he'd recently purchased at Richard's Sporting Goods Store in Marquette. He planned to teach Kristin how to shoot and then have her carry the little gun in her purse for protection when she had to leave work late and walk home alone in the dark. For the next few days, he decided to carry it in his pocket at all times. Not a lot of firepower, but enough at close range.

The next morning Klaus checked to see that all the first story windows in the house were locked, then locked both the front and side doors as he left for work. As soon as he got to his office, he called Eino and Richard and asked them to sign his will as witnesses. Then he turned his attention to a review of plans for the construction of two new horizontal tunnels at Level 3 of the Mather D mine. At four o'clock, he left the office and walked to his car. As he exited the parking lot, he spotted a car that looked like the one Jürgen had driven the previous night. But this car didn't follow him, prompting him to remind himself there were a lot of dark colored five-year-old Chevrolets in town. Arriving home, he first circled the house looking for, but failing to find, footprints in the snow or any sign of a possible forced entry through a window. However, when he went inside, it was apparent someone had been there. Pillows on the sofa had been moved and a cabinet door in the kitchen wasn't completely latched.

That evening, the weather report on radio station WJPD warned of a major snowstorm beginning late Wednesday afternoon or evening with an expected accumulation of fifteen to eighteen inches by Thursday noon. Klaus decided that would be a good time to put his plan into action. He called the Northland Hotel in Marquette. When the desk clerk answered he said, "I wish to leave a message for Mr. John Abercrombie. Please tell him Mr. Gustmann expects to receive the items he ordered after work on Wednesday and will meet him at the Mather Inn for dinner at seven." The clerk repeated the message. Klaus thanked him and hung up the phone.

The next morning, Klaus reported to work as usual, but at noon told Ruth he felt unwell and was taking the rest of the day off. This time, he left the parking lot at the back using an unpaved alleyway that led into a fenced area where the company kept several construction vehicles. At the far end was a gate, although locked at night, was now open. Driving through, he turned right onto a little used road, then headed north through a forested area. No one lived along there as the land on both sides belonged to the CCI. Slowing briefly as he crossed a road on which a right turn would take one to downtown Ishpeming, he continued north for another half mile.

Klaus pulled over, parking next to a dirt track that entered the woods to the east. From the trunk of the car he retrieved a shovel, a pickax, and a backpack. Then he followed the track for half a mile to where it ended. Turning north, he cut directly through the woods for another eighth of a mile. The going was easy as the snow was only a couple inches deep. He was counting on that changing dramatically by Thursday morning. His objective was a rocky hill on the far side of a small clearing. At its base, mostly obscured by a large pine tree, was the entrance to a small, long-abandoned iron mine. Its main shaft, more properly called an adit, since it was nearly horizontal, was less than fifty yards long. At two points the original miners had begun to dig horizontal drifts, but both ended after just a few yards. Clearly, only a small amount of ore could have been taken out before the mine was abandoned. The rails on which small ore cars had once been pulled into and out of the entrance by mules had long been removed for use elsewhere. It seemed a perfect place to hide a treasure. That was exactly what Klaus wanted Jürgen to believe.

Being on the lee side of the hill, the area directly in front of the entrance held almost no snow, but it was thick with leaves and brush. Klaus set to work and after half an hour was satisfied with the result. Returning to his car, he drove home. In his mailbox he found a short note from Jürgen acknowledging the message he'd left with the hotel clerk and saying he looked forward to their meeting at the Mather Inn.

That evening, Klaus took Kristin and Anna to dinner at the Northwoods restaurant to celebrate her thirty-fifth birthday. Later, after Anna was in bed, he sat with Kristin in her living room, watched the flames dance in the fireplace, and listened to a recording of the Glenn Miller orchestra. Klaus felt awkward and conflicted. It was a long time since he'd had a romantic relationship with a woman. There had been nothing since Magda died except for that single night with the prostitute in Latvia. He wanted to tell Kristin how he felt, that he cared deeply for her. But could he ever tell her who he really was? Would he always have to be Otto Krummel to her? Would she understand and forgive him if he did tell her the truth about himself? Somehow, that didn't seem likely. But whatever he was going to say to her he needed to do it soon. Even if he dodged the threat from Jürgen and could manage to sell one of the eggs to the Siegelman-Friedland Gallery in Chicago, he was almost certainly going to have to move again and perhaps assume yet another false identity. After an hour, he rose, kissed Kristin discreetly on the cheek, wished her happy birthday again, and left.

In the morning, Klaus washed, shaved, ate his breakfast, and left for work as usual, the loaded .32 caliber Beretta secure in the right-hand pocket of his parka. Leaden clouds presaged the coming snowstorm. At the office, he looked over plans for new excavations to be initiated at two other CCI mines. Then he scheduled for the next morning an inspection of a recently completed lateral tunnel at Level 3 of the Mather D mine that had begun to show some overhead cracks.

At four o'clock, Klaus left the office, drove out of the parking lot by the front entrance, and followed a circuitous route through several streets in Ishpeming. Checking the rearview mirror, he was reassured to see a dark blue Chevrolet following a couple blocks behind. Driving west out of Ishpeming, he stopped at a pullout a half mile east of the intersection he'd crossed going north the day before. No road entered the woods at this point, but he knew a fast fifteen-minute walk to the north would bring him to the abandoned mine. Jürgen would surely follow him, but since he wouldn't want his quarry to know he was being followed, he could be counted on to hang back and take somewhat longer to arrive. At the mine, Klaus entered and positioned himself to one side so he could keep out of sight but still watch as Jürgen approached. Ten minutes later, he heard the sound of footsteps on the thin crunchy layer of snow stop as his follower reached the clearing. In the gathering darkness, he could make out only a vague outline of the man.

Klaus held the Beretta ready as Jürgen approached. Something extended from his right arm, and as he edged closer Klaus could see it was a pistol, a pistol with a long barrel. Then Jürgen called out.

"Klaus are you in there? It's Jürgen. I came to help you."

"You're a surprise, Jürgen. I didn't expect to see you until this evening. But I'm glad you came. It's dark in here and my damned flashlight just failed. Have you got one? I'm having trouble finding my way about."

"Yes, I have one."

Klaus saw Jürgen take from his left coat pocket and hold up a large multi-cell flashlight, one heavy enough to use as a cudgel. As he did that, Jürgen turned slightly to the right, still holding but obviously hoping to keep his pistol out of sight.

To encourage Jürgen forward, Klaus shifted his pistol to his left hand, stepped to one side, then briefly revealed himself in the mine entrance and waved with his right hand.

"Stay between those slag piles, Jürgen. There's a narrow but fairly flat pathway leading to the mine entrance."

Jürgen started forward slowly, holding the flashlight away from his body with its bright beam aimed at the mouth of the mine entrance rather than his path. *You're being careful, Jürgen, holding your flashlight so it'll blind me if I step out and try to shoot you, but you can't really see where you're walking. Very good.*

Jürgen advanced cautiously. Now he stood just a few yards from the entrance. One more step and...Suddenly the lower part of his body disappeared from view, followed by a scream of pain.

"Help! Oh God! Help me!"

Klaus stepped forward, turned on his flashlight, which hadn't failed at all, and trained it on Jürgen. He'd broken through the brush-covered path into a depression holding a large bear trap that now dug deep into the flesh of his right leg. Jürgen's face was contorted in pain. He bent over, clutching at the injured leg with both hands. Having lost hold of both as he fell, Klaus could see Jürgen's flashlight lying in the brush to his left, his pistol to the right. Klaus picked it up, a .22 caliber Ruger semi-automatic, but with a difference. The barrel had been lengthened several inches through the addition of a cylindrical device, a homemade silencer. Playing his light over the pistol Klaus saw that the registration number had been filed off.

"This is an assassin's weapon, Jürgen. You were going to kill me once you got what you wanted."

"No, no. That's not true. Help me. For God's sake help me. I can explain."

"I'm afraid it's too late for that." Klaus held Jürgen's pistol in his gloved hand and pressed the muzzle against the man's forehead.

Jürgen screamed, "Noooooo…" and jerked his head to the right just as Klaus fired.

Convulsing once as the bullet entered his left temple, Jürgen lay limp. "Goodbye, Mr. Holzer, or whatever your name may really be."

Klaus knelt, pulled the dead man out of the depression, then pried open the jaws of the bear trap he'd set the previous day. Searching the man's clothing, he found matches and half a pack of Pall Malls in one coat pocket. In the pants pockets he found car keys, a key for a room at the Northland Hotel in Marquette, and a wallet. The wallet held $178 as well as an Illinois driver's license issued to one Anatoly Zaretsky with a Chicago address. No picture, but the license described the holder as a Caucasian male, thirty-five years of age, five feet seven inches in height with brown hair and blue eyes, a fair description of the man who'd introduced himself to Klaus as Jürgen Holzer.

Klaus pulled Zaretsky's body into and along the adit for about fifty feet, turned right, and left it along with the pistol in the first of the shallow drifts. Recovering the bear trap, he filled in the depression with brush. Then he carried the trap to the edge of the clearing and threw it as far as he could into the woods. Hidden in the mine, he supposed Zaretsky's body possibly might never be found or, when eventually discovered, might be hard to identify if animals got to it first. There were coyotes in the area, and Klaus had seen signs a bear had once used the mine as a den.

By now it was quite dark, and snow had begun to fall in earnest. Klaus began the half mile walk back to his car, using his flashlight to find and follow the tracks he and Zaretsky made coming in. He was leaving a clear trail, but by morning, those tracks would be completely obliterated. Klaus felt relieved. His plan had worked. Unlike what he'd done in Berlin, Klaus felt no guilt at all for having killed Anatoly Zaretsky, alias Jürgen Holzer.

Back at the road, Klaus's first task was to search and then move Zaretsky's car. Wearing gloves, he opened the doors and checked the front and back seats. In the glove compartment he found a highway map and a registration card issued by the State of Illinois to Gerhard Nelson at a Chicago address different from that on Anatoly Zaretsky's license. He wondered if Zaretsky had stolen the car or only borrowed it. Next he checked the trunk and found nothing other than the jack and spare tire. He planned to ditch the car behind a disintegrating log cabin at the end of a quarter mile long dirt track that took off from the main road and headed south into a wooded area a couple hundred yards to the east. But he did need to hurry. The car didn't have snow tires or chains, and given the rate at which snow was falling, it would soon be difficult to navigate the track leading to the cabin. He started the car, turned it around, and fifteen minutes later parked it behind the cabin. Then he removed the license plate and vehicle registration card, placed them in his backpack, and jogged back to his car.

Looking ahead through the darkness, Klaus felt a surge of anxiety at the sight of another car parked behind his. It was an Ishpeming city police car with a flashing red light on top. He saw the officer look at the license on his car, then walk around to the driver's side door, open it, and examine the interior with his flashlight. *Now what?* He gripped the pistol in his pocket, then thought, *Don't be an idiot, Klaus. Relax. Your pistol is legal, registered, and it hasn't been fired. There's no reason the police can possibly know why you're here. Think of something reasonable to tell the cop.*

"Hey, officer, what's up?"

The officer turned his flashlight on Klaus and said, "Is this your car, sir? Have you had a breakdown?"

"Yes, it's mine, and no, there's nothing wrong with it. I was just about to put my dog back in the car after a training exercise when he spied a rabbit and took off. I've been back in the woods calling him, but so far no answer. Now it's too dark to see his trail and the snow is getting pretty deep. I'm worried about that damn beagle, but I think I've got to give it up for now. I hope Buster makes it through the night. I'll come back and look for him in the morning."

"Yeah. I wouldn't worry too much. It's snowing hard, but it won't get very cold tonight. Your dog will probably dig a little hollow in the snow to spend the night and be out here in the morning looking for you and his breakfast."

The officer wished him good night and good luck. Klaus breathed a little sigh of relief, but his nerves were on edge. He felt no remorse for having dispatched Anatoly Zaretsky but knew he couldn't just sit back and relax. He needed a plan, but first he needed a drink, a stiff one. He got into his car and drove back to town.

Back at the house, Klaus poured himself a double measure of schnapps. Then he opened a bottle of Pabst to chase it and sat in his recliner to think.

Zaretsky's car would eventually be found, hopefully later rather than sooner. Clearly, the MGB now knew where he was. They were waiting for him to show up with the treasure and to hear news that an unfortunate guy named Otto Krummel had been shot and killed in Ishpeming in the course of a botched burglary. When that didn't happen, someone else would surely come to see what had happened. Maybe, if he was lucky, he could make them think Zaretsky had done a runner with the treasure. That would give him a little more time to plan his next move.

Klaus decided to call his office in the morning, tell Ruth he was feeling sick again, suspected it was flu, and might not make it in for the rest of the week. He decided to tell her to cancel the safety tour of Level 3 in the Mather D mine and reschedule it for the following week. In the meantime, she should have the area cordoned off until the risk of a collapse could be assessed and repairs made. Then he would call the gallery owners in Chicago and ask if they could see him the day after tomorrow. He would take his egg, catch the "400" to Chicago, hopefully sell a couple pieces of jewelry outright for cash and maybe get the gallery to either buy the egg outright or at least give him a written appraisal regarding its authenticity.

Picking up the phone, Klaus asked the operator if she could find a number for a Gerhard Nelson in Chicago, giving the address on the vehicle registration he'd found in Zaretsky's car. After a short pause, she came back on the line, gave him the number, and asked if he would like her to connect him.

"No, thank you. Not right now. I'll place a call to Mr. Nelson at a more convenient time tomorrow."

Klaus decided to call Nelson in the morning using a pay phone rather than his own. He had no way of knowing at this point whether Nelson was in on Zaretsky's mission to kill him and steal the treasure or not but hoped to get some sense of that from how the man responded to his phone call. With that, he retired to bed and slept poorly.

CHAPTER 14

Klaus was just about to call his secretary when the phone rang.
"Hello, Otto Krummel speaking."

"Hi, Otto. This is Tom Corker."

Who? The voice was familiar, but he couldn't think of anyone he knew by that name.

"I was just calling to ask if you were able to find Buster?"

Then it came back to him, and Klaus's heart skipped a beat. Tom Corker was the cop he'd spoken to last night. *Corker must have run my plate to identify me, and then looked up my phone number.*

"Um...you were exactly right, Tom. That damn dog found his way back to the main road and dug out a little hollow in the snow to spend the night. I got out there a little after dawn, and he was standing by the roadside, whining and hungry."

"Well good. I'm glad you found him. Incidentally, my uncle is Vice President of the Ishpeming Beagle Club. If you're interested, I'm sure he'd be willing to talk to you about a training regimen for Buster. Maybe you'd even like to consider joining the club?"

"Uh...maybe so. Give me your uncle's name and phone number, and I'll think about getting in touch." At that moment the dog belonging to his next-door neighbor, a beagle, began to bark at a squirrel just outside the kitchen door. Klaus turned, held the phone up against the door, and yelled, "Quiet,

Buster. Keep it down," as the neighbor emerged and took the dog back into the house. "Well, sometimes Buster does obey me. Thanks for your call, Tom."

Klaus hung up the phone, took a deep breath, then picked up the phone again and called his secretary. Someone else answered and told him that Ruth had called in sick that morning. Muffling his voice a bit and managing a fake cough, Klaus said, "I think we both must have the same bug. I'm not feeling at all well and now I have a fever, so I won't be coming into the office today or tomorrow. Hopefully, I'll feel better by Monday."

Next, Klaus drove to a gas station three blocks away that had an outside phone booth. Inserting a coin, he asked the operator to connect him to the number he'd obtained the night before for Gerhard Nelson. The operator came back and asked him to deposit two dollars. Once he had, she put the call through.

"Mr. Gerhard Nelson?"

"Yes."

"My name is Klaus Gustmann. Yesterday, a man named Jürgen Holzer came to my home. He said he was from ODESSA and had come to help me go to Rio de Janeiro where a job had been arranged for me with a consulting engineering firm there. He told me his assistant in Chicago would help arrange transportation and the other documents that I'll need."

A pause at the other end of the line, then "I, uh…well…what else did Jürgen tell you? Did he say I was to make those arrangements?"

Good enough. Nelson had implicated himself.

"Yes, he said you and I were to meet in Chicago next week, but then suddenly something went horribly wrong. I was about to give to him what I'd promised to ODESSA when he pulled a gun and tried to shoot me. The gun misfired and we fought, but then he used the gun like a club and knocked me out. When I came to, he was gone and had taken *everything* I had. I think…"

The line went dead. Gerhard Nelson had hung up. The MGB now knew he was still alive, but that Zaretsky had grabbed the treasure. As long as he had it, it didn't really matter whether Klaus Gustmann lived or died. They knew there was nothing he could do. He certainly couldn't go to the police. Zaretsky's handlers would expect him to return to Chicago to deliver the goods, and when he failed to show up, Klaus was banking on them thinking he'd gone rogue and kept it for himself. For a while, at least, Klaus hoped the MGB would focus on their own man and not on him.

Klaus drove back home and placed a call to the Siegelman-Friedland Gallery in Chicago. Mr. Siegelman's secretary answered.

"This is Mr. Otto Krummel calling from Ishpeming, Michigan. Mr. Siegelman and I have previously done business. I'll be traveling to Chicago tomorrow by train and could bring with me a piece in which he and Mr. Friedland have previously expressed great interest. Might it be possible for them to see me at the gallery late in the afternoon? My train is scheduled to arrive around three o'clock?"

"Please hold, Mr. Krummel, while I confer with Mr. Siegelman."

A minute later she was back and said, "Unfortunately, Mr. Siegelman has commitments all day tomorrow that extend well into the evening. However, he is most eager to meet with you and view the piece you mentioned. The gallery isn't normally open on weekends, but he asked me to inquire if it might be possible for you to meet him there at ten o'clock Saturday morning? Mr. Friedland can also be present then. Would that time work for you?"

"Yes. I can meet then."

"Very good. Is there anything else I can do for you, Mr. Krummel? Perhaps a hotel reservation?"

"Yes, I'd appreciate that. Please check if the Morrison Hotel on South Clark Street has a room available. That's where I stayed last month."

"I'll do that now and call you back as soon as I'm able to confirm your reservation."

CHAPTER 15

Klaus's meeting at the gallery was a success. If Messrs. Siegelman and Friedland had been pleased with the diamond and emerald necklace he brought to them in January, they seemed ecstatic when he unveiled his Fabergé egg. The two men took turns carefully examining it, consulted plates and text in several reference books, and conferred with each other in hushed tones that Klaus couldn't quite hear. Clearly, they were interested, but as Siegelman was about to tell him, it was necessary to temper that interest with a lot of caution.

"Mr. Krummel, I realize you're not able to provide compelling evidence regarding the egg's provenance, but it is of superb quality, and we believe it was definitely produced by the House of Fabergé sometime around 1900. It could *possibly* be one of the missing Imperial eggs, but we can't tender a more definite opinion without further study. Decent photographs are available for only two of the missing eggs, with a very grainy one of a third. Written descriptions of the others exist, but experts don't all agree on their authenticity. We must be very careful here. Many copies of the Imperial eggs based on those written descriptions have been made. Most are cheaply made and easily discerned, but some are of surpassing quality. In fact, a few are so well crafted as to demand a substantial price among collectors in spite of being known to be false."

Friedland added, "In fact, we now have in the gallery two quite impressive eggs Fabergé created in the 1890s, although not for the Tsar. We'll show them to you and point out features that serve to differentiate them from those created for the Tsars, as we think your egg *might* be." He went to a locked vault at the back of the gallery and returned holding two velvet-lined cases. Each held an ornate, gold and enamel, jewel encrusted egg-shaped object about three inches long. Siegelman pointed to several differences in the fine structure and certain materials used to construct the eggs, as well as maker's marks impressed in the base that helped distinguish them from his egg. Klaus could see and understood the differences as they were shown to him, but quickly realized how utterly dependent he was on the experts to determine the actual provenance of his egg.

Siegelman spoke. "Unofficially, we've heard one of the missing Imperial eggs may already have been found and acquired by a wealthy collector in Russia."

Klaus tensed but made no comment. His thoughts turned to Dieter, whose bullet-ridden body he'd passed in the street as he escaped from Berlin. Then he thought of his sister Gerda and the egg he'd left for her to find in his apartment in Berlin and later give to Horst. *Could that be one of those two? Which?*

"Mr. Krummel?"

"Yes."

"If we can authenticate your egg as one made specifically for the Tsars, it would be extremely valuable, possibly as much as a million dollars."

A million dollars! Klaus couldn't help but express pleased surprise. "What has to happen to achieve that?"

"Mr. Friedland and I will prepare our own assessment in writing, but beyond that we'll need to seek consensus from an international panel of experts. We would like to send your egg to the House of Wartski in London and ask them to arrange for such a review."

Klaus frowned. "So I'll have to leave it with you and allow it to be shipped to London for some unspecified period of time? How can I be assured of its safety?"

Friedland explained what the gallery did when a valuable art object had to leave an owner's hand and be shipped to another location. First, a contract was prepared under which the owner transferred possession of the object to the gallery and authorized it to act as his or her agent for a specified period. Under the contract, the gallery would have it insured against loss or damage for an agreed upon sum, which could be adjusted once a formal appraisal was completed.

"At present, based on our examination, but pending a review by an expert panel, the gallery is willing to insure your egg for $100,000. We will also give you a direct surety bond for $30,000, pending its safe return or sale. If the London experts concur in assessing your egg as one of these originally made to order for the Tsars, the insurance coverage will automatically be adjusted to reflect the new assessed value. At that point, per the contract, if you wish to sell the egg, we will act as your agent for 15 percent of the final sale price." He stopped and looked at Klaus. "What do you think, Mr. Krummel?"

Klaus looked at his hands and didn't respond immediately. He needed a minute to process everything. "How long do you think it will take to complete this assessment?"

"It's hard to say. My guess is six to eight weeks. To be safe, we ask you to give us up to three months to secure the assessment and then six more months to broker a sale that is to your satisfaction."

Three to nine months? I don't have that kind of time. Klaus realized he'd been utterly naïve to hope for a quick assessment and sale to the gallery owners. On the other hand, he hadn't reckoned on Siegelman's prediction that a single egg could bring as much as a million dollars. *A million dollars! Time versus money.*

Finally he looked up and said, "Gentlemen, I accept the terms you've outlined. Please prepare the contract."

"Excellent. We'll make out two copies of the contract now, one for us and one for you to take, including addenda consisting of the Lloyds of London insurance policy and detailed pictures of your egg."

"Detailed pictures? All I have is a single black and white photograph. That isn't sufficient?"

"Don't be concerned. We have equipment to take care of that right now." Friedland got up, opened a cabinet at the back of the room, and took out two lamps, a white screen, a piece of black velvet cloth, and a professional quality Polaroid Land camera. "With this we can take and immediately print a series of well-lighted, highly detailed, close-up pictures of the egg from several angles. They will be referenced in the main body and then attached as an addendum to the contract."

Klaus left the gallery a few minutes after noon and walked back to the Morrison Hotel. In a bulky envelope he carried the signed contract, the insurance policy, bearer bonds worth $30,000, as well as $2,500 in cash the gallery owners had paid for a pair of antique diamond earrings he's brought along with the egg. He was in a good mood, the only problem nagging him being the lengthy time needed to secure a definitive appraisal and find a wealthy buyer. And the longer he dwelt on that, the more uneasy he became. How much time did he really have before the MGB smelled a rat in his ruse about Anatoly Zaretsky? It seemed likely he might have to disappear quite soon to elude the Russians. But that brought a painful realization. Would he have enough time to explain or even say goodbye to Kristin and Anna? By the time he made it back to the hotel, his mood had soured.

Retrieving the small suitcase he had left with the bellman when checking out, Klaus added the envelope holding the cash and bearer bonds. Then he took a cab to Berghoff's for lunch. Afterward, he still had two and a half hours to train time, so decided to see if he could find something nice to buy for Kristin and Anna.

A block from the restaurant, Klaus looked in a store window at a model wearing an attractive red silk scarf and decided to buy it for Kristin. Two blocks further on, he stopped to study the window of a shop featuring antique and contemporary jewelry, plus an assortment of other art objects. His attention was immediately drawn to a set of four gold and enamel, bejeweled egg-shaped *objets d'art*, one of which superficially resembled the egg he'd just entrusted to the Siegelman-Friedland Gallery. Entering the shop, he sought out the proprietor.

"May I have a closer look at that set of ornamental eggs you have in the window? I've been reading about the ones made by Fabergé for the Tsars and suppose these are intended to be imitations? Where were they made?"

"Indeed. They are of the highest quality, crafted by artisans at a gallery in Paris, trained by one once employed at the original House of Fabergé in St. Petersburg." He took the eggs from the window and placed them on a piece of black velvet cloth under a light for Klaus's inspection.

Superficially they were impressive but close examination revealed flaws. Klaus's experience that morning at the gallery had already taught him a lot. These eggs were significantly lighter in weight than his, and he quickly surmised the gold wasn't solid but just plate. In fact the plating was uneven, and the small diamonds set into the gold work might or might not be real. Still, he thought, it would be amusing to display the imitation Fabergé eggs on the mantel of his fireplace while the real articles remained safely hidden away.

"I think I would like these if the price is reasonable."

"They are of the highest quality. The set is priced to sell for $800, but I can offer you a discount, $700."

"They are indeed attractive at a distance, but on closer inspection I must say the workmanship is only fair, certainly not excellent. Seven hundred dollars is way too much. I'll offer $300."

The man flinched and said, "I can't possibly sell for that price. Three hundred dollars is below my cost. However, I will accept $600."

"No," replied Klaus. "Four hundred dollars for all four. That is my final offer."

The proprietor shook his head, so Klaus turned and headed for the door. However, the man followed, finally saying, "Oh, all right then. Four hundred dollars. You must realize I am losing money, but times are hard. I need a sale."

Returning, Klaus returned, counted out $400, and placed the four faux Fabergé eggs, each now contained in a small velvet bag, in his suitcase. Then he noticed in one of the showcases featuring costume jewelry an attractive silver bracelet he thought Anna might like.

"How much is that bracelet? I believe my daughter would like it."

"Twenty-five dollars."

Klaus thought it likely the bracelet was worth half that, but as he'd already bargained the proprietor down on the larger purchase he said, "Fine, I'll take it."

Outside, Klaus hailed a cab and took it to the Chicago and Northwestern train station. In the snack bar, he bought coffee and two doughnuts, paid the seventy-five-cent tab with a five-dollar bill, and asked the cashier to include two dollars in quarters with his change so he could make a long distance phone call. At a pay phone, he dialed O and asked the operator to place a call to Kristin's number in Ishpeming. He heard the phone ring eight times, but there was no answer. Apparently, she wasn't home. He still had an hour before the train left, so resolved to try again in half an hour.

That time, Kristin picked up on the third ring.

"Hi, Kristin."

"Otto? Where *are* you? I called you yesterday evening and again this morning, but you didn't answer."

"I had to go to Chicago to do some personal business. I'll tell you about that later. I'm there now and just about to board the train back to Ishpeming.

I'll see you and Anna tomorrow. I assume we're still on for dinner at the Mather Inn tomorrow?"

"Of course, and Anna wants to go to the ski jumping competition in the afternoon at Suicide Hill. Are you up for that?"

"Sure. I'll come over to your place after I get some sleep and clean up from the trip. It's just about time for the train so I'd better go now. Can't wait to see you. Bye."

"Bye."

Two hours into the ten-hour trip Klaus bought two beers and a bad sandwich, then settled down to catch a little sleep as the train rocked back and forth. North of Green Bay the roadbed got rougher as it approached what local people sometimes called "God's Country." Some suggested that was because no one else would have it.

Several times Klaus dozed briefly, but real sleep was elusive. He spent most of the time thinking about how to deal with the MGB. He'd been lucky with Anatoly Zaretsky. Next time, he feared he would be looking at the barrel of a gun before he ever saw the face of the man holding it. Could he find a way to let Kristin know what was going on without losing her? If so, should he? That knowledge could put her and Anna in danger.

CHAPTER 16

The "400" pulled into Ishpeming at 2:11 A.M. Klaus got off with the only other two passengers still on the train. One was a middle-aged business-man, the other an elderly woman who'd told Klaus she was traveling from Milwaukee to visit her grandchildren in Ishpeming. Both were met at the station by family members. Looking around, Klaus didn't see a taxi, so he prepared to hike the mile and a quarter to his house on Iron Street. He thought of his first arrival in Ishpeming two years ago. It had been brutally cold then, and so it was again, the thermometer on the station wall registering -6°F.

Stepping from the station platform, Klaus heard a car horn and then spotted the light blue 1950 Ford coupe Kristin had just purchased. She rolled down the window and called, "Hi, traveler."

Klaus called back. "It's the middle of the night, Kristin. I didn't expect to see you. Where's Anna?"

"At home in bed, but she'll be fine. I told her I was going to meet you, and I'd only be gone fifteen or twenty minutes. I called the station a couple times tonight to find out if the train was on time."

Tossing his suitcase in the back, Klaus settled into the front passenger seat, looked at Kristin, and thought, *God, but I care for this woman.* The thought made him happy and sad at the same time.

As she turned into Iron Street Kristin said, "You probably didn't get any-thing decent to eat on the train. I'll make fresh coffee and heat up some of the lasagna Anna and I had for dinner. I also just made an apple pie."

Klaus smiled. "How can I say no to a beautiful woman who wants to feed me?"

After finishing one piece of pie and contemplating a second, Klaus said, "Close your eyes, Kristin. I've got a surprise for you." She complied, cheating just a bit. Klaus opened his suitcase, took out the red scarf, and placed it in her hands.

"Otto. It's beautiful. I love it. I'll wear it tomorrow night when we go to dinner." She leaned over and kissed him.

Klaus rose and looked at his watch. "It's almost three-thirty. I'd better go home and get some sleep. Anna wants to see the ski jumping competition to-morrow and cheer for her hero, Ralph Bietila. How about I pick you two up around one o'clock? We'll spend the afternoon at the hill, then come back here and still have time to get changed for our dinner at the Mather Inn."

Kristin took Klaus's hands in hers and said, "That all sounds good, Otto, but why don't you stay here tonight? Your place will be cold as ice. I suppose you had Jack stoke the fire and put enough coal in the furnace to keep the pipes from freezing, but it's still going to be really cold there right now."

Kristin looked intently at him, and Klaus held her gaze. Her message was clear, and yes, he really did want to stay, but...

"Okay, that would be nice. I'll pull out the sofa bed here, and you can bring me a couple of blankets."

Kristin gave him a raised eyebrow, turned, and pulled him toward her bed-room. "That isn't what I meant, you big ox, and you know it. Come on."

Kristin emerged from the bathroom wearing a pretty pink floral flannel nightgown, while Klaus had partly disrobed, keeping on just his shorts and undershirt. He embraced Kristin, kissed her, and the two then got into bed and pulled up the comforter. They continued to embrace and kiss. Kristin felt his tumescence and signaled she was ready. But nothing happened, and then she heard a series of repeated soft yet sharp expirations. It sounded almost as though...as though Otto was trying not to cry? She didn't know what to think or do. She'd been sure Otto cared for her, seemed to love her, even if he hadn't yet said so in so many words.

"Otto, are you okay?"

A delay, then a muffled "Yes." Otto continued to embrace her from behind but didn't say anything more.

Kristin couldn't think of anything else to say, so she just reached back and softly stroked Otto's leg. After several minutes, she felt Otto relax his embrace.

His breathing became deep and regular. He was asleep. Kristin lay awake for hours trying to make sense of what had or rather hadn't just happened.

When Kristin awoke in the morning, she was alone, but she heard voices and realized they belonged to Otto and Anna. She got up, put on a robe and slippers, and headed for the kitchen. Seeing her mother, Anna jumped up from the table, and said, "Look at the beautiful bracelet Otto bought for me in Chicago." It was attractive, sterling silver with several heart-shaped make-believe pink sapphires. Kristin made appropriate noises of appreciation, but her mind was focused on Otto.

Otto looked at Kristin, blushed, and said in a low voice, "I…I'm sorry. I was so tired last night I just couldn't stay awake. But I'm fine now. Anna's been helping me, and we've got fresh coffee, bacon, toast, and scrambled eggs ready for breakfast. Let's dig in. I'm looking forward to the afternoon at Suicide Hill and our dinner tonight at the Mather Inn." He gave Kristin a weak smile. Kristin resolved that she and Otto would have to have a talk in the very near future. Not now, of course. This wasn't something she wanted to discuss in front of her daughter.

That afternoon, the three of them watched the ski jump competition at Suicide Hill. Anna was happy to see Ralph Bietila, her favorite, take first place in the Seniors Division. She had pestered Otto to tie her toboggan to the roof rack of his car, so after the competition, they took two runs down the 1,200-foot iced toboggan slide.

Anna was in a bubbly mood that evening, proudly displaying to other diners in the restaurant the bracelet Otto had given to her. Her mother wore a new black dress and the red silk scarf Otto brought from Chicago. She looked great, but her mood was subdued. Anna noticed the conversation between her mother and Otto seemed strained and wondered why.

Later that night, after Anna had gone to bed, Kristin looked at Otto and said, "We really do have to talk." Her eyes stung, but she forced herself to say, "Otto, you have to be honest with me. Are you tired of me? Do you want us to break up?"

Otto looked back with a tormented expression that made her think he might cry again, but then vigorously denied that he was tired of her. "No, no, no, Kristin. You don't understand. I…I love you, and Anna too. I even hope… had hoped we might…become a family."

Present or past tense? What was Otto saying? It sounded like he wanted to propose to her or had wanted to propose, but...*Good God! Has something gone wrong with him medically so that he can't perform?*

Otto continued, "I was very much in love with my wife Magda, and when she died I...I couldn't at first see how to go on. But...finally, I decided I had to harden myself if I was going to survive and ensure a proud future for my young son."

"You have a son, Otto?"

"Yes. I do, at least I hope so." His voice broke. "I haven't seen or heard from Horst since 1942. He was living with my sister in Dresden, but she sent him to live temporarily with a cousin in Prague when she had to work nights at a munitions plant. At the end of the war, he didn't return home, and Gerda wasn't able to find him or her cousin Erica. After I was released from the POW camp in England, I went back to Germany and found Gerda, but then circumstances separated us, and now I've lost contact with her as well. I don't know where my sister and son are, or even if they're still alive."

Circumstances? Kristin wondered what those were. Otto had told her he'd been trained as a mining engineer, served in the German army, been a prisoner of war, and had come to the U.S. from a previous job in Sweden, but he hadn't volunteered and she hadn't pressed him for more. His revelation about a lost sister and son was news that raised a number of questions, but Otto's misery was now so obvious that she was moved to embrace him.

"I love you Kristin, but..."

"But what, Otto?"

A long pause, then, "I did something very bad during the war I regret every day but can never make right. And now I'm also being hunted by agents of the Russian government. During the war I found and took from Russia something of great value they are intent on getting back. My association with you puts you and Anna in danger, and I can't allow that. I love you Kristin, but for everyone's safety I think...I think I must leave you and go away."

Kristin stared at Otto, astonished and momentarily speechless. What had Otto done that he couldn't leave behind? And this danger he feared from Russian agents, danger he felt might extend to her and Anna? Was it even real or was it something he imagined? She'd seen how the horrors of war could cause psychological injury. Her best friend's brother, Michael Preston, came back from service as a marine in the Pacific Theater a broken man, a man who now wandered the streets of Ishpeming, always drunk, and terrified by dreams of what he'd seen and done during the battle for Peleliu. Kristin steeled herself. Michael Preston might be beyond recall, but she was damned if she was going to give up on Otto.

"Otto, I love you, and so does Anna, and that's what's most important. Don't leave us. I know horrible things happen during war. We can get help for you to deal with whatever nightmares you're carrying. And Russians? Really? You've got to tell me more about that. We'll stand with you. Everything will work out."

Kristin hugged Otto. Then she began to kiss and caress him, whispering endearments. For just a moment, he held himself away, but finally gave way and returned her embraces, gently at first, then with increased urgency. Kristin pulled away for a moment and stood. Removing her red scarf, she playfully tied it around Otto's neck, then unzipped and slipped out of her black shift. Their eyes met. This time there wouldn't be any hesitation and definitely no crying as she led him to the bedroom.

CHAPTER 17

On Tuesday, Otto Krummel, accompanied by Richard Maki, Eino Hakala, and Salvatore Lucci, descended the main shaft of the Mather D mine to Level 3 to inspect a new lateral tunnel that had developed some overhead cracks. They would have to decide whether the tunnel had to be shut down or could be shored up to render it safe for further extension.

Otto and his team examined and measured the overhead cracks, finding them more numerous and extensive than previously reported. They measured the angles between the sides and the tunnel roof as well as the curvature of that roof and considered whether fairly extensive wood or steel timbering could render the tunnel safe. Just then, the men sensed a trembling and heard a kind of grating noise. Within seconds, the noise grew in magnitude and became a deafening roar. Looking up, Klaus saw one of the overhead cracks increase before his eyes, allowing a large chunk of rock to fall directly on top of Richard Maki. Sal, who was further back in the tunnel, disappeared from view as a dust cloud blossomed, blinding and causing the other two men to choke and cough.

Reaching out, Klaus grabbed Eino by the arm and pulled him toward the main shaft as chunks of rock continued to shear off and fall from the ceiling. As they staggered toward the tunnel entrance, a rock struck Eino on the shoulder and a second one hit him in the back, knocking him to the ground. Klaus lost hold of Eino's hand. He was no longer able to see him because of the dust, but he heard Eino screaming in pain. Rocks continued to fall all around them. One grazed the left side of Klaus's face, causing a laceration that bled freely. He staggered, fell to his knees, and started to crawl toward the tunnel entrance, then stopped and crawled back, reaching out in an effort to locate Eino by feel. He found and grasped the man's left hand and started to pull, but stopped as Eino cried out in pain.

"Oh God, Otto, I think my left shoulder's broke. My back hurts too, and I can't move my left leg. It's caught under a rock."

Klaus couldn't see much because of the dust in the air, but at least the shaking and grinding noise had stopped. He crawled back a few more feet to find the flat piece of rock that lay across Eino's leg. Behind that, the tunnel was totally obstructed. With great effort he managed to lift the rock a couple inches, then push it aside just enough to get it off Eino's leg.

"Your leg's free, Eino. Now we've got to get you turned onto your back. Hold your left arm tight against your body while I roll you. Then I'll try to slide you over to the tunnel entrance by pulling on your good arm."

The next day, *The Mining Journal* carried a report about the accident at the Mather D.

TWO KILLED IN MINE COLLAPSE CAUSED BY RARE EARTH TREMOR

A rare earthquake centered twenty miles southwest of Ishpeming, which occurred yesterday at 10:37 A.M., was felt by residents throughout Marquette County as well as in several areas of adjacent Baraga, Iron, Dickinson, and Alger Counties. Rated 3.2 on the Richter Scale, it resulted in little damage and no serious injuries above ground. However, it caused a weakened area in a tunnel in the Mather D mine in Ishpeming to collapse, killing two and injuring two other members of a mine safety inspection team.

Workers reaching the collapsed area after the quake ended quickly found the injured men, Otto Krummel and Eino Hakala, and transported them to Bell Memorial Hospital for treatment. Only after removing substantial debris from the collapsed tunnel roof were they then able to reach Salvatore Lucci and Richard Maki, who sustained fatal injuries.

Treated for cuts and bruises, Otto Krummel has since been released, while Eino Hakala remains hospitalized in serious but stable condition with several broken bones.

The bodies of Salvatore Lucci and Richard Maki were taken to the Bjork and Zhulkie funeral home in Ishpeming where arrangements are pending.

All operations at the Mather D have been suspended until further inspections can be carried out and any unstable areas either reinforced or permanently closed off.

From his hospital bed at Bell Memorial Hospital, Eino Hakala told reporters he owed his life to Otto Krummel, who came back to help him when falling rocks had knocked him down and pinned him there. "Without a doubt, Otto saved my life." With that testimony, Otto became a local hero, his actions lauded by the mayor of Ishpeming and by Cleveland Cliffs management. Kristin told Otto she was very proud of him.

CHAPTER 18

Klaus had supposed Zaretsky's body might never be discovered or, when found, only after enough time had elapsed for decay and the work of animals to make identification difficult. The entrance to the old mine was almost completely obscured, and when he'd chanced upon it the previous summer, the only signs of past occupation had been some bones and animal scat on the floor. There was nothing hinting of recent human visitation, like cigarette butts, beer bottles, candy wrappers, or used condoms. So he panicked when he saw the lead story in *The Mining Journal* on Friday of the following week.

POLICE INVESTIGATE DEATH OF MAN FOUND IN OLD MINE

Yesterday afternoon the Ishpeming Police Department received a report that two teenagers had discovered the body of a man while exploring a long-abandoned iron mine in a forested area northwest of Ishpeming. Investigating officers found the body of a white male who had suffered a single bullet wound to his left temple. A .22 caliber Ruger pistol fitted with a homemade silencer lay next to the body. The pistol had been fired and was still loaded with only a single bullet missing from the clip.

The deceased, who has yet to be identified, was taken to Marquette for autopsy by the medical examiner. The body was well preserved with almost no sign of decay, but given how cold it has been, police speculate the man could have been dead for several weeks.

While suicide has yet to be ruled out, the police are treating this death as a possible murder. Anyone with information relevant to the case is urged to call either the Ishpeming Police Department or the Michigan State Police.

The next day was even worse for Klaus. He couldn't wait to have the paper delivered to the house but went to Olsen's News Agency to get a copy as soon as it came in. Once again, the dead man was front page news. This time the article included a photograph of the deceased and the results of an autopsy performed by the medical examiner in Marquette. *Scheissen!*

The dead man was described as a Caucasian male, thirty-five to forty years of age, five feet seven inches in height, and weighing 140 pounds. The autopsy confirmed that death was caused by a single bullet in the left temple, fired by the gun found at the scene. An effort was being made to trace the gun, but the forensic team found that the serial number had been filed off. They were also unable to lift any fingerprints from the gun, but fingerprints had been taken from the dead man and sent to the FBI for analysis. In addition to the fatal bullet wound, the medical examiner reported the man had suffered a significant, ragged wound on the lower part of his right leg. No identifying documents were found on or near the body, but the medical examiner noted the deceased had a tattoo of a snake on the inside of his right forearm. He also had on his left wrist a watch made by the Swiss manufacture Cortébert. This suggested he was probably right-handed, making it seem unlikely he shot himself in the left temple. The article concluded by stating the police were now definitely treating this as a case of murder, possibly a mob execution given the illegal weapon used. Anyone with information possibly relevant to the case was urged to call the Ishpeming Police Department or the Michigan State Police.

By the end of the week, the dead man in the mine had become a cause célèbre throughout Marquette County, with his murder being mentioned by newspapers as far away as Detroit, Milwaukee, and Chicago.

CHAPTER 19

Klaus slept poorly, rose early on Sunday, and paced restlessly until eight o'clock, then drove to Olsen's News Agency. The owner was just unloading copies of the Sunday *Detroit Free Press*, *Milwaukee Journal*, and *Chicago Tribune*, all printed Saturday evening, and then transported by truck overnight to the U.P. He bought copies of all three papers, scanned them quickly, and was dismayed to find each had a column about the murder with a picture of the deceased, plus a new item of information.

A desk clerk at the Northland Hotel in Marquette had recognized the dead man's picture as that of a businessman named John Abercrombie. He told the police Mr. Abercrombie had been a guest at the hotel during the third week of February but left without paying his bill. When the hotel tried to contact his employer, it learned the company didn't exist. The clerk recalled taking a telephone message for Mr. Abercrombie on 17 February 17 from someone named Gustmann concerning a dinner meeting the two men were to have the following night at the Mather Inn in Ishpeming. When contacted, the Mather Inn said it had no record of such a reservation under either name. The police now suspected both Abercrombie and Gustmann were pseudonyms for men engaged in some sort of criminal enterprise.

Klaus imagined Nelson or another MGB agent seeing this story and picture in the *Chicago Tribune* and immediately realizing that Klaus had lied, that Zaretsky hadn't taken the treasure and gone rogue with it. They were sure to come after him again. How soon? Tomorrow? The next day?

Klaus shook himself. He had to do something NOW. He considered calling J, thinking he should be interested to learn about Zaretsky's and Nelson's association with the MGB. But he didn't really trust the man. Aleksis had been sold out by an MI-6 double agent. Might J be playing both sides of the table as well? Could that have something to do with how Woodlawn, the man with the INS agent who'd interviewed him in Stockholm, had already known Klaus wasn't really Otto Krummel. If so, then J might even be cooperating with Zaretsky and Nelson and be happy to have them take him out. *God, Klaus! You're really getting paranoid. Still…?*

Klaus left Olsen's and drove back home. He retrieved the Beretta from his desk, checked that the clip was full, and chambered a round. What next? He'd watched as Senator Joe McCarthy and J. Edgar Hoover conducted their witch hunt in the U.S., accusing nearly everyone with liberal views of being a communist. He would bypass J on this but decided to call the FBI anonymously as a "concerned citizen" and tell them about Zaretsky and Nelson being agents of the MGB in Chicago. Maybe the FBI would raid and shut down their operation before anyone else could come after him. The FBI would surely try to trace the call, so Klaus decided to make it from a pay phone. He recalled a Sinclair station in West Ishpeming that wasn't open on Sundays but did have a phone booth at one side near the back.

Donning his parka and pulling his Green Bay Packers tuque low over his ears against the cold, Klaus left the house and drove a block past the station before parking on a side street. Then he walked to the phone booth, put in a dime, and dialed O. When the operator responded he spoke in an altered voice to conceal his identity. He told her he had critical information concerning agents of the Russian secret police operating in the United States and wanted to talk to someone at the FBI office in Chicago. From her hesitation he sensed she thought he was either a prankster or a drunk having a hallucination. But he persisted, repeated his message, and insisted she connect him with someone at the FBI in Chicago. Several times she asked him for his name, but he claimed he was operating under cover and couldn't reveal it to anyone but an FBI agent. Finally, she agreed to put the call through but still insisted he insert two dollars in coins since this would be a long distance connection. He complied and waited.

Two minutes later a man came on the line, identifying himself as Agent James Robinson of the FBI office in Chicago. Continuing to speak in a modified voice, Klaus quickly told him that two men named Anatoly Zaretsky and Gerhard Nelson were associated with a Russian MGB cell in Chicago. He went on to say he had knowledge that members of this cell had or might still reside at 11218 Lombardy Street in Chicago. He also read off the phone number at which he'd previously contacted Nelson, admitting he didn't know if it was still functional. Finally, he told Robinson that the body of the murder victim recently discovered near Ishpeming, Michigan, whose picture was in today's *Chicago Tribune*, was that of Anatoly Zaretsky. Along the way, and before he identified the murder victim as Zaretsky, something in Robinson's brief interjections and questions made Klaus think the FBI might already have had some knowledge of this cell. Twice, Robinson asked Klaus to give his name, but each time he declined, saying he feared for his safety. At that point, the operator cut in and brusquely said she would end the call unless he promptly put in more money. *Unbelievable!* Robinson came to his rescue, curtly telling her to shut up, saying the FBI would be responsible for any additional charge. Then he told Klaus to stay on the line while he got his supervisor to the phone. He wanted him to repeat his story but said it would take several minutes for his supervisor to get there. Recognizing this as a ruse to give the FBI time to trace the call and get the local police to detain him, Klaus quickly hung up and returned to his car.

Back home, Klaus paced the floor trying to decide how to stay safe. This time he was certain that anyone sent to get him wouldn't act like a friend. Most likely the guy would stay in the background until he could surprise and get the drop on him, force him to give up the treasure, and then kill him. Would the FBI act on his phone call and shut the Chicago cell down before that could happen? No way to know. *Maybe I can set a trap and kill him first. But how?* Glancing at the set of decorative eggs he'd purchased in Chicago, he got an idea. *No way to know for sure, but the bastard will almost certainly case the house first, then wait for darkness and break in hoping to catch me asleep. He won't find me, but I'll make it easy for him to find some 'bait' I leave when he does that.* Removing the eggs from the fireplace mantle, Klaus stowed three of them in his backpack, then placed one in the lower right-hand drawer of his desk. Next to it he added a copy of an old Ishpeming street map folded to show a northern segment of the city with a lightly penciled X at the end of Elm Street and a Yale key with an attached tab bearing the number twelve.

The next step was to set up a surveillance post where he could watch anyone approaching the house without them spotting him. Klaus retrieved his sleeping bag, air mattress, and extra blankets from the bedroom closet, then picked up a large thermos jug in the kitchen, filled it with water, and lugged everything to the loft of the single bay garage standing to one side but separate from the house. The roof of the structure was swaybacked to a point it looked at risk of collapse, while the floor inside lay littered with assorted car parts and other junk belonging to his landlord. Clearly, this wasn't a place where an assassin should expect to find him or anything else of value. Thinking if the Chicago cell was going to send another hit man after him, surely it would be soon. Klaus guessed he'd only need to watch from the loft for, at most, two nights. As for the 'bait' in the desk drawer, he supposed the guy would have been told what to look for, but as far as the eggs were concerned wasn't likely to be able to tell a fake from the real thing. Hopefully, he'd figure out from the map where the other eggs were supposedly hidden, then leave the house to look for them. As soon as he saw that happen, Klaus would leave the loft, take a shortcut through the woods, and arrive ahead of his pursuer. When the guy reached the cemetery and got to the end of end of Elm Street, he'd be waiting, hidden behind a nearby tool shed, gun at the ready.

Klaus kept thinking as he drove to the SuperValu store to buy a flashlight and some nonperishable food for his upcoming stint in the loft. *Not perfect. You still need to figure out what to do with the body. And…what if he should get there sooner than me…? Okay, okay, I just need to do one more thing to cover that. Maybe… maybe that would be even better. It could give me a little more time to try to work things out with Kristin.*

CCI still owed him a week of vacation. And since most people at the mine wanted to vacation at the same time in mid-summer, Klaus figured management would be happy to give him a little time off now. In the morning, he would call the office and ask for three days, saying he wanted to visit a cousin in Milwaukee newly arrived from Germany. To make that fiction more believable, he would also call Jack and ask him to come over once a day to stoke his furnace so the water pipes didn't freeze while he was gone. Finally, feeling a little guilty, he decided to tell Kristin and Anna at dinner that evening the company was sending him to Milwaukee for a couple days to attend another meeting.

CHAPTER 20

It was nearly noon by the time Klaus had everything ready, turned into Iron Street, passed Kristin's house, and approached his own place. Ahead he spotted a black Buick sedan with Illinois plates parked on the opposite side of the road two houses down from his. Two men were in the car, one of whom was looking at his house through binoculars. As Klaus passed they looked at him, and he saw their faces register a look of recognition. *Jesus, Maria, und Josef!* His call to the FBI had been way too late. The people in Chicago must have seen the *Tribune* story last night before the papers got trucked to the U.P. His plan to lay a trap was too late.

Klaus hit the gas, drove to the end of Iron Street, turned left, then headed south on Second Street, trying to think how he could lose the men if they tailed him. A look in the rearview mirror confirmed the Buick was in pursuit. There was no way his Plymouth could outrun that car on the open highway, but if he stuck to back streets and alleyways, maybe he could shake them. The chase around town went on for about twenty minutes, with Klaus doubling back several times, his effort aided by snowfall that had increased from light flurries to wind-driven flakes of such density that visibility was now little more than a block long. Finally, when he'd failed to see the lights of his pursuers after four successive turns, he pulled into an abandoned barn at the back of a small company that made precision machine parts on the southwest side of the city.

Klaus got out and stood just inside the barn, looking, listening, and fingering the Beretta in his pocket. After half an hour, he decided it should be safe to move but wasn't sure where to go. Definitely not back home. Had his pursuers returned to his house, or were they still cruising around hoping to come across him again and pick up the chase?

It was definitely time for Plan B, except there wasn't any. Klaus got back in the car and took a back road to the neighboring town of Negaunee. Along the way he kept a sharp lookout for any large black cars, the Beretta sitting ready on the seat next to him. It was snowing really hard now. There was almost no traffic, but at one point, he saw headlights approach rapidly in his rearview mirror and a large black sedan swung to the left to pass him. He feathered the brakes and grabbed his gun but relaxed when he saw it was a Lincoln driven by a young woman. He wondered how she could possibly see well enough to drive that fast in a storm like this and figured she was about to wind up in a ditch. But apparently she was lucky, because he didn't see her again.

Sticking to back roads, Klaus slowly made his way toward Marquette, thinking if he could drop out of sight for a couple days, the men now after him would likely return to Chicago. If they did, and the FBI used his telephone tip to raid the MGB operation in Chicago, then that would give him a little breathing room. As he approached Marquette on County Road 492 south of the intersection with US 41, Klaus made a decision. He would cross the highway, continue on Wright Street, and then drive north a couple miles toward Big Bay on County Road 550 to where an unnamed dirt track led to George Ballard's cabin. George lived just west of Detroit and only came to the U.P. in the summer to relax and fish. Klaus had been there twice for a cookout and beer after a day of fishing. The cabin would be closed now for the winter but that wouldn't be a problem. He could break in, get a fire going in the stove, and melt some snow for water. He would stop for a minute at the little store on the corner of Wright Street and County Road 550 just to pick up some instant coffee, milk, sugar, and cereal. That would stake him for a couple days until he felt it was safe to go back to Ishpeming and get in touch with Kristin. He hoped the accumulating snow hadn't gotten so deep that the store had closed or that he wouldn't be able to force his car far enough up the track toward George's cabin to shield it from the main road.

Those minor concerns were replaced by panic as he crossed the highway and saw the black Buick approaching on US 41 from the west. *Scheissen!* Klaus slammed the Plymouth into second gear, hit the accelerator and took off, fishtailing as his tires alternately caught and slipped in the icy slush on the road.

The driver of the Buick saw him, turned left, and followed. Quickly closing the gap between the two cars, the Buick pulled to his left, then cut back in and delivered a glancing blow to the rear of Klaus's car in an attempt to make him lose control. It almost worked. His car spun halfway around and started to slip toward the snowbank, but Klaus twisted the steering wheel hard to the right, downshifted, and managed to accelerate out of the skid.

In the rearview mirror, Klaus could see that after hitting his car the driver of the Buick had overcorrected. The Buick slid and ended up crossways of the road with its rear end hard up against a snowbank. He hoped they would be stuck there for some time, but as he approached the intersection of Wright Street with County Road 550, he again saw the Buick closing in. His plan to hide out in George's cabin wasn't going to work. He had to keep going and somehow find a way to shake them.

Passing by County Road 550, Klaus made a sharp right turn onto a residential side street. Had he lost them? No. Looking in the rearview mirror he again saw the Buick just one block behind and accelerating. Klaus turned left onto another street, then right. As he turned left again, the Buick closed in, and the front passenger side window opened. The man inside leaned out, apparently aiming for his tires, and fired three shots. But as he did, the Buick hit a patch of ice and skidded. One shot missed altogether, while the second hit the back window and the third penetrated the left rear window of his car. Klaus kept going, randomly turning left and right, continually looking in his rearview for following headlights, not realizing that once again the Buick had temporarily ended up in a snowbank.

By this time, the snow was falling so heavily Klaus no longer knew quite where he was. He made one more turn to the right, then a turn to the left and went straight for several blocks. Where was he? He hadn't seen any cars for a couple of minutes or any houses either. Then, through the driving snow, he realized Lake Superior was on his immediate right, and ahead, the outline of the LS&I ore dock began to come into view. *My God! I'm on Lake Shore Boulevard heading to Presque Isle. That's a dead end. If they trap me there…*

Approaching the entry to Presque Isle Park, Klaus checked the rearview mirror and saw a dim pair of headlights. No options left now. Lake Shore Boulevard turned to the left but came to a dead end in less than a mile. Klaus sped ahead onto Peter White Drive that circled the island park. How close were his pursuers? He checked the mirror again, but the snow was blowing so thickly he could barely see the road in front and nothing but white in the rear. He followed the road to the right, then to the left as he approached a short but steep hill and shifted down into second gear. The car barely made it, the tires alternately slipping and regaining traction. Finally, he topped out by the Kawbawgam memorial. Driving on another hundred yards, he suddenly realized the road ahead hadn't been plowed at all, and he was about to head into a foot and a half of snow. Hitting the brakes, the car slewed to the right, ending up with the front bumper hanging over the edge of a cliff, above Lake Superior. Holding the Beretta, he got out, crouched by the edge of a large spruce tree, and looked back in the direction from which he'd just come.

There seemed no escape now. There were two of them, and from the sounds he'd heard when they fired at the car, they apparently had large caliber pistols. He only had a .32 caliber pea shooter. For a moment Klaus thought he heard the Buick approaching, but no, maybe not, maybe it was just the wind. Maybe his pursuers had turned on Lake Shore Boulevard. But that would only delay them for a short time. As soon as they came to a dead end and learned he wasn't there, they'd realize he must have entered Presque Isle Park and be somewhere along the circle drive with no way to leave? Would they drive right up and come at him from the front, or would they split up, take their time, and maybe approach on foot from two directions?

Trapped! One hand held to shield his eyes from the blowing snow, his undersized pistol in the other, Klaus strained to see his pursuers approach, or hear them over the wind and sound of huge waves crashing on the rocks below. Not since Berlin, had death seemed so imminent. His mind raced, thoughts of Magda and Dieter, now both gone. Where were Gerda and Horst, and was Horst even alive? And his hope for a new life with Kristin, also gone because of his past and the damn treasure that now seemed more like a curse. He'd been a good, caring, considerate person until the war, then one disaster after another. Looking down at his pistol, the thought even crossed his mind of maybe saving the MGB hit men the trouble. If there really was a Hell could it be any worse than his life on Earth now?

Twenty minutes later two shots rang out, followed a minute later by a third that a person standing by Kawbawgam's grave marker might have been able to hear had the wind not been blowing at gale force. After that, nothing, except for the continuing snowfall and howling wind.

CHAPTER 21

That same day, Kristin and Anna stopped at the IGA on the way home from church to buy milk, coffee, a can of cranberry sauce, and a bunch of carrots. She'd invited Otto to join them for dinner later that afternoon and planned to roast a chicken and serve it with cranberry sauce, baked potatoes, and cooked carrots with a brown sugar glaze. Around two o'clock, she called to let him know dinner would be ready at five, and to tell him to come over whenever he felt like it, but he didn't answer. That surprised her. She decided to try again in an hour, but once again he didn't answer.

"Anna, it's snowing cats and dogs out there, but would you please run over to Otto's house? I've called twice, but he isn't answering his phone. Maybe he's doing something in the basement and didn't hear the phone ring. Tell him dinner will be ready at five and to come over whenever he wants."

Anna put on her hat, coat, and boots. Then she left but was back in just a few minutes. "I knocked on the door Mom, but Otto didn't answer. The door is locked and his car is gone."

Kristin frowned. Otto had told her he'd be home all afternoon. Had he forgotten and gone off somewhere? That wasn't like him, but he'd been awfully jumpy and distracted yesterday. She had a bad feeling about this, and muttered to herself, "Could he really be in danger?"

Anna looked up at her mother with alarm. "What do you mean, Mom? What kind of danger? I know you were worried when he got hurt in the mine two weeks ago, but he's okay now, and everybody says he's a hero for saving Eino Hakala. What's wrong now?"

Kristin hadn't shared with Anna what Klaus had told her during their late evening talk after their strange experience of not quite making love, and she didn't feel she could tell her now. She scolded herself for having upset her daughter and said, "Oh, honey, I'm just a worrywart sometimes. I'm sure there's a simple explanation for why Otto isn't home right now. Hopefully, he'll be back by five."

By five o'clock the chicken was done, and Kristin still hadn't heard from Otto. She called one more time and again he didn't answer the phone. Kristin set aside a portion to reheat for him if he showed up later, then she and Anna ate in silence, both feeling something wasn't right and worrying about it. Around six o'clock, she tried for a fourth time to call Otto and got no response. This time, Kristin put on her parka and boots and walked through the blowing snowstorm to Otto's house. As she approached, she saw lights on both downstairs and in an upstairs bedroom. His car was gone, but a large black Buick sedan with Illinois plates was parked in front of the house.

Kristin thought, *Maybe Otto had car trouble and got a ride back home from the person who owns this Buick.* She mounted the steps to the porch and was about to knock when she looked through the window and saw two strange men tearing open drawers and cupboards, looking under sofa cushions, tipping over bookcases, and pulling pictures off the wall and checking the spaces behind. As she stood there, one of the men looked up, spotted her, and pulled a pistol from his coat. Kristin froze, then turned and ran as fast as she could. The two men burst from the house a moment later, but instead of following her, they jumped into their car and quickly drove away.

Breathless, Kristin ran back to her house, locked the door behind her, and yelled, "Anna, call the police. I just saw two strange men inside Otto's house, and one of them had a gun. They saw me, and I was afraid they were going to chase me here. Thank God they didn't. When I looked back, I saw them get in their car and drive away." Anna called the Ishpeming Police Department and then handed the phone to her mother, her eyes wide and questioning. Still breathing hard, Kristin told the answering officer what had just happened. He told her two patrol cars would be sent right away. In the meantime, she was to remain in her house with the lights off and the door locked. Two minutes later, their red lights flashing, the cars pulled into Iron Street. One contained two officers who continued to Otto's house, while the second stopped in front of Kristin's home. Officer Tom Corker got out, walked to the front door, and knocked.

"Mrs. Albrecht, I'm Officer Tom Corker. Please let me in." Kristin, who'd been sitting in the dark holding her daughter, got up, turned on the living room lights, and opened the door.

"Are you and your daughter okay? The dispatch officer said that one of the two men involved in this break-in spotted you and displayed a gun."

"Yes, I…I'm okay. We're both okay. But I was terribly scared. I'm still scared. When I saw the gun I thought he going to shoot me. I ran back here as fast as I could to call the police. I was afraid they were going to follow me, but instead they got in their car and drove off. What if they come back?"

"Not likely. Sounds like you interrupted a burglary attempt. You probably scared them and they just wanted to get away. Still, we've got two officers searching the house now, and we'll have a patrol car come through here at regular intervals for the rest of the night."

Pulling a notebook from his pocket, Tom took a seat and said, "Please start at the beginning. Tell me everything you can remember about these guys. What did they look like, size, features, clothing? Have you ever seen them before? What about their car? Did you recognize the make and model? Did you get a look at the license plate?"

Kristin closed her eyes and did her best to comply. She started with the reason she decided to walk to Otto's house in the first place, that she'd called him several times during the afternoon and became concerned when he hadn't answered. When she got there, she saw his car wasn't in the driveway. However, there was a black Buick four door sedan, a new 1953 model she thought, parked directly across the street, and there were lights on in the house. And the license plate? She remembered the car had an Illinois license that read in part TH 13… but she wasn't able to recall the rest of the numbers. And the men she saw in the house? Kristin told him she'd only seen them for a couple of seconds before they looked up and saw her. They seemed to be tearing the place apart, looking for something. She hadn't had time to notice a lot about their features, only that both men had on dark clothing and that one was bald and wore glasses.

"That's good enough to put out an APB on the car and the guys driving it. Now, do you have any idea where Mr. Krummel might be since he wasn't at home?"

Kristin hesitated. She couldn't quite decide what to tell him.

"Mrs. Albrecht?"

"Sorry. No. I...I really don't know, but I'm worried. I was sure he was going to be home today, and we expected him for dinner. He works at the Mather D mine, but I can't think he'd be there on a Sunday evening. I can tell you what his car looks like. It's a green 1947 Plymouth coupe with license number UT3666."

Tom looked up. "Oh. I remember that car and license, and now I remember Mr. Krummel. We met a couple weeks ago on West Hematite Road during a snowstorm. He'd just lost his dog Buster. I told him not to worry too much. It wasn't that cold out. The dog would likely just burrow in the snow overnight and be waiting in the morning."

"Otto doesn't have a dog."

That brought a puzzled look. "What? He told me he did. I called him the next day to check, and he said he'd gone out that morning and found Buster just where I thought he would."

Kristin tensed. Had Otto made up a story about a lost dog named Buster to hide his real reason for being at that place at that time? The best response she could think of to say was, "Well, his neighbor has a dog, a beagle, but I don't know his name. Maybe Otto had his neighbor's dog with him."

CHAPTER 22

The storm that had wracked the U.P. on Sunday afternoon and evening dropped more than a foot of snow accompanied by gale force winds, and generated waves as high as ten feet in Lake Superior. But by midnight all was calm again. When Zeke Hanlon got up Monday morning, he decided this would be a good time to try out his new snowshoes. Leaving his apartment near Northern Michigan College of Education, he drove cautiously to Presque Isle Park. The city had plowed Lake Shore Boulevard and a small portion of Peter White Drive leading into the park after the snow stopped, but it hadn't yet had a chance to spread sand and the road was slippery in places. Twice, his car hit a patch of ice, one time skidding into the left lane and the other time lightly sideswiping a snowbank on the right before he regained control.

The road around Presque Isle had only been plowed a short way beyond where it topped out by the stone marking the grave of Chippewa chief Charles Kawbawgum. Zeke parked near the grave, got out, strapped on his snowshoes, and headed northeast. He'd gone only a short way when he noticed the faint track of a car, now mostly obscured by snow. He saw its obscure track had suddenly slewed to the right, ending at the very edge of a bluff overlooking the lake below. He approached with caution, aware that in places like this wave action had sometimes eaten away at underlying rock and soil to a point where there wasn't much holding up the last couple feet at the edge. He'd heard there was a plan to close this part of the road and replace it with a new one further in next summer.

Cautiously peering over the edge, Zeke's stomach clenched as he saw how deeply the lake had eroded the bluff on which he was standing. It looked like a forty to fifty foot drop to the basin below where the water looked pretty deep. To the left of the basin were several large boulders but submerged in its center...*My God! Is it a car? Yes, a car upside down on its roof, with both doors open.*

Turning around, Zeke quickly returned to his car, and drove to town as fast as he could. Halfway to his apartment, he spotted a Marquette Police car, flashed his lights, and pulled over to tell the officer what he had just seen.

Two hours later, after the city sent a truck to plow the road to the point of Zeke's sighting, three police officers stood and watched as a diver in a full wet suit dropped over the stern of a U.S. Coast Guard harbor tug to take a closer look at the submerged car. Following a brief examination, the diver surfaced, holding a jacket and a set of keys. On board the tug he turned the items over to a crewman and said, "It's a light green 1947 Plymouth coupe with Michigan plate number UT3666. There's no one inside, but both doors are sprung wide open, so if anyone was inside he or she probably got thrown out and washed away when the car flipped and sank."

In Ishpeming, Kristin had spent the night alternately pacing or staring out the window of her living room. As promised, a patrol car slowly cruised by the house every hour or so. Earlier, after answering Tom Corker's questions about the men she'd seen in Otto's house, he'd asked her to walk through the place and tell him if anything was obviously missing. Kristin had tried to comply, but she was so anxious and distracted by the chaotic way in which furnishings and accessories had been thrown about the place that she hadn't been of much help. In the bathroom, the sight of a wadded-up washcloth stained with what appeared to be blood on the floor by the bathtub put her in a panic. She'd screamed, and Corker, who'd been talking to one of the other officers, came running to find her shaking and pointing at the washcloth.

"Oh, oh, something awful must have happened to Otto. Those men... they must have beat him, maybe even killed and taken him somewhere before coming back to search the house."

Corker reached out, took her by the arm, and said, "Whoa, easy, Mrs. Albrecht. We don't know that anything like that happened. Maybe Otto cut himself while shaving or when he was working on something." But he put on a latex glove to pick up the towel and place it in an evidence bag.

In the morning Kristin didn't feel up to going to work, but she insisted against protests that Anna attend school. After Anna left, Kristin knew she had to do something to pass the time, or she'd go crazy. She got out her broom, vacuum cleaner, sponges, mop, toilet brush, bucket, bleach, and a bottle of Spic and Span, determined to clean the house from top to bottom. But all the time, she couldn't think about anything but Otto.

Around two o'clock, Tom Corker pulled up in front of Kristin's house, got out of his patrol car, and walked slowly to the front door, accompanied by a second man. When Kristin opened the door, she looked at Tom's expression and knew the news was bad.

Tom inclined his head toward the other man. "Mrs. Albrecht...Kristin... this is Detective Alan Jackson of the Michigan State Police."

Jackson, looking solemn, nodded at her, extended his hand, said, "Mrs. Albrecht," then looked back at Tom.

"Kristin...I'm terribly sorry to have to tell you this, but Otto Krummel's car was found early this morning, submerged in Lake Superior off the northeast side of Presque Isle Park in Marquette. It appears he was driving there sometime yesterday during the storm. We're not certain what happened. Maybe he lost control, and it plunged off the cliff into the lake, but..."

Jackson broke in, "It doesn't look as though this was just a tragic accident, Mrs. Albrecht. Once we raised Mr. Krummel's car from the lake we found bullet holes in the rear window and in two windows on the driver's side. So we believe Mr. Krummel was shot or at least shot at before his car went over the cliff, perhaps by the same men you saw trashing his home last night."

Kristin felt dizzy, whispered, "Oh no, no, it can't be...," and fainted. Tom caught her on the way down, carried her into the house, laid her on the sofa, and then went to the kitchen to get a glass of water. When she regained consciousness, she looked up at Tom and whispered, "Otto?"

Tom replied, "The Coast Guard diver who examined the car found no one inside, just a jacket. It seems likely he was ejected when the car hit the water, since both car doors were open. If he wasn't already dead when he hit the water, surely he must have drowned. The police and the Coast Guard are searching the area, but...Lake Superior is very cold. It isn't unknown after a drowning never to recover..."

Tom didn't finish the sentence. He didn't have to. Kristin just shook and cried and cried. He waited for her to regain some control and then urged her to drink the water he'd brought from the kitchen. They still had questions they had to ask.

Kristin felt numb. At first she couldn't speak. She just looked at Tom Corker and Alan Jackson, clutched herself with both arms and rocked back and forth. Finally she croaked, "Murdered? Oh God! I knew something was wrong. Otto's been so distracted lately, and frightened. A few days ago, he finally told me that during the war he'd found and taken something valuable for which he was now being hunted by agents of the Russian government. I tried to get him to tell me more, but he wouldn't. He said he didn't want to put me in danger."

CHAPTER 23

Kristin and Anna were in mourning. She frequently dreamed of Otto and sometimes awoke thinking for a moment he was still there with her. But as soon as reality set in, she quickly fell into a black state of mind, quite like the depression she'd had to work through years before when Richard had been killed in the mining accident. At least Anna was old enough now that she and Kristin could give each other support. When Richard died, Anna had only been three years old.

The two men who had invaded Otto's house and were presumed responsible for his death were soon identified, but both died before they could be arrested and interrogated. The same morning Otto's car was discovered in Lake Superior, Gerhard Nelson was shot and killed in a small town in northern Wisconsin by a homeowner who surprised him and his partner, Anton Sokolov, after they abandoned the Buick stolen two days earlier in Chicago, and then attempted to steal the man's car. Sokolov managed to get away with the car but was later intercepted by police just outside Chicago. During a high-speed chase, he lost control, crashed into a bridge abutment, and was killed.

Three months later, based on the weight of forensic evidence and perhaps influenced by a lawyer representing a Chicago art gallery, District Judge Malcolm Johnson was persuaded to issue a certificate of presumptive death for Otto Krummel, listing the date of death as March 8, 1953. An officer of the court was authorized to open Otto's safety deposit box at the Hematite Bank.

In it, he found a handwritten will, a life insurance policy, and a diamond ring. A date was scheduled for the will to be read and probated. As Klaus had intended, the text proved very confusing to the court and all who heard it, but the judge duly appointed an executor and charged him with trying to locate the designated beneficiaries, Gerda and Horst Gustmann.

Kristin, who now knew her lover's real surname was Gustmann, not Krummel, decided not to share that information. Touched to learn she was the beneficiary of his life insurance policy, she couldn't hold back tears when given the diamond ring he had left to her. Had he lived, it might have become her wedding ring.

Kristin coped pretty well through the summer and early autumn. But as the colored leaves and blue skies of September and early October gave way to the cold, gray, rainy, and snowy days of late October and November she felt herself slipping back into a state of depression. She needed to get away, so after talking it over with her daughter, she decided to take her annual vacation coincident with Anna's Christmas break from school. On December 19, using some of the proceeds from Otto's life insurance policy, the two boarded the "400" to Chicago for the first leg of a two-week trip to sunny Arizona.

Two weeks later, they returned home tanned and looking somewhat happier. But in May, Kristin told friends she still felt haunted by past events. She told them she and Anna had decided to leave Ishpeming and move west, perhaps to southern California where two of Richard's cousins now lived. In June, she put her house up for sale. It sold seven weeks later, and in late August, with the 1950 Ford coupe and a top carrier packed to the gills, she and Anna headed west out of Ishpeming on US 41.

PART II

2013 – 2015

CHAPTER 24

Horst Gustmann rose early and started a fire in the woodstove. Then he poured a little water from one of the two-gallon jugs into a metal basin, using it to wash his face and hands. The second of October had dawned clear and cold. Outside the cabin the grass and ferns wore a silver coating of frost that complemented the scarlet leaves on a nearby stand of sugar maples. He was glad he'd decided to remain in Vermont just a little longer than usual before heading back to Montreal.

Horst's daughter Eva, a physician with a practice in California, thought her seventy-eight-year-old father was crazy to live by himself four to five months every year in a remote cabin with no electricity or source of potable water. On top of that, his only means of getting to and from town was the occasional ride he was able to cadge from someone driving along the dirt road that passed by his place. She kept telling him it was downright dangerous, that he was being incurably eccentric, and that he should move to California and live there with her. Horst loved his daughter, but he also loved the frugal life he lived during the summer and fall in this thinly populated piece of northern Vermont. After much vain effort, Eva finally managed to convince her father to at least get a basic flip top cell phone. The bad news was cell coverage near his cabin was very spotty, and besides, Horst often neglected to even turn the thing on.

Horst poured a quart of water from his meager supply into a saucepan and set it on the stove to heat. As soon as it boiled, he poured a little into a tin cup, added a packet of instant oatmeal, some raisins, and a spoonful of brown sugar. To the rest he added three rounded tablespoons of coarse ground coffee and let it boil for a few minutes. After allowing the grounds to settle, he poured the strong coffee through a fine sieve into a large mug and added two heaping teaspoons each of coffee creamer and sugar. Two tart apples from a wild apple tree completed his breakfast.

Horst read for an hour, then putting his book aside, he walked the narrow, winding trail to where his mailbox stood by the dirt road leading to Johnson. Inside was a copy of the *Burlington Free Press* and, to his considerable surprise, a letter from the Restoring Family Links (RFL) program of the International Committee of the Red Cross. Over the years, he'd sent multiple inquiries to RFL, always hoping some new information might have come to light that would help him locate his aunt Gerda. So far, nothing, but considering his own age he supposed wherever she'd gone she might well have passed away by now. Could it possibly be there was new information? If Gerda was alive, she'd be ninety-four now. Horst tore open the envelope, read the letter, and was amazed. It said the RFL had located a woman named Gerda Brighton whose maiden name had been Gustmann and whose birthdate matched that which Horst had provided many years ago. This Gerda Gustmann had married a U.S. Army sergeant named George Brighton in 1952 and now resided in Worcester, Massachusetts. *Unbelievable!* His aunt had been living in the U.S. all these years, just a couple hundred miles from where he stood right now.

Racing back to the cabin, he threw a change of clothes into his duffle bag, returning to the road as fast as he could. He was in luck. Dean Smyth was just leaving his vacation cottage on the other side of the road and gave him a ride to Johnson. Once there, he put a call through to the number for George Brighton provided in the RFL letter. The phone was answered by a man who said in a quavering voice, "Mr. Brighton speaking." Horst introduced himself, telling the man about the letter he'd just received, suggesting Mrs. Brighton might be his long-lost aunt.

There was a pause, and then George replied in a voice strained by emotion saying Gerda, his wife of sixty-one years, had often spoken of Horst and had tried hard to locate him. Now, she lay desperately ill with cancer. He urged Horst to come with all speed as the hospice doctor thought she probably had only days to live.

Horst thumbed a ride into Morrisville, and from there took a series of buses, first to Montpelier, then to Boston, and finally to Worcester. Arriving very late, he found a cheap place to spend the night. The next morning he stepped from a taxi in front of 153 Lombardy Lane, a small white Cape Cod house. Excited at the prospect of seeing Gerda after a lifetime of separation, he also felt grief knowing their reunion must be very brief. As he stood looking at the house, the front door opened, and a very old man supported by a walker gestured for him to come in. Horst extended his hand and introduced himself. "You must be George. There's so much I want to know and to tell you and Gerda. I'm so sorry to learn she's now terribly ill."

George led Horst to the living room where his aunt lay in a bed provided by the local hospice organization. Her eyes were closed, but as he approached, they opened and looked at him.

"*Ist es wirklich du Horst?*" (Transl. Is it really you Horst?)

"*Ja, Tante Gerda, hier ist deine kleine Horst.*" (Transl. Yes, Aunt Gerda, here is your little Horst.) Then he took her hand and began to cry.

Reverting to English, Horst, Gerda, and her husband George sat together exchanging stories of their lives over the past six decades. Within an hour, Gerda grew visibly fatigued and asked her husband to bring to her a certain small box from the upper right-hand drawer of her dresser. Horst asked what it was. Gerda said she didn't know, but when she'd last seen his father in 1949, he'd given it to her, saying if he didn't return he wanted her to give it to Horst as a legacy. She'd kept it ever since. She said the box was locked, and she didn't think it would have been right for her to open it.

Horst's first feeling was one of gratitude for his father's gift and his aunt's unselfish stewardship. But then he felt confused. *Nineteen forty-nine? That can't be. After Erica and I came to Canada we managed to get a list of German soldiers killed during the Battle of Berlin in 1945, my father's name was on it.*

"Aunt Gerda, how could you possibly have seen my father in 1949? You must be mistaken. I was told he was killed action in 1945."

Gerda seemed to turn an even paler shade of gray. Looking at her husband, she whispered, "George, I must speak with Horst privately. Please give us some time alone." George threw her a questioning look but said nothing and shuffled away to the kitchen.

Gerda now turned to Horst and, with tears in her eyes, in a whispering voice told him, "Your father wasn't killed in the war after all. Finding his name on a list of the dead was a mistake, but to no one's credit, an intentional one.

And he wasn't, as you may have been told, a regular foot soldier in the army, i.e., the *Wehrmacht*, but a field artillery officer serving on the Russian front and later in Latvia and Poland in the military arm of Hitler's *Schutzstaffel*. When the Russians finally closed in on Berlin during the last days of the war, he was with one of the units assigned to the innermost circle of defense. Utterly depressed, his spirit broken, and knowing with certainty the war was lost, he later confessed to me his mind snapped as from a bunker in the Reichstag he watched a patrol of Russian soldiers march a group of captured SS officers into the plaza, make them kneel, then machine gun them to death so there was nothing left of their heads. He completely lost control, turned, and shot his own aide, a regular *Wehrmacht* soldier who looked very much like him, exchanged uniforms and identification cards with the man, then hid, later escaped from Berlin, and surrendered to the Allies." Gerda stopped trying to talk. Tears running down her cheeks, she closed her eyes and slumped, her breath coming in small gasps.

Horst sat stunned by what he's just heard and struggled to pay attention as Gerda recovered her breath after a few minutes and continued to talk about his father. She said that in 1949 his father had suddenly appeared at her apartment in Dresden and told her of a stash of gold and valuable jewelry he'd found in Leningrad and later hid in Latvia before the Russians invaded and pushed the German army all the way back to Berlin. He was heading back to Latvia to recover it and after that planned for the three of them; himself, Gerda, and Horst, to move to South America. He was devastated to learn she'd lost contact and been unable to find Horst after sending him to live with her cousin in Prague, and swore he'd return to find him. In the meantime, he put her on the train to West Berlin, told her to stay in his apartment there, told her where to find money he'd hidden, and gave her the box she was to keep for Horst if something went wrong and he wasn't able to return.

"Three weeks after your father left Dresden, I got a letter he mailed from Stockholm. He seemed to be all right, but something must have gone wrong because I knew he hadn't meant to go there. I sent a letter back and waited for further word. Two weeks later, I had to move because the building where I was living was slated to be torn down. As soon as I got another apartment I sent a second letter to Stockholm giving my new address, but it was returned marked 'undeliverable.' After that, I never saw or heard from your father again.

"I kept asking the Red Cross for help, but they were never able to find you. I was very sad and frustrated, thinking you might have died or been deported to a work camp in Russia. I continued to live in Berlin and got work there as a secretary. In 1951, I met George, who was serving in the U.S. Army. We became friends, then lovers. In 1952, we married, George left the service, and we moved here."

Totally exhausted now, Gerda stopped talking a second time. Horst just looked at her, speechless, trying to process everything, feeling overcome with shame at what he'd learned about his father.

That night at the hotel, he couldn't sleep at first, finally drifting into a disturbed slumber around two in the morning, later waking to the sound of the phone ringing. The clock on the bedside radio said 5:28 A.M. He answered to hear George tell him in a faltering voice that Gerda had passed away just an hour earlier. "Somehow, I don't know how, but when she knew you were coming, she managed to hang on just long enough to see you."

CHAPTER 25

The lights on the set were hot. During a brief break, Professor Derek Todson wiped perspiration from his face, hoping it hadn't looked too shiny while he'd been in front of the camera recording during his appearance on this episode of the Vermont PBS program, *Understanding Science*. Then the call, "Back on in five seconds…Five, four, three, two, one, live."

Looking directly at the camera, the program narrator, Jenni Johnson, said, "I want to thank Professor Todson for appearing on our program today and helping us understand what the science of epidemiology is and does to protect public health."

Then, as the camera panned back to pick up both of them, she looked at him, smiled, and said, "I must confess that before I prepared for this program I was thoroughly ignorant about the field and might well have embarrassed myself by asking Dr. Todson what sorts of skin diseases he treats in his practice."

Derek smiled outwardly but groaned inside at her reference to a common misconception that an epidemiologist was some sort of dermatologist. Hopefully, his presentation would put that one to bed for anyone who watched the program next week when it was scheduled to be broadcast.

"Professor, we have just a few minutes left. Would you please briefly just summarize one more time for our watchers what the epidemiologist studies and the kinds of questions to which he or she seeks answers?"

"Certainly. Our work encompasses all sorts of specific diseases and problems that impact our well-being and longevity, from infectious diseases like viral influenza, to chronic diseases such as heart disease and diabetes, as well as problems like car or workplace accidents, drug abuse, domestic and gun violence, and mental illness. Whatever the focus of a particular study, we look at the frequency, the distribution, and the determinants or causes of the problem in a specified population and think about what we can do with that information to improve public health. As I mentioned earlier, we look for answers to questions about the 6Ws: who, what, where, when, why, and how. We have that in common with investigative journalism and police investigations. To sum up, I like to say I think of the epidemiologist as a kind of disease detective."

As soon as the taping session was over, Derek said goodbye to Jenni and left the VPBS studio in Colchester. Back in his car, he stripped off his sweat-soaked white dress shirt and tie, replacing it with a lightweight short-sleeved golf shirt. Friday, the fourth of October, was turning out to be a classical "Indian Summer" day in northern Vermont, with bright blue sky, sun, and a temperature approaching 70°F. Opening both the driver's side window and the sunroof on his Subaru, he took Route 2A to Route 15 and headed east toward his cabin a few miles north of Johnson. He had two days to enjoy the autumn color and close up the place until returning for a winter trip to ski and snowshoe.

Traveling the last mile of the dirt road leading to his cabin, Derek was surprised to see a pair of crossed U.S. and Canadian flags still attached to the roadside mailbox that belonged to his friend and summertime neighbor, Horst Gustmann. Horst mounted them whenever he was staying at his primitive cabin some hundred yards into the woods where he spent each summer. Usually, Horst returned to his apartment in Montreal by late September, not returning until the following June. This year, Derek knew Horst also planned a brief winter visit when his daughter Eva, a physician who'd taken a leave of absence from her practice group in California to work with *Médecins Sans Frontières* in Ghana, would be returning home. He'd convinced her to spend a week with him in Vermont for a brief ski vacation. He wanted her to spend it with him at the cabin, but she'd told him she was having none of that, after working most of a year under primitive conditions. She'd told her father the price of having her stop in Vermont was that he arrange accommodation for them at the Trapp Lodge in Stowe. Horst had since invited Derek to join them for a couple days. He'd accepted and was looking forward to meeting Eva.

CHAPTER 26

The last of four buses Horst took returning from Worcester dropped him in Morrisville late Sunday afternoon. From there, he thumbed a ride to Johnson with a logging truck driver. Then he stood at the corner of Route 15 and Pearl Street hoping a local would take him to or at least close to his cabin. A few minutes later Derek Todson saw him and stopped.

"Yo, Horst. I'm surprised you're still here. I stopped by your cabin yesterday morning, but you weren't there. Get in."

Horst nodded and got in but said nothing and looked strangely solemn.

Derek frowned. "Whoa. What's wrong? You okay?"

Horst didn't answer immediately. Then he said, "I'm just returning from my aunt Gerda's funeral. I've told you how she cared for me as a child before we became separated during the war. Over the years I tried many times to find her without success. Then just days ago, I received a letter from the International Committee of the Red Cross telling me Gerda and her husband, a man named George Brighton, have been living for many years in Worcester, Massachusetts. All this time, she was so close and I didn't know. I called immediately, only to learn she was extremely ill and not expected to survive. So I went to Worcester. She recognized me, we talked, and then…she passed away later that very night."

"I'm so sorry, Horst. No wonder you're depressed."

"Yes." Horst fell silent for full minute. "But…there's more."

Derek looked at his friend whose face was a mask of misery.

"Just before she died, Gerda told me things I didn't know about my father, terrible things that bring shame upon our family. I always thought he was a soldier in the regular German army, simply a patriotic German who felt obliged to fight for the homeland in an idiotic war the bastard Hitler started, and that he was killed as the Russians finally captured Berlin. But I was wrong. I learned he actually served as an officer in the military arm of Hitler's SS. And he didn't die in Berlin. He only escaped being killed by the Russians by hiding after killing and exchanging uniforms and identification papers with a man who very much resembled him, an ordinary German soldier named Otto Krummel. He hid, managed to escape from Berlin with some other soldiers, and later surrendered to the Allies, still posing as Otto Krummel. He told all this to a surprised Gerda in 1949, then left her and went to Latvia to try and recover some sort of treasure he'd discovered in Russia and hidden away. Gerda received one letter from him later posted from Stockholm. After that, she never heard from him again."

Horst fell silent, slumped in his seat, and covered his eyes. *Wow!* Derek tried hard to think of something to say to comfort his friend. "I…well, just wow, Horst. I'm so sorry. Obviously that came as a terrible shock, but war makes people do hideous things. You may not be inclined to forgive him, but you can never really know the feelings that make a man do what he does under terrible stress. In any case, you mustn't try to shoulder his guilt. You're a good man, Horst. You've given a lot of time and money doing good, helping refugees gain asylum and resettle in Canada. Grieve for Gerda. Grieve for your father but don't look back. Live proud for yourself and for your daughter."

Horst nodded but didn't answer.

Derek slowed the car and said, "Hey, how about we turn around and go back to Johnson? I'll buy dinner."

Horst shook his head. "Thank you, Derek, for your words and the offer, but no. Tonight I just need to sit, think, and get the cabin ready for winter. Tomorrow I'll go home to Montreal. Could you perhaps drive me to Burlington in the morning?"

"Of course."

At the cabin, Horst built another fire in the wood stove and lit his two ancient kerosene lanterns. Then he took from his duffle bag the small wooden box Gerda had given to him. Even though it was locked and there was no key, it seemed remarkable that in all those years she'd never tried to open it. What if he hadn't found her? He doubted George knew the box even existed until Gerda told him where to find it. It was nothing much to look at. He could imagine George setting it out with a dozen other knick-knacks at a garage sale or even tossing it in the trash when the house was cleaned out now that Gerda was gone.

Horst forced the blade of his hunting knife between the top and base of the box, twisted it to break the lock, and lifted the lid. Inside, in a black velvet pouch, he discovered an exquisite gold and green egg-shaped object inlaid with what appeared to be diamonds and emeralds. *Are they real?* Four images of the double headed Imperial Russian eagle, sculpted in gold, circled the egg at its midpoint. It rattled when he picked it up, so there must be something inside. He supposed the jeweled egg was meant to be opened but couldn't find a button or lever to release the top. He could only guess at the object's value. It must be substantial.

What to do with a legacy from a father of whom he was now ashamed? Part of him was tempted to cast it in the trash, but that obviously made no sense at all. Most people would tell him to appreciate his good luck and just enjoy the wealth it could bring. But that didn't seem right either. He wasn't most people. He lived a simple life. He didn't even own a car anymore, had never yearned for expensive possessions, and frankly didn't know what to do with the prospect of sudden, unearned wealth.

Horst decided to put the egg aside and wait until his daughter came to Vermont in February. First, he had to decide how to share with her what he'd just learned about his father, her grandfather. After that, she could help him figure out what to do with the thing: a curse or a boon?

Horst was excited at the prospect of Eva's visit. It would be his first wintertime visit to Vermont in many years. Even at seventy-eight years of age he was still in good condition and looked forward to cross country skiing and snowshoeing with his daughter and Derek. At her insistence, he'd finally agreed to book rooms at the Trapp Lodge in Stowe, although he thought the cost was outrageous.

Horst got out the small digital camera Eva had given to him the previous Christmas. He was amazed at the quality of pictures it took, but had only used it a few times so still felt compelled to check the instruction manual to make sure he knew what he was doing. Placing the egg on a piece of white shelf paper, he arranged the kerosene lamps on either side. Then he took close up pictures from several angles. Satisfied, he placed the egg back in its velvet pouch, thought for a few minutes, then decided to hide it in a place he felt quite sure no one would think to look.

Just after dawn, Derek left his cabin and drove down the road to find Horst already standing by his mailbox, duffle bag in hand.

"Morning, Horst. Feeling any better today, I hope?"

"Still struggling, Derek, but I know I've got to deal with this and also find a way to share with Eva what I've learned."

As Derek turned onto Route 15, he said, "How about we stop for some breakfast at the Mix in Jeffersonville? There'll still be plenty of time for you to catch the 10:05 A.M. Greyhound to Montreal."

Over coffee, Horst said, "Just before Gerda died, she gave to me a small locked box, saying it contained a legacy my father left for her to give to me if he didn't return. I only just opened it last night and found something I'm sure is very valuable. But now I feel it would be dishonorable for me to keep it. I'm going to wait until Eva visits in February to help me decide, but my inclination is to sell it and give the proceeds to a good cause."

Derek supposed Horst had the object in his duffle bag, but he was too polite to ask, and Horst didn't offer to show it to him. He was also tempted, but resisted the urge to ask his friend why he always was so damn altruistic.

CHAPTER 27

In Montreal, Horst resumed the volunteer work he'd been doing for several years after retiring as a professor of European history at McGill University. Three days a week he taught ESL classes to new immigrants to Canada and also worked with a group at his church to help them find employment and housing. But the wartime actions and ultimate fate of his father were never far from his mind. During the last week of January, he decided to see if he could find out anything about the postwar life of Otto Krummel. On his way home from a class, he stopped at the Grande Bibliothèque to see his friend Uwe Reinhardt, a reference librarian. He told Uwe he was trying to trace a relative with whom the family had lost contact many years ago. He told him Otto Krummel had been a much older brother of his late wife Elsa and had surely passed away some time ago but was last known to have been in Stockholm in 1949 when he was about forty years old. It made him feel guilty to make up such a story, but he was nowhere near ready to admit who Otto Krummel really was. He told Uwe that his daughter Eva was trying to reconstruct her family tree and wanted to learn what she could about this uncle that neither he nor she had ever met.

Uwe acquainted Horst with several ancestry search engines. Then starting in 1949 and going forward sixty years, they searched Swedish death records. They found a number of Krummels, but none named Otto. After that they searched Swedish marriage records over a twenty-five-year period starting in 1949, as well as birth records for any children bearing the surname Krummel.

Again, a couple hits, but none in which the groom or the father bore the first name Otto.

"If your brother-in-law was in Sweden in 1949, it seems clear he didn't die, get married, or father a child there. He must have gone somewhere else, back to Germany perhaps? Or maybe he left Europe and went to North or South America, even Australia? If so, we might be able to find him by looking at shipping manifests from that period. That could take a while, but if you want, I'll look into that."

"Please do that, Uwe. I really appreciate your help."

Two days later, Uwe called Horst to tell him he had what looked like a promising hit.

"I found a shipping manifest showing that an Otto Krummel, age forty-one, traveled from Sweden on the SS Gothenburg to New York City in February, 1951."

CHAPTER 28

On February 4th, an episode of *Treasure Finders* on cable channel ZX featured the recent rediscovery, near destruction, but later recognition and sale of an egg-shaped *object d'art* that Fabergé had crafted for Tsar Alexander III in 1887. The egg's owner and its whereabouts had been unknown since 1922. In 1964, it was put up for sale at an auction in New York City, but its provenance wasn't recognized, and it sold for the paltry sum of $2,450. After that, the egg disappeared until 2004 when a precious metals scrap dealer discovered it in a "bric-a-brac" market and bought it for $13,302. Once again, the new owner didn't recognize what he really had. He planned to resell it for something above $15,000, his estimate of the minimum value of the embedded jewels and the melt value of the gold. Failing to find a buyer, the egg remained intact but forgotten in his home for several years. That changed dramatically in 2012 when he happened to search the internet using both the words "egg" and "Vacheron Constantin," the latter being the maker of a lady's watch found couched inside the hinged egg. His search turned up an article published the previous year about the so-called Third Imperial Egg. It included a picture that matched his egg, and its current value had been estimated at THIRTY-THREE MILLION DOLLARS! Astounded, but afraid to believe at first, the dealer rushed to have his egg appraised. The appraisal confirmed its provenance, and it was subsequently sold to a private collector for an undisclosed sum.

The program went on to tell viewers that the Third Imperial Egg was just one of fifty-two that Tsars Alexander III and Nicholas II had commissioned the House of Fabergé to create between 1885 and 1917. Fifty of those were delivered before the Bolsheviks executed Tsar Nicholas II and his family. After that, the eggs, along with other Romanov family possessions of value were removed to the Kremlin Armoury in Moscow. Some of the eggs, including the Third Imperial Egg, were later sold by the Soviet government. However, eight of the eggs went missing. Currently, seven were yet to be accounted for. What happened to them? Were they destroyed, quietly appropriated by some high Soviet official, sold without proper documentation, or were they just lying around somewhere waiting to be found? The program closed with a tantalizing message suggesting there might be a fortune waiting to be discovered at the nearest garage sale. Not a program that ever scored much of a Nielsen rating, at least a portion of this episode happened to be viewed by three individuals whose lives would soon intersect.

In Philadelphia, Derek Todson stood before his bathroom mirror, feeling a bit of dread at the approach of his fiftieth birthday. In fact, the image coming back really wasn't all that bad. It showed a reasonably muscled guy with hazel eyes and dark brown hair, albeit sprinkled with a fair bit of gray and beginning to thin in the front and on top. Derek stood six feet tall and weighed just over 200 pounds, but there was no denying the recent emergence of a small pair of "love handles" at his waist.

Checking his to-do list for the evening, Derek decided he needed to complete his abstract for the upcoming American Public Health Association meeting, then edit and return to Bill Brenner an application they were jointly preparing for a grant to track mutational changes in the RNA genome of the Hepatitis E virus. But before that, he had time to watch the news and channel surf a bit before getting down to business. First he listened to Diane Sawyer summarize the major national and international headlines on WPVI, then switched to WHYY to catch a piece of the news from the BBC point of view.

After the news, Derek clicked through a series of channels looking for something interesting but found nothing other than an unending series of ads until he landed on cable channel ZX where the narrator was talking about the recent recovery of the Third Imperial Egg. Watching the rest of the program, Derek lazily imagined what it would feel like to trip across something of really tremendous value at a garage sale, like maybe a previously unrecognized Picasso painting?

In Montreal, Horst Gustmann was sitting on his sofa, half asleep, as the announcer droned on about political issues in Ottawa, conflict in the Middle East, and finally the local weather forecast. Then, like Derek in Philadelphia, Horst also decided to surf through the channels and happened to land on channel ZX just as the narrator was again showing a close up of the Third Imperial Egg and saying, "Remember, folks, you're looking at thirty-three million dollars, and there may be seven more Imperial Fabergé eggs out there waiting to be found. Good luck and good night." Horst thought, *Is it barely possible the egg my father left to me could be one of those and worth something like that?*

In New York City, Sergei Yakushin, a *Capo* in the Russian mafia, also known as the *Bratva*, poured a second shot of vodka and relaxed in his Manhattan condo overlooking the East River. He was waiting for Vasily to call and report on the latest shipment of Romanian girls who assumed they had been contracted to work as housemaids in the U.S. Sergei actually was a fan of the program *Treasure Finders* and tuned to channel ZX right as the program devoted to the Third Imperial Egg began. He watched with interest and immediately thought of a story his great uncle Gennady had told him more than twenty years ago.

In 1991, as the Soviet Union was dissolving, retired Colonel Gennady Yakushin, eighty-six years old, and now cursed with a bad heart, was living in an expensive dacha near Moscow. Having no children of his own, he'd invited his twenty-six-year-old grandnephew Sergei, a rapidly rising member of the *Bratva* in Moscow, to move in. In the evening, over shots of vodka, Gennady entertained Sergei with stories about his experiences in the army during WWII and later as an officer in the MGB and the KGB. One story concerned a captured German SS officer he'd interrogated and found to possess what appeared to be one of the missing Imperial eggs created by Fabergé for Tsars Alexander III and Nicholas II.

"With a little *persuasion*, Sergei, he confessed that he and a colleague had discovered six of them along with a quantity of jewelry and several bags of gold rubles when looting the Catherine Palace. They hid their stash, including four of the eggs, somewhere near Riga, Latvia. In the man's wallet, I found a photograph of his friend, an SS major by the name of Klaus Gustmann. Across the back was scrawled a line of letters and numbers. I suspected it was code and finally got the man to admit it told where their treasure was hidden."

"So did you force the Nazi shithead to tell you what the code said?"

Gennady muttered a curse. "No, I was about to do that when my adjutant came to the door with a message. I turned away for just a moment and the SS dog jumped up and pushed me aside. He literally threw himself out the window into the street, landed on his feet, and started to run away. Before I could stop him our own damn sentry cut him down with his machine gun. But I did get the one egg he'd been carrying in his dispatch case."

Sergei knew his uncle had always seemed to have plenty of money. He had owned expensive cars and a boat, as well as the dacha in this exurb of Moscow favored by a number of high-ranking Soviet officials.

"Well, Uncle, it appears you did well with the one egg you did find."

"Indeed, but don't repeat this anywhere. As far as the world is concerned, that egg is still missing. I sold it to a private collector for a very substantial amount of cash, a bonus being that a sizeable portion was in U.S. dollars and British pounds, not just Russian rubles."

Sergei's appreciation for his uncle's business acumen soared.

"For some time I tried to find the other eggs those SS officers had stolen. At first, it appeared this Major Gustmann had been killed during the fighting in Berlin. My own men found his body, but when I examined it, things didn't look right. The face of the dead man did resemble the picture on his ID papers and the photograph I'd just taken from the other man, but it wasn't a terribly good match. And on closer inspection, I found at the base of his neck a small tattoo that read OKRUMMEL. I concluded Major Gustmann had escaped our net and assumed the identity of a dead man named Krummel, first name beginning with the letter O: Oskar, Otis, Otto, Oswald?"

"So, what then, Uncle?"

"Officially, Major Klaus Gustmann was dead and was reported so in a list we compiled of German soldiers killed during the battle for Berlin. But four years later, when I was with the MGB in the Soviet zone of Berlin, a routine border crossing report caught my attention. An Otto Krummel crossed by car from the American into the Soviet zone on his way to Dresden. In the meantime, having learned Krummel was a rare surname in Germany, I thought it worthwhile to have this man followed."

"And?"

"We were already a day behind. We managed to locate his car in Dresden, but we couldn't find him. Then, several weeks later, I heard from MGB sources in Latvia about the arrest of some senior members of a guerrilla group called the Forest Brothers. The leader had in his possession several bags of uncirculated fifteen-ruble gold coins. Tortured before they sent him to Siberia, the man finally admitted he'd gotten the coins from someone named Klaus Gustmann."

"The same Klaus Gustmann who became Otto Krummel?"

"Absolutely. Gustmann was like a chameleon. He was Otto Krummel when it suited him, but when he went to Latvia to recover the treasure he'd hidden during the war, he traveled as a Swiss mining engineer named Ruedi Bachmann. Our MGB agent had managed to infiltrate the ODESSA cell in Latvia that was helping Gustmann. The night he arrived in Riga, our agent jumped his real contact, dispatched him, and took his place. He was all set to accompany Gustmann and then kill him once the treasure was in hand. Even though I already knew the treasure included jewelry and those missing Imperial Fabergé eggs, for some reason our agent in Riga only knew about the gold and thought it was gold bullion. Somehow, Gustmann smelled a trap and managed to get away with the aid of a Forest Brother leader he'd known during the war. That's how the man came to have that gold when we arrested him."

"Did you ever manage to track him down?"

"We did, but it took a long time. We finally found him living modestly as Otto Krummel in a small town in the northern part of the United States. At first I wondered if he hadn't managed to get most of the treasure out of Latvia after all, but then I decided maybe he was just keeping a low profile until he could find a way to turn the jewelry and eggs into cash without drawing too much attention."

Gennady continued, "Well before the end of the war, we'd been organizing communist cells in a number of U.S cities. I got in touch with the head of the one in Chicago, gave him some background, and got him to send someone after Gustmann, a.k.a. Bachmann, a.k.a. Krummel, to retrieve this Russian treasure and then kill him."

"He wasn't successful?"

"The first agent wasn't. Gustmann saw through him and killed him first. After that, the Chicago cell sent two men to do the job."

"No better?"

"Only sort of. Apparently they did manage to corner Gustmann, shoot him, and push his car off a cliff into a big lake up there. But one of them got into a confrontation with a local who shot and killed him when he tried to steal the man's car. His partner got away but was intercepted and chased by the police as he returned to Chicago. He lost control, crashed, and was killed. I was never able to find out if they got their hands on any of Gustmann's treasure or not. The police didn't report finding anything in the car, but you never know." He chuckled. "If I'd been one of the officers investigating that wreck, evidence of *that kind* would have quietly gone home with me. So, nephew, keep your ears open if you ever hear of a Gustmann with an Imperial Fabergé egg." Rising, Gennady walked stiffly to his desk, picked up an old black and white photograph, and handed it to his nephew. "Here."

The morning after watching *Treasure Finders*, Horst walked to the library to learn more about the missing Imperial Fabergé eggs. Of those, he'd been able to find decent pictures only for two, and a very grainy shot of a third. None of them closely resembled his egg, but it did have features in common with a sketchy written description of the Alexander III Egg Fabergé had created for Tsar Nicholas II in 1902. Could his egg possibly be the real thing? Only an expert would be able to tell.

Horst fantasized. He was an old man with few needs. With several million dollars he could set up a foundation and fund in a big way the refugee projects he'd been supporting with his time and small monetary contributions.

Horst spoke to several high-end jewelers and the director of a respected local gallery with some knowledge of Russian art, who urged him to contact Arkady Rubenstein, owner of the Rubenstein Gallery in New York City. That evening, he composed a lengthy email message, describing his egg and explaining how he had come to possess it. Having previously learned from Uwe how to do it, he added copies of the pictures he'd taken in Vermont and sent his message to the email address he found for the Rubenstein Gallery, marked, Attention: Mr. Arkady Rubenstein. The next day he received an enthusiastic reply from Rubenstein himself saying he would be very interested to see Horst's egg. He even offered to come to Montreal to view it if Horst would call and let him know when such a meeting could be arranged. Horst called Rubenstein to tell him the egg wasn't in Montreal. However, he suggested that he and his daughter would be glad to bring it to the gallery in New York at the end of February.

Next, Horst composed a brief email message to his daughter. He wanted to let her know about the egg, but he wasn't yet prepared to tell her everything about it and the shameful things he'd learned about his father. He wanted a quiet, serious, face-to-face discussion with her about that. Mulling over what to say and not to say, he typed the following message.

Dear Eva,

It's only a short time until we are together again. I can scarcely wait. I booked the rooms you wanted at the Trapp Lodge. A nice place to be sure, but $$$$!! Attached is a picture of an ornate egg-shaped object your aunt Gerda gave to me just before she passed away last fall. A Mr. Rubenstein in New York has expressed interest in possibly buying it. I'm counting on you to help me make a decision about that when you get here.

Love,
Dad

CHAPTER 29

At 7:30 P.M. on Friday, February 14th, Horst bid goodbye to the students in his latest ESL class. It would be three weeks before the next one was scheduled to start. Now, he could think of little else except the upcoming week with Eva in Vermont. On the way to his apartment he stopped at Rossini's to pick up the salad and lasagna he'd ordered for supper.

After eating, Horst read for two hours and then prepared for bed. Just as he was about to turn out the lights, there was a knock at the door. Peering through the doorscope, he saw two men in business suits. Leaving the chain on, he opened the door just a crack, and inquired, "Yes, gentlemen. Can I help you?"

The large, older man replied, "My name is Michael Bradford, and this is my colleague Richard Sobel. We work for Mr. Arkady Rubenstein at the gallery in New York. Since we were already in Montreal this afternoon for a meeting, Mr. Rubenstein asked us to contact you and make a preliminary appraisal of your Fabergé egg. I apologize for the late hour, Mr. Gustmann. We stopped earlier, just after six o'clock, to ask if you would like to go out for dinner, but apparently you weren't yet at home."

"Yes, I was teaching a class that didn't end until seven-thirty." But then Horst thought, *Rubenstein knows I don't have the egg here. Something's wrong.* He tried to close the door, but the big man lowered his shoulder and hit it with great force, breaking the chain and knocking Horst to the floor.

Inside, Sergei Yakushin and Vasily Kozlov tied Horst to a chair. Then they pistol whipped him and threatened worse if he didn't give up the egg about which he had written to Rubenstein as well the others they knew he must have. Horst was stunned and frightened but also confused. *What other eggs?* When he didn't immediately respond, they beat him some more and proceeded to trash the apartment, hoping to locate them on their own. Finding nothing, they threatened more violence, to include his daughter, whose picture they'd found on his desk, if he didn't cooperate. At that, Horst told them the egg was in Vermont.

"Vermont? In a safe deposit box in a bank there? Which bank? Where? Give me the key to the safe deposit box. We'll take you there now. In the morning, my friend," Sergei nodded at Vasily, "will stay with you while I recover the egg. If all goes well, you can go free. If not, then think of your daughter."

"The egg…isn't…it isn't in a bank. It's…it's at my cabin outside Johnson, Vermont."

"Your cabin?" Sergei was incredulous to hear that something worth millions of dollars could have been left in a cabin in the boondocks of northern Vermont. He threatened Horst's daughter once again, thinking the old man must be trying to throw them off the track, but Horst was adamant. Finally, he forced Horst to draw a map and explain exactly how to find his place. After that, Sergei looked at Vasily and nodded.

Taking a syringe from his pocket, Vasily withdrew a quantity of liquid from a vial he carried in another pocket and plunged the needle into a vein on the back of Horst's hand. In less than a minute, Horst was unconscious. Then the two men half carried, half dragged their prisoner outside and to a black Mercedes-Benz SUV parked in the alley behind the apartment building.

Leaving Montreal on Route 10, Sergei crossed the St. Lawrence River on the Pont Champlain. Then he headed east toward Sherbrooke. A little south of Sutton, he turned onto a graded dirt road, drove for two miles, and finally turned onto a primitive dirt track that ended after half a mile. The border between Canada and Vermont lay about two hundred yards away, across mostly open snow-covered country. Sergei was confident the SUV could handle the crossing, having previously used the same route to smuggle drugs into the U.S. and illegal South American aliens into Canada. Just over the border was a short stretch of dirt road leading into the small town of Richford, Vermont.

Sergei glanced in the rearview mirror at Horst slumped against the door, unconscious. "How does he seem, Vasily? Is he breathing okay? Do you really think Gustmann has it hidden in his summer cabin? If it were mine, I'd keep it in a safe deposit box in the bank."

"Yeah, it seems strange, but I don't see how it could help him to lie to us about it. He's old and weird, so I guess he probably buried it in the back yard or something."

"If it isn't there, and if he also doesn't tell me what his father did with the other eggs, then he must know he's a dead man."

Vasily gave Sergei a wolfish smile. "He's a dead man even if he does help us isn't he, Sergei?" *And so are you once I've got the egg and learn where the others are hidden.*

Horst remained unresponsive as they approached Johnson.

"Christ almighty, Vasily. How much shit did you give him? He's still breathing, isn't he?"

"Yeah, yeah, Sergei. He'll be okay, but it's going to take a little longer for him to come out of it because he's old, you know. Maybe another half hour."

"Well, it's cold as sin right now. I don't want to sit in an unheated cabin and freeze my ass off while he sleeps off your overdose, but I guess we might as well drive on to the cabin."

Sergei turned on the map light and studied the map Horst had drawn showing the location of his cabin some six miles northwest of Johnson. Twenty minutes later, he slowed the Mercedes as he spied the old barn standing across the road from the trail that led to the cabin. Just beyond the barn, Sergei turned into a snow-filled track and drove in a short way to shield the SUV from view. Then he turned and looked at Horst.

"Okay, old man. Wake up, it's time to take us to your cabin."

Horst, half awake now but still very groggy, feigned unconsciousness and didn't move or reply.

"Damn, Vasily! You must have given him a huge hit. It's lucky you didn't kill him outright. Slap him a bit. Wake him up. Now I've killed the engine, it's getting cold. Let's get this done and get out of here."

Vasily shook Horst, then slapped him several times across the face. This elicited a low moan but no other response.

"I guess we'll have to drag him to the cabin. Maybe the cold air will bring him around. Come on."

The men grabbed Horst, one on each side, and dragged him through the snow along the narrow trail leading to the cabin. Sergei released his grip to get out a small flashlight and the ring of keys he'd forced Horst to give up in Montreal. Focusing his light on the Yale padlock on the front door, he searched for the right key. Meanwhile, Vasily let Horst collapse in a heap in the snow. Now almost fully awake, Horst continued to pretend being unconscious while desperately trying to think of a way to escape.

Sergei pushed open the door and looked inside. The cabin was primitive all right, no electricity and no source of heat, except a wood stove halfway between the front door and the back wall. *Not a problem because we aren't staying any longer than it takes for the old man to give up the egg.* But maybe it was going to be a problem. Horst still didn't seem to be coming out of his drug induced stupor, and until he did they were stuck in an icebox with nothing but one small flashlight whose batteries were starting to give out.

"Vasily, bring the old man in and toss him on the bed over there until he comes around. In the meantime, I'll see what I can find. He must have some sort of light source when he stays here, maybe a battery or gas lantern."

Vasily pulled Horst from the snowbank, dragged him into the cabin, and threw him on the bed. Then he pulled him upright into a sitting position and slapped him several times across the face, hard. Horst emitted an incoherent mumble but kept his eyes closed and fell limply back on the bed.

"Shit! He must have no tolerance at all. If it was me, I'd be ready for another hit already."

Sergei finally found Horst's light source. *Christ! What century are you living in, old man?* On the metal kitchen table stood two old-fashioned flat wick kerosene lamps and a gallon can of fuel. Sergei fueled the two lamps and lit them. Their light was faint compared to that cast by a decent gasoline or propane lantern, but it was enough to allow a closer look at the interior of the cabin.

Picking up one of the lamps, Vasily walked over to a sideboard on the south wall and inspected all the shelves and cabinets. To the right of the sideboard was a box of dry firewood. He picked that up and dumped the contents out onto the floor. *Nothing hidden there.* To the right of the box was a door opening to the back yard. This one was bolted shut from the inside. Horst's bed and a small dresser stood in an alcove extending out a few feet on the west side of the cabin.

Vasily checked Horst once again but still elicited only a vague moan when he slapped the man. So pulling a bottle of vodka from his coat pocket, he suggested to Sergei they have a drink to fend off the cold. Returning their lamps to the table, the two sat at the kitchen table in a pair of mismatched chairs and shared the bottle.

"We know for certain Gustmann has at least one of the missing Imperial eggs, and my uncle Gennady told me he forced a captured SS major to admit that he and a friend named Klaus Gustmann had several more. You saw how he reacted when I showed him that photograph. He clearly recognized his father, but then he said he didn't know anything about other eggs or what those letters and numbers could mean. I don't believe that. We'll beat the truth out of him before you give him that final shot, Vasily."

As he continued to play the beam of his faltering flashlight around the cabin, Sergei finally noticed that a rag rug just inside the front door had been displaced, revealing a seam in the underlying floor. Getting up, he lifted the rug and underneath found a small hinged door in the floor.

"Vasily, I think this could be it."

The two men knelt on either side of the door. Sergei grabbed the depressed ring at the top and pulled the door open. Underneath, his flashlight weakly illuminated a SentrySafe steel security box in the space below.

"Hot damn!" While Sergei sorted through the ring of Horst's keys for one that might fit the lock, Vasily lifted the box up to the floor. Intent, neither man noticed as Horst rose from his bed, slowly and quietly unbolted the back door, and slipped outside.

Still focused on the box, Vasily reached for it, but Sergei grabbed it first and carried it to the table to get a better look by the kerosene lanterns. After trying three keys, he inserted one that fit the lock, turned it, took a deep breath, pulled the lid open, and…

"WHAT THE FUCK?!"

The case was empty.

The men jumped up, spun around, and lunged toward Horst only to find the bed empty and the back door ajar. Enraged, Vasily pulled open the door and spotted Horst in the moonlight. He was wading as fast as he could through the snow and about to disappear into the woods. Pulling out his pistol, he screamed, "I'll kill you, you lying son of a bitch," and fired two quick shots. Horst flinched as one bullet hit him high in the shoulder and felt a deep burning pain as the second struck him lower down in his back. He nearly fell but forced himself to keep moving toward the cover of the woods.

"STOP!" Sergei cried. "Vasily, you damn fool. Don't shoot him. We'll get him and find out where the eggs are hidden. He's an old man and leaving tracks in the snow. Run after him."

But Vasily's blood was up. Standing in the doorway, he took aim and was about to fire a third time.

Christ! They told me he has a crazy temper. Sergei lunged forward, grabbed Vasily, spun him around, and screamed, "I said stop! You stupid shithead! Put the gun away and go after him."

But Vasily had just snorted a large line and was in a cocaine-fueled rage. Pushing Sergei away, he screamed, "I'll get him back right after I take care of you, asshole." Then he fired, hitting Sergei in the left thigh.

Grunting with pain and surprise, Sergei staggered and fell back onto the sofa. Still purple with rage, Vasily raised his gun to shoot again, but before he could Sergei pulled out his own, a Kahr CW45, and fired twice. One round missed and went out the back doorway, but the other struck Vasily square in the chest. For a moment, he didn't move. Then dropping his gun, Vasily collapsed against the table, knocking to the floor and breaking open both lit lanterns as well as the open can of kerosene. The pungent odor of kerosene filled the cabin, followed a moment later by a sheet of flame as a puddle of the flammable liquid on the floor ignited and spread.

Just short of reaching the woods, Horst heard the third and fourth pistol shots, but felt no impact. *Keep going, keep going.* He forced himself to keep moving, but the pain from his wounds was bad. A hundred yards into the woods brought him to a shallow creek. Horst hesitated for a moment. Then he stepped through the thin coat of ice at the edge and waded a short distance downstream in the freezing water to where the lower branches of a large pine hung out over the creek. Just beyond it, he painfully pulled himself from the stream, hoping the branches would shield his tracks from the view of anyone following on the opposite side. *So cold now, but must keep going, keep going.*

Back in the cabin, Sergei forced himself to stand, probing his thigh where Vasily had shot him. A flesh wound. Apparently the bullet hadn't hit bone or an artery, but it still hurt like hell. Cursing, he looked about for something to put out the growing fire. He didn't see a fire extinguisher, but limping to

Horst's bed, grabbed a blanket, and tried to use it to beat out the flames. It was too little, too late. The burning kerosene had spread across the floor and was now igniting both the sofa and the base of the curtains over the window on the east wall of the cabin. He had to get out.

Sergei limped out the back door of the cabin and considered trying to follow Horst. After all, he was old and probably wounded. He couldn't have gone far. He just hoped the old man wasn't already dead. But after limping only a short way the pain in his thigh grew worse, and the fire in the cabin was becoming an inferno. He needed to leave.

Cursing his luck and the dead Vasily in particular, Sergei turned and slowly worked his way back to the SUV, where he fashioned a crude bandage, tying it tightly around the wound to retard the bleeding. He decided he'd better head back to Manhattan where there was a doctor who owed him a favor and would patch him up without feeling compelled to report a gunshot wound. The *Bratva* also ran a shop nearby. It would quickly get the merc on a ship and out of the country so it couldn't be traced back to him. However, New York was 350 miles away, nearly a six-hour drive if he didn't blow the speed limits. He sure as hell didn't want to be stopped by a cop. For about twenty minutes after leaving the cabin he passed no other cars, but as he approached Morrisville he was noticed.

Bored and in desperate need of a cigarette, Doyle Holloway, the night clerk at the Sunset Motel, decided to take a five-minute break. It was cold as hell outside, but that was okay because the office inside was like a steam room. Hoping the phone wouldn't ring, he put on his coat and went outside to light up. There had been very little traffic all evening on Route 15, especially the big trucks that used jake brakes to slow down as they passed the reduced speed limit sign at the edge of town. He hadn't heard one do that for more than two hours. Now, as he stood outside the motel office, Doyle saw a large black SUV approach from the west, slow down, and stop briefly on the other side of the road. A car fanatic, he recognized it as an upscale G550 Mercedes-Benz. *Sweet!* He figured it must have cost something north of a hundred grand. He wished he could have a ride like that instead of the trashy little Subaru Justy he had to drive.

Sergei's wound was already hurting so much now he knew he couldn't make it all the way to Manhattan without help. As he approached Morrisville he decided to call a doctor in Manchester, New Hampshire, a guy who was in on the drug trade the *Bratva* ran from Montreal to Burlington to New York. *What was the guy's name, Cantrell or maybe Connor? Time to call in a favor.* Pulling over for a minute, Sergei got out his phone, found the number, and speed dialed it. When a very sleepy voice answered, he was told in no uncertain terms to be ready in three hours' time to quickly and quietly remove a bullet from his thigh. Then, swallowing three tabs of ibuprofen and gritting his teeth against the pain, he drove on through Morriville toward St. Johnsbury, where he could pick up Interstate 93 and put on some speed.

CHAPTER 30

USAirways Flight 638 from Philadelphia touched down at the Burlington International Airport at 8:10 P.M. Ten minutes later, Derek stood by the luggage carousel waiting for his bag. The day hadn't started well, beginning with his discovery that the Subaru had a transmission problem. *Damn!* Well, that wasn't going to stop him from spending the next week and a half at his cabin in Vermont. When he tried to get a rental, he learned the local car rental companies were completely sold out of AWD vehicles because of the heavy snow and freezing rain that had pounded Philadelphia over the past two days. *Double damn!*

Okay, plan C; fly then drive. Checking with Alamo, Derek confirmed AWD vehicles were available in Burlington. Then he went to the USAirways website, and for an obscenely high price got a seat on a flight leaving at noon. Just enough time to grab his duffle bag and catch SEPTA to the airport. Once there he learned the flight had been delayed thirty minutes by a minor mechanical issue. Finally, two hours later the gate agent announced the mechanical issue had turned out to be a larger problem and the flight had been cancelled. Lining up with others, he managed to get one of the last seats on a flight scheduled to depart at 4:30 P.M., but at 4:00 P.M. yet another delay. *Unbelievable!* This time, the problem wasn't the airplane, but a heavy snow squall that had temporarily closed the airport in Burlington. Finally, at 6:30 P.M., passengers were allowed to board for the eighty-minute flight to Burlington, and the plane did take off. At which point his seat mate turned to him, rolled her eyes, and said, "I guess if you've lots of time, and you don't care, go by air."

Now, as the baggage carousel began to move, Derek saw the first item to appear was actually his own duffle bag, and muttered under his breath in Latin, *"Tandem, parva Victoria."* Grabbing it, he walked to the Alamo counter and in a few minutes was on his way in a new Subaru Outback.

By now, the storm that shut the airport for nearly two hours had quickly moved east and was rapidly being replaced by a front of frigid air from Canada. Many local roads remained snow covered, but the commuter rush was long over, so Derek quickly cleared the city and was soon heading toward Johnson on Route 15. Stopping for a few minutes at the Price Chopper in Essex Junction, he picked up a six pack of Otter Creek Copper Ale, milk, cereal, bananas, bread, cheese, lunch meat, batteries, and a cheap ice chest. No need to buy ice. He could just stuff the chest with snow to keep things cold, and he already had a stock of coffee and sugar at the cabin. The checkout clerk was chatty, told him it was predicted to drop as low as –15°F overnight. She wished him a good rest of the day and a warm night.

Route 15 had been plowed, but a mile east of Jeffersonville, windblown snow on a curve hid an underlying patch of ice. The Subaru fishtailed, and Derek gave his full attention to not sliding off the road, briefly slowing down to well below the posted limit. Twenty minutes later, he stopped at Wicked Wings in Johnson to grab a burger before heading to the cabin. Ellen, whose tattoo always made him think of something drawn by Escher, recognized him from previous visits and chatted a bit before taking his order. Then, as he nursed a beer and waited for his food, Derek found his thoughts growing dark again.

It was three years since he'd lost Julie to cancer. Three years, but he still couldn't quite accept that his wife was gone and often found himself slipping into a depressed state of mind. Work afforded some defense against that, but too many sixty-hour weeks in the office and laboratory left him exhausted. Worried about him, his daughter Kate kept urging him to take a break. She'd encouraged him to get out, do some fun things with friends, maybe join a group like Single Professionals of Philadelphia, where he could meet new people and perhaps find someone special. Last summer he'd been persuaded to try a dinner date with an attractive forty-two-year-old lawyer who worked with Kate at Barnham, Olds, and Stanton LLP. But it hadn't gone very well, and Derek told Kate he didn't feel quite ready to get "back in the mix."

So now he was getting away from the office, if not quite in the way Kate had in mind. Part of his brain told him his daughter was right. He ought to be looking for new social outlets, but another part pulled him in a different direction. He'd decided to try a week and half of "suck it up" therapy involving a lot of physical exertion, cross-country skiing and snowshoeing in the woods of northern Vermont, although he wouldn't be on his own for the entire time. Next week, he would join his friend Horst and Horst's daughter Eva for some ski outings and dinner a couple times before heading home. Indeed, he was looking forward to meeting Eva. During the summer, Horst hadn't been shy about saying he thought Derek and his daughter might be a good match.

Leaving Wicked Wings, Derek drove north past Johnson State College and a few minutes later turned left onto the gravel road that ended just beyond his cabin. It hadn't been plowed since the latest snowfall, but that wouldn't be a problem for the Subaru. The real problem on roads like this occurred in March and April, when alternate periods of freezing and thawing resulted in mud on top of deep icy ruts. That could make the best AWD vehicle lose control and slowly slide into a ditch when heading downhill or around a turn.

On his right, Derek passed the small Crawford dairy farm and wondered what the older couple who owned it planned to do in the future. In the family for four generations, it was now up for sale, testament to the fact a small operation like that couldn't compete with the large corporate farm milk producers. A little further on, he passed two singlewide trailers. The less battered one looked to be occupied, a flickering light in a window suggesting the operation of a TV set. Outside, a rusty green F150 pickup sat parked next to a child's broken swing set. The second trailer appeared to be beyond salvage, with a serious dent in one side, a hole in the roof, and broken windows all around.

Beyond the trailers, no tire tracks showed in the snow-covered road. Half a mile on, Derek passed a marshy area bordering a large pond where he knew that a pair of loons spent the summer. After that, the road curved left and ascended a steep hill at the top of which stood a small white house belonging to Ed and Vera Lonergan. The house was dark with no smoke coming from the chimney, so Derek supposed Ed and Vera were likely in Florida visiting their daughter.

A quarter mile past the Lonergan place, Derek passed a weathered barn, and across from it, a tiny cemetery that contained a dozen gravestones dating from the mid-to-late 1800s. During the summer, volunteers from Johnson cut the grass, planted flowers, and placed small American flags on the graves of three men who had fought for the Union during the Civil War. After that, the road curved to the right, descended into a narrow hollow, and rose again to a plain that once held two small farms, now abandoned and given over to second growth forest. Here, he passed Horst Gustmann's mailbox.

Derek reflected on the last time he'd seen Horst in October, his friend in a state of shock and grief over having just found and then immediately losing his long-lost aunt Gerda, as well as a feeling of shame over her deathbed account of his father's actions during WWII.

A half mile on, Derek finally came to the track that led to his cabin, just ahead of where the road now ended. At one time, it had continued another third of a mile, but that section had later been abandoned. Now, there was only a rough trail, ending at an abandoned farmhouse and barn once used as a squat by a band of hippies in the 1970s. He and Julie had explored the place years ago, finding an array of old bottles, rusted cans, a cooking pot, broken dishes, the odd hand tool, discarded clothing, and some animal bones. The barn roof sagged to such a degree it probably wasn't safe to enter, but the house at the time looked as though it might still be salvageable. Inside, they'd discovered a rug and two blankets of recent origin, and guessed the place might still be used for amorous teenage trysts.

Derek was pleased to see Abner Perkins had plowed the track to his cabin earlier in the week, so he now only had to negotiate the six inches of snow dropped by the recent storm. Unlike Horst's place, his had several modern amenities, including a propane fueled electric generator used to power a well pump, electric lights, small appliances, a circulating fan to distribute heat from a gas fireplace insert in the winter, and, on the occasional hot day, a small window air conditioner. However, it still made do with just a primitive "necessary house" some twenty yards behind the cabin.

The cashier's prediction in Essex Junction seemed right on. It was cold enough that his boots made a squeaking noise in the snow as Derek carried his groceries and duffle bag in from the car, the thermometer on his porch reading -8°F. Overhead, the moon was full, stars glittered in a black sky, and the breeze made a sighing sound in the crowns of the surrounding pine trees.

Inside the cabin it was as cold as outdoors, so Derek's immediate priority was heat. He planned to start a fire in the wood stove, turn on the gas fireplace and an auxiliary electric heater, then make coffee on the gas stove and wait for the cabin to reach a tolerable temperature before going to bed. But first he had to crack the valve on the propane tank out back and start up the electric generator. Opening the back door, he plodded to the propane tank, then uttered a curse loud enough to be heard half a mile. "Damn, damn, damn you, Cleo Lambert!" The broken valve Cleo had solemnly promised to fix last October had yet to be serviced. Now the gas fireplace and electric generator were useless until he could get someone from Northern Propane to come out. The wood stove would have to serve as the only source of heat, and he couldn't activate the well pump to get water. Apart from fresh snow, the only water he now had was a one-liter bottle he'd purchased before boarding the plane in Philadelphia and hadn't used.

Derek put paper and pieces of fatwood in the firebox of the wood stove, lit the tinder, and added progressively larger pieces of wood until he had a roaring fire. Then he put some coarse ground coffee in the strainer basket of an old aluminum percolator, added half a liter of water from his bottle, and set the percolator on the stove top to heat.

Still wearing his parka, Derek added fresh batteries to his portable radio and a battery powered lantern, and pulled both his bed and Morris chair to within a few feet of the stove. Tuning to WCVT FM 101.7, he settled back to listen to Vivaldi's *Four Seasons*. By eleven, the cabin had reached a tolerable temperature. He added more wood to the fire, shed his parka, and got ready for bed. Zipped up in his down sleeping bag, he listened to the crackling of wood burning in the stove and the soft sound of the wind in the pines outside. Finally, he fell asleep, but soon suffered an unsettling dream, one he'd had before.

In the dream, he was with Julie. She was young and beautiful and running toward him. Suddenly, she stopped and began to change, turning older and shrunken before his eyes, pulling away, fading away, and finally disappearing completely. Derek awoke with a start. Was it the dream or had he heard something? The fire no longer crackled, and the wind had ceased. He lay still, tense, and alert, listening intently, but for what? Looking at his watch he saw it was just past one. Gradually, he relaxed and was almost asleep again when a sharp crack brought him fully awake. A gunshot? No, surely not. He thought a moment and decided it must have been the long beam in the cabin roof suddenly contracting with the cold.

Sleep now seemed a long way off, so Derek got up, turned on the battery powered lantern, and relieved himself using what Julie had enjoyed calling the *pot de chambre*. No way was he walking out to the privy in the middle of a night this cold. Then he added several more pieces of wood to the fire, opened a bottle of Otter Creek Copper Ale, and sat down to read a bit of Craig Johnson's latest novel about Wyoming's indestructible Sheriff, Walt Longmire.

CHAPTER 31

Numb from the cold and fighting for breath because of fatigue and blood loss, Horst staggered out of the woods just east of Derek's cabin. Drawing hope and a final measure of strength from a dim light in a window, he half walked, half dragged himself across the short clearing, collapsed against the heavy wooden front door. In a fog of pain, and lacking the strength to call out, he scratched repeatedly at the door.

Inside, Derek tensed at the sound of a thump and a subsequent scratching noise. Putting aside his book, he walked to the door and said, "Is someone there?"

No reply. But more scratching noises, and what, the sound of breathing? Could there be an animal out there? Maybe a bear? Derek took his flashlight to the window and tried to shine light on the porch by the front door, but the angle was too great. The door could be locked from the inside by both a chain and a sliding bolt, but he hadn't bothered to set either one. Now he quickly attached the chain so he could open the door a couple of inches without letting in whoever or whatever might be out there.

Retrieving his old 20-gauge single shot shotgun from the closet, he loaded it with a #6 shotshell. Pretty light ammunition if the visitor was a bear or a human intruder bent on doing something bad, but plenty effective at very close range. Then he went to the door and opened it just a crack. On the porch lay a large figure. Not a bear, but a MAN! Clearly, he was injured. There was blood on the porch and because of the moonlight he could also see traces of blood in the snow beyond. How had he come here? Had there been an accident down the road? Unhooking the chain, he opened the door all the way, bent to examine the man, and felt a shock of recognition. *HORST!* The man on his porch was Horst Gustmann.

"My God, Horst! What happened?"

Horst tried to lift his head. He extended his hand and whispered something, but Derek couldn't make it out. He focused the beam of his flashlight on his friend, listened to Horst's labored breathing, and saw blood continuing to ooze onto the porch from the back of his jacket. No time to lose. As gently as possible, he pulled Horst into the cabin to better assess his injury and call 911.

Inside, Horst looked up and seemed to recognize Derek. He began to whisper urgently. Derek listened, but at first had trouble understanding. Some of the words were in English, but then he realized his injured friend had mostly reverted to the German of his childhood.

"Derek? *Ja?* Help, *bitte...zwei Männer...Russen...entführt...*beat...shot me...*wollte das Ei.*" Horst paused and struggled to get his breath.

Derek saw that Horst had multiple bruises on his face and the right arm of his jacket was soaked with blood. When he unzipped and folded back Horst's jacket, he also saw blood still seeping from a bullet wound in his friend's right shoulder. Gently turning him a bit to the left, Derek saw even more blood on the back of the jacket around the entry hole made by a second bullet. Horst moaned with pain.

Derek felt a knot of fear in his gut. What had happened? Was someone out there right now in the dark trying to track Horst down? He got up, picked up his shotgun, closed both the chain and bolt locks on the cabin door, and returned to Horst's side. He listened for just a moment but heard nothing. Then taking his phone to the southwest corner of the cabin where he could usually get a decent cell phone signal, he called 911. The call was answered on the third ring by a woman who sounded sleepy but quickly woke up when he told her what had happened.

"My name is Derek Todson. I'm with a critically injured elderly man who's been shot at least twice. He's lost a lot of blood and is only semi-conscious. Furthermore, he's been outside for a while. He's ice cold and is fighting for breath."

"Understood, Mr. Todson. What is your location?"

Derek replied, giving specific directions so the EMTs could find his cabin.

"Please stay on the line, Mr. Todson."

As he waited, Derek grabbed two pillows from his bed, gently raised Horst up, and stuffed the pillows in behind his back in the hope this would help him breathe. Horst moaned in pain as Derek did that, but his breathing seemed to improve a bit.

Two minutes later, the 911 dispatcher was back on the phone.

"Mr. Todson, an ambulance is being dispatched from Johnson with an ETA of fifteen minutes, and there is a medivac helicopter on standby at Fletcher Allen Hospital in Burlington. The Lamoille County Sheriff and the Vermont State Police have also been contacted and are sending officers to your location. What is the condition of the victim? Is he still outside in the cold?"

"No, I've pulled him into my cabin and covered him with my sleeping bag, but I'm afraid he's going to go into shock."

Horst's face looked ashen. Derek rolled up the blanket he'd used on top of his sleeping bag, rolled it into a ball, and used it to elevate Horst's feet. Then he took a hand towel from his duffle bag and folded it, intending to use it to apply compression to the wound on Horst's back that continued to seep blood.

"Horst, don't talk. An ambulance is coming. Just hold on. Help is on the way." He tried to give his friend a sip of water, but Horst pushed it away, and in his barely conscious state seemed intent on talking more.

"Derek, *Die Russen*...threatened...*Eva zu töten*...unless...I..." More coughing and words Derek couldn't make out. "*Die andere Eier.*" After another brief pause and several more labored breaths, Horst continued in a whisper that Derek was scarcely able to hear. "They find...*Geldschrank*...I...I ran... *zum Wald...dann...dann...schiessen sie mich...*" Horst's breathing grew more labored. His eyelids fluttered and closed.

"For Christ's sake, Horst, shut up. Don't talk anymore. Conserve your strength."

But Horst had one more thing he was determined to say. Opening his eyes once again and summoning a last reserve of energy he clasped Derek's hand and whispered, "*Hilfe Eva...schützen. Schau...*" Another cough. "*Schlupfwindel...Ecke...kleinen Ort...unter...unter den Balken.*"

"Shut up, Horst. That's an order." Derek could hear the siren of the ambulance in the distance. "Just take it easy and hold on, man."

Suddenly, Horst's body went rigid. He muttered, *"Kalt...sehr kalt..."* His eyes rolled back in his head, he let out a single long sigh, then nothing. Derek gently placed a finger over his friend's carotid artery: no pulse.

His phone still on, Derek heard the 911 dispatcher say, "Mr. Todson, how is the victim?"

"He just stopped breathing, and I can't detect a pulse, but the ambulance is almost here. I'm going to start CPR."

Two minutes later the ambulance pulled up in front of the cabin. Derek interrupted the chest compressions just long enough to pull open the door for the EMTs. He told them Horst had stopped breathing two minutes ago and that he had started CPR. Then he stood aside to let the EMTs take over. One started an I.V. line with a saline drip while the other applied a heart monitor, which showed no pulse, only a flat line. The first EMT placed an AMBU bag over Horst's face and mouth and began to pump air into his lungs, while the second EMT set up their AED, hoping to shock and restart his heart. Twice the AED was triggered, causing Horst's body to stiffen, but his heart failed to start. The EMTs looked at each other and at Derek. "Okay. One more time." The AED was triggered a third time. Still no response. Horst Gustmann was dead.

More sirens and flashing lights as the Lamoille County Sheriff pulled up by the cabin, followed a couple minutes later by a Vermont State Police cruiser. Sheriff Amanda Tate and Deputy Sheriff Dave Cole entered the cabin. "We weren't able to save him, Sheriff," said the senior EMT. "We shocked him three times, but it didn't work. He's been shot twice and lost a lot of blood." Derek felt dizzy but stepped forward to talk to the sheriff.

"Sheriff, my name is Derek Todson. I called 911 about twenty minutes ago to report finding Mr. Gustmann injured and lying on my doorstep. I got him inside and tried to slow the bleeding from his shoulder wound a little, but I couldn't do anything about internal bleeding caused by the bullet that hit him in the back. He stopped breathing just a couple minutes before the EMTs arrived."

"You called the victim Mr. Gustmann. So you are acquainted with this man?"

"Yes, I've known Horst for years. He's a Canadian citizen who has a cabin less than a mile from here. Normally he only comes to Vermont in the summer and lives the rest of the year in Montreal. But this year was different. His daughter is about to return to the U.S. after spending a year in Africa. He was going to meet her in Burlington, and they were going to spend some time together skiing in Vermont. But that wasn't supposed to happen until a week from now."

Corporal Ed Bradshaw of the Vermont State Police arrived as the EMTs were repacking their gear and calling in a report to the ED physician at Fletcher Allen Hospital in Burlington. After conferring briefly with Sheriff Tate, Derek and the EMTs were told to wait in the second room of the cabin and remain available to give formal statements while the officers inspected Horst's body.

Away from the wood stove, the second room of the cabin was still very cold. Derek put his parka on again and paced back and forth with the two EMTs as they all tried to keep warm. In his mind he kept going over the words Horst had whispered just before he died. So much didn't make sense. Who were these Russians and what was this about an egg? Horst had used the German word *das Ei*. Then there was his concern about his daughter Eva being in danger, his plea to Derek to protect her, and his admonition to look someplace, the *Schlupwindel*? What the heck was that? Apparently it was something in the corner (*Ecke*) of a small something (*Ort*) under something (*den Balken*). He would have to look up the meaning of those words when he got the chance.

Sheriff Tate called Derek back to the main room. She directed Dave Cole to take statements from the two EMTs in the other room, who were told they could then leave but to leave the victim's body in place. The medical examiner had been summoned, and after a preliminary exam would transport it back to Burlington for an autopsy. She and Corporal Bradshaw would interview Derek.

Sheriff Tate said, "Mr Todson, you told me you know the victim as Horst Gustmann. Please tell us exactly what happened before you called 911."

"Yes. Horst is...was...a friend and a sometime neighbor during the summer months. Earlier tonight I had trouble sleeping, so I got up and was reading when I heard an odd sound, a thud, like something heavy hitting my front door. After that, I heard a scratching sound. I wondered whether, even though it's midwinter, it might possibly be a bear. With the chain on, I opened the door just a crack and saw instead it was the body of a man. Looking closer, I was shocked to realize it was Horst. He was bleeding and barely conscious.

In the moonlight, I could see the track he'd left in the snow as he approached my place from the woods just east of here. Horst seemed to recognize me and attempted to speak, but I couldn't understand what he was saying at first. I pulled him into the cabin, saw that he'd been shot at least twice in the back, and called 911."

Corporal Bradshaw said, "So far, your statement is all we have regarding his identity. Sheriff Tate and I found nothing on his person to verify who he is, like a passport, driver's license, or a credit card. Perhaps his wallet and passport were taken from him or maybe they're in his cabin. We'll go there next to look. We definitely want to know where, when, and how he came across the border from Canada. We'll be checking with customs."

Derek nodded. "As I said a few minutes ago, I was surprised to see him here now because his daughter isn't scheduled to come until next week. When he tried to tell me what had happened to him, he used the German word *entführt*. It's been a long time, but I had German in college, and I think that translates to something like 'lead away.' I think he was telling me he was kidnapped in Montreal and brought here forcibly."

A moment later, Deputy Dave Cole returned from the other room, having taken statements from the EMTs, who then packed up their gear and headed back to Johnson. Sheriff Tate asked Dave to put on his cross-country skis and check out the trail Horst had left as he approached Derek's cabin. She and Corporal Bradshaw had additional questions for Derek as they waited for the medical examiner to arrive.

Corporal Bradshaw said, "Do you own a gun, Mr. Todson?"

Derek flinched. *Whoa! Jeez! Do they think I shot Horst?* Then he showed Bradshaw his 20-gauge shotgun loaded with birdshot. He told him he'd been nervous when he heard the sounds outside, so had been holding the gun when he opened the door.

"How about a rifle or pistol, Mr. Todson?"

"No. Just the shotgun."

"But you won't object if we examine your car, your luggage, and the cabinets in the cabin?"

"No, of course not."

"Before he died, did Mr. Gustmann say anything else besides that German word you thought might mean he'd been forcibly taken from his home?"

"He did. I kept urging him to keep still and conserve his strength, but as long as he was conscious he insisted on talking to me. It must have been the shock of what happened, but much of what he uttered was in German, the language he spoke as a child. I didn't understand everything but enough to learn that two Russians had beaten and shot him."

"What else? Did he mention their names or the name of anyone else? Try to remember exactly what he said."

"If he knew his assailants, he didn't say so. He only said there were two Russian men who were after his egg—he used the German word *das Ei*—and they seemed to think he either had or should know about additional eggs. He also told me they threatened to harm his daughter, and he asked me to protect her. Then he said that I or we, I'm not really sure, should look for something in a particular place, using several words whose meaning I'm not sure of. I'll have to look them up."

"Those other words, can you remember them?"

"He said to look in or for something called a *Schlupfwindel* apparently located in the corner of a small something under something called *den Balken*. I'll have to look up and confirm the meaning of those words to see if I can make any sense out of what he said."

Sheriff Tate and Corporal Bradshaw wrote down the words.

"And *das Ei*, the egg those men were after, does that mean anything to you?"

Derek was just about to say no when he suddenly recalled the episode of *Treasure Finders* he'd watched the week before last. *Really? Could the legacy Horst told me his father left for him be one of the missing Imperial Fabergé eggs that program talked about?*

"When I last saw Horst in October, he told me his dying aunt had just given to him a legacy left by his father, something she'd held for many years hoping to find him after they became separated during the war. He didn't tell me what it was, but the week before last I watched the last few minutes of a program on TV about some incredibly valuable jeweled egg-shaped *objets d'art* that had been custom designed and crafted by the House of Fabergé for Russian Tsars Alexander III and Nicholas II. When the Bolsheviks killed Nicholas II and his family, they took those eggs and put them in the Soviet Armoury, but several went missing. It seems like a real stretch, but since Horst's legacy was something his father discovered in Russia while serving in the German army, I wonder if *das Ei* could possibly be one of those missing Fabergé eggs."

Sheriff Tate and Corporal Bradshaw both looked skeptical but wrote down what Derek had just told them.

A short time later, the medical examiner arrived, examined Horst's body, and rendered a preliminary opinion that death had resulted from internal bleeding caused by the bullet that struck in the middle of Horst's back on the right side and probably damaged his kidney. A complete autopsy would be performed the next day.

As Horst's body was being loaded for transport to Burlington, Amanda Tate's radio came alive. Dave Cole was calling in to report what he had found.

"Sheriff, I followed the victim's track through the woods for at least half a mile to a point where it ends by the edge of a creek. Up to this point he clearly was alone, so the shooting must have occurred somewhat further away on the other side of the creek. It's amazing to me that a man his age could make it as far as he did in this cold with the wounds he sustained. What do you want me to do now?"

"Come back, Dave. I'll have Mr. Todson lead us to Mr. Gustmann's cabin. It seems more than likely that's where his assailants shot him."

Riding with Tate and Cole in the sheriff's car, Derek guided them to the trail leading to Horst's cabin, with Bradshaw followed in his VSP cruiser. Across the road from where they parked, he noticed a set of tracks left by a vehicle that had entered and later backed out of the unplowed driveway that led to Dean Smyth's place and called Tate's attention to them.

"Sheriff, those tracks weren't there when I drove by just past ten last night. Whoever made them may have seen or even been involved in what happened to Horst."

"Okay. Let's have a look. Whoever used that driveway must have been driving a vehicle with high clearance and all-wheel drive. The snow there looks pretty deep."

"It leads to a vacation cottage belonging to a Burlington physician named Dean Smyth. I'd be very surprised if he was here today. As far as I know, he drives a Toyota Corolla and doesn't use the place at all in the winter."

Equipped with high intensity spotlights, the three officers and Derek walked over to examine the tire tracks. Dave Cole measured the width of the tread and took several close-up pictures. He also photographed footprints apparent in the snow on both sides of the vehicle. One set to the left, but two and maybe even three sets on the right. They then crossed over to follow the trail leading to Horst's cabin. Again, they saw three pairs of footprints, or more precisely, two well defined pairs and a track between them that looked as though someone or something had been dragged in between. They also saw one pair crossing over the others, heading back in the direction of the road. Once again, Dave Cole took close-up pictures.

The smell reached them well before they saw it. Emerging from the woods into the small clearing where Horst's cabin stood, they immediately saw that it had burned to the ground. The roof was completely gone, and the walls had collapsed inward, leaving just piles of smoldering debris. The footprints they'd been following led to where the front door had once stood, while at the back two sets of footprints could be seen. One set began where the cabin's back door had been, crossed a short open area before turning right, then disappeared into the forest perhaps twenty-five yards away. The second set also emerged from the back door, went a shorter distance in the same direction, then turned, and made a wide circle heading back in the direction of the road.

Sheriff Tate and Corporal Bradshaw approached to take a closer look at the interior of the cabin. From the back Corporal Bradshaw could see broken remains of what appeared to have been two old-fashioned kerosene lamps and a partially melted kerosene container. He supposed that must have been the source of the fire and wondered if it had been accidental or set on purpose. Meanwhile, standing where the front door had once been, Sheriff Tate looked in and spotted on the floor a small strong box, the top open and empty.

With the aid of his own flashlight, Derek approached what had once been the east wall of the cabin. Directing the beam inside, he saw the blackened and partially melted remains of Horst's metal kitchen table and next to it on the floor a large dark object. With a feeling of nausea, he realized it was a body, burned beyond recognition, and called to the others.

Focusing her spotlight on the remains, Sheriff Tate called to Bradshaw and said, "You'd better call the ME again and also arrange for a CSI team and someone from the VBCI Fire Investigation Unit. They'll need to process this scene before we do anything more than set up a perimeter of crime scene tape."

It was now 4:30 A.M. Derek and the officers headed back to the road, taking care to step only in the tracks they had made going in. Light from the moon made it fairly easy to see the way.

Bradshaw and Cole returned to the VSP cruiser to wait for the ME and the CSI team, while Sheriff Tate offered to drive Derek back to his cabin. She said, "Are you okay, Mr. Todson?"

"No, I'm really not. I mean…this has been a terrible shock, and I don't feel like staying in my cabin right now. I…I think I'll drive into Morrisville, get something to eat, check into the Sunset Inn, and then try to get some sleep."

"Sounds like a good idea. I'll take you back so you can get your car, then I'll follow, check in by radio with Dave and Bradshaw, and also go on to Morrisville to get them something to eat."

At Dunkin Donuts, Derek ordered a coffee and a toasted sesame bagel with cream cheese, while the sheriff got a Box O' Joe and half a dozen bacon egg and cheese sandwiches to take back to the team working the crime scene. Derek was halfway out the door with his order when she called him back.

"Mr. Todson, I'm going to need you to come to my office in Hyde Park tomorrow to submit a formal written statement and discuss what you know about Mr. Gustmann with a detective from the Vermont Bureau of Criminal Investigation. Since you say he was a citizen of Canada and may have been kidnapped, this investigation will certainly involve the RCMP and likely the FBI as well. How about two o'clock? That should let you get a few hours of sleep."

The night clerk at the Sunset Inn clearly thought 5:30 A.M. was a weird time to be checking in. However, Derek didn't feel at all like filling him in on the night's events, and the clerk didn't press the issue. In his room, Derek ate his bagel and drank his coffee. Then he went to bed but sleep eluded him. He lay awake staring at the ceiling, re-living over and over finding Horst on his porch and hearing the words he'd had whispered to him just before dying. Finally, he drifted into a restless sleep. He awoke at eleven-thirty, took a long hot shower, dressed, and turned on the TV to see if the noon news on WCAX in Burlington had anything to say about the murder.

It was mentioned, but only very briefly. The news anchor reported that overnight the Lamoille County Sheriff and the Vermont State Police had responded to a 911 call from a rural area northeast of the town of Johnson to find an elderly man dead from two gunshots wounds at a neighbor's cabin. An active investigation was underway, and a press conference was scheduled for three o'clock that afternoon at the office of the Lamoille County Sheriff in Hyde Park.

CHAPTER 32

Derek arrived at Sheriff Tate's office just before two, where he signed a statement concerning the events of the previous evening. After that, he was introduced to VBCI Detective John Evans and spent twenty minutes telling him everything he knew about Horst Gustmann. A few minutes before three, Tate and Evans headed outside to prepare for the press conference. Reporters and cameramen from the network TV stations from the Burlington area were there, as well as reporters from several local papers: *Burlington Free Press*, *Barre-Montpelier Times Argus*, *Stowe Reporter*, *Morrisville News and Citizen*, and the *Waterbury Record*. Sheriff Tate spoke first and then introduced Detective John Evans as the VBCI officer in charge of directing the investigation going forward. Because of his role as a prime witness, they knew the press would have liked to question Derek, who now sat in Tate's office, but they weren't ready to let anyone talk to him. They only said the shooting victim had been discovered by a neighbor who then alerted authorities. But Derek, curious to hear about what was being said out front, slipped out the back, walked all the way around the block, and stood across the street behind a handful of local residents as the TV people filmed and the two officers spoke and then took questions from the reporters.

Sheriff Tate began by reading the following statement:

"An elderly man was fatally shot last night north of Johnson. A neighbor discovered the victim at the front door of his cabin and called 911 to summon an ambulance and the police. Unfortunately, the man died just as the EMTs arrived. An autopsy is now being performed by the ME in Burlington.

"The victim has tentatively been identified as Horst Gustmann, a Canadian citizen who lives in Montreal. However, final confirmation is pending receipt of further information from the RCMP, since the victim had no identifying documents on his person, and U.S. Customs has no record that Mr. Gustmann recently entered the U.S.

"Evidence suggests this crime was committed at or near the deceased's cabin located a little less than a mile away from where he died. Officers approaching the cabin discovered the footprints of three persons, the impressions from one set matching boots worn by the deceased. When they arrived at the cabin, they found it burned to the ground, and inside, a badly burned body that has yet to be identified and is now being autopsied by the medical examiner.

"The identity of the person or persons committing this crime is unknown, although evidence suggests the prime motive may have been theft of a very valuable object.

"Police are seeking to locate and question the third person who left the cabin and apparently drove away around two or three this morning in a truck or SUV equipped with tires having a 265 mm width and a tread consistent with that of a Yokohama model Geolander HT. Anyone who saw such a vehicle last night or who has any other information possibly relevant to this crime is urged to call either the office of the Lamoille County Sheriff or Detective John Evans at the Vermont Bureau of Criminal Investigation."

With that, Amanda turned the meeting over to John Evans who told the assembled reporters that future bulletins and press conferences regarding the case would be organized by and held at his office in Waterbury.

Several reporters tried to get either Sheriff Tate or Detective Evans to say something more about the identity of the person who discovered Mr. Gustmann, the nature of the valuable object that might have been the cause of his murder, and the possible identity of the person or persons who killed him, but they were waved away and simply told additional information would be released at an appropriate time so long as it wouldn't compromise the investigation.

With that, everyone dispersed. The TV reporters especially needed time to pare down their videos to a minute or less to show on the six o'clock news.

However, one newspaper reporter hung back and watched as Derek walked back to his car in the lot behind Sheriff Tate's office.

Jenni Johnson, the narrator four months earlier for an episode of *Understanding Science* that featured Derek explaining the science of epidemiology to be broadcast later on Vermont PBS, was now working as a reporter for the *Burlington Free Press*. Derek hadn't noticed her, but she had spotted him standing in the background listening to what Sheriff Tate had to say. Now charged with writing a piece about the murder for the Sunday edition, she wondered if Derek might possibly have some inside information about the incident. From a conversation they'd had prior to the VPBS taping, she already knew he had a cabin a few miles north of Johnson and he was here now. She decided to seek a conversation with him before her midnight deadline.

CHAPTER 33

Jenni followed Derek as he left Hyde Park, drove to Morrisville, then stopped at Price Chopper, emerging a few minutes later carrying a small bag of groceries. From there, he drove to the Sunset Inn. She wondered, *Is he just stopping for a moment or is he actually staying there?* Apparently the latter, because she saw him park in front of room twelve, pull a key from his pocket, unlock the door, and carry his groceries into the room.

Deciding on the direct approach, Jenni parked her car next to Derek's Subaru, looked in the mirror to check her makeup, then walked over to room twelve and knocked on the door.

Inside, Derek was just about to call his daughter Kate but put down the phone to answer the door. Peering through the peephole, he didn't immediately recognize Jenni, who stood turned to one side, her face partly shielded by the hood of her parka.

Derek opened the door. "Yes, miss?"

Jenni turned and said, "Derek Todson, don't you remember me?"

Derek looked at the attractive auburn-haired, green-eyed woman and replied, "Well sure. Jenni. Jenni Johnson. "It's nice to see you, but…" He looked at the ski pants and parka Jenni was wearing and realized it looked exactly like the outfit he'd seen from the back on one of the dozen media people standing close to Sheriff Tate as she read her statement regarding Horst's murder. *Oh, crud! Watch it. She's damned attractive, but stay aware, she's just here to pump you for information you're not supposed to give out.*

183

Jenni had been smiling. Now her demeanor changed. She became serious and said, "I wanted to offer my condolences on the death of your friend, Horst."

Derek wasn't sure how to respond. He recalled having told Jenni about his cabin a few miles from Johnson during one of the breaks when they were taping *Understanding Science*. Had he also mentioned Horst? If not, then…

"It must have been terrible to find your friend like that, beaten, shot and dying on your doorstep."

"Why do you think…?"

Jenni tried a ruse, saying, "I have good information you were the neighbor who found Horst."

Derek thought, *Can't be the police. Maybe one of the EMTs. They were still there when I first spoke to Sheriff Tate.*

"I wondered why Sheriff Tate didn't identify you this afternoon. Did you ask her not to?"

"No, but if she put my name out there, then you and everybody else would be at my door wanting details, as you are now. Surely, you can appreciate the police need to keep a cover on things and restrict loose and speculative talk that might jeopardize the investigation."

"Of course, I understand. I certainly don't want to hurt the investigation, and I really don't want to make you uncomfortable. But I'm preparing an article about the murder for the Sunday edition of the *Burlington Free Press*. I really do want to be as comprehensive and as accurate as possible. I think you and I worked really well together on that episode of *Understanding Science*. I was hoping you'd help me put together a really good understanding of who Horst was. And I'll be honest, I really would like to know what he was able to tell you last night and whether you or the police know anything more than what the Sheriff Tate just said about the person or persons who attacked Horst being after something very valuable."

"I guess I can give you some background on Horst. I don't think I should do more than that."

Jenni smiled. "I'll be grateful for anything you can tell me. Look, let me do something nice and treat you to dinner tonight."

Derek thought, *Hmmm, she's playing you for sure, but after all that's happened, a nice dinner in the company of someone who looks as good as she does would be nice. Just make sure you don't give away the store.*

"Okay, Jenni. I accept."

"Wonderful! Do you know the Foxfire Inn in Stowe?"

"Sure."

"Meet me there at six. They have a scrumptious entree, chicken stuffed with gorgonzola, pancetta, and figs with a cream sauce. I super recommend that along with a bottle of good Tuscan wine." She smiled. "Of course, you can have whatever appeals to you."

A double entendre? Nah…not really likely.

After Jenni left, Derek called his daughter. The receptionist at Barnham, Olds, and Stanton LLP connected him immediately when he told her he was Kate Todson's father.

"What's up, Dad? This is only DAY ONE of your 'come close to killing yourself outdoor fitness program.' You exhausted already?"

"I am, Kate, but not for the reason you might think."

Derek told his daughter what had happened overnight. She offered condolences over Horst's death. Then, following her professional instincts, suggested he consider retaining legal counsel while the investigation was going on. Derek told her he didn't think he needed that. He said he'd already signed a sworn statement and that the police were treating him as a witness, not as a suspect.

"They've asked but haven't ordered me to stay in the area for a while during the investigation. I'll scan and send a copy of my statement to you. Check the evening news on WCAX Channel 3 in Burlington for a summary of the murder."

"So what's your plan, Dad? Are you going back to the cabin?"

"I'll go back tomorrow. I want to be around when Horst's daughter Eva gets here. The police reached her early today, and she immediately got a flight out of Ghana to Amsterdam. From there, she's supposed to fly to Kennedy, and catch a connecting flight to Burlington late tomorrow afternoon or evening. I plan to be there when she meets with the authorities the day after that. I'm the last person Horst spoke to. He told me the men who shot him also threatened his daughter and asked me to protect her. I owe him that, and I want to help any way I can."

Derek was already waiting when Jenni pulled into the parking lot of the Foxfire Inn five minutes early. Inside, the host showed them to a table in the

Garden Room. Only a handful of tables in the restaurant were occupied at that hour, just one of those being in the Garden Room. They'd be able to talk freely with little fear of being overheard. Jenni ordered a bottle of Camerano Cannubi San Lorenzo Barolo, 2008, and crostini caprese appetizers to begin.

Derek thought, *Impressive. This girl must have a decent expense account.*

"I have to submit my story by midnight so I can pass it through the copy editor and be ready when the paper goes to press at two in the morning. I've already prepared a draft based on what Sheriff Tate said this afternoon, but I'm hoping you can tell me more about Horst Gustmann. You do know, don't you, that the RCMP has now formally confirmed your identification of Horst that Sheriff Tate categorized this afternoon as provisional?"

Derek nodded. "Yes, the sheriff called to tell me that just as I was leaving to come here, so I guess I'm free to talk to you some more about him."

"My assistant at the paper has been working like crazy for the past hour. I already know he once was a professor at McGill University, that he was a widower, and that his daughter Eva is a physician who has been working in Africa. Tell me how you came to know Horst and what else you know about him."

Over the main course, Jenni's questions veered back to what Derek knew or thought about the crime. He had to consider carefully what it was safe to say or not say, so he began telling her something Sheriff Tate had told him during their recent phone conversation.

"Sheriff Tate just told me that when the RCMP entered Horst's apartment in Montreal, they saw had been it ransacked. His passport and wallet were still there, and the wallet contained several hundred dollars. Assuming the people who broke into the place were the ones who shot him in Vermont, it seems clear they were looking for something a lot more valuable than some cash."

"I agree. So I think I can safely write that based on information obtained from the RCMP, Horst was forcibly removed from his apartment, smuggled across the border, and taken to his cabin because his assailants were seeking something of great value they thought he kept there. Sheriff Tate only referred to the person or persons who committed this crime. However, it definitely had to be persons, at least two, because the police found one dead in the burned cabin and someone else obviously got away in that truck or SUV whose tread marks were found near his cabin."

Jenni gave Derek her most earnest look. "So please, Derek, did Horst tell you what they were after, and did they find it? If you tell me, I promise to hold your answer in confidence. I can see that publishing that particular bit too early could compromise something the police are planning to do, but I'd really, really love to know."

Derek hesitated. He'd already told Sheriff Tate and Corporal Bradshaw that Horst's dying reference to *das Ei* referred to a legacy from his father and suggested it could possibly have been a bejeweled egg-shaped object once owned by one of Russian Tsars. They had seemed skeptical, and Derek was having some trouble believing it himself. Still, Horst had clearly used the German word for egg to describe what his attackers were looking for, and his kidnappers were convinced he had others as well. They had threatened violence against his daughter if he didn't give them up. His last words to Derek had been a plea to help Eva. Derek began to think of a way that Jenni's article might help him do that. He decided to tell Jenni about Horst's legacy but not say at this point exactly what he thought it must have been.

"Derek? Earth to Derek."

"Yes, Horst did speak to me. He said the men who kidnapped and shot him were after a very valuable object his father had set aside many years ago as a legacy. I'm not sure exactly what that was, but I suspect his killers may have found it because the police discovered a safe box standing open and empty in the burned cabin. Horst also said his attackers seemed convinced that he possessed other items of value, and they threatened violence against his daughter if he didn't give them up. He specifically asked me to help his daughter and then mumbled some more German words just before he died, whose meaning still isn't clear to me. I want to help Eva and think you might be able to help me do that by planting a little misinformation in your article tomorrow."

"You have my full attention, Derek."

"How about saying in your write-up that just before he died, Horst managed to tell me the legacy from his father that his kidnappers were after was hidden in a place no one else knows about. But leave it at that. That will put me in the frame as someone who might or might not have information the killer wants, but hopefully it diverts some attention from Eva. When she gets here and talks to Sheriff Tate and Detective Evans we'll find out if she actually knows anything about her dad's legacy and whether she can make sense of the few words he actually whispered to me before he died."

Jenni's expression changed from avid interest to one of alarm.

"Whoa! If we print that, you've as good as made yourself the next target of the guy who just killed your friend."

"Look, I'm not really into the role of dead hero, but if I don't put myself out there a little, then I'm afraid this guy is going to target Eva. There ought to be some way to get the killer to shift his attention away from her and show himself without completely offering myself as a sacrifice."

"You saying or asking?"

Finally, Derek said, "I guess I've got to take the chance."

CHAPTER 34

Rising early, Derek showered, dressed, and walked to the motel office to check out. Inside, Doyle, the night clerk, was watching the morning news on Channel 3. As Derek entered, he jumped up and shouted, "Man! I saw him. I'm sure I did. I saw him."

"Saw what?"

"The SUV that murderer was driving. I just saw on the news the guy who murdered Horst Gustmann is thought to have left the scene in a high clearance four-wheel drive truck or SUV equipped with 265 mm width Yokohama model Geolander HT tires. I was here all night Friday. There was almost no traffic most of the time, but around two-thirty I went out for a smoke and saw this beautiful black Mercedes-Benz G550 SUV come by the motel heading east. It pulled over and stopped for a minute just across the road. I think maybe the driver was making a phone call. Anyway, I know cars. That was one sweet ride, costs maybe 100k, and I know it comes equipped with the kind of tires I just saw the sheriff mention on TV."

"Did you get a look at the driver?"

"Nah, not really, other than it was a guy and he looked big."

"What about a license plate?"

"Too far away, but I could tell it was white, so maybe Quebec."

"You should call Sheriff Tate and tell her what you saw. I'm sure she'd like to know."

"Right. I'll do that now." Doyle looked around for the phone book but couldn't seem to find it.

Derek pulled out his phone and handed it to Doyle. "Here, use mine. I have the sheriff's number here on speed dial."

Derek waited as Doyle excitedly told the person answering the phone about the black Mercedes-Benz SUV. As soon as he had finished and Derek got his phone back, he checked out and headed over to Dunkin Donuts for breakfast, then asked the girl at the counter to fill his thermos with coffee. Driving to the cabin, he passed Lamoille County Sheriff and VSP cars that were still parked alongside the trail leading to Horst's cabin, now blocked by yellow crime scene tape.

Derek built a fire in the wood stove, sat down to drink some coffee, and waited for Cleo Lambert to show up. He'd stopped at the Northern Propane office in Morrisville on his way to Hyde Park yesterday to complain about Cleo's failure to fix the valve on his propane tank and received a profuse apology from the woman behind the counter, who promised to contact Cleo immediately. She must have done so, because a few minutes later Cleo called him and promised to be at the cabin the following morning at nine sharp. At a quarter to ten Derek finally heard Cleo's truck turning into his driveway. *Vermont time.*

"Morning, Cleo."

"Ayuh. Mornin', Mr. Todson. Got tha' valve you need. I'll put 'er in now and get yer tank filled directly. I hear'd theyah was wicked goins here night afore lahst, an' just read more about it in the papah this mornin'."

Cleo reached into the cab of his truck, withdrew a copy of the Sunday *Burlington Free Press*, and handed it to Derek. The front page carried Jenni's story about the murder, the fire at his cabin, and the other body found in the charred remains.

Derek read quickly, anxious to see if Jenni had inserted the "bait" he'd asked her to put in her article. *Ah, there it is.* In the second to last paragraph, she'd written that just before he died Mr. Gustmann confided to his friend his attackers had been after part of a legacy left to him by his father, but he had more of it hidden in a place no one else knew about.

The last paragraph said police in Vermont were now working with the RCMP in Montreal where Gustmann had been kidnapped. Neighbors and other acquaintances there were being interviewed for possible clues. The article also noted that Mr. Gustmann's daughter Dr. Eva Gustmann had been notified of her father's death and was expected to arrive back in the U.S. that afternoon from Africa to meet with the police.

Cleo watched as Derek read, obviously hoping for a first-person account of his experiences that night, but Derek wasn't in the mood for that.

Handing the paper back to Cleo and said, "Thanks for letting me see this, Cleo. I haven't had time to get my own copy. Yes, it was a terrible thing to see my friend die."

"Yer roight. Brings to mind when brotha' Clarence drownt up to Mil-un Lake." He waited a moment to see if that got a response, and when it didn't, said, "So, what you be doin' next?"

Deciding to employ a little local vernacular himself, Derek replied, "Hard tellin', not knowin'," and just stood there with his hands in his pockets.

Taking the hint, Cleo finally said, "Okay, then. I'll just fix yer tank propah now and be on muh way."

As soon as the propane tank had been made functional, Derek turned on the electric generator and the gas fireplace. Then, feeling a little nauseous as he looked at the bloodstain on the floor, he turned on the pump, filled a bucket with water and detergent, and set about scrubbing it clean. Restless after finishing that, he stepped outside and chopped more wood for the stove. An hour later, arm muscles aching and his shirt wet with sweat, Derek put the ax away. Inside, he popped a bottle of Copper Ale, sat in his Morris chair, and thought some more about Horst's last words. Could the legacy *really* have been one of those missing Fabergé eggs? It seemed almost, but not completely, beyond belief. If so, did Horst have any idea about its actual worth? And if he did, why on earth would he have left something like that in his cabin? The logical thing would have been to take it to Montreal and put it in a safety deposit box at a bank. Derek decided Horst either didn't recognize the value of what he had, or had been so ashamed by what he had learned about his father that he'd been unable to think logically about it. Maybe it was some of both, and what about Eva? Did she know anything about the legacy? He supposed he'd learn soon enough when they met tomorrow at John Evans's office in Waterbury. His reverie was interrupted by a phone call from the office of the Lamoille County Sheriff.

"Hello?"

"Derek, Dave Cole here. Sheriff Tate asked me to let you know Eva Gustmann has run into trouble with her flight from Europe. Bad weather cancelled the flight she was supposed to take to New York yesterday and stranded her overnight in Amsterdam. She's now booked on a flight out of Schiphol to New York tomorrow morning, but she won't be able to make it to Burlington until late afternoon or evening depending on what sort of connection she can get out of Kennedy. Our meeting with Evans has now been rescheduled for ten o'clock Tuesday morning. You want to ride with me, or would you rather drive there yourself?"

"Thanks for letting me know, Dave. I think I'll take my own car. Just give me the phone number and the address of Evans's office."

Dave gave him the number and address, then said, "Oh, one more thing. Sheriff Tate asked me to ask you what the hell you were thinking in allowing that reporter for the *Burlington Free Press* put that thing in the paper about Gustmann telling you there was more to his legacy hidden in a place that nobody else knows about? Did he really do that, and if he did why would you want to let his killer know? It puts you in the guy's sights."

"Sorry, Dave, but yeah, I did that on purpose. Tell Sheriff Tate and Detective Evans I'll say more about that when we get together on Tuesday."

Derek drove to Johnson for lunch. Half an hour after he returned, his phone rang again. This time it just showed the call was from code 212, a number he didn't recognize. *Probably somebody promising to help me with my credit rating, wanting to sell me replacement windows, or telling me my car warranty is about to expire.* He almost let it go, but after the fourth ring did decide to answer.

"Hello."

"Professor Derek Todson?"

The voice had an accent he couldn't quite place.

"Speaking."

"Oh, Professor. It's Eva, Eva Gustmann. I…I just landed at Kennedy Airport." The voice sounded strained, as though she were trying not to cry. "I'm trying to get a flight to Burlington but there are problems. One has been cancelled and another is full. I just read the story in the *Burlington Free Press* on my iPad. Please, I am so torn up, I can't wait. Please tell me what my father said to you that night."

At Kennedy Airport? Really? Dave Cole just told me Eva was stuck in Amsterdam until tomorrow morning.

"Uh…Eva, I'm terribly sorry about your dad, but I'm sure you're tired and need a rest. We can meet tomorrow. And I hate to ask, but since you had to leave on such short notice, were you able to bring with you the Ebola cultures we talked about last month?"

"Yes, of course I have them, but oh, I just can't wait until tomorrow. I'll rent a car and drive. I know it will be very late before I can get there, but…

There was a click and the connection was broken. Derek looked at his phone. Who was that? It obviously hadn't been the real Eva Gustmann. *Ebola samples? Really? How dumb are you, lady? Was this a prank call or something else?* Derek immediately called the office of the Lamoille County Sheriff again, got Dave Cole on the line, and told him about the call he'd just taken from a fake Eva Gustmann.

"Thanks. I'll pass that on to Evans. I guess I know now why you asked that reporter to slip in that bit about what Horst said to you into her article. Too bad they cut the connection. We might've been able to set a trap if you'd managed to set up a meeting. We'll try to trace the call, but if it really came from Horst's killer it was probably made on a throwaway. In the meantime, really watch yourself. You can't be sure when or how this guy may show up."

As Derek was speaking to Dave Cole, a more heated exchange was taking place in Manhattan between Sergei Yakushin and his girlfriend, Tatiana.

"Jesus, Sergei! Why did you grab the phone and turn it off? I'm pretty sure he was about to agree to a meeting."

Sergei's thigh wound hurt and he was in a foul mood. "You stupid cunt! He was testing you. He asked if you brought the Ebola samples, and you said yes. For Christ's sake, Tatiana, you should know no one would ever be allowed to carry samples of that deadly virus on board a commercial airliner. He suspected and now obviously knows for sure you weren't Dr. Gustmann. If you had set up a meeting, it would have been a trap. We'd have walked right into a nest of cops."

"Well." Tatiana pouted, flounced away, and poured herself a drink at the bar. "You should have prepared me better. How was I to know his question didn't make sense? I don't know crap about this Ebola stuff. I'm not a doctor."

"Yeah, okay baby, that was a shot in the dark and it didn't work. I've got to find another way to learn what Gustmann may have told Todson or his daughter about the egg that wasn't where he said it was and what others he must have hidden away as well."

Tatiana brought a double shot of vodka to Sergei, who downed it in a single swallow.

"If it hadn't been for that bastard Vasily, I'm sure I could've made the old man give up everything."

Tatiana sat on the arm of the sofa and massaged Sergei's neck. "Yeah, that Vasily was a little shit all right, a real crackhead. You're well rid of him, baby, but be careful. He had friends who may not be so forgiving about what you had to do. Like Fedor. I heard he's been talking that maybe he'd do a better job than you at running the business here. Did you know he's a second cousin to Vasily?"

CHAPTER 35

Eva Gustmann finally made it to Burlington late Monday evening, a day later than planned. The cancellation of her KLM flight from Amsterdam to New York on Sunday hadn't been her only problem. After landing at Kennedy and clearing customs, she learned the connecting JetBlue flight she was to have taken to Burlington had been cancelled due to a mechanical problem and a later flight was already fully booked. *Damn!* In a moment of pique, she pulled out her credit card and hired a limousine to drive her the entire way. Once in the back seat, she promptly fell asleep.

In Burlington, Eva checked into the Sheraton Hotel. The desk clerk handed her a note from Detective John Evans saying he would meet her there for breakfast and then take her to his office to meet with others involved in the investigation of her father's murder.

Derek hadn't ever met Eva in person, although they had exchanged emails and he'd spoken to her in the course of a couple conference calls two years ago. At that time her practice group in Palo Alto was interested in conducting a study comparing the sensitivity and specificity of a new diagnostic test with two currently licensed test procedures. Knowing his friend had experience designing and conducting clinical trials, Horst had urged his daughter to run some thoughts about the study by Derek for advice. But Horst had a *sub rosa* reason as well. He'd decided to play matchmaker between a distressed daughter recently jilted by an unfaithful fiancé and a friend still having trouble adjusting more than a year after losing his wife to cancer. Sometime after the pair had conferred by email and phone, Horst gave Derek a picture of Eva and a little pep talk about how he thought that she and Derek might make a good couple. He did the same thing in correspondence with his daughter. Horst had still been looking for a way to have them get together when Eva suddenly decided to take a leave of absence from her practice group and spend a year working with *Médicins San Frontières* in Africa. Now, the two were about to meet, but not under happy circumstances.

Seeing Eva as she sat in Evans's office made Derek think of the Australian actress who played the role of an adventurous lady detective from the 1920s named Phryne Fisher. Like her, Eva had her dark hair cut in a short bob. She had a pretty, heart-shaped face, a slightly pug nose, and a gaze that made you think she knew what you were thinking. But today, her green eyes were reddened by grief and fatigue, and Phryne's trademark bright red lip color was missing.

Evans introduced everyone. "Dr. Gustmann, this is Amanda Tate, Lamoille County Sheriff." Then, gesturing to Dave and Derek in turn he said, "This is Deputy Sheriff Dave Cole, and this is Dr. Derek Todson. Dr. Todson found your father wounded in front of his cabin and called 911 to alert the police and get an ambulance."

Eva shook hands with Amanda and Dave and said, "Please, just call me Eva." To Derek she said, "I feel I already know you from those phone calls we had before I went to Africa. I know you and Dad were good friends. I'm so grateful you could be with him, someone he knew…and…" She began to tear up.

Derek touched her lightly on the arm. "Eva, I'm so sorry about Horst. He didn't deserve this. His last thoughts and words were about you."

Waiting a moment for Eva to compose herself, Evans continued, "I've given Dr. Gustmann a brief summary of what happened and what we know so far. She's also seen the article in the Sunday *Burlington Free Press* and a report from the RCMP about what was found at her father's apartment in Montreal. They recovered a tape from a CCTV camera at the back of the building showing three men approaching and getting into a dark colored SUV at 10:37 P.M. last Friday. It was too dark to get a clear view of their faces, but the men on either side appeared to be holding up the one in the middle. The guy on the left was tall and had a heavy build, while the one on the right was shorter and lighter. They must be the two Russian men Horst said kidnapped and later shot him. And based on a note the ME just sent over, I suspect the John Doe we found in the cabin is likely the smaller guy on the right side in that CCTV image." Turning to his computer, Evans opened a document and read aloud.

"The badly burned body found in the cabin north of Johnson is that of a Caucasian male, perhaps thirty to thirty-five years of age, five feet seven inches in height and of slight build." He stopped for a moment. "And here's the interesting part. It appears he wasn't killed by the fire but rather by a large caliber bullet in the chest. Looks like maybe his partner decided not to share whatever it was they found."

"ID?"

"Not yet. The body was burned beyond any possibility of lifting fingerprints, but the ME extracted some pulp from one of the victim's molars for DNA analysis. That'll take a while, but once we get results, we'll check them against criminal databases in the U.S. and Canada. If we get a hit there, that *might* give us a lead to the person who was with him."

Evans turned from his computer and fixed his gaze on Derek. "Dr. Todson, you said in your statement Mr. Gustmann managed to tell you several things using a mix of both English and German words, possibly because of the shock of what had just happened to him. I want to go over one more time *exactly* what it was that he said, in part…" picking up the paper with Jenni's article, "in part because I didn't see anything in your signed statement about Mr. Gustmann confiding to you the hiding place of the rest of his legacy as this article seems to suggest."

Derek colored a bit. "Guilty as charged but let me reiterate what Horst did say and why I urged Jenni Johnson to put that bit about Horst's legacy in her article."

As soon as Derek started to repeat Horst's last words, Eva started. "*Das Ei.* That's what Dad had, a green egg-shaped object surrounded by bands of gold inlaid with what looked like diamonds and emeralds. He sent an email with a picture of it to me last week. He told me it was something his aunt Gerda gave to him just before she died, and that a Mr. Rubenstein in New York might be interested in buying it." Eva opened her briefcase, pulled out a copy of Horst's message, and put it on Evans's desk. Then she turned to Derek. "So you're saying this is what Dad's attackers were after, and that it's something my grandfather Klaus set aside for him before he was killed at the end of the war?"

"Yes. When I last saw Horst in October, he'd come back from attending Gerda's funeral in Worcester, Massachusetts, and was really depressed. That made sense to me, but it turned out he was also upset by something more than her death. He told me Gerda had given him a small wooden box just before she died. She told him it contained a legacy his father Klaus gave to her in 1949 and charged her with keeping safe until she could pass it to Horst. That nearly didn't happen."

Eva looked puzzled. "1949? That doesn't make sense. Dad checked years ago and found his father's name on a list of German soldiers killed in Berlin in 1945. How could he have given the box to Gerda in 1949? She was an old lady and terminally ill. She must have mixed up the date."

"Horst said it didn't make sense to him either, but then Gerda told him Klaus hadn't died in Berlin after all. He was living under an assumed name, Otto Krummel, and paid her a surprise visit in Dresden in the spring of 1949. He told her he was on his way to Latvia to recover treasure that he and a friend had found and cached there during the war. Then she confided to Horst something that made him terribly upset. His father hadn't been a regular soldier in the *Wehrmacht* as Horst had always thought, but an SS officer. Even worse, as the Russians closed on the center of Berlin, when he witnessed Russian soldiers summarily executing any officers found wearing an SS uniform, Klaus panicked. He killed and took the identity of an of a regular *Wehrmacht* soldier who resembled him. That man was Otto Krummel."

Eva was stunned. "That's awful. No wonder Dad was depressed. He told me he was only seven years old the last time his father came to visit, but he loved his *Vati* and always thought of him as a hero."

Derek continued. "Horst did tell me his attackers were after his egg, *das Ei*. He also said they thought he had others, *andere Eier*, and if he didn't give them up they threatened violence against you, Eva. He asked me to help you. I don't have any reason to know if he could have had more than the one egg, but I'm worried the guy who killed your dad might now come after you. I asked Jenni Johnson to say in her article that Horst told me the rest of his legacy was hidden in a place no one else knew to put me in the frame and take some attention away from you. It almost worked." Derek looked at Evans. "I guess Dave Cole told you about the call I got from a fake Dr. Eva Gustmann the other day, saying she couldn't wait to get here and begging me to tell her exactly what her dad had said before he died. Possibly that was just someone playing a prank, but if not…"

Evans shook his head. "Yeah, Captain America, we couldn't trace the call, so your ploy didn't work out so well, and now you've really got to watch your tail." Turning to Eva, he said, "This picture your dad sent to you in his email may be what we need to break this case. I'll call Sergeant McConnell at the RCMP. He can start tracking and interviewing people your dad might have spoken to about the egg in Montreal. He can also check out your dad's phone calls and emails on his computer. We definitely need to talk to this Mr. Rubenstein in New York and set up surveillance to see if the egg comes up for sale. Of course, the thief may well go to ground and keep his head down for a while. Another discouraging possibility is that this might've been set up as a contract job to get the egg for some very wealthy collector."

After the meeting broke up, Dave Cole and Amanda Tate headed back to Hyde Park, while Derek offered to take Eva to her hotel in Burlington. Evans was already on the phone to his RCMP contact in Montreal, but he waved as they left and promised to call later if he learned anything new.

CHAPTER 36

On the way to Burlington Derek said, "It's a shame your dad only managed to find Gerda just before she passed away. He told me he'd tried many times, but I guess his search hit a wall because he didn't have any inkling Gerda might have married an American soldier, changing her name by becoming Mrs. George Brighton and moving to the states. He was only able to connect with her at the last minute because someone in the RFL program of the International Red Cross decided to have one more shot at what the police would call 'a cold case.' Anyway, I wonder that Gerda didn't manage to find Horst. I'm sure she must have tried."

"She probably failed because for some years after the war Dad told me he was officially known by the name Václav Kovach. He didn't manage to get back his true identity until he'd been in Canada quite a while."

"What was that all about?"

"In 1944, Gerda started working a double shift in the munitions factory. Neighbors had helped her care for Horst when she only worked a single shift part time, but that was no longer possible. So Gerda sent Horst to live with her cousin Erica in Prague. In retrospect that seemed like a really good idea after Dresden got firebombed. Erica had a son named Václav, who was the same age as Horst, and Dad told me they got on really well together. But toward the end of the war, Erica's husband was killed in action and soon after that her son Václav got diphtheria and died. When the Russians occupied

Prague, they weren't friendly to residents with German surnames, so Erica presented Horst as her son, Václav Kovach. After the war, the two of them ended up in a DP camp for quite some time in the Russian controlled zone of Austria. There, at least, Erica felt Horst wasn't at risk of being shipped to Siberia with some family having a German surname."

"Was that really necessary? Horst was only what, ten or eleven years old while they were stuck there? Would the Russians really have done something awful to a German kid that young?"

"I'm guessing not, but Erica was pretty paranoid. Dad told me that he was already much taller and heavier than most kids his age, and the Russians rounded up and deported a lot of male Germans to Siberian work camps, some as young as twelve or thirteen."

"Okay. But later? Gerda was still in Dresden in 1949. Surely she'd been trying to find Erica and Horst since 1945?"

"I'm sure she did. Dad told me Erica also contacted the Red Cross multiple times trying to locate Gerda, but without success, only managing to learn Gerda's apartment building had been completely destroyed and many of the residents killed. On the other side, Gerda's inability to find Horst was surely due to Erica's decision to move him to Canada, still identifying him as her son, Václav Kovach."

"Why did she keep calling him that?"

"Dad told me Erica had both his and Václav's papers but felt she needed to keep saying he was Václav because of a mistaken impression that though Canada was welcoming Czech refugees they might still ban Germans. After they settled in Canada..." Eva stopped in mid-sentence, her eyes starting to close. Jet lag was having its way, and she was feeling overcome with fatigue.

"Eva?'

"What? Whoa. Sorry. I'm just so tired."

"I get it. Let's get a little lunch and some strong coffee. Then I'll take you to the hotel."

At Leunig's Bistro, Eva ordered a double espresso plus a Waldorf chicken salad sandwich to split with Derek. Five minutes later the caffeine supplemented with some sugar began to have some effect.

"I needed that. Now, what was I just saying?"

"Forget it. We can talk later."

"No, I remember. When Erica and Horst finally got settled in Canada, she learned her fear that Horst might be rejected because he was German had been baseless. But now the poor woman feared telling the truth, thinking both she and Horst might be expelled if the authorities learned she'd brought him into the country using a false identity. Dad told me it took several years before he was able to convince her to present his real identity papers to the Canadian immigration authorities. If fact, that did create complications, but eventually he got things worked out and officially became a Canadian citizen under his proper name, Horst Dieter Gustmann."

They worked on their sandwich for a couple of minutes. Then Eva said, "What about *die andere Eier* you said Dad's killer seemed to think he had?"

"I only just recently learned something about them on a TV program. Apparently, over a number of years the House of Fabergé was commissioned to create a series of unique, bejeweled eggs that Tsars Alexander III and Nicholas II presented as gifts to their wives and mothers. After the revolution in 1917 these were all confiscated by the Soviets but later eight of them were reported as missing, and as far as the world seems to know, seven still are. Were they destroyed or are they in private collections the public doesn't know about? Maybe they were misplaced and are just lying around waiting to be found. But if the egg in the pictures your dad sent to Mr. Rubenstein really is one of those seven, then it seems possible your grandfather might have found some or all the others. Frankly, I'm not convinced Horst had or knew anything about those, but as we discussed this morning, just before he lost consciousness, he whispered those other words I still don't understand about looking somewhere for something…"

"Okay. I got that we're supposed to look in a small place under something, but *Schlupwindel?*"

"Yeah, when I put that into Google Translate I got 'slip diaper.'"

"Slip diaper?"

"Yeah. Go figure."

Eva stared for a minute. Then she stood up and swayed a bit. "I'm going to the ladies' room. When I get back you'd better take me to the hotel before people start to think the three glasses of water I just had with lunch were all spiked with vodka."

"Roger." Derek signaled to the waiter to bring the check.

In the car, Eva fell asleep almost immediately. When Derek pulled up at the hotel entrance, he gently shook her awake. For a moment her gaze was uncomprehending, but then she replaced it with a faint smile.

"Thanks, Derek. I'll sleep now. Hopefully, I'll be more myself tomorrow."

"Do that. I'm in Vermont all week. I want to do whatever I can to help, Eva."

"Tomorrow, please take me to Dad's cabin. I want to see it." He gave her a questioning look, but Eva nodded. "I *need* to see it."

"Okay. I'll meet you for breakfast. Say nine-thirty? After that, we can go to your dad's place if you really want to."

A new front was coming in from the northwest and the temperature was again dropping fast. As Derek left Burlington, the thermometer on the Northwoods Bank read 2° F. The forecast was for a low of –15° F that night and a high of only –5° F the next day. Hardly great weather for Eva to go tramping around her dad's place in the light clothing she'd brought from Africa.

CHAPTER 37

The next morning, Derek called Eva's room from the lobby.

"Five more minutes, Derek. I'm almost ready."

She emerged from the elevator attired in hiking boots, ski pants, a sweater, and carrying a new red parka. She didn't look tired anymore, and Derek realized he wasn't going to dissuade her from heading to her dad's place just because it was –6° F outside.

"After I got a few hours of sleep and could think straight, I realized I obviously had to get some different clothes. It's going to be cold in Montreal too when I go there to talk to the RCMP and sort through Dad's apartment. So I took a cab to the L.L. Bean store to get provisioned. I would've bought this stuff in any case if…" her voice caught, "…if I'd come here next week to stay with Dad."

Eva was eager to get started, so Derek stopped at a McDonald's for coffee and two breakfast biscuits they could eat along the way.

Three and half days after the fire, the smell of burned wood still hung in the air as they approached the cabin site. The footprints left by Horst and his assailants were now obscured by those of the CSI team as well as the track of the snowmobile and sled used to remove the body of the burned man.

At the sight of cabin's remains, Eva tensed and stopped for a moment.

"You sure you want to go on? There really isn't anything left to look at."

"Yes. I need to. This place was terribly important to Dad. It's going to be hard, but I wouldn't feel right if I didn't come here one more time."

As they approached the charred remains, Eva said, "If the killer thinks Dad had other eggs besides the one he found here and that you or I know where they are, then we're his logical next target." She looked around nervously. "Do you suppose it's possible he could be watching even now?"

"I very much doubt it. The guy who left the cabin that night was wounded, maybe seriously. I figure he's well away from here and, as Evans suggested, likely to keep his head down for a while. But since he at least *thinks* your dad had other eggs, you and I do need to watch out."

Eva shivered and said, "I'd feel better if I had my pistol with me."

Derek looked at her with surprise. She was reminding him even more of the Phryne Fisher character. "Really? I guess I never figured you for a person who went around heeled."

"Not something I really wanted to do, but our clinic has been broken into three times by people looking for drugs, and there have been several assaults in the neighborhood where I live. So I finally got one, and I've learned how to use it."

Walking slowly around the remnants of the cabin, Derek kept looking, hoping to see something that might help identify and catch Horst's killer. He was thinking of Locard's exchange principle, that the perpetrator of a crime will usually bring something into the crime scene and leave with something taken from it, both of which can be used as forensic evidence. With Eva looking on, he pointed out the open, empty strongbox Horst had kept hidden under a trapdoor in the floor he had normally used to stow his passport, checkbook, extra cash, and other items of value he didn't wish to carry everywhere during his summers in Vermont. The police had spotted it right away. With its top thrown open and nothing inside, it seemed his killers must have found what they were looking for.

At what had been the back of the cabin, they looked at the two sets of footprints, now partially snow filled. The set entering the woods had to have been made by Horst. Eva followed them and Derek trailed behind. Perhaps something short of a hundred yards they ended by a creek, now completely frozen over.

Derek said, "Your dad must have waded some way down the creek, then got out on the other side and somehow managed to drag himself pretty near a half mile to my place. When I found him, his pants were covered with ice. I can scarcely imagine how he managed to do that. If only…" Derek took Eva in his arms and held her for a long moment.

Returning to the clearing bordering what had been the back of the cabin, Derek glanced at the two clothes poles Horst had erected some years ago, placed his hand on the nearer one, and chuckled. "Clothes poles! Your dad was something else, Eva. He could've washed and dried his clothes at the laundro-mat in Johnson for two bucks. But no, he had to scrub his clothes on a wash-board by that creek, then tote them back her to dry."

Eva smiled. "I know. Dad was eccentric, but I loved him for that."

Stepping away, Derek's mitten snagged on a splinter of wood. As he pulled it free, he saw the splinter was just one of several surrounding a small hole. A bullet hole! It didn't go all the way through, so the slug must still be inside. Something the CSI team had missed.

Returning to the road to get a cell phone signal, Derek called Sheriff Tate to tell her what he'd found. "Wait there, Derek. Don't touch anything and don't try to take the bullet out. I'll send Dave Cole out with a camera and an evidence bag, and you can show him what you've got."

Later, when Derek brought Eva back to the Sheraton, he noticed a poster in the lobby advertising a performance of Shakespeare's *Richard III* at UVM that evening. He suggested checking to see if tickets were still available, but Eva seemed hesitant.

"Hey, I know *Richard III* isn't the most uplifting play, but you really should get out and do something. Don't just sit in your room and feel terrible."

"Well…"

Assuming the hunchbacked posture of the play's leading character, Derek said, "Now is the winter of our discontent, to be made sweet again if milady would but accompany me to the theater this evening."

"You?"

"I'll have you know I played Richard III in college, and *humbly* suggest my interpretation to have been most excellent."

This made Eva laugh. She replied, "My liege, nothing so becomes a man as modest stillness and humility. I would fain satisfy thy plea."

"Very good, Eva."

"Well, you're not the only Shakespearean here. I played Desdemona in *Othello*."

"Impressive, but I hope we both do better in this life than the characters we've played."

"Amen."

After the play, Derek and Eva returned to the hotel and sat talking over a bottle of Sauvignon blanc in the nearly empty bar. She wore a simple black dress accented by an emerald necklace that complemented her green eyes. Derek had begun the day dressed in his Steve Jobs look-alike outfit, jeans and a black turtleneck, but after a quick trip downtown managed to find a gray tweed jacket to top it off.

Derek said, "You know your dad wanted us to get to know each other. He told me he thought we would make a good couple. I'm only sorry it's tragedy that's finally brought us together."

Eva nodded and held his gaze. "Yes. Dad told me the same thing. I suppose he also told you I was engaged for two years to a colleague in California. I really thought Jeff and I were good. I was looking forward to marriage, trying to figure out how to start a family before my biological clock ran out, and also keep my career going. Anyway, that all blew away when I learned he'd been having an extended affair with another woman, a very wealthy young widow with an artificial front and rear for God's sake. I did say *very wealthy*, right? That turned out to be what he really wanted. He didn't even act sorry when this all came out. He just told me he was moving on. I don't know how I was blind to that for so long."

"You had good reason to feel angry and hurt."

"I did. That's why I finally decided to take a leave from my practice group and spend a year in Africa. I figured I could still do useful stuff and help people while I tried to get my head straight, but I needed to get away and do that somewhere else. Ghana was definitely *somewhere else*. So, where are you right now, Derek?"

"Since your dad was working on both of us, I guess you know I was married for twenty-five years. Julie and I had a daughter, Katherine. Most people just call her Kate. She's a lawyer working in Philadelphia. Ours was a good marriage. I loved Julie very much. Five years ago, they found a lump. It was breast cancer. Julie had surgery, but the cancer spread, so surgery was followed by radiation and chemo. For a time we thought she'd beat it, but it came back. She passed away three years ago. I didn't...I still haven't completely dealt with that."

Eva didn't say anything, just reached out and covered Derek's hand with hers.

The next morning, Derek drove back to Burlington to have breakfast with Eva before taking her to the bus station. She was scheduled to meet later that day with Sergeant Malcolm McConnell of the RCMP, and after that planned to spend time sorting through her dad's things at his apartment.

CHAPTER 38

At six forty-five Sunday evening, Derek pulled into the garage at the Burlington International Airport and waited for Eva to call when her bus arrived at the station next door. He had just enough time to grab a coffee in the terminal before his phone rang. The bus from Montreal was early for a change.

He'd spoken with Eva every day she'd been in Montreal. Thursday evening she'd called to tell him the RCMP had found on her dad's computer a lengthy email with multiple pictures of the egg he had sent to the Rubenstein Gallery in New York, as well as a return email from Arkady Rubenstein expressing interest and urging a phone call to arrange a viewing in either Montreal or New York. Horst's phone records also showed that he had called and spoken for several minutes with someone at the number suggested in Mr. Rubenstein's email. That was the same day he later sent to her the email containing a single picture of the egg saying Rubenstein was interested in it. John Evans was now on his way to New York to interview Rubenstein and his employees along with a detective friend in the NYPD.

When Derek called Eva on Friday, he found her feeling pretty low after spending the morning making funeral arrangements and the rest of the day at the apartment deciding which of her dad's things to keep and which to give away or discard. But now, on Sunday evening, she looked positively buoyant as he pulled over to pick her up.

"Derek. I found him! I found Otto Krummel, or rather Dad did. I was going through some papers in his desk this morning and found a copy of a shipping manifest listing an Otto Krummel, age forty-one, as a passenger on a Swedish ship named *Stockholm*. It sailed from Gothenburg to New York in February, 1951."

"That sounds right. When I drove him to Burlington last fall, he said Gerda told him her last contact with Klaus had been a letter he sent to her from Stockholm. But Sweden definitely wasn't a place he'd intended to go. Something must have happened that forced a change in plans. That has to make me wonder if he was able to get the treasure out of Latvia. Maybe it's still there."

"No way to know at this point, but I'd really like to see what more I can learn about my grandfather's life as Otto Krummel. Do you suppose he stayed in the U.S.? Wherever he went and whatever he did there, he must be dead by now. He'd be 104 years old if he's still alive."

"Right. Let's go back to the hotel and get something to eat. Then we'll search through U.S. death records from 1951 on up and see if we can find one for an Otto Krummel."

Two hours later, Derek turned his laptop so Eva could see the screen, and said, "This could be him." Krummel wasn't a common surname, and his search had turned up only three recorded deaths in the U.S. since 1951 for a Krummel with the given name Otto. One referenced an individual born in 1887 who died in 1960 at seventy-three years of age in Syracuse, New York. Another was for a child born in 1973 who died in 1975 in Chicago, Illinois. The third was for a forty-three-year-old man listed as having died in March, 1953 in Ishpeming, Michigan.

"If the Otto who came to the U.S. from Sweden on the *Stockholm* is the same person who went to Ishpeming, Michigan, why did he go there, what did he do, did he marry, and did he have children? If he did, I might even have an aunt or an uncle or maybe some cousins I don't know about. And how, I wonder, did he die?"

Derek did a quickie search on Ishpeming, learning it was a small city of about 6,500 persons located in Marquette County in the central portion of the Upper Peninsula of Michigan, and that the city once had been a center for deep shaft iron mining.

"Maybe Otto got a job working as a miner in Ishpeming. But why go to a place like that if he had the treasure he hid in Latvia during the war? I'd have thought he'd head to a big city where he could quietly sell or pawn the stuff. Again, it makes me wonder if he might have been forced to leave Latvia without getting what he came for. As far as his cause of death, we can request a copy of the death certificate. We can also check to see if microfilms of the local newspaper from that period are available. If so, maybe we can find an obituary and see if he was mentioned in the paper during that period for any other reason."

"I absolutely want to do all those things, Derek. Although right now I've really got to get back to the practice group in Palo Alto. I called Joe Donnelly from Montreal this morning and told him about everything that's happened. He was very sympathetic and said I should take all the time I need, but I can't stand to just sit around waiting for the police to find Dad's killer. I…I hope maybe going back to work will help me stay sane, and we can work on Otto Krummel later as time allows."

Derek gave Eva a hug, turned back to his laptop, entered *USAirways.com*, and said, "Okay, let's get you back home."

The next morning, as they ate breakfast before heading to the airport, Eva got a call from Detective Evans. He had two things to tell her. One was that the RCMP had been able to identify a fingerprint lifted from a syringe found in a wastebasket in Horst's apartment. Residue in the syringe had been identified as a potent mix of heroin and fentanyl, while the fingerprint matched one belonging to Vasily Kozlov, a foot soldier in the Russian mafia. So Evans now figured Kozlov was almost certainly the smaller of the two men who abducted Horst and was the corpse found shot in the heart and burned beyond recognition in the remains of the cabin. That was something to be verified when they finally got results from the pending DNA analysis. In any case, Evans figured the other man was probably affiliated with the Russian mafia as well.

The other information Evans had was that he and his NYPD friend had interviewed Arkady Rubenstein and five of his seven employees at the Rubenstein Gallery. Mr. Rubenstein had been cooperative. He seemed genuinely surprised and disturbed to learn what had happened to Horst. He told Evans a tentative appointment had been made to see and look at the egg in New York after Gustmann suggested later bringing it to the gallery with his daughter. He denied knowing a Vasily Kozlov as did the other five employees they had been able to interview. Two other employees were currently out of town, one of them out of the country for a time, and would be interviewed in the future. Somehow, the information Horst gave Rubenstein had passed into the wrong hands, but as yet it wasn't clear when, how, or by whom.

An hour later, Derek drove Eva to the airport. At the entrance to the security checkpoint Eva said, "I'm glad you were with Dad at the end, and you've been very kind to me. Would you…that is…I'd like it if maybe you could visit me in California sometime."

"I'd like that a lot, Eva. How about the week before Easter? Franklin University is on spring break then."

"It's a date, Derek." She reached up, kissed him lightly, then turned away and joined the line of passengers being screened.

"Be sure to call me when you get home, Eva, and stay safe."

"You, too."

CHAPTER 39

A week and a half after his abortive attempt to steal Horst Gustmann's Fabergé egg, Sergei sat in his Manhattan apartment staring out the window at the East River. His wound was healing, but it still hurt enough to make him limp a little, and he was in a foul mood over how things had gone. His first thought in the morning and the last at night was pretty much the same. *STUPID FUCKING VASILY!* Sergei checked his laptop daily for any further reports from Burlington TV station WCAX or the *Burlington Free Press* concerning the death of Horst Gustmann. On Monday, two days after Sergei got back to Manhattan, the newspaper had printed a short piece stating that a clerk at the Sunset Motel in Morrisville had advised police he'd seen a black Mercedes-Benz G550 SUV, a vehicle often equipped with tires having a tread like those found near the murdered man's cabin, pass by, heading east on Route 15 around 2:30 A.M. Saturday morning. Police were now on the lookout for such a vehicle.

Sergei smirked as he read that, thinking it a good thing he'd ditched the vehicle as soon as he'd returned to the city. No big loss there. It was already on the way to Africa to fill an advance order from some warlord.

In a subsequent report two days later, both the *Burlington Free Press* and WCAX mentioned that the dead man found in Horst Gustmann's burned out cabin had yet to be positively identified. However, the ME had released a statement saying the deceased was a fairly young man, probably Caucasian, about five feet seven inches in height and of medium build, and that he hadn't been killed by the fire but rather by a bullet fired from a gun of a caliber different than that used to kill Horst Gustmann."

Nothing to lead the cops directly to me. Still, this left Sergei with an uneasy feeling. Sooner or later, the police would identify Vasily. Then it wouldn't be much of a stretch to connect Vasily to him. In spite of extensive involvement with criminal activities in both the U.S. and Canada, until now, Sergei had managed to keep his personal record clean. That was due in large measure to expert legal advice combined with the careful delegation of riskier activities to subordinates paid to take a fall for the boss, if necessary. But the venture with Vasily had been an impulsive thing. So far, he hadn't yet told anyone except Tatiana about what had happened to Vasily. Maybe he ought to let *certain* people know before the police announced a positive ID. But he had to be careful. As wild and crazy as Vasily was, he had friends in the *Bratva* who might not easily forgive him.

And the egg? Sergei knew the old man had had it, and he still wanted it. Recalling the story his great uncle related years ago, it seemed to have become an obsession. The pictures Gustmann sent to the gallery closely matched a detailed description of an egg described in a letter written to a friend by Empress Alexandra Feodorovna in 1905, a letter Rubenstein had somehow acquired, but about which the rest of the art world seemed ignorant. Copies of the letter and Gustmann's email to Rubenstein had been passed to Sergei by a contact at the gallery who was cooperating with the *Bratva* on another project. That had been enough to convince him to go after Gustmann, although he still found it hard to believe the old man would have kept something like that at his cabin. And the other missing eggs? That first write up in the *Burlington Free Press* seemed to hint Gustmann *might* have told his friend, Professor Derek Todson, something about them just before he died.

Sergei needed to find a way to learn what the Todson guy and Gustmann's daughter knew about her father's "legacy." With that in mind, he put a call through to Mikhail Filipov in Moscow.

"*Da*, Sergei?"

"Mikhail, I need a favor. There are a couple people whose thoughts and conversations are of great interest to me."

"You want me to bug their phones and computers?"

"Exactly."

"The computers? Easy. It may take a little time, but I'm sure I can get you in. The phones? That's easy only if you can get hold of them for a little while. Remotely, it's a much bigger challenge. If you're close, you can set up a fake cell tower to grab and listen to a call. The police and the KGB do that all the time. But to listen from a long distance, you need to get lucky, maybe convince your people to download a free app or use a public charging station loaded with spyware that quickly transfers to the phone."

"Okay, Mikhail. Hack into their computers and their phones if you can. I want to read their emails and texts and listen to their Skype conversations if they use that."

"First, tell me whatever you know about these people. I expect they're not the sort of complete idiots just waiting to respond to Mrs. Lovey Aberjidian, widow of the ex-Vice President of Walawalaland, who wants to share thirty million dollars in a secret Swiss bank?"

Sergei chuckled. "Yeah, Mikhail, they're definitely not that. One is a woman named Eva Gustmann, a physician with a practice in California who just came back from a year in Africa working for *Médecins Sans Frontières*. The other is a guy named Derek Todson. He's some kind of professor at Franklin University in Philadelphia."

"Okay, Sergei. I'll Google them, find out more about who they are, their backgrounds, what they do, and what professional organizations they belong to. One possible way to get in might be through a fake email message about an upcoming meeting of an organization they belong to with an attachment that looks like a meeting schedule or a registration form. If they click on that, we're in. Or I could send a fake notice that includes a picture with an embedded spy program. With that, the mark doesn't have to do anything to get infected. The spy program silently downloads while he's just reading the message and looking at the picture. Neat, huh?"

"Yeah, and scary, Mikhail. Now I don't want to use my own computer. But go ahead. I need to keep tabs on these two. Keep in touch."

"Of course, the picture thing can fail if the computer is on a network that scans all pictures for bad stuff before allowing it to be shown. But trust me. I'm an expert. One way or another I'll get you in. However, I am curious, Sergei. Are you going to tell me why it's so important to track these two? This is a custom job that may take a fair bit of time to complete. Am I going to…you know?"

"I can't say more right now, Mikhail. But don't worry. I'll make it worth your time."

CHAPTER 40

For Eva, getting back to the medical practice did help. She quickly became so busy during office hours she didn't have time to think much about her father's death. Nights were a different matter. She talked with Derek daily and looked forward to April when he planned to visit over a weekend. The heavy patient load at the clinic, together with Derek's teaching and research at Franklin University, had largely sidelined their efforts to look into Otto Krummel's past. But one evening, she told Derek she'd finally sent off a letter to the Michigan Department of Health and Human Services requesting a copy of Otto Krummel's death certificate. In return, he told her he'd finished researching U.S. marriage and birth records but could find no evidence Otto had married or fathered any children between 1951 and 1953. He'd also learned that Northern Michigan University in Marquette, Michigan, maintained microfilm copies of *The Mining Journal*, a local paper that would have covered news from Ishpeming and the surrounding area during the time Otto lived there.

"Once you get the death certificate, we should plan a trip to the Upper Peninsula of Michigan. We can find out where Otto is buried, see what Ishpeming looks like, and maybe even find someone who knew him. And in Marquette we can search through microfilm copies of the newspaper for 1951 to 1953 to see if we can find an obituary or any other articles about him."

"I'd really like to do that. Right now, I'm totally booked and putting in like sixty hours a week for about forever. It'll be quite a while before I can get more than a day or two off. At least it won't be that long before I get to see you again."

Two weeks later, Derek texted Eva as his flight from Philadelphia pulled into its gate at SFO. A few minutes later he was in a Super Shuttle van heading to Palo Alto. At the clinic, Derek introduced himself to the receptionist then settled into a chair to wait until Eva got a free minute. A few minutes later she walked out just long enough to let him know it would be another hour.

"No problem. I've been looking at local restaurants for dinner. How does the INDO on El Camino sound at seven-thirty?"

"It's a good one. I ought to be done here by seven."

The Thursday evening crowd at INDO was light, and they were able to score a quiet candlelit table in a far corner. Derek looked at his date. She had on the same simple black dress and emerald necklace she'd worn for the production of *Richard III* at UVM in Burlington. Once again, the female detective character, Phryne Fisher, came to mind. Well, he and Eva were definitely working a mystery. So did that cast him as Inspector Jack Robinson? On *Miss Fisher's Murder Mysteries*, it seemed something always happened to prevent the attraction Phryne and Jack obviously had for each other from developing fully. He hoped that needn't be the case here.

From the wine list, Jack selected a 2010 Freemark Abbey Cabernet Sauvignon, and Phryne nodded her approval. After studying the menu for a few minutes, they settled on chicken satay, a salad of grilled prawns and spinach with toasted coconut and peanuts, and braised Australian lamb shank for an entrée.

With their plates cleared and coffee ordered, Eva opened her briefcase, took out a document, and put it on the table. "This came yesterday. It's Otto Krummel's death certificate and there's a surprise. It says he was murdered."

Derek scanned the document. A box labeled **Date of Death** contained the date *March 8, 1953*, but the entry in a subsequent box labeled **Pronounced Dead On** was *June 17, 1953*. Under the heading **Occupation**, the certificate listed *mine safety engineer*, and under the heading **Marital Status**, it said *widowed*. There were no entries under **Father's Name** or **Mother's Name**, but someone named *Kristin Albrecht* was listed in a box bearing the heading **Informant**. The answer to the surprising discrepancy between the dates listed under **Date of Death** and **Pronounced Dead On** was explained later in a section entitled **Cause of Death**. It didn't simply list a primary cause and possible secondary contributing causes of death, but devoted a full paragraph of text stating that this was a certificate of presumptive death issued in the absence of a body. It went on to explain the certificate had been issued based on forensic evidence suggesting the deceased had suffered a bullet wound that might have been fatal. And if not killed by the bullet, then Mr. Krummel would have surely drowned when thrown from his car, discovered upside down, doors open, submerged in the frigid waters of Lake Superior. District judge Malcolm Johnson's signature appeared at the bottom of the certificate.

Derek looked up. "Murdered! The evidence for that must have been pretty compelling for the judge to authorize this certificate after just a few months."

"It's creepy, but I remember reading that in very cold water the bacteria that generate gas as a body decomposes aren't able to grow. It's possible a body can remain almost completely preserved at the bottom of a cold lake for years."

"Not a pleasant thought with which to finish off a nice dinner."

"Sorry. Do you suppose, like my dad, he was murdered by someone after his Russian treasure?"

"Possibly, but we need to know more. Now I'm really eager to have a look at old issues of *The Mining Journal* to see what they might tell us. We need to schedule that trip, Eva."

A look through their respective calendars offered scant hope of doing anything in the near future. Finally they settled on the third week of June. Derek's last class at Franklin University ended on Friday, June 13. He was free to travel the following week. Eva figured she could get free at that time if she agreed to do double duty the previous week, covering both her own patients and those of Joan Callahan, who was hoping to take that week off. She would offer and ask Joan to cover for her the third week of June.

Friday and Saturday were great. Derek and Eva spent the time being tourists in and around San Francisco and getting to know each other better. But Sunday came too soon. At 7:00 A.M., as Derek was waiting at the gate for his flight back to Philadelphia, his phone buzzed. It was Kate.

"Hi, Counselor."

"Hi, Dad. So how was it?"

"What do you mean?"

Kate chuckled. "What do you mean by that, Dad? You spent the weekend with a beautiful woman. So how did it go?"

"I…well…"

"Not badly, I hope." Her voice took on a note of concern.

"No, we had a good time. At least I did, and I think Eva did, too. We talked a lot, ate a lot, and did typical tourist stuff. We walked through part of Golden Gate Park and went to the Japanese Tea House. After that, we went over by the piers, got chocolate at Ghiardelli's, had a lunch of chowder in a sourdough bread bowl at Boudin's, and took a tour of San Francisco Bay on one of the Blue and Gold boats at Pier 39. When we got back from that, we finished off the afternoon spending a whole bunch of quarters at the Musée Méchanique. After that, we returned to Eva's place in Palo Alto, made spaghetti, and shared a great bottle of cabernet sauvignon. How's that for a travelogue?"

"Cool. And then?"

"Jeez, Kate! Let's just say we didn't do anything for which I'd be arrested if she was underage."

"Sorry, Dad. I know I shouldn't push. It's just that you've been so down for so long. I've been hoping you'd meet someone you really like. I know you didn't care for Rachel."

"I didn't *dislike* Rachel, Kate. We just didn't click, you know?"

"Yeah. Of course, I haven't met Eva, but in the picture you showed me she looks really pretty, foxy even, and it seems like you guys have a fair bit in common professionally."

"I like her a lot, Kate."

"Good luck, Dad."

"Thanks. Maybe this'll go somewhere. But give us a little time. Okay?"

"Got it. Love you, Dad. See you tonight for dinner. We're reserved at seven at the City Tavern."

"Sounds good. They're calling my flight now. Bye."

CHAPTER 41

Taking converging flights from San Francisco and Philadelphia, Eva and Derek met in Detroit the afternoon of June 15. There, they boarded a one-hour flight to Sawyer International Airport (MQT). The small facility seventeen miles south of Marquette had a fantastically long runway because it had once been part of K.I. Sawyer, a SAC airbase that closed in 1995. But there was only a single terminal building with just three gates, only two of which appeared to be used on any regular basis. As Derek waited by the carousel for their bags, Eva walked over to the Hertz counter to claim their rental car. Five minutes later they were on their way in a white 2014 Impala parked just a hundred feet away in slot number two.

Eva said, "There's something to be said for a place like this. Virtually no lines and your plane is always the first in line to land or take off."

"Yup, though I'm guessing this could sometimes be a tough place to get to or away from in the midst of winter. If your flight gets cancelled by weather or mechanical problems, there aren't many options. Delta has just two flights a day from Detroit, and American has only one from Chicago."

Twenty-five minutes later, Eva pulled into the new Hampton Inn adjacent to Lake Superior on the south side of Marquette. After check-in, the desk clerk pointed out the breakfast room where they could get coffee or tea 24/7, and the platter of complementary cookies by the elevator. Thus provisioned, Derek and Eva headed upstairs to their room overlooking the lake.

Even though Eva had made the arrangements for both the car and their room, she now looked a little uncertain. Looking at each other from the opposite sides of the king bed, she actually blushed a bit. Derek didn't say anything but allowed his imagination free rein. He wasn't going to push, just wait to see if there was a signal.

The weather was perfect, sunny, blue sky, 72°F, and low humidity. The girl at the reception desk had urged them to get out and enjoy it, recommending a walk downtown along the lake and a waterfront restaurant named L'attitude. An hour and a half later, after a dinner of Lake Superior whitefish tacos, coconut shrimp, and a local beer, Derek and Eva strolled through Mattson Park fronting Marquette's lower harbor. There they bought Mackinac Island Fudge ice cream cones and sat for a while, watching other people walk by.

In June, at latitude 46.5° N, it didn't get dark in Marquette until well past ten o'clock. Returning to the hotel, Eva and Derek got coffees, took them to the outdoor patio, and sat, looking at the lake and a flock of noisy seagulls on a rocky islet next to the old ore dock. Then Eva returned to the room, returned with a bottle of the same wine they'd enjoyed at INDO in Palo Alto.

An hour later, they called it a day. Upstairs, he quickly scanned the current edition of *The Mining Journal* as Eva hung up the blouse and skirt she planned to wear the next day. Tomorrow they planned to go to the university to search through microfilm copies of *The Mining Journal* from the early 1950s. Eva headed to the bathroom, emerging a few minutes later in a sheer blue babydoll nightie. Walking across the room, she pulled the drapes shut, turned, and gave Derek a little smile.

Oh wow! And blue for heaven's sake, just like in the TV ads. Derek stood and turned out the light.

CHAPTER 42

The next morning, Derek and Eva sought out the archivist at the Northern Michigan University Learning Resource Center, received her permission to review microfilms of *The Mining Journal* for the years 1951-3, and spent the next several hours scrolling through hundreds of pages. In 1951 they found a single reference to Otto Krummel, a brief entry in the February 21 edition that mentioned the promotion of two Ishpeming-based Cleveland Cliffs administrators and the hiring of a mine safety engineer with that name. A review of papers published in 1952 yielded two more references. In one brief report, Otto Krummel was cited as having caught the second largest bass in a fishing contest at a lake near Ishpeming. The second article concerned a group of five Cleveland Cliffs employees, including Otto Krummel, who were being honored for helping restore a summer camp used by local brownies and girl scouts. That one included a picture allowing Eva to confirm it did look like the man in the old photo her dad had had of his parents.

In 1953, they hit the jackpot. As Derek scanned through papers published in January and then February, he noticed an article in the one published on February 25 concerning a tunnel collapse at the Mather D mine triggered by a rare, though mild, earthquake. The collapse and buried and killed two workers, while two others, including Otto Krummel, survived but sustained injuries. Six days later, the paper published on March 3 showed a picture of Otto Krummel receiving congratulations from the mayor and the local head of CCI operations for having saved the life of his colleague, Eino Hakala.

Continuing on, Derek paged through more editions, stopping briefly to scan a story published on Friday, March 6. "Hey. Here's an interesting story, although it doesn't mention Otto. A couple kids found a body in an old mine just north of Ishpeming. It says here the body was that of a man recently killed by a single shot to the head from a gun found at the scene. It doesn't say why, but the police seem to think it was a murder rather than a suicide."

A follow-up article published the next day provided a more detailed description of the dead man, along with a picture and an explanation as to why the police felt this was a murder; although the man appeared to be right-handed, he'd been shot in the left temple. *The Mining Journal* didn't have a Sunday edition, so the next issue Derek scanned was the one published on Monday, March 9. Again, there was no mention of Otto Krummel, but a follow-up article concerning the murder, including a new item of information that sent a jolt of electricity through him.

"Wow! Eva! Listen to this. It says here a reception clerk at the Northland Hotel in Marquette recognized the picture of the dead man published in the Saturday edition of the paper and identified him as a businessman named John Abercrombie, who'd been registered at the hotel during the third week of February. He's quoted as saying Mr. Abercrombie disappeared on February 18 without checking out or paying his bill."

"So?"

"Here's what! The clerk recalled taking a telephone message on February 17 from someone named Gustmann, concerning a dinner meeting the two men were supposed to have the next day at the Mather Inn in Ishpeming. The article goes on to say the police found no such reservation existed. They think both Abercrombie and Gustmann were pseudonyms, not the real names of these men."

"That must have been my grandfather. Do you really suppose he could have killed that man? But why? And why would he have used his real name?"

"My guess is Abercrombie, whoever he really was, already knew that Otto Krummel was really Klaus Gustmann. Somehow, I'll bet he knew about the treasure Klaus had found and either planned to kill him once he got it, or maybe he knew too much about Klaus's history during the war, and decided to take a blackmail approach, threatening to leak his true identity to the authorities if he wasn't given a big payoff. Either way, Klaus would've have had a good reason to want to get rid of him."

Eva looked over Derek's shoulder as he advanced the microfiche reader the March 10 issue of the paper. "Whoa! There it is." The reader showed side by side front page articles about Otto Krummel. The first one was titled, **Ishpeming Man Missing and Presumed Dead—Car Found Submerged in Lake Superior**, while the header for the second read, **Police Investigate Invasion of Missing Man's Home**. Derek pushed the button to print a copy of the screen. Then he and Eva quickly read through both reports.

"It says here Otto Krummel's car was found submerged in Lake Superior off Presque Isle in Marquette early Monday morning, March 9. That's consistent with the March 8 date shown on his death certificate."

"With no body, it's obvious my grandfather isn't buried in Ishpeming, so I suppose it isn't worth checking with the Ishpeming cemetery. Still, do you suppose his friends might have put up some sort of marker as a memorial? I keep wondering about this Kristin Albrecht, the person listed on his death certificate as 'informant'."

Derek stretched. "We can keep looking through more issues of the paper. There might be something there about a memorial service or marker. I'd also like to find out if the police were able to track down the guys who broke into your grandfather's house. Presumably they're the same ones who shot him. Right now I'm seeing double and it's already past noon. How about we get some lunch and come back tomorrow? Let's drive to Ishpeming, see if the place where your grandfather lived might still be standing, and maybe find someone old enough to have known him." The article describing the break-in at Otto's home in Ishpeming gave his address as 176 Iron Street. Eva put the address in her phone and asked the GPS to plot a route.

The house at 176 Iron Street was still standing, but in desperate need of repair. At one time it had been white, but now much of the paint had peeled away, leaving a checkered pattern of dirty paint and areas of naked gray clapboard. The roof sagged in the middle, a number of shingles were missing, and the rest were worn to a point where they retained hardly any of the original pebbling. The glass in a small attic window facing the street had been replaced by an unpainted square of plywood. What had once been a single car garage at the end of a cracked asphalt driveway had collapsed completely and was just a pile of rubble. For all that, the place appeared to be inhabited. A rusty blue Ford 150 pickup sat in the driveway. And in the front yard, a little blonde, blue-eyed girl happily rode her spring-mounted, pink bouncy horse. She smiled and waved at the two strangers as they sat in their car and looked at her house. Eva waved back.

"I guess I didn't really expect to learn anything here, unless we happened to find a nice ninety-year-old couple sitting on the front porch who knew my grandfather. The people living here now can't have been there very long. So what's next?"

"I'm thinking the police station would be a logical place to start. Not that we're likely to find someone really old there, but since the police were involved with Otto's disappearance and the break-in at his home, maybe we can learn if any of the officers involved at the time are still alive, living in the area, and might be willing to talk to us."

The desk sergeant at the station was a woman who looked to be in her thirties. She had never heard of Otto Krummel and was pretty sure no one in the current department would have any knowledge of a murder that had happened as far back as 1953. However, she suggested they contact Bill Bullock, the recently retired chief of police. At seventy-two he would have been only eleven when Otto was murdered, but she thought he *might* recall something about it. When he was the chief of police, she said Bullock had managed to solve a couple "cold cases" from the past.

Eva called the number the desk sergeant gave her. A woman answered, Eva introduced herself, and asked if it she could speak to Mr. Bullock.

"Are you that Eva from the credit card company, the one always trying to sell us some service we sure as heck don't need?"

"Uh, no ma'am. I'm Dr. Eva Gustmann, a physician from California, and I'm in Ishpeming with a friend trying to find out more about my grandfather who once lived here and was murdered in 1953. Sergeant Mattson at the police station told me that Chief Bullock recently retired, but he'd been much interested in working on cold cases and might be able to tell me something more about the death of my grandfather."

"Oh yes, of course. I'm sorry, Dr. Gustmann. Please hold and I'll ask Bill. Since he retired he's been as restless as a bear in the spring. Right now he's in the back yard taking out his frustration on some blocks of wood with an ax."

A minute later, she returned and said, "Bill said he'd be happy to talk to you about an old unsolved murder. Would you like to come here?" She gave Eva the address and directions for finding the house.

When they pulled up ten minutes later, Bill was waiting at the curb, a tall and somewhat corpulent but well-muscled man with a florid complexion and a shock of white hair. Eva introduced herself and Derek. She first told Bullock about her father, Horst Gustmann, being kidnapped and killed by two Russian men, who stole a valuable jeweled object originally left to him as a legacy by his father, Klaus Gustmann. Klaus and Horst had become separated during the war and never managed to find each other again. Now, having lost her father, she was trying to learn more about her grandfather Klaus. Apparently, he came to the U.S. in 1951 and lived in Ishpeming under an assumed name, Otto Krummel, and two years later was murdered.

"Otto Krummel," said Bullock. "I do recall reading about that case. Two men broke into his home and tossed it looking for something. The next day, his car was found submerged, upside down, in Lake Superior. The body was never recovered, but they found several bullet holes in the car windows and in the collar of a jacket inside the car."

"That's what we learned just this morning by looking through old issues of *The Mining Journal*. But we only got part way through March of 1953 before we decided to take a break. Can you tell us if the police ever figured out what those men were looking for and if his murder was ever solved?"

"As far as I know, the police never did find out what those guys were looking for and whether they found it or not. The next morning, they abandoned the stolen car they'd been driving outside Kingsford, Wisconsin. Then they tried to steal another one, but the owner caught them at it. There was a shoot-out. He killed one of the burglars, but the other guy managed to get away with the car."

"Was he ever caught?"

"Yes and no. The police had a description of the car and put out an APB. They got several reports from people who thought they'd seen it. Apparently, he sort of seesawed back and forth on a bunch of rural highways. Eventually the police caught up with him on the outskirts of Chicago. There was a high-speed chase. He lost control, hit a bridge abutment, and was killed."

"Leaving no one left to question about the break-in or my grandfather's murder?"

"Right. So case closed? Maybe. But there was something that intrigued me about it. I read everything I could find and talked to some people who had known Otto Krummel. The guy killed back in Kingsford, Wisconsin, was named Gerhard Nelson. His buddy was named Anton Sokolov. Rumor had it that both were affiliated with a communist cell in Chicago run by an agent of the Russian KGB. It was called the MGB back then."

"So, the Russians were after my grandfather in 1953, and more than sixty years later my dad is kidnapped and killed by a member of the Russian mafia. Can that be a coincidence?"

"Makes you wonder. One thing I learned is that the police in Ishpeming questioned whether there might have been a connection between the two guys who broke into Krummel's house, and a murdered man named Anatoly Zaretsky. His body was found by a couple kids in an old, long abandoned mine north of town just a couple of days before the break-in and Krummel's disappearance. Rumor had it Zaretsky was also affiliated with that communist cell in Chicago."

"Were the police able to confirm that?"

"Not definitively. Jack Bennett, who was chief of police at the time, left some notes in the case file. He passed away before I joined the force, but I had some conversations with Tom Corker, another officer on the case. He told me Bennett contacted the FBI, asking them to confirm if Zaretsky, Nelson, and Sokolov had been affiliated with a communist cell in Chicago."

"And?"

"Stonewalled. The FBI refused to confirm or deny the rumor. They just told him 'Fuhgeddaboudit.' Of course, that kind of non-answer from the Feds only serves to convince you they almost certainly were. As for Krummel, the local police began to wonder if he might somehow have been working under-cover for the government to get involved with and then report on the activities of this supposed cell. Maybe his cover somehow got blown, and Zaretsky was sent to take him out. Krummel got to him first, but when Zaretsky's body was discovered, Nelson and Sokolov were dispatched to do the job, and this time they got him. If that's what happened you can imagine the Feds wouldn't be eager to admit losing one of their own."

Bullock continued, "When Krummel's car was found in the lake, Tom Corker was sent to break the news to his girlfriend. She told him Krummel had been very nervous recently, and that when she pressed him, he finally told her agents of the Russian government were looking for him, trying to recover something of great value he'd found during the war."

"Did she tell the officer what that was?"

"I don't think she knew."

"Is Tom Corker still living?"

"He is. He must be about ninety years old now and has to use a walker to get around, but he's perfectly clear in the head. I visit him once in a while. He's living at the Southside Manor Retirement Home in Marquette."

Eva took out her phone. "Can you give me his number? I'd really like to call and ask if he'd be willing to talk to us."

"Sure." Bullock went into his office and came back a minute later with a scrap of paper bearing the address of the home where Tom Corker now resided and his phone number. He handed it to Eva, then said, "Why don't I call him and give him a heads up summary of our conversation? I'm sure Tom will be happy to talk to you."

Eva and Derek waited as Bullock talked to Tom Corker on his cell phone, telling him who they were and their interest in finding out more about Eva's grandfather. Finally ending the call, he said, "Tom's looking forward to meeting you folks, suggested five o'clock for a meeting."

Back in the car, Derek said, "What do you hope to learn from this guy, Eva?"

"I'm not really sure, but Bullock said my grandfather had a girlfriend, so I'm curious about that. Do you suppose she was the Kristin Albrecht identified as informant on Otto's death certificate? I'd really like to get a better sense of who my grandfather was as a person. He looks like a decent guy in the two pictures we saw in the newspaper. But then, there are the awful things Gerda told Dad about him. I can't help wondering, did he also have a good side?"

Eva looked sad. "Now that Dad's gone, I don't have any living relatives I know of. That makes me want to know as much as I can about the people I came from."

"What about your grandparents on your mother's side?"

"Mom was adopted. Her adoptive parents were good to her and to me, but I only got to know them just a little before they passed away. Mom never knew her birth parents. I tried, but I haven't been able to trace them."

Tom Corker was already standing in front of the main entrance to the retirement home with his walker as Eva pulled into the parking lot. Like Bullock, he had a thick shock of white hair, but in build was as lean as Bullock was stocky. He waved as Derek and Eva got out of the car.

"Over here, Dr. Gustmann. Pleased to meet you. Please come inside." Tom led them inside to a corner of the lounge by a table holding urns of coffee and hot water for tea.

"I spent nearly forty years as a cop in Ishpeming, working all kinds of shifts, and that turned me into a real coffee addict. I was also pretty much into having doughnuts with the coffee. Got a special fondness for the frosted ones covered with shredded coconut. That sort of behavior turned a couple of my buddies into three-hundred-pound copies of Jabba the Hutt, but I've always been blessed with a high metabolic rate so managed to escape that fate." He sighed, looking with disdain at a plate holding the small sugar-free cookies the home set out for residents and their guests. "Unfortunately, you can't get a decent doughnut in this place."

Derek said, "Hey, Tom. How about having dinner with us? I've heard good things about the restaurant at the Landmark Inn. We could have a drink, talk awhile, have dinner, and hang out as long as you'd like."

"Offer accepted, Derek. That is, if your car has a trunk big enough to accommodate my assistant here." He pointed to his walker.

"Not a problem."

"Great. Give me five minutes to freshen up and put on something presentable for the occasion."

Seated at a corner table in the restaurant, Eva sipped a glass of Kendall Jackson chardonnay, while Tom and Derek each worked on a Coconut Brown from the local Black Rocks Brewery.

"Chief Bullock said you were directly involved in the investigation of my grandfather's murder and the break-in at his home. Would you tell us what you saw and heard at the time and what you think was going on?"

"Sure. Officially, the case is considered closed, mainly because the FBI refused to give us anything when we tried to get more information about Nelson and Sokolov. We figured they must've trailed and shot Krummel in Presque Isle Park in Marquette before driving back to Ishpeming where they tossed his house. At the time we were already working on the murder of another guy identified as Anatoly Zaretsky, who was also rumored to be connected to a communist cell in Chicago. I don't much believe in coincidence, so we began to suspect Otto Krummel must've been involved in some way with all three guys. Bill told me your grandfather's name was actually Klaus Gustmann, and that just helps confirm what we guessed at the time. I presume you saw that piece in the paper stating that a clerk at this very hotel remembered taking a message for a Mr. Abercrombie, which turned out to be pseudonym for Anatoly Zaretsky, from someone identifying himself as Gustmann?"

"We did. So why do you suppose the FBI stonewalled you when you asked them for help working things out?"

"Hard to know for sure, but I'm thinking the agency was embarrassed and didn't want to officially admit that an illegal Russian spy operation had been going on for some time right under their noses."

"Chief Bullock also told us my grandfather had a girlfriend, and that you talked to her at the time. What can you tell us about her?"

Tom's eyes took on a faraway look. "Her name was Kristin Albrecht, a pretty widow who lived with her daughter Anna on the same street as your grandfather. I gather they met shortly after Otto got to Ishpeming, when she went around the neighborhood with Anna selling Girl Scout cookies. Kristin had been married to a guy named Richard, who went to high school with my older brother. Richard married Kristin just before the war and was drafted soon afterward. He came home on leave in 1942, just long enough to get Anna started before they sent him back into combat. The ironic thing is Richard survived the Battle of the Bulge without a scratch, but a year later when he came home and got a job in the mine, he was killed in a cave-in. Kristin was left alone with a three-year-old child."

"Was the relationship between my grandfather and this woman serious?"

"Oh yeah, I definitely think so. Kristin was scared stiff when she saw those goons tossing his house, but she was more terrified by the fact that Otto had gone missing. He was supposed to come to her place that afternoon for dinner, but he never showed and didn't call. She tried to call him twice and sent Anna over to check in mid-afternoon before going over herself and seeing those guys in the house. The following day when I had to go tell her we'd found his car shot up, upside down with both doors open in the lake, she completely lost it. Then, when she finally got hold of herself, she told us that two days earlier he'd finally let her know he was being hunted by the Russian MGB over something very valuable he'd discovered and taken during the war."

Eva and Derek looked at each other and nodded. *The eggs.*

Tom continued, "Kristin and Anna were terribly grieved by Otto's death. My initial contacts with them were official, but…even though she was older than me, I found myself really attracted to her. I decided to offer any help and support I could outside my official role as a cop, hoping she might become interested in me."

"And?"

"She was always friendly and grateful for whatever I did for her. But no, it was pretty obvious Kristin was stuck on Otto. He was pretty much all she could think about, even a year after he died. She wasn't anywhere near ready to get involved in another relationship.

"Several months after they pulled his car out of the lake, while unusual, the judge decided there was enough evidence to warrant issuing a certificate of death for Otto Krummel. When that happened, Kristin did ask me to go with her to a session of the Probate Court as a friend to hear Otto's will read."

Eva and Derek said together, "His will? Otto left a will?"

"He did, and it was damn strange. As far as anybody knew he didn't own anything worth giving away. But when they opened his safe deposit box at the Hematite Bank, they found a fancy diamond ring, a life insurance policy for $5,000, and a handwritten will, so it had to be probated. It turned out he also had a savings account at the Hematite Bank with a balance of $1,200. Kristin, to her surprise, was named sole beneficiary of the life insurance policy and the intended recipient of the ring. The rest of his estate was to be divided equally between Gerda and Horst Gustmann, described in the will as Otto Krummel's cousin and her son. Apparently, this only consisted of the $1,200 in his savings account and perhaps another $400 if the insurance company was prepared to pay for the loss of his car."

Eva said, "Of course, Gerda wasn't his cousin. She really was his sister, and Horst, my father, wasn't her son, but actually his son. So even in death my grandfather felt compelled to conceal his true identity. But apart from there seeming to be almost no estate left to distribute, what did you mean by saying the will was strange?"

"It said nothing about the actual substance of the estate that Gerda and Horst were to inherit. That's okay, I guess, but what was really strange is it ended with what appeared to be a child's verse in German, followed by a series of verses taken from the Bible. I remember looking at Kristin and asking if the rhyme and those verses meant anything to her, but she had no clue."

Tom continued, "I really began to think Otto must have been involved in some sort of clandestine activity involving the Russians, perhaps as an agent of the FBI or the CIA. I thought maybe those verses were meant to convey a message that would only make sense to the guy running him. I did notice a stranger sitting at the back of the court room taking notes when the will was read."

"What did the court do?"

"The judge was as puzzled by the will as anybody, but following protocol, he appointed an executor and told him to try to locate Gerda and Horst Gustmann. The will gave their last known locations. For Gerda, an address in Berlin. For Horst, an address in Prague."

"Well, we know the executor never managed to find my father or Gerda."

After dinner, Eva and Derek drove Tom home. It was a warm evening, so they stood in the parking lot for a few minutes while Tom enjoyed the rare cigarette his doctors kept advising against.

"Hell, I'm ninety-one years old. I think I oughta be allowed the occasional pleasure. Speaking of which, thanks again for the dinner, drinks, and company."

Eva hugged him. "Thanks, Tom, for everything you were able to tell us about my grandfather. I really appreciate it. We enjoyed meeting and having dinner with you. If Derek and I get back here we'd like to see you again. Okay?"

"Ya' sure. You betcha'." Tom crushed out his cigarette and waved goodbye.

CHAPTER 43

They hadn't bothered to draw the drapes, so when Derek woke up he stood and looked out at the lake just as the sun began to rise. Then he turned and quietly watched Eva as she slept.

Given what Bill Bullock and Tom Corker had told them, it no longer seemed necessary to spend time looking through any more microfilm at the university. Their big find was learning that Klaus Gustmann, as Otto Krummel, had written a will, weirdly worded in a way he'd obviously hoped would make sense to Gerda and Horst, but not to anyone else. Their first priority should be to go to the Marquette County Courthouse and obtain a copy. Eva agreed, but first wanted to visit Presque Isle Park where she now knew her grandfather's car had been found submerged in the lake.

The weather was perfect with no prediction of rain until the next day. Upon mentioning their plans to the man at the hotel desk, he suggested they consider renting bikes to ride there and maybe pick up a pasty for a picnic along the way.

"You can't be an honorary Yooper until you've had an Upper Peninsula pasty."

Derek said, "Okay, but first, what's a pasty, and second, what's a Yooper?"

"It's a sort of meat pie the early Cornish miners brought to the U.P. The other ingredients include potato, onion, parsley, and especially rutabaga," then holding his hands together in a certain way he said, "all wrapped up in a Dshaped crust so you can eat it out of your hand. Fresh baked and wrapped in a few layers of newspaper, it'll stay warm for hours. The miners took them to work in the morning so they could have hot food for lunch."

"Sounds good. We'll try them. And Yooper?"

"Oh, yeah." He smiled. "That's our name for people like me born and raised here as opposed to being from south of the Mackinac Straits bridge. In that case, our name for you is Troll. If you have time, drive a little west of Ishpeming, and check out a place called 'Da Yoopers Tourist Trap.'"

A little past noon, Derek and Eva parked their rented bikes next to a picnic table on the south side of the park and attacked their pasties, whose aroma had induced hunger pangs as soon as they picked them up. Noisy seagulls circled, waiting for something to drop that they could scavenge. Derek tossed a bit of his pasty into the grass and watched the birds compete with one another.

"Don't encourage them, Derek. You'll just attract more."

Looking across the bay to the south, she noticed a large lake freighter approaching the tall rust colored dock. On top of the dock stood a line of hopper type rail cars full of pelletized iron ore soon to be transferred to the ship's hold through a series of chutes.

Eva said, "Can you read the name on the prow?"

"M…something." Derek squinted and shaded his eyes. "Okay. Now I can make it out. Michipicoten. Wonder what that means?" Derek pulled out his phone, typed in "Michipicoten," scrolled down, and selected a *Wikipedia* entry.

"It's an Ojibwe word meaning 'big bluffs.' The ship is owned by a Canadian company. They also own another one called the Giiwedin, again an Ojibwe word meaning 'north wind.'" They watched the Michipicoten finish pulling alongside the dock. Then they walked a short way to gain a better view of a long breakwater with a light at the end. It served to protect the inner harbor from the tremendous waves storms over the lake sometimes produced.

"Look at this, Derek." Eva stood by a bronze plaque near the top of a stairway leading to the rocky beach. "So sad, and hard to imagine on a beautiful day like this, but when my grandfather was killed during that storm, it must have been a terrifying place." The plaque spoke of the deaths of two students at Northern Michigan University. One drowned when he was washed off the breakwater by a huge wave during an early October storm. His friend had entered the water in a failed effort to save him and also died.

Returning to their bikes, Derek and Eva rode the road encircling the park. At the top of a short but steep hill, they paused by a stone memorial marking the graves of Charlie Kawbawgam, last chief of the local Chippewa tribe, and his wife Charlotte.

"Tom said that in the fifties the road around the island came to within a few feet of the edge in several places. They finally closed it and built this new one further in." Eva pointed to the northeast. "If we walk over there, we'll probably be close to where my grandfather's car went over the cliff. A few minutes later they stood and looked down from the edge of a sharp drop-off to where the dark blue-green water of Lake Superior washed against and continued to slowly eat away at the base of the cliff.

"Today it's beautiful. But I'm thinking what it must have been like when he was trapped and killed here by those two men during a violent storm. Did they kill him and then push his car over the edge? Or was he just wounded, lost control, and the car plunged over the edge as he tried to get away?" Derek watched Eva as she stared down at the water, then shuddered and said, "Okay, that's enough. Let's go back."

After returning the rented bikes, they drove downtown to the County Courthouse. In the office where wills were filed, Eva told the clerk, Debbie Maki, she wanted to obtain a copy of her grandfather's will, Otto Krummel, which had been probated in Marquette following his death in 1953. Debbie entered Otto's name and date of death into the computer, waited a moment, then frowned and said, "I'm afraid we have a problem."

"What?"

"We had an electrical fire in the archives two weeks ago. The good news is the automatic sprinkler system worked so none of the documents stored there got burned. The bad news is they sustained an awful lot of water damage, especially those in the section holding wills and other legal documents from the period 1950–59. We've got a student intern in the basement right now carefully peeling away a page at a time, drying it, reassembling the complete document, and then refiling it. But it'll be weeks until he's done. Right now the best I can do is promise to send a photocopy once Mike finds the original and dries it out, if it's still legible." Disappointed, but realizing they had to wait Eva paid in advance and gave Debbie her address in Palo Alto.

As it was only a little past two, Derek suggested they spend a little more time being tourists. Heading west out of Marquette on U.S. 41, they stopped in Negaunee and toured the Michigan Iron Industry Museum. Then they drove on to Ishpeming to the place recommended that morning by the hotel clerk, "Da Yoopers Tourist Trap." There, they bought matching trucker caps bearing icons of the Upper Peninsula and a bit of Yooper speak, "Say Ya to Da U.P."

On the way back to Marquette, Derek proposed having supper *al fresco* on the hotel patio. "We could pick up a pizza at Aubree's and finish the rest of that bottle of wine you brought from California. What do you say?"

"Sound good to me."

The next morning, Derek woke to the sound of a violent thunder and wind storm. Lightning streaked the sky, the very short intervals between flashes and subsequent booms suggesting nearby hits. What a change. It'd been so pleasant the night before, they hadn't bothered to close the window or pull the drapes. Now, a strong wind drove rain through the open screened window, making the drapes on each side dance. Sprinting to the window, he closed it, returned to bed, and snuggled next to Eva, waking her.

"Our plane doesn't leave until three-thirty, so we've got the morning. Any ideas?"

Eva said she wanted to go to Presque Isle one more time. Yesterday, when they'd been at the park, they'd talked to a sixtyish Yooper skipping rocks across the water next to the breakwater. He told them they really ought to see the place during a storm. With a heavy wind out of the northeast, he said he'd seen waves hit the breakwater that cast a wall of water more than ten feet high.

Two hours later, Derek and Eva stood by the breakwater, drenched in spite of their umbrellas, taking a close-up look at the wrath of Lake Superior in a storm. Eva shivered and thought, *That guy wasn't kidding. This must have been what it was like for my grandfather that day.*

CHAPTER 44

Each time she fell asleep that night, Eva had a dream where she saw her dad and he seemed to be okay. But then she saw him gasping for breath and heard the German words he'd whispered to Derek just before he died: *Schlupwindel, Shau, unter den Balken, Ecke.* The words kept cycling round and round in her brain like musical chairs until suddenly all but one disappeared. Each time that happened, she woke up. For the third time that night she hit the Indiglo button on her Timex to check the time, 2:57 A.M.

Finally giving up, Eva got up and went to the living room to look for something to read. But just twenty minutes into a new detective novel, she couldn't stay interested. Instead, she decided to turn on the radio and began to page through one of her albums of family photos. In one, there were three pictures of her as a teenage cowgirl on a paint horse named Jellybean. She'd taken classes and later competed briefly in junior class barrel racing at several local rodeos, once even placing third and winning fifty dollars. But her career as a rodeo cowgirl came to a sudden end when Jellybean stumbled at full gallop. Fortunately, he was okay, but when she hit the ground she fractured her right arm. After that, her parents had vetoed further rodeo participation.

From Jellybean, Eva's thoughts drifted to a summer three years earlier at the cabin in Vermont, where a local farmer had taught her the first rudiments of horseback riding on a pony named Pokey. She didn't have a picture of Pokey, but as her mind summoned an image of the little black and white equine, in the background she heard the radio playing, 'Everything That Glitters' by Dan Seals. She'd loved that song during her brief tenure as a cowgirl. Now she joined Dan singing the final stanza:

...Everything that glitters is not gold

The next song wasn't to her taste, so Eva buttoned the radio to its next preset, an oldies station currently playing 'Memories' by the Platters. She was still thinking about her early teen years and horses, and absently humming the song 'All That Glitters,' when her brain called her attention to a line the Platters were just singing:

...Childhood days, wild wood days...

Childhood days, wild wood days. Eva pictured herself playing behind the cabin in Vermont soon after her dad had bought it. She'd explored the woods, imagining she had to look out for hostile Indians. Exploring the creek in woods to the west of the cabin she'd found several small rocks embedded with flecks of gold. Her dad told her they were quartz and that the gold flecks were iron pyrite. He called it fool's gold. Well, *he* might think it wasn't real, but she was sure those flecks were REAL GOLD. And as she recalled trying to convince her dad they needed a safe place in which to keep her newfound wealth, her ear picked up another line as the song came to an end.

...Among the birds and bees...

This time, the word jogging her was *bees*. Well not bees, actually, hornets. Maybe her dad's killer hadn't found the egg after all. *He might have hidden it in the secret place he made to hold my gold-flecked pebbles.* The more she thought about it the more she was sure that was what he must've done. She had to call Derek. Eva looked at her Timex again. *Damn, only 3:41 A.M.* Derek might not be up yet. With difficulty, she forced herself to wait awhile before calling. Her adrenaline was running high, and she felt full of energy. She made coffee, not because she needed any, but just as something to do to pass a little more time. Then she turned to her laptop to check out flights to Philadelphia.

In fact, Derek was already up when Eva first thought of calling. He'd made himself get up at the ungodly hour of 5:00 A.M. to complete a critical piece of work, before heading north for a long Fourth of July weekend in Vermont. Attired in running shorts and a sweatshirt, but with dry underwear, pants, and a shirt in his daypack, he jogged to the office, stopping just long enough at the all night deli to pick up two chocolate croissants and get his thermos filled with coffee. At 9:08 A.M. he finally finished proofing the last paragraph of a grant application that was due the following Monday. Then he poured his third cup of coffee and went to work on the second croissant. Ten minutes later he was halfway out the door when his phone rang, showing an incoming call from Eva. It was still early, just 6:18 A.M. in California.

"Yo, Eva. You at work already?"

"No, I'm still home. My first patient isn't scheduled until nine." Her voice was excited. "I have something I've just got to tell you."

"Did Klaus's will come?"

"No. No word on that yet. But listen. I didn't sleep much last night. I kept waking up and thinking over and over about those words you said Dad whispered to you, words that just didn't seem to make any sense."

"Yeah?"

"Derek, I know where the egg is. At least I think I do. I don't think the Russians found it after all. I think it's still in Vermont where Dad hid it. He tried to tell you where to find it, but he was confused, going back and forth between English and the German he spoke as a child."

"But we looked all around and inside the burned cabin in February. I was with the police when they found his strongbox open and empty. You saw it, too."

"I know. I know. But suppose Dad didn't put the egg in that box. You know the police haven't heard even a whisper of a rumor that any missing Imperial Fabergé egg has been found and put up for sale in either a legitimate or the underground black market. That could mean Dad's killer never got it."

"Possible, I guess. But remember, the absence of evidence for something doesn't mean the opposite is true. Remember, Evans thought the thief might go underground for a while or that the job might have been done under contract for a collector so the egg may never show up for sale."

"I remember, but I'm just convinced Dad didn't hide that egg in the strongbox, and I'm pretty sure those scarcely intelligible words he whispered were an attempt to describe where he did put it."

"Okay. So, tell."

"You told me one of the words was *Shau*, which means 'look.' Then he seemed to say *Schlupwindel*. That really threw us off since that translates as 'diaper slip.' What the heck is that? The best we could come up with was that maybe he wrapped the egg in some kind of cloth. We also didn't know what to make of the word *Ecke*, which could possibly translate as 'angle' or 'nook' or 'corner' depending on context, followed by the words *des kleinen Ort*. One translation of that is 'small village.' From that, you might wonder if perhaps he stashed the egg in a safety deposit box in a local bank. But I don't think he had time. You told me he'd just returned from Gerda's funeral when you gave him a ride back to his cabin. So I think the words *des kleinen Ort* only means something like 'small place.' Finally, we've got *unter den Balken*, which we interpreted as 'under the joists.' So in the end we decided he must have been talking about the special space between the joists under the floor of the cabin where he always kept his strongbox. And since the strongbox was open and empty, the Russians, or at least the one who wasn't killed and burned to a crisp, must have gotten away with the egg."

"I'm with you so far. What's changed?"

"Those words kept going through my head all night long, and I wasn't getting anywhere. Finally, I got up, and started leafing through an old family photo album while half listening to the radio. It's weird, but a picture combined with some word you hear at the time can summon a memory that leads to another and then to another. I suddenly remembered something from almost thirty years ago that gives those words new meaning. This really should have occurred to me when you first took me out to look at the burned cabin and I saw the empty strongbox, but somehow it didn't."

"So give, girlfriend. I'm listening."

"We need to look in *das Nebengebäude*, the 'outhouse.'"

"The outhouse? How do you figure? Actually, the police did check it out the next day, but they didn't find anything of interest."

"They didn't know where to look, Derek. I'm pretty sure I do. I've just got to go there now and check this out. I've got patients all day today, but then

I'm free until Monday. If I can get an early morning flight to Philly tomorrow, can we drive up to Vermont together?"

"Thursday traffic is going to be just awful. I was just about to leave for Vermont now to beat that. Let me check and see if I can get you a ticket through to Burlington instead. I can meet you there and we can spend the weekend together."

Derek went to the USAirways website and searched for round trip flights between SFO and BTV starting July 3 and returning July 6.

"Here's one that ought to work. USAir Flight 817 leaves SFO at 8:30 A.M. and gets to Philly at 4:45 P.M. Then you take Flight 3297 leaving at 6:15 P.M. and get to Burlington at 7:40 P.M. I can meet you there. I'll try to get us a dinner reservation and also see if I can book a nice place to stay for a couple days, although that may be tough this close to the Fourth of July."

"The flights sound okay, and I'll definitely be ready for dinner, but don't kill yourself looking for a hotel. We can stay at your place. What are my return options on Sunday and what is this trip going to cost?"

"Let's see. Here's a pair of flights that get you back to SFO at 7:35 P.M. You leave Burlington at 11:25 A.M. After a longish wait in Philly your flight to SFO leaves at 4:11 P.M. Now the price. Wow! It's really steep, twice what it'd run if you booked well in advance, but after all, it's the Fourth of July weekend. Hold on, I've got a bunch of frequent flier miles. Let's see if I can use them."

A few minutes later, he was back on the line. "Got it. Your transportation is in hand." He gave her the reservation number. "So now, love, tell me where and why you think your dad hid his egg in the outhouse?"

Eva giggled. "Nope. I'm going to keep that a secret for now and just show you when we get there."

"I'll tickle it out of you."

"I'm looking forward to that."

CHAPTER 45

Eva nudged Derek. It was barely dawn on the Fourth of July. "Unghhh. God! What time is it?"

"Five-thirty. Let's go. There'll be plenty of light by the time we get there."

Derek dragged himself out of bed and wiped the sleep from his eyes. Trying to tickle the truth out of her the night before had been pleasant enough, but otherwise unproductive. Eva still wouldn't tell him what to expect when they looked in *das Nebengebäude*.

Twenty minutes later, Eva pulled open the door of the unpainted outbuilding some sixty feet behind the burned remains of the cabin. It was a classic ancient "two-holer" to which Horst had added come modern accouterments: a pair of white plastic seats with hinged covers and silver colored toilet paper holders mounted on each side wall.

Inside, Eva climbed up between the seats, and then, with one foot on either side of the seat on the left, extended her right hand up to and behind the largest hornet nest Derek had ever seen.

"Whoa, Eva. That thing's humongous. Long dead, I hope. What are you doing?"

Eva grinned. "Years ago when Dad bought this place, the nest was already here and already dead. But he had a sense of humor. Instead of getting rid of it, he decided to preserve it and let it scare visitors. He sprayed the thing with a lot of some sort of plastic coating material to strengthen and waterproof the paper mâché-like material so it wouldn't shred over time and fall apart."

"Wow. I visited Horst a bunch of times over the years, but I never had occasion to use this facility. It surely would have scared the *s…t* out of me if I'd sat down, looked up, and seen that over my head in the summertime."

"Mom didn't approve. She thought it was in terribly poor taste but couldn't convince Dad to take it down. I was just eleven years old, and I thought it was really cool. Back then I loved to go exploring in the woods, pretend I was a pirate, and bring back my treasures. I was convinced the flecks of iron pyrite in little pieces of quartz I found by the creek were real gold. I told Dad I had to have a place to hide my treasure, so he hollowed out a space in the back of this nest, sprayed some more of that plastic stuff to strengthen the inside and put my gold there."

Probing the at the back of the nest, Eva withdrew three small pieces of white quartz containing gold colored flecks and showed them to Derek.

"See. And I felt something else in there."

Eva probed the nest one more time, withdrawing a small velvet bag with a drawstring at the top. With Derek's help, she stepped back down to the floor, opened the bag, and squealed..

"I was right! I was right! This is it. Dad's egg."

The object Eva took from the bag was about three inches long and felt fairly heavy for its size. Clearly, the hornet nest had been able to serve as an adequate hiding place only because of the treatment Horst had applied to both its surface and interior years ago.

The body of the egg's surface looked to consist of some sort of hard marbled material, light green in color. Multiple bands of gold filigree inset with small diamonds and dark green emeralds wreathed its upper and lower portions, while a band of four gold images of the double-headed Imperial Russian eagle encircled the midsection. As he took the egg from Eva, Derek heard a rattling sound. Clearly, it must be hollow with something inside. Just like the egg he'd seen featured on that episode of *Treasure Hunters*.

Derek said, "I read that all the eggs Fabergé made for the Tsars were designed to open up and reveal a 'surprise' inside, so there must be a way to open this one. And even though there aren't any validated photographs, two brief written descriptions I found online make me think this could be the missing Empire Nephrite egg, named for the pale green jade from which it was supposedly made. It's also sometimes called the Alexander III Medallion egg, because there's supposed to be a medallion inside showing his likeness."

Derek and Eva took turns looking for the button or latch that would let them open the egg and see what might be inside. Finally, Eva noticed that the crown above the twin heads of the Imperial Russian eagle in one of the four images was separated by a narrow seam. A gentle upward push on that crown released an internal lock and allowed the top of the egg to swing open. Inside, they found a gold, emerald-encrusted medallion bearing an image of Tsar Alexander III, as well as several loose diamonds and emeralds and a scrap of paper bearing two lines written in longhand:

Schau hier mein Sohn wenn ich nicht zurück komme

Og⊙ev.K-85G2200-5G65Va-65G127Oz-310d80SG

Eva looked and the words and slowly translated the German: "Look… here…my son…if…I…don't…come back. That looks like some sort of code. Do you think…no, it must be my grandfather left this message for Dad and Gerda to find if he was never able to get back to them."

"Sure seems like it. We'd better let Tate and Evans know what we've found. It belongs to you now, Eva, but I'm thinking Evans may need to take temporary possession of it as evidence pending the arrest and trial of your dad's killer."

Derek looked at his phone. "Crud! Just like last winter. No signal. This place is a dead zone. Your dad told me you complained that he rarely called you on that phone you gave him, but it was generally useless right here."

Returning to the road, Derek finally got a decent signal and put a call through to the office of the LaMoille County Sheriff. Jessica answered and told him Sheriff Tate was out on a call, but she'd try to patch him through to her car. A minute later, "Mr. Todson, this is Sheriff Tate. What have you got?"

"Sheriff, Eva had an inspiration a couple of days ago about those German words her dad whispered to me about the egg his assailants were trying to steal."

"Trying? I thought we decided they succeeded."

"Well, Eva flew here from California yesterday, dragged me out to her dad's place just past dawn, and found it in a place you wouldn't believe."

"What? Where?"

"The egg. Eva found the egg where her dad had hidden it, in the *outhouse* of all places. She's holding it in her hand right now."

"Have you advised Evans?"

"Not yet. We just found it and weren't quite sure what to do next. I called you first. I'll put a call through to Evan's office now."

"Given it's the Fourth of July, he may not be on duty, but I'm sure you can get a message to him, and I know he'll want to see it." A pause, "You say you're by the path to Gustmann's place now?"

"Yes."

"I'm only four miles away. Stay where you are and I'll come to you. It shouldn't take me more than ten minutes."

While Derek called Evan's office in Waterbury, Eva opened the thermos of coffee he'd insisted on making before leaving the cabin that morning.

"I'm getting a busy signal at Evan's office. I'll have to try again later."

A few minutes later he saw the sheriff's car crest a rise a couple hundred yards down the road. Amanda Tate pulled to a stop and got out.

"Let's see what you have. I managed to get Evans on my radio while driving here and gave him a quick head's up. He wants to meet all of us at his office as soon as possible."

An hour later, Eva, Derek, and Amanda Tate sat with John Evans at his office in Waterbury. Eva told how she'd suddenly remembered the secret hiding place in the outhouse behind the cabin, and because of that at least some of the words her dad had whispered to Derek began to make sense. The large, reinforced hornet nest in which Horst had hidden the egg was in the corner (*Ecke*) of a small place (*kleiner Ort*), although it wasn't located under floor joists (*unter den Balken*) but rather the rafters of the outhouse for which *Sparren* would have been a better word choice. The word that had really thrown them off was *Schlupwindel*, which translated as diaper slip. Eva realized Derek must have misheard. She thought her dad either must have said or meant to say *Schlupwinkel*, a word meaning hideout or hiding place.

"It's a shame Dad didn't just say *Wespennest* or *Hornissenest* instead of *Schlupwinkel*. I would have picked up on that right away."

Evans thought, but didn't say out loud, *Weird! You think you've seen and heard everything, then this. Too bad the poor guy couldn't manage to mutter all that in English, but considering the state he was in.* Then he reached into his desk and took out a camera.

"I'm going to take some close-up pictures and add a detailed written description of the egg. Then I'll ask you all to sign and date that as witnesses. Since this egg appears to be the reason Horst was kidnapped and killed, it will be relevant evidence when we finally get a suspect to trial. However, I don't think I have to impound it so long as it's kept in a secure place."

Evans paused. Then he said, "I've got a friend who manages the Merchants Bank in downtown Burlington, and he owes me a favor. I'll call Bruce now, ask him to meet us at the bank *tout de suite*, and put this thing in a safe deposit box."

Bruce was less than thrilled at having to leave the family Fourth of July picnic, but apparently Evans's argument was persuasive. An hour later they were all at the bank, and shortly thereafter, Horst's egg was safely locked away there. As they left the bank, Eva turned to Evans.

"What now? I feel good about finding the egg, but what I really want is to catch Dad's killer. It's been almost five months. You identified the man whose body was found in the burned cabin, but do you have anything at all on the other one, the tall heavyset guy on the CCTV tape?" She sighed. "We might be better off if he had found the egg. Then we might have heard something about it being sold and been able to use that information to track the bastard down. I'm terribly frustrated. I'm afraid you'll never find Dad's killer."

"Dr. Gustmann, Eva, I'm not going to sugarcoat it. We haven't made much progress yet. However, we're definitely not going to quit working on it. I'd really hoped for a lead when we interviewed Arkady Rubenstein and his employees, but so far nothing. As I told you, Rubenstein himself looks clean. A couple of his employees acted pretty nervous, but that could just be normal jumpiness at being questioned by a cop. We plan to have another go around with them soon, including the couple who were not available the first time. I'm almost certain there has to be some connection with a person at the gallery."

"You told me the dead man in the cabin, Vasily Kozlov, was affiliated with the Russian mafia, so supposed the other man was, too. What have you been able to learn about Kozlov's associates?"

"I'll tell you this much, but this you *absolutely must* keep it quiet. The NYPD and ICE have a deal going with a guy inside the New York City Russian mafia.

He's agreed to pass on information about their operations. I got my friend at NYPD to introduce me a couple months ago, and he asked his informant to tell us whatever he might hear from the inside about Vasily Kozlov. Right off the bat, he tells me Kozlov hasn't been seen for several months, so most members of the *Bratva* guys there assume he may be dead. He had a reputation as an unstable hophead, and they figure he probably overdosed somewhere. If that's the case, then they just figure it's his fault. But we know Kozlov was actually killed by a .45 caliber bullet like the one Derek found buried in a post behind your dad's cabin."

"So how does that help? If you tell your informant what you really know, do you think he'd be able or willing to identify the person most likely to have shot him?"

"It's not that simple. If our informant were the one to let the rest of the cell know that Kozlov was murdered, they'll wonder how he got that information, and I'm afraid he'll wind up at the bottom of the East River. We've got to wait a little longer and see if we can't learn more about who Kozlov worked with before he 'disappeared.' But if that doesn't happen pretty soon we'll eventually release a statement identifying him as the man found last February in your dad's cabin and publicize the fact that he'd been shot."

"And then?"

"We might just find the body of a man as big as the one the CCTV showed taking your dad out of his apartment, or better, somebody will give us a tip as to where we can find and arrest the guy."

Eva nodded, but inside, she wasn't feeling satisfied. Maybe the police would hear something, maybe not. Their approach seemed too passive. She had another idea.

"Detective, couldn't we set a trap? Carefully leak some information that I've found the egg and see if we can prompt the killer into making another attempt to steal it."

Everyone looked askance at Eva. Amanda spoke first.

"Are you serious? This is one really bad dude. To draw him out you'd have to create a story that not only convinces him this isn't a trap, but that you'll have the egg in your possession at a time and place where he can safely heist it. I'm having a tough time imagining what that story would sound like, but if you did succeed, you could wind up losing your life. Not a good idea, girl. Way too dangerous."

Eva didn't respond, but her tight-lipped expression suggested she was far from satisfied. Derek saw it and got an uneasy feeling his "Phryne" might well charge ahead on her own and try something risky.

The group split up. Detective Evans and Sheriff Tate returned to their respective offices, while Derek and Eva headed back to his cabin.

"It could work, Derek."

"You mean your plan to make the killer show himself?"

"Yes, I know there are risks, but if we're careful, I'm sure we could work things out so no one gets hurt except that Russian bastard. Help me think this out, Derek."

Derek looked at Eva, feeling conflicting emotions of admiration and fear. Over lunch at Wicked Wings, he leafed through a copy of the *Stowe Reporter* looking for something to divert her. "Any thoughts on what you'd like to do tonight? Movie? Oh, hey, here's something that might be fun. There's an outdoor concert tonight at Johnson State College."

"What sort of music?"

"Two bands are listed. I'm guessing it's maybe a combo of folk or country music and rock. The first band is a local all-girl group called the Contented Cows.

"Hmmm."

"The second one is listed as a tribute band to several of the classic soft rock bands from the seventies. It says here they play Crosby, Stills, Nash and Young stuff like 'Judy Blue Eyes' and Led Zeppelin's 'Stairway to Heaven.' They call themselves 'EIAC.' Oh my! I'll be damned."

"What?"

"EIAC stands for Eastern Artificial Insemination Cooperative. That was the name of a company, no longer in business, that stocked and sold bull sperm for the artificial insemination of cows. I remember seeing it on a building next to the Cornell University campus back in the nineties. I thought then it would be a great name for a rock band."

"Yeah, right. Do you suppose a joint appearance of the Contented Cows with Eastern Artificial Insemination Cooperative at the same event is a coincidence? Sounds like a ploy by some clever male event manager at Johnson State College. But, okay. I'm game. Let's pack a picnic and go. I like that seventies stuff even if it is from way before my time."

"Well, technically it's before mine, too. Most of that genre really took off from the gathering at Woodstock."

"So, Derek, what were you doing at the time of Woodstock?"

"Um…pretty sure I was mostly excited about getting ready to attend kindergarten. And you?"

Eva laughed. "That's five years before I became a gleam in Dad's eye."

CHAPTER 46

Eva nursed a cup of coffee and scanned the calendar as she waited for her first patient of the morning. Monday, August 4, a month since they'd found the egg and also a month since Evans had urged her to be patient about the investigation into her dad's murder. Again, she felt consumed by a need to do something now. The case was going cold. She couldn't stand the idea the murderer might go unpunished.

With the egg safe in the bank in Burlington, Eva kept wondering if some carefully scripted disinformation could lure her dad's killer out of hiding. Evans and Tate had done their best to completely scotch the idea. Still, she thought, *Damn it, I'm going to do it. I just won't tell them until it's out there. Then I'll apologize and work on convincing them to follow through by setting up surveillance nearby in the woods. It won't be the first time I got something done by asking for forgiveness instead of permission.*

Although Derek had mostly avoided talking about it after Eva had floated her idea with Evans and Tate, she knew he also opposed putting herself at risk. She was going to do it, but they'd grown so close she didn't want to blindside him. Pulling out her phone she thought, *I have to tell him, and he won't be happy.*

Two hours later, informed that a Dr. Eva Gustmann was calling from California, Arkady Rubenstein responded immediately. He inquired politely after her well-being and expressed sincere condolences over the death of her father. Privately, he was surprised to hear from her and curious as to the purpose of her call. So far as he knew, Horst's killer had succeeded in stealing the Fabergé egg. The police had already interviewed him and his staff concerning communications they had had with Horst Gustmann and had urged him to report immediately any rumor he might hear of an attempt to sell the egg on the stolen art black market. But so far, nothing. Surely Dr. Gustmann had been kept apprised of this disappointing lack of information. Why was she calling him?

"Mr. Rubenstein, the last email message my father sent to me included a picture of the Fabergé egg his father left to him. In it, he mentioned you might be interested in buying it and said he wanted me to help him make a decision about that."

"Yes. We set up a tentative appointment when he suggested that you and he would be willing to bring the egg here to the gallery for an appraisal. Just a moment while I check my calendar…Yes, we agreed on 10 A.M. Wednesday, February 26th for a meeting. I'm so sorry. It's tragic what befell your father."

"I know where it is."

"Excuse me?"

"I know where the egg is."

"But it was stolen."

"That's what everyone thought, including me, because we found my father's strongbox open and empty in the remains of his cabin. But the egg wasn't stolen. It's still hidden near his cabin in Vermont. Yesterday, while sorting through papers I took from his apartment, I found a note telling me where he hid it. I'm certain I now know where it is."

"That's wonderful, amazing, Dr. Gustmann. I certainly remain most interested and am completely at your disposal if you would still consider bringing it to me for appraisal."

"Thank you, Mr. Rubenstein. I'm making arrangements now to fly to Burlington on Friday. I'm going to go to my father's place Saturday morning to collect the egg. After that, my friend Dr. Todson and I plan to drive to New York. Would it be possible for you to meet us early Sunday morning at the gallery? I realize that's an odd time, but I have a full slate of patients at my practice on Monday, so I need to fly back to California Sunday afternoon."

"Yes, I can definitely meet with you then, Dr. Gustmann."

"Wonderful. As soon as I book my flights and a hotel in Manhattan for Saturday night, I'll send that information to you. What's the best address to use, *RubensteinGallery.com*?"

"Yes. That would be fine. I'll ask my staff to arrange for your hotel. I'd also like to host you and Dr. Todson for dinner Saturday evening."

"Thank you. Please book something close to the gallery. You can send a copy of the confirmation to me at *Egustmann51@gmail.com*. And thank you for the dinner invitation as well, but I think we'd better decline. I'm really not sure when we'll get to New York Saturday evening."

Pleased at the unexpected news, Rubenstein thought nothing of the slight click he heard just as he was hanging up the phone. Then he turned to the intercom to let his secretary know about Dr. Gustmann's pending visit.

In California, Eva turned to her computer to make flight arrangements. She settled on a pair of USAirways flights that would get her to Burlington just before 11:00 P.M. Friday, then booked a return nonstop flight on Sunday leaving Kennedy at 5:00 P.M. After that, she sent copies of her flight itinerary to both Derek and Arkady Rubenstein. And since Eva wanted to make sure her message got to the *right* person at the gallery, if that's where the previous leak had occurred, she also sent to Rubenstein an email reiterating the substance of their phone conversation. A short time later, a message from Rubenstein's secretary appeared in her inbox confirming a reservation at the Peninsula Hotel on Fifth Avenue. It also confirmed Mr. Rubenstein's agreement to meet her and Derek at the gallery at 10 A.M. on Sunday, August 10.

CHAPTER 47

Derek called just as Eva was deplaning.

"Hi, Derek. I'm off the plane and in the jetway. I'll be there in just a minute."

"Big problem, Eva. I'm still at the cabin. Something's wrong with my car. It won't start. It seems like a bad battery, although that doesn't make a lot of sense as it was only replaced three months ago. I called AAA, but they told me their truck was out on another call and would get to me as soon as possible. I called again fifteen minutes ago, and they said it would still be another hour before they can get here."

"Damn! Oh well. I'll just go check with the Alamo desk and rent something. I ought to be able to get to your place a little past midnight."

"I'm really sorry, Eva."

"Hey, when it rains it pours. See you soon, *mon amour*."

An hour later, Eva was headed north out of Johnson on Clay Hill Road. *Just four more miles to Derek's place*. As she entered the long curve half a mile past the intersection with Plot Road, her headlights picked up a man standing on the left side of the road holding a flashlight and waving his arms. His vehicle, a beat-up green Ford 150 pickup, was half off the road, its right front fender hard up against the trunk of a large tree.

Eva pulled over, turned on her flashers, opened the window, and called out, "Hey. Are you okay?"

The man walked toward her, stumbling a bit. "No ma'am. I'm hurt. Truck blew a tire, went off the road an' hit that tree." He pointed. "Muh head hit the windshield. I'm kindah dizzy an' bleedin' some." He shined the light on the left side of his face. Eva could see blood streaming from a scalp wound.

"Okay. I'm a doctor. Sit on that stump over there and let me have a look." Eva got out of the car and turned to get her medical bag from the back seat. As she did so, another set of headlights approached from the south. The driver of that vehicle, a white utility van, pulled to a stop behind her car. Leaving his headlights on, he got out of the van and called, "You folks needin' help?"

Shielding her eyes, Eva turned to reply and was immediately grabbed from behind by a strong pair of arms. She struggled and started to scream, but the man from the van strode forward, struck her hard in the face, then pulled out a large dirty kerchief and tied it tightly around her eyes and mouth. She continued to struggle, but was thrown to the ground, where one man held her down while the other pulled her arms behind her back and applied a pair of flex cuffs. Then they taped her ankles together, carried her to the van, and threw her in the back. Outside, Eva heard the men talking.

"Jake, yer a sight with that fake blood. Call the boss now an' tell him we got her."

"Ay-uh. It all went roight good, Evan."

A moment later, the van door opened. The driver got in, started the engine, and took off, spinning his tires as he executed a sharp U-turn. Eva was thrown hard against the inside wall making her cry out. The driver called back, "Shut up an' lay quiet, girlie, an' you won't get hurt. We're goin' for a bit of a ride yet."

At first Eva was stunned, then terrified, but gradually that emotion morphed into burning anger. She'd been kidnapped. No question in her mind, this had been set up by the same bastard who'd killed her father. *So the ploy worked. Somebody at the gallery must've passed my message on to the bastard, but he decided not to wait for Saturday. Damn it! He's probably had me followed since the airport.* What she couldn't know was that Mikhail Filipov, having hacked both of their computers, had finally managed to hack Derek's cell phone as well when he'd recently driven up for a long weekend and tethered it to his computer to access the internet at his cabin. His subsequent phone conversations had since been captured and recorded, giving Sergei enough information to know the egg had been found and that Eva was on her way to Vermont to meet Derek and then take the egg to the Rubenstein gallery.

Getting kidnapped before she even got to the cabin definitely hadn't been part of the plan. She'd hoped to lure the killer to watch for her, then move in and try to take the egg as she apparently found it in the outhouse. But she wouldn't actually be there. Her place was to be taken by a plainclothes, dark-haired, female VSP officer able to pass for her at a distance. Sheriff Tate, Deputy Cole, and Detective John Evans would be lying in wait nearby with a second VSP officer, all ready to arrest the man when he showed himself.

So what had gone wrong? The killer must have believed she knew where the egg was hidden, but suspected a trap at the cabin so decided to grab her and make her tell him where it was. If she told him the truth, what then? Would he hold her at ransom and demand the egg as payment for letting her go? But would he really let her go? Not likely.

Although her hands were manacled behind her back, Eva thought, *If I can just stretch a bit to the left and down, maybe I can reach my phone.* The effort hurt, but on the third try, she made it, and slipped the phone from her back pocket. At that moment, the van rocketed around a curve so fast it threw her against the inside wall. She lost hold of the phone, and it slid away across the floor. *Damn!* Unable to see anything through the kerchief in the dark interior, she rolled back and forth, finally finding it again by feel. The phone was equipped with GPS and software that sent a continuous signal to the carrier. If someone was looking for her, they could track her precisely, but the critical question was whether anyone would be looking. *Derek's got to be wondering where I am.* She'd called him when she left the airport. He'd be expecting her by now.

Eva couldn't see to make an outgoing call. She kept hoping Derek would call her. But then she worried. If he did, would the driver hear it ring? Then she remembered it was still set only to vibrate, not ring. Road noise combined with the country music the driver had blasting on the radio made her doubt he could hear much of anything. She'd be able to feel rather than hear an incoming call, then answer it by touch without having to look at it. But could she get close enough to the phone to whisper intelligibly through the damn kerchief tied around her mouth? *Call me, Derek. PLEASE CALL ME!*

It was hard to tell how much time had passed, maybe twenty minutes, when Eva felt the phone buzz. She tapped the face in what she hoped was the right place to take the call, then inched her body around to get her face close to the phone and whispered, "Derek?"

"Eva? Where are you? You're late. What's wrong? Why are you whispering? What's all that noise I hear?"

"Derek, keep your voice down and listen. I've been kidnapped."

"Oh, my God!"

"They grabbed me at a fake accident scene just a few miles from your place. Right now I'm blindfolded and handcuffed in the back of a white utility van going fast, but I don't know where. Call the sheriff and the state police. I've got GPS on the phone. They can track me."

"Are you…"

"Right now, Derek. Hurry. Please."

"Of course."

Eva closed her eyes and prayed Derek would reach the police soon enough to locate the van before it got wherever it was headed. The loud music from the radio was now joined by the smell of cigarette smoke as the driver slowed and turned onto a road rougher than the one on which they'd been traveling. *Oh Lord. Are we getting close already?* But after banging through some potholes, the road got smoother, and the van picked up speed. After what seemed like another half hour, she couldn't really tell, the van slowed almost to a stop, turned, and continued at a slower speed along what felt like a gravel road.

Eva's phone buzzed again. She tapped the screen twice and whispered, "Derek?"

"Eva. I'm with Sheriff Tate right now, and we're in touch with Detective Evans. The Vermont State Police have your signal and are locked on your GPS position. They've scrambled a helicopter, and there are two VSP cruisers and an Essex County Sheriff's car closing in just a few miles from where you are."

"Essex County?"

"Yeah. He's taken you into the Kingdom. It looks like you probably went north on Route 100C, then east on Route 58. Now you're heading in the direction of a small town called Island Pond. You are still moving? Yes?"

"Yes, but slowly. We've been on a couple of gravel roads, and this one feels rougher then the last."

Perhaps ten minutes later, Eva suddenly heard a throbbing sound. *The helicopter?*

From the front of the van a loud exclamation, "SHIT!"

The van braked to a stop so abruptly it slewed sideways. Eva was tossed against the inside wall for a third time and once again lost hold of her phone. Then, as the driver opened his door and jumped out, she heard a siren and an amplified voice ordering him to raise his hands and stand where he was. The driver was having none of it. He took off running as fast as he could into the woods.

A minute later the back door of the van opened, and a police officer, his gun drawn, focused his flashlight on Eva. "Dr. Gustmann, are you all right?"

Eva replied as best she could through the kerchief still tied round her mouth. Her emotion now one of pure anger, she spit out, "I hope you got that bastard. Did you?"

Having expected a shaking, terrified woman rather than an enraged tigress, the officer hesitated a moment, then replied, "Uh…not yet. He ran into the woods, but the helicopter is trying to spotlight him, and two officers are in pursuit. The main thing is you're safe. Let me get that rag off your face, the tape off your ankles, and cut those flex cuffs."

Once able to see and speak more intelligibly, Eva looked at the name tag of her benefactor and said, "Thank you, Officer Nordstrom. I apologize. I'm sorry I spoke harshly."

"No offense, ma'am."

"But I'm certain the two men who kidnapped me were doing it for the man who murdered my dad last February. You've just got to get them so we can find and arrest him."

Then, remembering her phone, Eva looked around, found it on the floor of the van, and heard Derek's anxious voice saying, "Eva, are you there? Is everything all right? Answer me, Eva. What's happening?"

"I'm here and I'm okay, Derek, but the van driver took off into the woods. The police are looking for him now." Suddenly, the extra adrenaline that had fueled her for the past hour failed, and she started to cry.

Two and a half hours later, Eva sat next to Derek in his cabin along with Sheriff Amanda Tate and Deputy Dave Cole, while Detective Evans joined the group by phone from his home in Waterbury. Eva felt exhausted, relieved, and chastised all at once. Evans had started out giving her both barrels, harshly reminding her she was lucky she hadn't gotten herself killed without helping the police get any closer to identifying and apprehending her father's killer.

The consensus was that Eva was still in danger, even back home in Palo Alto, California, if the killer had reason to think she possessed the egg or knew where to get it. So Derek proposed they now send it by special courier to Wartski's in London, the house that had handled the vetting and sale of the Third Imperial Egg a year ago. Then they could release a story to the media. That should convince Horst's killer that prize was finally out of reach, although the question of *die andere Eier* was still out there.

Having agreed to that, conversation turned to the prospect of getting a break in the case. As soon as they captured and interrogated the van driver, they hoped to learn who had hired him to kidnap Eva. Detective Evans and his friend in the NYPD would also take another very close look at Arkady Rubenstein and any gallery employee who might have overheard his conversation with Eva or read the email she sent to him.

By now, everyone was exhausted but resolved to hang on a bit longer hoping to learn if the police had captured the van driver. Evans was getting constant updates from the search site. At 4:00 A.M. they learned the helicopter had managed to light up the driver several times as he ran north through the forest for more than a mile, but then lost him when he descended into a heavily wooded swampy area. In the meantime, the police brought in a German Shepherd tracking dog, let him take scent from a handkerchief and a hat the driver left on the front seat of the van, and then released him to follow the man's trail.

At 5:15 A.M. Evans came back on the phone and said, "They found him."

Eva said, "Wonderful. Now we can find out who hired him."

"Not so wonderful, Dr. Gustmann. He's dead."

"What?" Eva was furious. "Don't tell me the police shot him."

"Not us, someone else. Our guy went around in circles for quite a long time, but the dog finally tracked him to a small cabin about two miles from where he quit the van. Officers surrounded the place, lit it up, and called for him to come out. No answer. Then they broke in, guns drawn, only to find him dead on the floor, a bullet hole in his head. We assume this was where he was supposed to take you and that his boss was waiting there. When he showed up without you and told him what happened, the boss decided to make sure he could never tell who hired him. He shot him and made a quick exit. That couldn't have occurred much more than ten or fifteen minutes before we got there."

"Well, what about the other man, the one who got me to stop at the fake accident site. You've got to find him."

"We'll try. Tell me again as much as you can remember about him."

"It was dark, but my impression is he was fairly young, maybe in his late twenties, a little shorter than average, with dark hair and a wispy mustache. The left side of his face was covered with what I thought was blood from a scalp laceration, but after they threw me in the van, I heard his partner call him Jake and say something about how realistic the fake blood looked. The truck he'd supposedly driven off the road was a beat-up green Ford 150. What else? When he spoke he had a marked rural Vermont accent. You know, saying Ay-uh instead of yes and roight instead of right when he was talking to his friend, Evan."

"No chance you got the license number on the truck?"

"No."

"Well, that's something, but certainly not a lot to go on. However, as soon as we ID the van driver, look at his record, and find out who his friends were, maybe we can zero in on this Jake character. In the meantime, I'm going to call Doug Collins at NYPD, tell him what happened tonight, and arrange for the two of us to have another session, a surprise one this time, with Arkady Rubenstein and his employees. We'll question everyone again, and this time Doug and I are going to separately interview each individual, then get together and compare their stories."

With that, the group broke up, Sheriff Tate and Deputy Cole heading back to the Lamoille County Sheriff's office, while Derek and Eva went straight to bed. Derek fell asleep immediately, while Eva, exhausted as she was, lay on her back just staring at the ceiling.

Later that morning, Eva called USAirways, and for an extra $150. was able to change her ticket for the New York to San Francisco flight on Sunday to one for a pair of flights that would take her from Burlington to SFO via Philadelphia. There was no need for her to contact Rubenstein again. Evans and his NYPD friend were taking care of that. She'd resolved to let the police carry the ball, for now at least.

On Sunday, his car restored to working condition, Derek drove Eva to Burlington to catch her early morning flight to Philadelphia.

"Promise me you'll call as soon as you get home, Eva. Once the report about finding your dad's egg and sending it to Wartski's gets published on

Monday, you ought to be at least somewhat safer, but I'm still going to worry."

"I promise Derek. I'll be as careful as I know how when I have to go anywhere by myself, and from now on I'm going armed."

Derek made a sucking sound through his teeth. "I know you showed me you know how to use that pistol, Eva. But damn it, if someone really is lying in wait is it more likely you get to use your gun on him or he gets to use his on you?"

They drove on in silence for a few minutes. Then Derek said, "It definitely isn't over yet."

"Of course not. Dad's killer is still out there."

"For sure, but I mean the other treasure your grandfather mentioned to Gerda, not just the egg he left for Horst. The men who kidnapped your dad were after his egg, but they seemed sure there were others and that Horst either had them or must know where they were. In fact, I don't think he did know anything about those eggs and other treasure. You remember the piece of paper we found inside the egg with the words *Schau hier mein Sohn wenn ich nicht zurück komme* and that line of symbols, letters, and numbers? I'm pretty sure Horst never saw it. It took us a while to figure out how to open the egg. Your dad was curious enough to take several pictures, but I'm guessing he never opened it. He was so overwhelmed with feelings of guilt and shame about his father, I think he just decided to put it away until you got there to help him decide what to do."

"Are you thinking my grandfather might not have managed to recover all the treasure he hid in Latvia?"

"I just don't know. Possibly. And I think your dad's killer may be starting to have second thoughts of the same kind. We can't know what made him so sure Horst had the other eggs. As soon as we publish that we've sent the one egg to Wartski's for appraisal, but don't say anything about any others, he's got to question if his assumption about the others was wrong."

"So you want to go to Latvia and take a look?"

"Yes, if we can figure out that code. I'm already scheduled to go to Warsaw at the end of September for a meeting of the World Congress of Epidemiology. If we can break the code, then as soon as the meeting is over I could make a quick side trip to Latvia and try to find where Klaus initially hid his treasure."

CHAPTER 48

Derek yawned and stretched. He'd spent hours pouring over the code he and Eva had found on the scrap of paper inside Horst's Fabergé egg.

Og ⊙ ev.K-85G2200-5G65Va-65G127Oz-310G80SG

He'd learned the circle and dot symbol had been used over time to stand for all kinds of things: the alchemical sign for gold, the Egyptian hieroglyphic for gold, the Ojibwe symbol for spirit, the Australian Aborigine symbol for waterhole, the Blissymbol for eye, the Freemason symbol for an Entered Apprentice, and in modern times, the trademark of Target Corporation. But none of those, with the possible exception of gold, seemed to make sense here. He was sure Klaus had intended the symbol and the following letters and numbers as a guide telling Horst where to look for the treasure if he failed to return with it himself.

Continuing his search, Derek finally found a meaning that made sense, learning a circle and dot was often used on road signs in Europe to designate the city center. If that was what Klaus had intended, then could **Og** perhaps be the first two letters of a city? An alphabetic listing of cities in Latvia quickly showed that only one, Ogre, began with those two letters. Was Klaus telling Horst to begin his search in the center of Ogre?

Next, Derek puzzled over the letters **ev.K**, supposing them to be an abbreviation for another Latvian place name, such as a local district or a particular street. Googling a street map of Ogre, he blew it up large and searched for any that might be abbreviated **ev.K** , but drew a blank. Then he wondered if the letters might be some sort of German abbreviation. An alphabetic list of common German abbreviations gave **ev** as an abbreviation for the word *evangelische*, which means protestant, and in Germany most commonly referred to Lutherans. By itself, Derek didn't find the letter **K** listed as an abbreviation for anything in particular, but he did know *die Kirche* was the German word for church, so guessed **ev.K** might refer to a Lutheran church in or near the center of Ogre.

Bingo! A further internet query told him that the Ogre Lutheran church, built in 1930, was located near the city center. Derek felt he was beginning to get somewhere. Maybe Klaus had hidden his treasure somewhere near or even in the church itself. If that was true, the rest of the line after the abbreviation **ev.K** should point to the precise location.

Direction and distance. Four composite blocks of numbers and letters followed the letters **ev.K**. Each block began with a number followed by a **G**, followed by another number. In the first block it was followed only by a number, but in the last three blocks it was followed by a number and two more letters. Derek imagined standing at the front of the church and tried to think how these blocks of numbers and letters could point to a secure hiding place inside the building. What was the unit of distance? It must be metric. Centimeters? Possibly. Two thousand two hundred centimeters should get you all the way to the back of the church. What about meters? In that case the church could only be a point of reference with the treasure hidden more than two kilometers away. And what about direction?

Stuck at this point, Derek took a break and went to bed, but shortly after midnight he woke, felt too warm, and decided to turn on the AC. The thermostat on the hall wall read 77°F. Turning the mode to cool, he set the desired temperature to 72°F and had an inspiration. *Degrees! Could the first part of each block of numbers and letters in Klaus Gustmann's line of code be a direction expressed in degrees?* Derek dug out his German dictionary to confirm that the preferred word for degree was *der Grad*. He also learned that *die Gradzahl* referred to a compass direction.

With this revelation and thinking of the church as a point of reference rather than the actual hiding place, Derek took a new look at the first block of numbers and letters. Could 85G2200 possibly refer to a location 2,200 meters from the church at a compass angle of 85 degrees? Turning on his laptop, he called up the street map of Ogre again. On it he traced a road leading approximately two kilometers to the east from the location of the Ogre Lutheran Church and saw that it passed by a symbol indicating a cemetery. That seemed like a great place to securely hide something in wartime. If he was right so far, then the subsequent blocks of numbers and letters should point to the exact place where the treasure had been cached.

Derek returned to bed but couldn't sleep. Finally he got up, read for a couple hours, then made coffee and waited impatiently until it was almost, but not quite, legitimate to call Eva. He picked up his cell phone only to realize he'd forgotten to plug it in, and the battery was dead. Okay, he'd call on the house phone that rarely got used. Eva's phone rang seven times before she picked up, her voice heavy with sleep.

"God almighty, Derek. It's 4:55 A.M. What's up?"

"I'm sorry, I just couldn't wait any longer." Then he told her he was pretty sure he'd just broken the code they'd found in Horst's egg.

CHAPTER 49

Derek's discovery a year earlier that a genetically engineered strain of Hepatitis E virus had been responsible for an outbreak of unusually severe hepatitis among members of a Muslim family had triggered an investigation involving the Philadelphia Health Department, the CDC, and the FBI. It turned out the strain had been created legitimately as a research tool and stored in a P3 level biosafety laboratory at the University of Pennsylvania, but an audit subsequently revealed a vial of it was missing. Subsequent detective work finally linked the loss and the later outbreak of illness to a rabidly anti-Muslim man who had once been a maintenance worker at the facility, and later used the virus to contaminate a yogurt-based dish where the family was having a reunion dinner.

A key factor in cracking the case had been his team finding that apart from one individual, the only persons suffering illness were members of the family who had eaten a portion of the yogurt-based dish, but had also arrived late because of a delayed flight. A survey of all foods served and consumed by each member of the afflicted family revealed that first batch of the suspect dish had been fully consumed before the late group arrived. It was then replaced by a second batch brought to the table by a new server who had just come on duty. The second batch was consumed by some but not all the late arrivals as well as a single earlier diner who went back for a second serving. Under persistent questioning, the man who brought that dish to the table finally admitted to having stolen the virus and using it to contaminate the yogurt in the hope of killing Muslims. He was arrested, tried, subsequently convicted on a federal charge of terrorism, and sentenced to a lengthy term of imprisonment at the U.S. penitentiary in Florence, Colorado.

Derek was now making last-minute edits to a talk about this case that he was scheduled to give during a session on forensic epidemiology at the World Congress of Epidemiology in Warsaw. It wasn't a new field, but the growing threat of bioterrorism was giving increased emphasis to the need to better prepare public health professionals to look for evidence of crime and to work more effectively with law enforcement officials.

As soon as that was over, Derek planned a quick side trip to Latvia. He kept telling himself not to get too excited. He now knew Klaus had survived, had managed to get out of Latvia, and eventually made it to the United States via Sweden. But had Klaus really been able to recover the other eggs and valuables he'd discovered during the war before going to Sweden? Derek supposed he probably had. Right? Well, possibly not, or maybe not all of it. Clearly, something had gone wrong. Klaus was never able to reunite with his sister and son and move them all to South America as Gerda later told Horst he'd planned to do. Instead, for reasons they might never know, he'd ended up in a small town in northern Michigan before being murdered, apparently by agents of the Russian government. How did that all make sense, and where was the treasure now?

In Warsaw, Valery Morozov woke to the sound of an incoming call on Skype, a highly encrypted version whose use he restricted to a very short list of clients.

"Sergei?"

"Valery. A job for you."

"Who's the mark?"

"An American scientist. A guy named Derek Todson. Nothing heavy this time, at least I don't think so. But I want you to watch him closely for a couple of days. Let me know where he goes and what he does. He's scheduled to arrive in Warsaw the day after tomorrow for a meeting of the World Congress of Epidemiology at the InterContinental Hotel. I want to know where he goes, who he talks to, and especially what he finds, if anything, during a trip he's taking to Riga on Friday and Saturday. Use that shotgun microphone of yours and record any conversations he has with people there. I'll send you his picture, a copy of the reservations for his hotel in Riga, and the flights he's taking from Warsaw to Riga and back."

Valery pursed his lips. "And he sent all this to you in advance to make it easier, Sergei?"

"Yeah, he gave me the password to his email account. He just doesn't know that."

Two days later, jet lag notwithstanding, Derek's talk Tuesday evening went well. The next day, following a decent night's sleep, he felt alive again, and worked pretty much straight through from 08:00 to 17:00 with the Forensic Epidemiology Study Group. After that, he ate a light, early supper at the hotel, then checked out and asked the doorman to call a car to take him to Chopin Airport. His flight to Riga on Air Baltic was scheduled to depart at 19:55. After clearing security, he still had an hour, so bought a coffee, then sat near the departure gate to skim a copy of the *Financial Times*.

Somewhat surprisingly, a stranger sat next to him in the sparsely populated lounge and proceeded to engage in casual conversation. At first, Derek supposed he might be an American tourist, but then noted the man's fluent English had a decided accent he thought sounded Russian.

Arriving in Riga at 22:30, Derek took a taxi to the new Mercure Riga Centre Hotel. At check-in, he asked the concierge to arrange for a car and driver who spoke English, telling him he wished to be driven to the city of Ogre at 09:00 the next morning. Then, since his supper in Warsaw had been both light and early, he headed to the hotel bar for a snack and a liter of weissbier. He was still there fifteen minutes later, so failed to see the man with whom he'd spoken in Warsaw and was on the same flight to Riga, enter the hotel. Valery had changed clothes, now wore a pair of wire rim glasses and had on a dark brown wig that concealed his natural blond hair.

To the reception clerk, Valery said, "I have a reservation for two nights. I expect my good friend Dr. Derek Todson from America checked in just a short time ago. We had planned to meet at the airport, come in together, and take adjacent rooms, but unfortunately there was a mix up. Would you please check if there is a room available adjacent to his and in the meantime connect me with him on the house phone over there?"

Valery put the phone to his ear as the desk clerk rang Derek's room before turning back to speak with another guest. Of course, Derek didn't answer, but Valery pretended he had and conducted a quick one-sided conversation, saying the clerk was checking to see if they could have adjacent rooms before hanging up. Luck was with him; as he hung up the desk phone, the clerk told him he'd given him Room 307. Valery tendered his credit card, signed the register, and headed upstairs. He hadn't directly asked, and the clerk hadn't actually told him Derek's room number, but now he surmised it should be either 305 or 309. He would put up listening devices on the walls his room shared with those rooms.

The next morning Derek rose early, took breakfast in the hotel dining room, and was waiting when his car, a Volvo S90 sedan, arrived. He was a bit startled but not displeased to see that his driver, Maija Irbe, bore more than a slight resemblance to his own Eva.

Derek told her the story he'd been rehearsing. "As a child my aunt Gerda lived in Ogre during the war. But when the Russians began their westward advance in 1944 and threatened to retake Latvia, the family decided to leave the area. Just before they left, her brother Stefan contracted a fatal case of pneumonia and was buried in the local cemetery. Gerda and her brother had been very close. She told me that she always meant to come back one day and visit his grave, but one thing led to another. The family eventually emigrated and went to the United States. Gerda is now very old, not in good health, and no longer up to the trip. But when I told her I was going to a meeting in Warsaw, she begged me to make a quick side trip to Latvia. She wants me to visit Stefan's resting place, take pictures for her, and leave on his grave a little remembrance she made years ago."

As they approached the city center of Ogre, Derek asked Maija to stop so he could walk about and take a few pictures for his aunt before looking for the cemetery. Fifteen minutes later, he returned to the car having found and photographed the Lutheran Church.

Derek told Maija his aunt had been a little vague after all this time, but she thought the cemetery in which Stefan had been buried was about two kilometers east of the city center. Maija expanded the map of Ogre on her GPS and showed it to him. "Look here. The map shows a shaded area about two kilometers east of here located just north of Turkalnes Street, also called Route V968, and just south of a river and reservoir called Norupe. I think that must be the cemetery you're looking for."

Maija drove southeast on Brīvības Street, then bore left on Turkalnes Street and immediately passed a sign pointing east that said Kapsēta Street, the Latvian word for cemetery. Within a few minutes, she turned into the cemetery entrance.

"Did you aunt remember enough to tell you where to go from here?"

"Yes, well I think so, but I may have to explore a bit. Please wait for me here."

Derek entered the cemetery as though he knew where he was going, then stopped briefly, took out his pocket compass and set about using it to follow the course defined by Klaus's line of code. Looking at the second block of numbers and letters, 5G65Va, he headed five degrees east of due north, stopped after sixty-five paces, and surveyed his surroundings. His heart skipped a beat as he spotted a small mausoleum to his right bearing the name Vanags. The next block of code read 65G127Oz. Derek counted out 127 paces along a more easterly course of sixty-five degrees and was excited to see a large monument that bore the name Ozols. *This is it, Derek. You've got it.*

Just one more segment to go, 310G80SG. Turning to the northwest, 310 degrees, Derek began to pace another eighty meters. Then, *What the...?* Halfway there, he reached the edge of a lake extending north and west for at least a couple hundred meters. *Maybe Klaus wrote 310G by mistake.* Perhaps he meant to write 210 degrees. But no, that didn't make sense because that would pretty much take him back in the direction from which he just came. Still, he decided he'd better try. Returning to the Ozols monument, he took a southwesterly orientation of 210 degrees and paced off eighty meters. From there he walked increasing circles around the graves looking at the names on the monuments. Nothing. There were no monuments bearing the name Gustmann or anyone with first and last names beginning with S and G, respectively.

Derek walked back to the Ozols monument one more time. Klaus must have made some other mistake when he wrote that last block of code. If not 310 or 210 degrees, might it be 110 degrees? At least that wouldn't take him back into the lake or back in the direction where he'd started. Orienting himself 110 degrees east southeast of north, he once again paced eighty meters, stopped, and looked around. He was standing amidst numerous memorial markers and headstones. Two above ground mausoleums, one bearing the name Liepa, the other Gulbis, stood nearby to his left and right, respectively. Well, a G at least, but no SG, and Derek felt pretty sure Klaus must have cached the treasure in a grave topped by a monument bearing those letters. Once again, he walked a series of enlarging circles, carefully checking the names on each grave marker. No SG and no Gustmann! *Damn!*

Discouraged, Derek slowly returned to the cemetery entrance. He checked the name on each marker as he passed, even though his path no longer bore any relationship to the angles and distances specified in Klaus's line of code. Just inside the entrance, he spotted a man wearing work clothes and holding some tools in conversation with another man standing in the doorway of a small stone building. *Caretakers.* Maybe they could help him find a grave bearing the name Gustmann. He waved and approached the men, hoping at least one would know some English.

"Hello."

The men looked at him. The workman said nothing, while the man in the doorway replied, "Hul-lo."

"I wonder if you can help me. Do you speak English?"

The man shrugged, raised his hands palms outward, and replied, "*Piedo-diet. Es nesaprotu.*"

Derek thought a moment, then partially raised his right hand, palm forward with his index finger pointed skyward, hoping that in Latvia, as in the U.S., this would be interpreted as a "please wait a moment" sign. Then he went to fetch Maija and told her he hadn't been able to locate the grave of Stefan Gustmann. Would she please ask the man in the building whether the cemetery had records showing the location of any graves for persons of that name? He wasn't in fact sure if Stefan's full name was on the marker; it might just have been inscribed as S. Gustmann.

Maija did as he asked, translating from English to Latvian and back again. The man in the doorway invited them in to what turned out to be the cemetery office. Consulting a file cabinet, he finally found a folder bearing the name Gustmann and uttered something that sounded to Derek vaguely like "A-ha." But when the man opened it and began to read, his face took on a puzzled expression. Looking up, he spoke at some length to Maija. She turned to Derek and translated.

"Mr. Arājs says that according to this file the cemetery had a grave recorded for a Gustmann buried in 1944. The name on the low stone marker wasn't Stefan Gustmann but rather Säugling Gustmann, which suggests the deceased was an infant, or at least no more than two years of age. In any case, the reason you couldn't find the grave is that the original site is now under water. A lake formed there ten years ago when the Norupe River was dammed to prevent the frequent flooding of low-lying areas on the eastern and southern edges of Ogre. When the dam was built, sixty-three individuals had to be disinterred and reburied in another location. Säugling Gustmann was one of those."

"Ah, so that's why I couldn't find the grave based on what Aunt Gerda told me." *I wonder what they found when they dug up the grave?*

"And that is why Mr. Arājs looks so perplexed. The relocation of those graves occurred before he became caretaker, but the report in this file says that when workmen opened Säugling Gustmann's grave they found no coffin. What they did find were several empty German army ammunition cases and a bag holding a large number of Russian fifteen-ruble gold coins."

Both Maija and Mr. Arājs looked expectantly at Derek, as though he should be able to explain this mysterious finding. Derek, thinking he knew exactly what that finding meant, had no intention of explaining anything. Doing his best to assume a convincing look of surprise, he tried to improvise a plausible response.

"Why…I…I've no idea what that could mean. I'm beginning to think my Aunt Gerda may have been confused about a couple things. I know she had a brother named Stefan; I've seen his picture, and he did die young. But in the picture I saw he was definitely more than two years of age. I'm thinking maybe Stefan died some time after the family left this area. And Gerda, you know she's really very old now and sometimes has trouble remembering things. Of course, that in itself wouldn't explain what the workmen found when they dug up the Gustmann grave. Perhaps…perhaps the Gustmann family created this false grave as a hiding place for their valuables, removing them, but somehow missing one, when they finally left the country as the Russians reinvaded Latvia. I'm really just guessing. I'll ask Gerda when I get back home, but she may no longer remember."

Maija turned and translated Derek's remarks to Mr. Arājs, who listened carefully, then looking a little disappointed, shrugged his shoulders. No one in the group noticed the dark-haired man standing nearby, partially hidden behind a mature gingko tree next to a white marble mausoleum. Valery lowered the shotgun microphone he'd been aiming at Derek, Maija, and Mr. Arājs, and turned off his pocket recorder. He didn't know what to make of the conversation he'd just heard but figured this had to be what Sergei had wanted to know about.

Two hours later, after stopping in Ogre for lunch, Derek was back at the Mercure Riga Centre Hotel. He thanked Maija for her service as a chauffeur and translator, gave her a fifty-euro tip, and entered the hotel. His first thought was to call Eva to tell her what he'd just learned but then remembered she was at a medical conference in Hawaii. With the time difference he figured it would be 3:00 A.M. there. Not a good time to call. Instead, he wrote and sent off an email message that Eva could read whenever she got up.

The next morning in New York, Sergei read the email Derek had sent to Eva and saw it only confirmed what Valery had already conveyed to him. With the exception of a bag of gold coins, Klaus Gustmann must have recovered all the eggs, jewels, and gold he and his friend buried there during the war. Sergei felt encouraged and discouraged at the same time. Gustmann's treasure was almost certainly stashed somewhere in the United States just waiting to be found, but apparently Derek Todson and Eva Gustmann had no better idea than he did as to where it might be.

CHAPTER 50

A day and a half after returning from Warsaw, Derek was still suffering jet lag. He fell asleep before sunset on Saturday, woke up in the middle of the night, and then couldn't get to sleep again. Early Sunday morning he was sitting in his office, holding his second cup of coffee, and trying to focus on the text of a grant application due the following week. When his office phone rang, he picked it up without taking his eyes off the computer monitor and said, "Hello, Professor Todson speaking."

"My, we're formal this morning, Professor."

"Oh, Eva. I'm at the office and didn't see the number before I grabbed the phone. I suppose you must've tried calling my cell first, right? I'm still fighting jet lag and forgot to bring it with me to the office."

"Yeah, good old cell phones, wonderful if you remember to take them with you and also when they work. The battery on mine just quit last night. So I'm also talking to you on a house phone I hardly ever use." Then her voice took on a note of excitement. "It looks like we've got a break. Evans called last night and told me he's pretty sure he knows the identity of Dad's killer."

"Whoa! Someone at the Rubenstein Gallery?"

"Uh-huh, but sort of indirectly. It turns out ICE has had the place under surveillance for quite a while because they think the Russian mafia has been using it to launder some of its illegal money. Apparently the gallery buys and sells tens of millions of dollars' worth of Russian jewelry and art objects annually.

Evans and his NYPD buddy Collins arranged with an ICE agent for the three of them to make a surprise visit to the gallery. This time they managed to catch everyone, including the pair who'd been away before, and this time each of the three quizzed each employee separately, then got together to compare stories."

"And…?"

"Patience, I'm getting there. Once again, Rubenstein was nothing but helpful and consistent, and once again several of his employees acted pretty nervous. As Evans said before, that doesn't have to mean a whole lot, since being questioned by the cops can make anyone jumpy. But this time they finally got to interview one individual, the bookkeeper who'd been out of the country during the first round of interviews, and got missed again the second time they went because she was home sick. She seemed collected when Evans and his NYPD friend interviewed her. But when she learned the third guy was from ICE and asked her some different, very tough questions, she realized she'd been busted, and just confessed everything.

"Everything?"

"She confessed to having had an ongoing role in the money laundering operation. But the part we care about is she admitted to having known Vasily Kozlov. Turns out he'd been her regular contact with the Russian mafia for about a year and the person to whom she'd passed along essentially everything she learned about any high-value stuff coming to the gallery that the mafia might want to buy with their dirty money and then resell later. She didn't know Vasily was dead but hadn't seen him in a long time, and last spring she was introduced to a new contact named Tatiana Alliluyeva. She admitted to also passing to Tatiana a copy of the email I sent to Arkady Rubenstein just before I was kidnapped."

"This is getting to be a really long story. Give, Eva. WHO?'"

"Evans told me they learned Tatiana Alliluyeva is the live-in girlfriend of a guy named Sergei Yakushin who's long been suspected of being a *Capo* in the Russian mafia. Apparently he splits his time between condos in New York City and Montreal. As soon as they had that information ICE raided Sergei's condo in Manhattan and arrested Tatiana. Sergei wasn't there, and Tatiana claims she doesn't know where he is, so now they've asked the RCMP to look out for him in Canada. Evans feels sure Sergei must be the guy who was with Vasily Kozlov when Dad was kidnapped."

Eva took a breath and raced on. "And that's just the beginning. When I got back from Honolulu last night there was a pile of mail in my box. I just started to work through it this morning and guess what I found?"

"A letter from Publisher's Clearing House saying you've won $5,000 a week for the rest of your life?"

"Shut up, Derek, and get serious! A copy of the will."

"It sure took them a long time to get it to you."

"Yeah, but I guess I'm glad it was found at all. Debbie Maki enclosed a note of apology about the delay but went on to say not only had it been badly soaked by the sprinkler system, but also somehow ended up in one of two document boxes that got shunted into a closet with other stuff scheduled to be shredded and was only found again and rescued just a couple weeks ago. The ink ran pretty badly, making it difficult but not quite impossible to read. I just scanned it and sent a copy as an email attachment. I hope you have your computer with you."

"Sure. I'll look at it right now. Maybe we can figure out what he did with those other eggs after all."

Derek saved and closed the draft of his grant application. Then he signed on to his account and printed off a copy of the will Klaus Gustmann, a.k.a. Otto Krummel, had written more than sixty years ago. Remembering Tom Corker's comments, he quickly scanned the nursery rhyme written in German followed by twelve bible verses.

> Hoppe, hoppe, Reiter,
> Wenn er fällt, dann schreit er.
> Fällt er in die Graben,
> Fressen ihn die Schlangen.
> Fällt er in den Sumpf,
> Macht der Reiter plumps!
>
> Proverbs 1:8
> My son, hear the instruction of thy father, and forsake not the law of thy mother.
>
> Proverbs 13:22
> A good man leaveth an inheritance to his children's children: and the wealth of the sinner is laid up for the just.
>
> Ezekial 28:4

With thy wisdom and with thine understanding thou hast gotten thee riches, and hast gotten gold and silver into thy treasures.

Proverbs 10:2
Pleasures of wickedness profit nothing: but righteousness delivereth from death.

Ecclesiastes 8:10
And so I saw the wicked banished, who had come and gone from the place of the holy, and they were forgotten in the city where they had so done: this is also vanity.

1 Kings 20:38
So the prophet departed, and waited for the king by the way, and disguised himself with paint upon his face.

Deuteronomy 27:23
Cursed be he that lieth with his sister in law. And all the people shall say, Amen.

Matthew 15:39
And he sent away the multitude, and took ship, and came into the coast of Tiberias.

Psalm 5:9
For there is no faithfulness in their mouth; their inward part is very wickedness; their throat is an open draught; they flatter with their tongue.

Ezra 10:31
And the sons of Harim; Eliezer, Elijah, Malchiah, Shemaiah, Simeon.

1 Chronicles 2:47
And the sons of Jahdai; Regem, and Jotham, and Gesham, and Japhlet, and Ephah, and

Shaaph.

<u>Daniel 2:43</u>
And whereas thou sawest iron mixed with miry clay, they shall assemble themselves with the seed of men: but they shall not cleave one to another even as iron is not mixed with clay.

"Have you got it, Derek?"

"Yeah, and I can translate some of the words in the rhyme, but I'll have to check out a few of the others." He got up get his German dictionary.

"Don't bother. I know it by heart. Dad used to put me on his knee, bounce me up and down, and sing *Hoppe, hoppe, Reiter* more times than I can count."

Then she read from memory in English.

"Hop, hop, rider, If he falls he will cry.

"If he falls into the ditch, He will be eaten by the ravens.

"If he falls into the mud, The rider makes a thump."

Then, "Whoa, wait a minute. Something's wrong. This isn't quite right."

"What?"

"The last words in the fourth line Dad sang to me was always *die Raben*, the ravens. This says *die Schlangen*, the snakes. I'm *certain* he never sang it that way."

"Hang on a minute. Let me check something." Derek typed *Hoppe hoppe Reiter* into his browser, opened the first reference that popped up, and quickly skimmed through the text of the rhyme shown there. "Okay, the first reference shows just what you said. It lists the fourth line as *Fressen ihn die Raben*, but just below the rhyme it goes on to say several other variations of the rhyme are known. Do you suppose…?" But as soon as he began to say it and Eva started to object, he stopped, thinking it didn't make sense Klaus would have written out a version of the rhyme different than the one that Horst and his aunt Gerda should know. Was it conceivable Klaus could have forgotten which version he used to sing to Horst and accidentally replaced *die Raben* with *die Schlangen* from an alternate version he'd heard at some time? Possible, but he didn't believe it. Derek felt sure Klaus meant this change to help guide Horst and Gerda, but no one else, to the treasure he'd managed to bring back from Latvia.

With that in mind, the amateur detective couple went back and forth, trying out and rejecting possible messages the rhyme might have been meant to convey. Coming up dry after an hour, Eva suggested they take a break, get something to eat, skip the rhyme for a bit, and take a look at the Bible verses.

Derek left his office and walked three blocks to Dario's where he ordered a cheesesteak and a diet coke. Then he sat in a small park to eat and continue thinking about the rhyme. *What the hell could either ravens or snakes have to do with the location of the treasure?* Then, he thought, *The words of the verses themselves don't have to mean anything! It's just the fact they're different from what was expected that's important. He's using the rhyme to tell Horst and Gerda to look at the Bible verses for* wrong *words. Somehow that'll help them find the treasure.* Derek quickly finished lunch and hurried back to his office.

Minutes later, with the page of the will in hand on which Klaus had written the twelve Bible verses, and Eva on the phone with a KJV Bible she'd taken from her father's apartment, they proceeded to test Derek's hypothesis. Turning to Proverbs 1:8 in her bible, Eva read aloud as Derek scanned his copy of the will. No difference at all! Disappointed, he told Eva to go to the next one, Proverbs 13:32. Again, the text as written in the will was exactly the same as that in the Bible. Giving it one more try, Eva flipped to and read aloud from Ezekial 28:4. Once again, the Bible and the will read the same.

"Damn! It looks as though my idea doesn't wash."

Stymied, the two spent most of the next hour trading and rejecting ideas before Eva hit on something useful.

"Derek, the more I look at them, the more it seems like the first three verses are just a kind of preamble telling my Dad and Aunt Gerda to pay attention, he's set aside a significant inheritance, and if they think about it they should be able to figure out where it is. But in doing that I think maybe he made the text of those three verses exactly match the Bible to also foil and to discourage someone else, like us for example, who get their hands on the will and try to decode it. Let's keep going and look at the next nine verses in the will. If I'm right, that's where the key information has to be."

"Well...okay. Klaus has done a pretty fair job of discouraging me so far."

Consulting the Bible again, Eva read aloud from Proverbs 10:2. "Treasures of wickedness profit nothing: but righteousness delivereth from death."

"Whoa, Eva! There's a difference. That line you just read starts with the word *Treasures*, but in the will it starts with *Pleasures*."

"You're right!"

Eva read from her Bible each of the next eight verses Klaus had written in the will, and in each case they spotted a single word where the text as written in the will differed from that in the Bible. Derek typed out a column of the substituted words alongside the correct words from the Bible, and immediately saw what he thought must be the clue they'd been looking for.

Will	KJV Bible
Pleasures	Treasures
Banished	Buried
Paint	Ashes
Sister	Mother
Tiberias	Magdala
Draught	Sepulchre
Elijah	Ishijah
Japhlet	Pelet
Assemble	Mingle

"I think we've got it, Eva, or at least part of it. Listen. Treasures buried ashes mother Magdala sepulchre Ishijah Pelet mingle."

Eva was silent for a moment. Then she said, "Huh? That makes it sound like my grandfather was telling Dad and Aunt Gerda their inheritance is buried with my grandmother Magda's ashes. But that doesn't make any sense."

"Why not?"

"Two good reasons. Dad told me his mother died of pneumonia in 1938 and was buried in the Gustmann family mausoleum in a suburb of Dresden. He recalled being taken there by Gerda, and once showed me a picture of the family mausoleum where she was interred with his grandparents, Axel and Ericka Gustmann, and Klaus's younger brother Erik. At that time the family was Catholic, so I'm pretty sure Magda's body would have been entombed intact, not cremated, so the reference to ashes doesn't ring true. Apart from that I see no reason at all why he would've gone back to Dresden, which was then under Soviet control. We know he'd already gotten Gerda out of Dresden and over to the American Sector of Berlin, and later communicated with her there from Sweden before coming to the U.S. I'm guessing he had the treasure with him the whole time, so what do these words tell us? To whom do these *Magda's ashes* belong, and where were they when my grandfather wrote this will in 1953?"

"Maybe...they don't belong to anyone. Klaus used a false grave to hide the treasure in Latvia. Maybe he did that again. I'm thinking he might have hidden the eggs and maybe some other small items like jewelry in a funerary urn in a grave bearing the name of his dead wife Magda."

"So where is it?" Eva quickly read off the original KJV words for which Klaus had inserted substitutes when writing out the final three Bible verses Klaus in his will. "*Ishijah, Pelet, mingle.* The first two words appear to be personal names followed by the word mingle. So, something about two guys getting together? That's not giving me any insight."

Derek offered, "You don't suppose he might have intended for his son and sister to cross back to the will and look for meaning in the substitute words he used there, *Elijah, Japhlet,* and *assemble*? Once again, there are two personal names, and while mingle and assemble don't mean exactly the same thing that both seem to hint at people coming together."

"God, Derek, I don't know. This is getting really Byzantine." Eva fell quiet for a time, then started to say the three words she'd read out loud before, but slower this time, then even slower with emphasis placed on the first syllable of each word. "*Ish-i-jah, Pe-let, min-gle.* **Ish**-*i-jah,* **Pe**-*let,* **min**-*gle.*"

"Whoa! You've got it, Eva. Just add the **g** at the end and you have Ishpeming, the town where Klaus lived the last two years of his life. That's got to be where he hid the treasure, and I'll bet it's hidden in a fake grave marked with the name of his wife Magda."

Eva said, "I'll call the cemetery tomorrow and ask if they have a record of a Magda Gustmann being buried there. No, wait a minute...I almost forgot my grandfather was living as Otto Krummel. I'd better ask if the cemetery has a record of a grave for Magda Krummel."

CHAPTER 51

The next morning, Eva called the phone number she'd found for the cemetery in Ishpeming, Michigan, and spoke to the sexton, a man named John Auvinen. She told him she was tracing her family history and had recently learned her *maternal* grandfather, Otto Krummel, had been living in Ishpeming and died there in 1953. She'd heard that Otto brought with him from Germany the ashes of his wife Magda, who'd passed away some years earlier. Could he please check and tell her if Otto's and Magda's remains were interred in the Ishpeming cemetery? She'd already tried looking on *www.findagrave.com* but drew a blank.

John Auvinen put her on hold, returning a couple minutes later to say a funerary box containing the ashes of Magda Krummel had indeed been interred in March 1951 in niche number twelve of a columbarium located on Elm Street in the southwest corner of the Ishpeming cemetery. The record showed that her husband, Otto Krummel, had also purchased niche number thirteen for his own use at a future time, but there was no record of his remains being interred there or anywhere else in the cemetery. To Eva, the sexton sounded like a fairly young man, someone unlikely to know anything about the circumstances surrounding Otto's death in 1953. With no body, of course there would have been no burial. Eva thanked him and ended the call after learning the columbarium was unlocked and open to visitors during regular cemetery hours, 11:00 A.M. to 5:00 P.M. Then, she sent a three-word email to Derek that said, "Ishpeming says YES!"

Had it been up to Derek, he'd have taken off the next day. On sabbatical leave from Franklin University during the fall term he was pretty much free to travel at will. But Eva already had a full load of patients scheduled at the clinic through October and in to most of November. Finally, after promising to cover Joe Donnelly for three days around Thanksgiving and by making a similar deal with Amy Blomquist for two days just before Christmas, she was able clear her calendar for November 14–20. As they had in June, the detective couple agreed to meet in Detroit and fly from there to Marquette.

Meanwhile, Sergei, disguised as Jussi Eskola, a Finnish businessman, was biding his time in a hotel in the suburbs of Montreal. Tipped off just in time about Tatiana's arrest by ICE in New York, he'd slipped out of New York and into Canada, using one of two false identities he always carried for such emergencies. Temporarily cutting off communication with other *Bratva* members in New York and Montreal, he was staying out of sight and contemplating his options. Sergei cursed his bad luck and cursed himself for ever having worked with Vasily. Tatiana knew all about that, so he had to suppose she would eventually break and spill information linking him to the kidnapping and murder of Horst Gustmann. And for what? He hadn't gotten the old man's egg or enough information as to know where the others were. Thinking again about the story his uncle Gennady had related years ago about Klaus Gustmann and the eggs, he realized he hadn't really had good reason to assume Horst Gustmann would've ever had more than the one egg. The old man had vigorously denied knowing about any others. And as his uncle had told him, after the two MGB agents finally cornered and killed Klaus Gustmann and were themselves killed shortly thereafter, there'd been no mention of the eggs or any other valuables being found in the agent's wrecked car. Maybe they had been found, the discovery kept quiet, and the eggs sold privately in sales never made public. Or maybe they were still hidden somewhere waiting to be found. *Damn it all.* Sergei sighed, poured himself another drink. What to do next? He had considerable cash stashed in several locations, but it wouldn't last forever.

A moment later one of his burner phones rang, the one he'd let Mikhail in Moscow know about. Should he answer it? He debated a few seconds, then took a chance thinking, or at least hoping, the only reason Mikhail would be calling was to pass on some potentially useful information he'd managed to glean by spying on Eva's and Derek's computers.

Indeed, Mikhail's message gave Sergei a glimmer of hope. Apparently, Klaus Gustmann, alias Otto Krummel, had left a will, leaving his entire estate to Horst and Gerda Gustmann, describing them as cousins, and yesterday Mikhail had detected Eva Gustmann sending a copy of that will to Derek Todson. What was the significance of these two communicating about a will written more than sixty years ago? Was Eva Gustmann just interested in the will as a piece of family history or something more?

"Mikhail, what was the accompanying message with the will Gustmann sent to Todson?"

"Nothing, really. There was just a title line that said. 'Here it is.'"

"But you have their phones monitored, no?"

"Yes, but apparently they weren't using their cell phones at the time. However, the next day Gustman sent an email to Todson saying 'Ishpeming says yes' with the yes in caps. The next day Todson called her and said, 'Leave now?' and Gustmann replied, 'I wish, but I've got way too many patients right now. It'll probably be several weeks before I can work something out.' Does all that mean anything to you, Sergei?"

"Not right away, Mikhail." To himself thinking, *Ishpeming, Michigan, is where my uncle told me the MGB finally caught up with Gustmann and killed him. If those two are excited to go there maybe it could mean…* "But I really want to see that will. Circumstances…uh, make it necessary to stay off the internet for a while, so print a hard copy of that will as soon as possible, and keep monitoring their computers and phones, especially anything mentioning the will or their travel plans."

"Okay, Sergei, but maybe only for a little longer. This is taking quite a lot of my time. You mentioned large compensation, but now I'm hearing you're, shall I say, indisposed."

"This is temporary, Mikhail. I *will* pay you."

"Yes, I certainly hope so. You know you don't want to cross me, Sergei."

With that, Sergei let Mikhail know the pseudonym under which he was currently living, the address of the hotel where he'd be for the next few days, and then gave him the number of a different phone on which to reach him the next time.

Three days later, with a hard copy of the will in hand, Jussi Eskola checked out of the hotel, became a Canadian named Alex Norton, ditched the used burner phone in a trash bin, bought two more, and took a bus west to Ottawa. Once there, he settled into a rarely used apartment supplied with a substantial hidden cache of cash where he could study the will and impatiently wait for more information from Mikhail. For three days he poured over the will for hours at a time, finally throwing the damned thing on the floor in frustration. He wasn't a patient man.

CHAPTER 52

Their flights from San Francisco and Philadelphia both arrived in Detroit on schedule, allowing Eva and Derek time for dinner before the connecting flight to Marquette at 10:00 P.M. However, thirty minutes past the time when boarding should have commenced, the gate agent told the waiting passengers their plane had a mechanical problem that *might* be fixed in another hour. Finally, at 12:10 A.M., they were allowed to board. Twenty-five minutes later it took off and at 1:40 A.M. touched down at Sawyer International Airport. An hour later, after checking in at the Landmark Inn, the two promptly crashed and slept until nearly ten the next morning.

Over a late breakfast with multiple cups of coffee, they talked through when and how they could gain access to Magda Krummel's niche in the columbarium. Although the main entrance to the building was open every day until 5:00 P.M., the individual niches were of course locked. They had no key and the odds seemed slim to none Eva could simply persuade the Sexton to give her one. Derek supposed the best thing they could do was to first just go there to verify that niche number twelve was in fact labeled as holding the ashes of Magda Krummel. After that, he supposed they would have to go to the court in Marquette on Monday, find out how to ask for Otto's will to be formally reexamined, submit documents establishing Eva as Horst Gustmann's legitimate heir, and get an order to have Magda's ashes examined. God knew how long that would take.

But Eva surprised him, confiding she possessed a skill he'd always pretty much associated only with magicians and criminals. Leaning forward with a grin, she whispered, "We don't have to wait for all that to find out what's in there. I can pick the lock!"

Derek looked askance, but Eva assured him she'd only taken it up as a hobby and had never used the skill to do anything illegal, not until now anyway. Now she said she just couldn't resist. She wanted to try picking the locks to niches number twelve and number thirteen in the columbarium. If they found what they hoped, she promised to leave everything in place, relock the niches, and then start legal proceedings to claim the Fabergé eggs and any other valuables her grandfather might have hidden there.

By eleven o'clock, a leaden sky, gusting wind, and snow flurries were already providing notice of an approaching nor'easter that forecasters expected to peak in another twenty-four to thirty-six hours. Officially, sunset was at 5:16 P.M., but the sun wasn't visible even now, and Derek figured it would be quite dark by four. That seemed like a good time to try their luck at the columbarium. In the dark, with deteriorating weather, few if any people other than the caretaker were likely to be at the cemetery.

Shortly after four, Eva turned into the main cemetery entrance, and from there navigated two internal lanes to the southwest sector where the columbarium was located. As she prepared to park, Eva noticed a pair of headlights approaching in the rearview mirror.

"Damn it, we aren't alone after all. Do you think we should put this off until tomorrow?"

However, the car, a silver-colored Cadillac Escalade with Wisconsin plates, passed them. It drove on another block, then turned left onto another lane and stopped after a short distance next to a large memorial marker. Eva and Derek watched, as the driver, leaving just his parking lights on, got out and studied the inscription on the monument using a flashlight. A moment later, they saw him reach into the back of the car, retrieve a bouquet of cut flowers, then kneel and lay them at the base of the monument.

Eva whispered, "I guess we should be okay. He's a fair distance away, and it looks like he's occupied. Let's go in." Quietly, they got out of the car and, without using their flashlight, entered the columbarium, and closed the door behind them. Inside it was pitch dark, but now Derek used his flashlight to find and illuminate the door to niche number twelve. Below the door to the niche was a bronze plaque that indeed read as they'd hoped.

Magda Krummel
Loving wife of Otto Krummel
Born 13 April 1909
Died 23 December 1938

Eva got out her tension wrench, hook pick, and rake pick. It took only a short time before she whispered, "Got it." Derek heard the lock's plug rotate and saw the door swing open. Eva withdrew the box, placed it on the floor on a piece of plastic sheeting, and opened the top. The box held no ashes, just three roughly spherical objects wrapped in several layers of flannel. Eva unwrapped one, and a golden, jewel-encrusted egg came into view.

"Oh, my God! We've got it."

At that moment the columbarium door opened, and they were temporarily blinded by the light from a large high-powered flashlight. Shielding his eyes, Derek could only discern the outline of a very large man, who held the flashlight in his left hand and a gun in his right. It was a .38 caliber pistol assembled from plastic parts that Sergei had been able to sneak past the TSA in carryon luggage.

"I will relieve you of those ornaments now, Dr. Gustmann."

Eva hissed, "You killed my father, you bastard, and then you tried to kidnap me."

"True." Sergei smirked. "And this time I'm getting what I came for."

Continuing to hold them at gunpoint, Sergei focused his flashlight to take a closer look at the egg Eva had unwrapped. As he did, his gun arm shifted, and Derek decided to take a chance. Dropping his flashlight, he threw himself at Sergei, grabbed his gun arm, and brought his right knee up as hard as he could into the man's groin. Sergei howled in pain and attempted to shoot him. Derek held on, forcing the gun away and up so that the bullet missed and struck the ceiling. Meanwhile, Eva picked up Derek's flashlight and attacked Sergei from the left, repeatedly striking him on the head. The combined attack might have succeeded against a lesser assailant, but Sergei was a bull of a man.

Sergei struck Eva a sharp blow to the head with his large flashlight, knocking her to the ground. Shifting his attention back to Derek, who continued to hold onto his gun arm, Sergei pulled his left knee sharply into Derek's groin and hit him hard on temple with his flashlight. Derek fell to the ground writhing and only semi-conscious. Pointing his pistol at Derek, he fired.

Then, turning to Eva, he pointed the pistol at her. She froze in fear as he pulled the trigger, but the gun jammed and failed to fire. Cursing, he hit Eva once again with his flashlight. Then he picked up the unwrapped egg and the other two wrapped ones still in the box and ran from the columbarium with them.

Stunned but conscious, Eva heard Derek moaning. Unable to see him in the dark, she reached around until she found the flashlight. The right side of his face was already turning purple where Sergei had hit him. But her main concern was the bullet wound. The slug had hit his upper arm and exited out the back. What was clear and frightening was it must have nicked an artery. Derek was bleeding heavily and at risk of soon going into shock. Eva pulled off her scarf, rolled it tightly to make a rope, and wrapped that around Derek's arm above the wound to use as a tourniquet. She tied a pen to her makeshift tourniquet, then twisted and locked it in place after applying enough compression to stem the bleeding. No time to lose now.

Eva called 911 and, as she waited, said, "Derek, can you hear me?"

His eyes remained closed, but he moaned and whispered, "Eva?"

"Stay with me, Derek. I've called 911. We'll get you to the hospital. You're going to be okay." *At least I hope so.*

The 911 dispatcher answered on the second ring. Quickly describing the situation, Eva gave her location and stayed on the phone as the dispatcher arranged for an ambulance and contacted both the Ishpeming City and the Michigan State Police. When he came back on the line, he told her the ETA for the ambulance was five minutes. Eva kept eyes on Derek, who was now looking very pale.

The ambulance and an Ishpeming Police car arrived at almost the same instant, followed a minute later by a Michigan State Police squad car. As the EMTs worked on Derek, Eva summarized events for the police. She described Sergei and told them he'd been driving a silver-colored Cadillac Escalade with Wisconsin plates whose leading letters she remembered because they were the same as her initials, EMG.

An APB was issued for the Escalade along with the sketchy description Eva had been able to give of the man who attacked them. State Police patrol cars were especially alerted to watch for the suspect car along highways US 41 and M 28.

Sergei was most of the way to Marquette when he heard the APB go out on the police scanner he'd brought with him. He needed to get off the main highway as soon as possible, get rid of the Escalade, and either get a different car or find some other means of getting out of the U.P. He'd used his good false Canadian passport for Alex Norton to go back and forth between the U.S. and Canada on several occasions. But he couldn't chance driving all the way to Sault Ste. Marie now. He thought about trying to fly to Detroit or Chicago. However, the weather had degraded to such a degree it seemed certain any flights would now have been cancelled.

He wasn't sure how good a look Gustmann managed to get of him, but he was afraid that by tomorrow a police artist might have put together a sufficiently good likeness to make it risky for him to pass through security at the airport. Maybe a bus? That also seemed risky. Only two buses went through Marquette each day. It would be too easy for a cop to board and briefly check out the riders. Then he'd be trapped.

Sergei figured his best chance might be to just stay out of sight in Marquette for a day or two, then change his appearance and turn back into Jussi Eskola again to match the other false driver's license he carried. The picture on that license showed him to have blond hair, and blue eyes (courtesy of colored contacts) as opposed to the dark-haired person with hazel eyes he was now. Then he could rent another car and get out of the area.

He needed time to think, so looked for a place to park the Escalade where it wasn't likely to attract a lot of attention. Approaching downtown Marquette, he turned north on 4th street, drove a mile, and decided to turn into the parking lot of St. Michael's Church, where parishioners were arriving for a Saturday mass.

Sergei thought for a moment, then decided to call and reveal himself to Viktor Ruchkin, a longtime friend in the *Bratva*. He told Viktor what he'd acquired and offered to make a deal. He was in a bind because a witness had survived when his gun misfired and had made him. His description and that of his car were all over the police scanner. Could Viktor help get him and his take out of the area or, preferably, out of the country? He promised to be generous.

Viktor agreed it made sense for Sergei to go underground for a day or two and then reemerge with a different identity. In the meantime, he had an idea for transporting the eggs to Canada without risking discovery when Sergei subsequently flew or drove across the border with his new identity.

"My boys bring horse into Michigan from Windsor, Sarnia, and Sault Ste. Marie. One of the camels is a cook on the lake freighter Giiwedin. Right now it's in Marquette taking on a load of taconite at the Presque Isle dock. It's due to leave at seven and deliver the ore to Essar Steel Algoma in Sault Ste. Marie tomorrow morning. An hour before departure Pyotr always gets a box of groceries delivered from a store in Marquette. And that's not all. Pyotr gives the van driver a new load of goods, and the driver gives him payment for the stuff he brought in the last time the ship was in port."

"Where are you going with this, Viktor? Are you seriously suggesting I send the eggs to Canada with this Pyotr?"

"Sure. I'll be happy to set that up. Just remember me when you cash them in, okay?"

"Damn it, Viktor. They're worth a fortune. I know squat about your Pyotr or the other guy who brings the groceries. What's to stop them from ripping me off? Did you hear about the trouble I had earlier this year with Vasily Kozlov?"

Viktor replied, "I did, but you didn't really know him very well, did you? Trust me, Sergei. I've worked a long time with these guys. They know the cost of screwing up. I'll admit, we had one guy last year who thought he'd divert and sell a little product on his own." Viktor chuckled. "The poor man lost his mind, literally."

"I still don't like it, Viktor. Look, is there some way you could get the goods *and* me on the Giiwedin?"

"I don't know. Well…maybe. I'll call Pyotr first, and then our guy who delivers for the grocer. I'll tell him to meet you at the Presque Isle dock in an hour and to give both the groceries and the payment to you. You take them on board and give them to Pyotr. Pyotr will take you to the galley and find some place for you to hide while the ship makes its run to Canada. If anyone asks, he'll say you got right off the ship after making the delivery, and if they care to look they'll see that the delivery van is no longer parked at the dock. I'll meet you later in Sault Ste. Marie. This is going to cost you, Sergei."

"I promise, Viktor. I'm good for it."

CHAPTER 53

Captain Colin Hampton looked from the bridge with some concern as the last carloads of taconite slid down the chutes into the holds of the Giiwedin. The wind had increased to an average of twenty miles per hour with occasional gusts to thirty-five, and increasingly heavy snowfall made it hard to see much beyond the end of the dock. Once again he checked with the Coast Guard and NOAA regarding current conditions in the eastern part of Lake Superior and how they were expected to change overnight.

The large low pressure system covering much of the eastern half of the country was spiraling counterclockwise, creating a giant nor'easter expected to result in blizzard conditions around the Great Lakes. Still, it wasn't supposed to peak until late morning tomorrow. Hampton knew it usually took eleven hours for the fully loaded Giiwedin to go from Marquette to Sault Ste. Marie. If he left now, the run could be a little rough, but he ought to be able to make it several hours before the lake really got dangerous. He signaled the crew to make sure all hatches were secure and get ready for departure. In the galley, Pyotr showed Sergei to a small storage room and told him to stay in it for the duration of the trip.

Six hours out, the Giiwedin was being hit by increasingly strong crosswinds and starting to fall behind schedule. Captain Hampton now estimated it would take at least thirteen hours to reach Sault Ste. Marie. Of growing concern was a problem he'd started to have with the control system for the ship's rudder. Electronic directions from the bridge to turn the rudder were taking an unusually long time to register and then sometimes failed to bring about as much change as needed. The engineer was working on the problem, but so far hadn't been able to correct the fault. Hampton was finding he had to order frequent overcorrections to remain on course. When the problem first started, he'd briefly considered heading back to Marquette but then decided to continue east. He should have turned around.

An hour later, there was no longer a question as to whether the ship was in serious trouble. The guidance system had become even more erratic, and the Giiwedin was starting to turn athwart the gusting northeast wind, wallowing and in danger of rolling over. Hampton directed his first officer to put a distress call through to the Coast Guard, then rang a general alarm and told crew members to stand by their stations and to put on their marine survival suits. In the storeroom off the ship's galley, Sergei had had enough. He'd become nauseated and scared by the rolling of the ship, and when he heard the general alarm, that was it. With Magda's funerary box held under his left arm, he entered the galley to find a panicked Pyotr donning his marine survival suit.

"Where's one of those for me?"

Pyotr stared at Sergei. "I…I don't know. There's just one assigned to each crew member. I…"

Pulling his pistol from his pocket, Sergei shot Pyotr in the head, having earlier changed the clip that had malfunctioned when he'd tried to shoot Eva. Then he started to put on Pyotr's survival suit but was having trouble as he was both several inches taller and heavier than the man for whom it was made. At that moment, the ship rolled precipitously, causing the funerary box to fall from the table. It opened and spilled the three eggs in different directions. Pausing, Sergei tried to pick up the eggs, but as he did, the ship pitched in the other direction and the eggs rolled away. The general alarm rang once again, and this time Captain Hampton shouted through the PA system.

"ALL HANDS. ABANDON SHIP! ABANDON SHIP!"

Gripped with panic, Sergei ran from the galley to a ladder leading to the main deck. Once there, he grabbed and pushed away two other crew members ahead of him. The pitch of the ship was too great to stand without support, so he stopped just short of the open deck and once again tried to completely close the suit. Then, stepping outside, he grabbed the portside railing for support.

A tremendous gust of wind made the ship roll even further. Looking up, Sergei saw an even larger wave about to crest as it approached. The ship rolled over. Its load shifted, and two of the aft hatches broke open. Water poured in, and the Giiwedin quickly sank, stern first.

Cast into the frigid water, Sergei didn't so much feel cold as complete shock. For a few seconds he still believed he was going to survive, but because of his size he hadn't been able to completely seal the survival suit. Within a minute, he was painfully cold, then numb, then sleepy, then nothing at all.

CHAPTER 54

The sinking of the Giiwedin evoked memories among many residents of the U.P. of a similar fate suffered by the lake freighter Edmund Fitzgerald thirty-nine years earlier. Over a two-day period, the nor'easter responsible for this latest tragedy buffeted the Upper Peninsula with high winds gusting to near hurricane velocity and covered it with a foot and a half of snow. When it finally abated and people began to dig out, the bodies of three crew members who had managed to don survival suits and reach the deck before the ship sank were discovered on the southern shore of the lake twenty miles east of Grand Marais. Two of the men were quickly identified, but the third was a mystery. News reports described him as a large, middle-aged Caucasian man in possession of two passports bearing different names, neither of which appeared on the Giiwedin's list of crew members. Pending further investigation, authorities declined to reveal those names or any other information about the man, a decision that only served to whet the appetite of the media. Numerous commentaries and speculations about the 'mystery man' immediately soon appeared in print, on TV, and on social media.

Three days after being shot, Derek was released from the hospital in Marquette, still feeling a bit shaky and very sore. Eva, sporting a large bruise on the right side of her face, but otherwise unharmed, drove him back to the Landmark Inn. They'd just settled into a corner booth at the hotel restaurant when Sergeant Michael Wolcott of the Michigan State Police entered and sought them out. He placed a picture on the table.

"Is this him?"

The photograph showed the face of a man wearing an orange marine survival suit. Eva looked and paled.

"I only saw his face briefly when we were struggling and I hit him with the flashlight, but yes, that's the man who attacked us."

"He's the 'mystery man' from the Giiwedin I'm sure you've heard about. He was carrying two different passports, one from Finland identifying him as Jussi Eskola, the other a Canadian passport identifying him as Alex Norton. Both turned out to be fakes, albeit good ones."

"Have you figured out who he really is? Is…is he the man who killed my father, Sergei Yakushin?"

"Yes, he is. We found the car he drove parked on a side road close to the Presque Isle ore dock. Apparently he went there knowing the Giiwedin was in port and arranged with someone to help him stow away and escape to Canada. We've identified the fingerprints of our 'mystery man' and those lifted from the car as belonging to Sergei Yakushin, long known to have been associated with Russian mafia operations in Montreal and New York but up to now never convicted of anything. The kidnapping and murder of your father, his attempt to kidnap you, Dr. Gustmann, and his assault on you and Dr. Todson last week doesn't smell like an organized mafia operation. It looks more like he went rogue, driven by some personal obsession to get his hands on those Fabergé eggs."

Eva shook her head. "Just an awful tragedy for the crew and their families, but for that bastard the sinking of the Giiwedin seems like the sort of rough justice he had coming."

"I guess, but a pretty expensive outcome for you. Assuming he had them with him, those eggs are now on the floor of Lake Superior under about nine hundred feet of water."

The next morning, Eva and Derek were about to head to breakfast when the room phone rang. It was Wolcott again.

"Dr. Gustmann, I thought you'd like to know that in addition to identifying Yakushin, we've now cracked open a Russian mafia drug operation. Last night, when we talked to the guy who brings groceries to the Giiwedin, he acted very squirrely. We kept working on him and eventually he admitted to being a drug mule for the mafia. He received drugs brought in from Canada by the Giiwedin's cook. His job was to distribute to local dealers, collect payments, and then deliver the money back to the cook the next time the ship came in to port. Last Friday, his boss called and said there'd been a change of plan. He was to meet another guy at the dock and give him the groceries and money to take on board the ship. He described the guy. Clearly it was Yakushin."

Wolcott finished by telling Eva that she and Derek should prepare themselves for a flurry of calls from the media. The police were about to hold a press conference making public the drug bust, the identification of Sergei Yakushin as the Giiwedin "mystery man" and the story behind his attack on Eva and Derek. Eva made a face at the thought but thanked him for the heads up. He hadn't exaggerated. Within hours of his call, they'd been contacted for interviews by reporters from WLUC-TV and *The Mining Journal*. That afternoon and the next day they fielded calls from newspapers and network TV stations in Milwaukee, Chicago, and Detroit.

Two days later, Eva took a call from someone with a 323 area code number. It turned out to be from a Howard Bernstein, producer and director of the program *Treasure Finders* that ran on cable channel ZX. "I've just seen the recent newspaper and network TV summaries about the experiences you and Dr. Todson had looking for the Imperial Russian Fabergé eggs that your grandfather found and hid away long ago. First, allow me to express sympathy for the loss of your father and the dangers to which you and Dr. Todson have since been exposed. But I'm also calling to ask if the two of you would be willing to tell your story on a future episode of *Treasure Finders*. It would make a wonderful sequel to the program we ran last February about the Third Imperial Egg."

Bernstein continued on, offering to fly them first class to Beverly Hills for a weekend taping session and to put them up, all expenses paid, in a deluxe suite at the Peninsula Beverly Hills hotel. Eva had had her phone on speaker so Derek could hear. Her first thought was to say no to the proposal, but then she glanced over at Derek.

"What do you think, Derek?"

Derek shrugged, then, "What the heck. Let's do it. Any time I can spend an all-expenses paid weekend with you in a luxury hotel…"

EPILOGUE

E va and Derek's story was shown on *Treasure Finders* the second week of March. A few days later, as Derek left the lecture hall, his phone pinged. It was a text from Eva.

In the office, he put a call through on FaceTime and a moment later Eva answered.

"Hey Eva, what gives?"

"Derek, I just had a really strange call from a woman in Mexico City who identified herself as Anna Vasquez. She told me she'd just seen our episode of *Treasure Finders* and has some very important information about my grandfather she's sure I don't already know. She said she's scheduled to be in L.A. next week at a conference for social service agency administrators and asked if we could meet her there."

"You think she's real or some kind of crank?"

"I didn't know what to think at first, but no, I'm fairly sure she isn't. I probed a bit, asked who she was and where she was calling from. She told me she lives in Mexico and was calling from a place called Lomas Verdes, a suburb on the west side of Mexico City. She said she's just retired as the administrative head of a children's orphanage there, and when she told me the name of the place it hit like an electric shock."

"Well?"

"*El Hogar Otto Krummel para Huérfanos.*"

"You're kidding! The Otto Krummel Home for Orphans?"

"Keep listening. She told me she once lived in Ishpeming, Michigan as a child, knew my grandfather at the time as Otto Krummel, and would I be interested to know he didn't actually die there?"

"Wow!"

"Derek, we've got to meet this woman and hear her story. She's staying at the Hyatt Century Plaza in L.A. from the sixth through the eighth of April and could meet with us any one of those days. I could be there on the sixth or the eighth, but not the seventh. What about you?"

"I've got a lecture on the eighth, but I'm free on the sixth. How about I fly to San Francisco on Good Friday? Maybe we could spend Saturday in Sonoma, stay overnight, then fly to L.A. Sunday afternoon, and meet her Monday morning."

At 7:10 A.M. Monday, April 6, Eva and Derek sat in the lobby of the Hyatt Century Plaza, waiting for Anna Vasquez to show for a 7:00 A.M. breakfast meeting. The door to one elevator opened, disgorging a bevy of young women wearing tags identifying them as attendees of a conference on early elementary education. Moments later, a much older, white-haired woman emerged from a second elevator. Of medium height, lean, and tanned, she wore a dark blue business suit, carried a leather briefcase, and approached with a slight limp favoring her left knee.

"Dr. Gustmann, Dr. Todson? I'm Anna Vasquez."

Eva replied, "Pleased to meet you, Mrs. Vasquez."

Derek extended his hand and said, "Please, no need for formalities. Call us Eva and Derek."

"Fine. I'm sorry to be late. I twisted my knee two weeks ago and it's been a real pain, literally. The doctor tells me I have a torn meniscus and will need arthroscopic surgery."

Derek replied, "I've been there. Both knees in fact. My doctor tells me I need to stop jogging and take up a less punishing form of exercise."

Eva added, "I'm trying to get him to try biking, but so far he just gives me a mournful little boy expression and tells me how much he really, really wants to run."

"Yes, my husband Jorge often gives me that look. I believe it's a common male trait."

The requisite small talk accomplished, Eva looked at the woman and said, "Anna, the truth is I was at first convinced you must be some kind of kook when you phoned and said you knew things about my grandfather you were sure I didn't know, especially that he hadn't died in 1953."

Anna nodded but didn't immediately respond.

"But when you said you'd been the head of a private nonprofit orphanage named *El Hogar Otto Krummel para Huérfanos*, that really blew me away. I Googled both you and the orphanage, found out it really does exist, was founded in 1955, heavily funded by an anonymous donor. I also read your bio, identifying you as the current director of the orphanage. It also mentioned you'd been born in Ishpeming, Michigan, and that your maiden name had been Anna Albrecht. That *completely* nailed it. When Derek and I looked into my grandfather's life in Ishpeming, we learned he'd had a close relationship with a woman named Kristin Albrecht and that she'd a daughter named Anna. I take it you are she?"

Anna nodded again and said, "You did exactly as I would have expected. Yes, I'm that Anna Albrecht, and my mother Kristin fell in love with your grandfather. We only knew him as Otto Krummel at the time. Let's get some breakfast in the restaurant, and I'll give you the whole story."

The waitress brought coffee and Anna began her tale.

"*Treasure Finders* isn't a program I normally watch. But I was bored that night, started to surf through the channels, and happened to land on the show as the camera panned in on the image of a Fabergé egg. I thought, hey, I know something about those, and heard the narrator say this one had recently been confirmed as the Alexander III Medallion egg, one of seven Russian Imperial eggs previously listed as missing since the 1920s. That caught my attention given what I already knew about three of the others."

Derek frowned. "You knew? How?"

Anna raised her hand. "Tell you in a minute. I continued to watch as the narrator introduced you and Eva, fascinated to learn her family name was Gustmann and that her father had been Horst Gustmann, a name I'd known for years."

Eva nearly interrupted, but Anna continued, "I was shocked and saddened to learn Horst had been killed by men attempting to steal the egg your grandfather had left for him. Then you explained how you and Derek had learned Klaus once lived in Ishpeming under the name Otto Krummel, that he'd written a coded will leaving an undefined estate to Gerda and Horst, which you finally managed to interpret. That was really something. You were talking about the Otto I knew, Mom's second husband, the man I came to call Dad. I…"

Eva interrupted, "Are you saying my grandfather and your mother were married in Ishpeming sometime before he supposedly died?"

"Not quite. They only married two years later, well after Otto had legally been declared dead. After that, they were together for nearly forty-five years until Mom passed away."

"Incredible!"

"The explanation, of course, is that Otto, or rather Klaus, didn't die in 1953. At first, all anyone, including Mom and I, knew was that his car had been found submerged in Lake Superior. Bullet holes in the windows and another in the collar of a jacket found in the car convinced police he'd been murdered, apparently by the same two men who'd broken into his house and were later found to have been associated with the Russian MGB."

"So you and your mom really thought Otto had been killed?"

"Oh yes, and we were devastated. Mom had fallen in love with him, and I'd already started to think of him as my second father. My real father was killed in a mining accident when I was only three. I barely remember him at all."

"So how and when did you learn he was still alive?"

"Some weeks after a memorial service at our church, Mom got a sympathy card from a man named Lars Aronson in Bisbee, Arizona. He wrote that he had been Otto's friend when they worked together in Sweden and had traveled with him to the U.S. to take jobs here. He said they'd exchanged letters every so often so he'd come to know how close Otto and Mom had become. His message ended with a little poem hinting at the two of them being reunited someday. The name Lars Aronson didn't mean anything to her as she'd never heard Otto mention him. But she was touched by the sentiment expressed in the poem and supposed Mr. Aronson must be a religious person as the poem seemed to suggest a meeting in the afterlife."

"I've got a feeling this Lars Aronson ultimately turned out to be my grandfather Klaus."

"Correct. Over the summer and fall Mr. Aronson sent two more letters. The second one included train tickets to Phoenix. In it, he urged Mom to visit him in Arizona during my Christmas break from school, saying he knew how bleak the weather could be during winter in the north and what a nice change Arizona would be at that time of year. He promised to take us on a tour of the desert, we could visit Mexico, I could ride a horse, and so on. Mom thought about it. It seemed strange, yet nice that a casual friend of Otto's, someone who really didn't know us, should be so concerned and solicitous. Finally, she decided okay, we'd go. She sent a return letter back to the P.O. box in Bisbee where Aronson had posted his letters, thanking him and confirming the date and time we would arrive in Phoenix. However, she made clear we had our own funds and in no way expected or would allow him to pay our expenses, so she included a check to cover the cost of the tickets he'd sent. He wrote back, promising to meet us at the railroad station, and described himself as being tall, with brown hair, a short beard, and wearing wire rim glasses."

Anna continued. "As soon as we got off the train in Phoenix, she spotted him right away at the other end of the platform. I lagged behind, looking at a toy poodle another passenger had had on the train, but Mom kept walking. Suddenly she stopped, stared at Mr. Aronson for a long moment, then shouted, "YOU SON OF A BITCH!" She turned around and rapidly walked back toward me. Then she stopped again, turned back, ran to Mr. Aronson, and hugged him. I didn't know what to think, but when I got a little closer I realized Mr. Aronson was Otto, Otto in disguise."

"Why did my grandfather disappear as he did and allow you to think he was dead? He must have known how much that would hurt you."

"We were hurt, and at first Mom couldn't decide whether she still loved him or hated him. Otto realized it was now or never. He persuaded her to stay long enough to tell us everything about a past he'd previously hidden out of shame, as well as a blow-by-blow account of the events that finally convinced him disappear without warning."

"Apparently that was good enough for your mom to forgive him since they later married."

"It took a while. After we got over the shock of just seeing him alive he drove us to the small house he was renting in Bisbee while working at the Phelps-Dodge copper mine. Along the way, he said he wished he could live under his real name, Klaus Gustmann, but that was no longer possible. The MGB now knew him both as Klaus Gustmann and as Otto Krummel. Then he told us about his wartime service as an officer in the SS and his fear of discovery and possible prosecution because of that. So now he was Lars Aronson and that was what we must call him. It took us quite a while to get used to that. Even now my brain first thinks Otto before my mouth says Lars. For you, who never actually knew him, of course he's Klaus."

Anna paused as the waitress approached to refill everyone's coffee and ask if they were ready to order. Derek said they just needed another minute or two to study the menu.

"Finally, hesitantly, and with great remorse, Lars confessed to us the murder he'd committed during the battle for Berlin, killing Otto Krummel and switching uniforms and identity with him, driven by a state of utter panic to escape capture and execution by the Russians while wearing an SS uniform."

"How did your mother take *that* news?"

"She was stunned. I was only ten at the time, old enough to know that what he'd done was absolutely awful, yet at the same time it seemed sort of unreal to me. For me, reality was the good times we'd had together over the past two years. I wanted him to be my dad. Mom wasn't sure what to say or do at first. She'd fallen in love with Otto, but now she had to wrestle with a huge moral dilemma. It wasn't really hers to forgive the crime he'd committed in the heat of battle. But she'd also seen him act selflessly in saving Eino Hakala when a tunnel collapsed in the Mather D mine. It took a lot of soul searching, but by two days before we were to return home, and then only with my concurrence, she decided we would try to forge a new life with Lars."

"A very heavy decision."

Anna looked intently at Eva and Derek. "Harder for Mom than for me, but it worked out. We never regretted our choice."

Derek said, "I guess Klaus's ruse may well have saved his life, but it also cost him the eggs he'd hidden in the mausoleum. And now we've lost them as well. At least Eva has the one egg he left as a legacy for Horst."

Anna nodded. "I'm glad for Eva. But you're wrong about the others. He didn't lose them."

"But we saw Yakushin take them. He was on the Giiwedin. The ship sank. Those eggs are on the bottom of Lake Superior."

"Those eggs yes, but they aren't the real ones. The eggs you found and Yakushin took were fakes."

"Fakes?"

"That Sunday, trapped on Presque Isle in a blowing snowstorm, at any moment expecting the two men who'd been chasing him to close in and kill him, after a short time he began to wonder if they had temporarily lost him. But he saw no way to safely go back, thinking if they didn't get him now, someone else was sure to be sent. He'd already dealt with one MGB agent, a man later identified as Anatoly Zaretsky."

"We know. Eva and I read about that when we scrolled through old issues of *The Mining Journal*. Are you saying Klaus killed him?"

"Yes, and as soon as Zaretsky's friends saw their dead friend's picture in the paper he knew they would know he'd been responsible and send someone else after him. He'd quickly hatched a plan to either let him trap and kill the next agent or at least fool him long enough to buy a little time to work things out with Mom and me before dropping out of sight. But as he returned home that morning to put everything in place he spotted two men already casing the house. They chased him halfway around the county in a heavy snowstorm, where he eventually made a wrong turn, ending up sliding off the road and trapped on Presque Isle, sure he was about to be killed. When fifteen minutes passed and nothing happened, it seemed his pursuers had briefly lost him, but he still knew there was no way to safely go back home. He'd been wearing a parka the whole time during the car chase but also had a lighter jacket in the car. So he put a bullet through the neck of that to suggest he'd been hit, and shot another two holes through the driver's side windows. Then he opened both doors and pushed it over the cliff. With the real treasure in his rucksack, he walked five miles through the snowstorm to the bus station in Marquette and caught a Greyhound to Detroit."

The waitress approached a third time looking hopeful, so Anna paused long enough to let everyone order something.

"By the time we went to visit him in Arizona, your grandfather had hatched another plan. After finally sharing his darkest secrets to us, he told us about a project for which he wanted to use much the money he hoped to gain from selling the eggs and jewelry as well as a packet of bearer bonds he'd received as a security deposit for one egg while still in Ishpeming he'd loaned to the owners of a Chicago gallery to be sent to London for a formal appraisal by experts. He told her he wanted to move to Mexico, thinking it would be easier to live 'under the radar' there than in the U.S. And once there, he wanted in some small way to amend for his actions during the war. He'd already met some people in Mexico City who'd helped him sell some of the jewelry he had. While he was there, he'd seen and been deeply affected by the abject poverty in the barrios, and especially the desperate state of so many street kids. He told us he wanted to establish and fund a home for those orphaned or rejected kids. He wished to stay anonymous as a donor, but would Mom help run the place? He'd already decided he wanted to call the place *El Hogar Otto Krummel para Huérfanos*. Another big decision, but as I'm sure you've heard 'in for a penny, in for a pound' so we signed on, and Mom served as Director of *El Hogar* for the first thirty years. After that, I took over. Lars, or Klaus, I should say, cashed the bearer bonds to get things started. Over time he found buyers for the eggs and the jewelry, and every couple of months we'd also go to coin dealers or other intermediaries and sell a handful of the gold coins he'd found to help keep the place going."

Reaching down to her briefcase, Anna pulled out a small cloth bag and handed it to Eva, saying, "This is for you. There aren't so many left after all these years, but I felt you should have some." Opening it, Eva saw the bag contained a couple dozen gold fifteen-ruble coins.

Eva said, "We'd wondered about the gold. The men who came after Dad only seemed to know of or be concerned about the other eggs, and of course that's all we'd found in the mausoleum when Yakushin surprised us. We decided not to mention that on *Treasure Finders*, but before we worked out the message in Klaus's will, Derek had managed to decode a line of symbols, letters, and numbers Klaus left written on a strip of paper inside the egg that my dad had. It gave directions to the grave in Latvia where he'd hidden the treasure. Derek went there and spoke to the cemetery caretaker through an interpreter. He learned the grave was one of a number that had to be moved for a construction project, but to everyone's amazement, the workmen found no coffin or body but had found a torn bag containing some gold coins. We had no idea how much gold Klaus had had and what he might have done with it. We thought if the amount wasn't too great, then perhaps he might have stashed in the niche next to the one supposedly holding Magda's ashes. After the shooting, we persuaded the cemetery to open the other niche, but there was nothing inside."

Anna smiled. "There's an interesting story about the coins. When Mom and I were just about to board the train back to Ishpeming, Lars asked if she knew what had happened to his piano. Mom was surprised he cared. He'd paid almost nothing for it and had rarely played it. She told him she'd hired two high school students to move it, his desk, and his lounge chair over to our house after the 'sonofabitch' landlord threatened to dump all his stuff on the curb just a week after the police pulled his car from the lake. He smiled at that, and in a whisper told us there were sixteen sacks of uncirculated fifteen-ruble gold coins hidden inside the back of that piano."

"I'm guessing the first thing you did after getting home was to recover them and plan another trip south?"

"You bet. Mom put the house up for sale. She told friends and neighbors we wanted to leave old unpleasant memories behind and were going to relocate somewhere in the southwest, maybe in or around San Diego, California. The first part of that explanation was true enough, but our actual destination was Mexico."

Eva shook her head. "An amazing story, Anna. I'm so glad you called, and we were able to get together."

"Me, too. I only wish your grandfather had managed to find Gerda and Horst during all those years. He knew when he took the eggs and jewelry from the mausoleum that made his will irrelevant, so he kept searching for Gerda and Horst."

"My grandfather and your mom. When..."

"Lars, I guess I should say Klaus, I came to always call him just Dad, died in 2003, Mom in 2000. They're buried together in a cemetery near where I live. You know, I'd be happy to have you visit sometime."

"We will."

Derek said, "Just one more thing, Anna. You said Klaus sold the real eggs, but the world doesn't seem to know anything about that. Except for Eva's egg they're all still listed as missing."

"For the rest of his life, Klaus felt compelled to stand in the shadows. The jewelry wasn't so hard to fence at value, but he decided he didn't want to risk the exposure that would attend the formal vetting of his eggs as members of those Fabergé made specifically for the Tsars. He managed to sell them clandestinely to collectors who recognized them as high-quality Fabergé products from an early period but very likely didn't know precisely what they were getting or maybe suspected but wanted to keep the deal quiet. I know he got a substantial sum for the eggs but probably just a small fraction of what they'd have brought if their true provenance been known."

Early the next morning at LAX, Eva and Derek sat together waiting for their respective flights to SFO and PHL.

"What's next, Eva?"

"For the egg or for us?"

"Both."

"As soon as I get back home I'm going to tell Wartski to sell Dad's egg and use the proceeds to create the Horst Gustmann Charitable Trust."

"What will the trust do?"

"Dad never forgot he was a refugee at one time and needed a lot of help to get established after he came to Canada with this cousin Erica. After he retired from McGill University, he spent a lot of time during the winter months helping newly arrived refugees find housing and employment, teaching them English, and preparing them for citizenship. That stream of refugees is now growing larger, and the need is great. I'm going to honor his memory by using the trust to fund programs helping those refugees."

"That sounds good, Eva. So what about us? Shared tragedy and terror put us together, but I feel…at least I hope, we've got something beyond that. Okay, I'm beginning to feel like a tongue-tied teenager, but…I really care for you, Eva. Do we…do you think we have a future together?"

Eva looked at Derek and smiled as his earnest gaze brought a fleeting memory of Chocolate, the Labrador she'd had as a child. She looked away for a moment, then turned back and took his hands in hers.

"I love you, Derek P. Todson. There, I said it and I mean it. But I don't know if we can work it out to become, you know, get married and have a real family life. I've got my practice in California. You've got your professorship in Philadelphia. I suppose long distance relationships can work, but it's a tough challenge. Still, I don't want us to break apart either. I want to keep seeing and being with you whenever we can manage it."

"Okay. I'll go with that for now. I love you too, Eva."

The gate agent across from where they were sitting made a final call for passengers to board Flight 68 to SFO. Eva got up.

"I've got to go now, Derek." She kissed him.

Derek followed and called out as Eva approached the jet bridge.

"It's really not too late for a family, you know. Your mom had you when she was four years older than you are now."

Eva stopped, looked back at Derek, and cast him a "stink eye." Then, with an evil grin she yelled back, "Call me as soon as you get back to Philly, you old goat."

"Ma'am?" Eva was the last passenger in line, and the gate agent now stood, hand extended, waiting for her boarding pass.

"Oh! Sorry. I was just saying goodbye to my boyfriend." Eva gave her pass to the man, who scanned it and wished her a pleasant flight.

Derek watched Eva go and felt a surge of optimism. An advertisement he'd seen in many in-flight magazines came to mind. IN BUSINESS YOU DON'T GET WHAT YOU DESERVE, YOU GET WHAT YOU NEGO-TIATE. *Maybe that applies to love as well?*

QUESTIONS FOR READERS TO CONSIDER

We often must choose between two or more courses of action. Usually, the path taken has few if any long term consequences. Not so for Klaus Gustmann when confronted by several unplanned and unwanted life threatening situations. Do you try to talk your way out, run away, hide, fight, kill, or what? How do you imagine you would have reacted to those situations and why?

How do you perceive sudden, unearned, unexpected wealth; a wonderful thing, a bad thing, something else? Did this story change your perspective in any way?

In the past, Sergei Yakushin has succeeded in keeping himself beyond the reach of the law by having lesser minions carry out and take responsibility for his criminal schemes. So why do you suppose he decided to insert himself so personally in the effort to steal Horst's Fabergé egg and others he initially supposed Horst had?

Upon finally meeting her, Derek is immediately attracted to Eva. He wants to stay close, offer solace in her grief, and help in any way he can. Joining forces, they manage to learn more about her grandfather, solve the mystery of Horst's Fabergé egg, and find his killer. In doing so, romance blossoms, and by the end of the story they've expressed love for each other. Still, it isn't clear what their future really holds. What do you think should happen (the author is pondering the same question for possible use in a future story)?

Derek and Eva prove adept at solving coded puzzles. Consider this one. DEATH, FAMINE, WAR, and CONQUEST or GLORY are names given to the Four Horsemen of the Apocalypse in Revelations 6, Chapter 1 of the Bible. From within those words can you identify a behavior that could help avert the human tragedies symbolized by these mounted specters?

<u>Hint</u>: See below one of several possible ways the number of times each letter in the words below could be used.

D(3)**E**(1)**A**(1)**T**(1)**H**(1); **F**(1)**A**(1)**M**(0)**I**(0)**N**(1)**E**(2); **W**(0)**A**(1)**R**(2);
C(1)**O**(1)**N**(2)**Q**(0)**U**(1)**E**(0)**S**(2)**T**(1); **G**(0)**L**(0)**O**(1)**R**(2)**Y**(0)

Was there a point in this story where you began to anticipate something like the way in which it actually worked out in the end? What gave you the hint?